ANOTHER TIME

by

Jared Vaughn

To Mary,
Keep shining!
Jared

This is a work of fiction. Names, characters, businesses, places, events and incidents are either the products of the author's imagination or used in a fictitious manner. Any resemblance to actual persons, living or dead, or actual events is purely coincidental.

Printed in the United States of America
First Printing, 2020
ISBN 978-0-578-75220-4

Thanks to Makenzi and Celestina for providing some of the characters' names. Thanks to others who will find their names and/or birthdays sprinkled throughout the book. Thanks most of all that these and an ever-growing number of friends and family have encouraged me and wouldn't let me give up. Many wonderful things have happened in the three years since *The Longest Time*, but this is only the beginning. My motivation for finishing this book wasn't just to satisfy the ones waiting to read it, but to fulfill my own purpose. Just as Charlie needed to find his, I believe that I found mine. My hope is that everyone who reads this won't just be entertained, but will be encouraged to love people more. It's simple, but it's desperately needed now more than ever.

"Love changes everything."

CHAPTER 1

It all started with a boy who loved a girl. Their lives were filled with challenges to get to this point of their story, but they never gave up. A new challenge was imminent. Charlie Jordache looked at his reflection in the mirror.

"I'm Charlie. I can do this. I can do anything. Because I'm Charlie. I am who I am."

He took a deep breath.

"Besides, this is what I wanted. It's finally happening. Nothing will ever be the same."

He made a small adjustment to his hair. He smiled.

"I can do this."

He headed for the door. As he put his hand on the knob, he said, "This is the time."

After exiting the bathroom, he took a drink from the fountain. When he finished, he turned to see a familiar face.

"Tracy!"

"Hey, Charlie!"

"You look so beautiful."

"Thanks, Charlie. You clean up pretty good yourself. Very James Bond-like in that tux."

He spun in a circle and pointed at her.

"The finger guns!" Tracy said with a laugh. "Now it's complete."

Charlie laughed.

"I'm surprised that you're not nervous," Tracy noted.

"Oh, believe me, I'm nervous."

"You're doing a good job of hiding it."

"I've always done that. I don't always show what I don't want you to see. Underneath this confident exterior is a bundle of nerves."

"I guess I have known you to be that way sometimes. I knew you loved Lisa since we were kids. There was no way you would ever admit it, but I could tell."

"Oh, really? Why didn't you say something?"

"Some secrets are good. Knowing something before you should know it kind of takes the fun out of it."

Charlie smiled. "I remember that."

"I always saw something in you that was deeper than it was with other kids. I saw the same thing in Lisa. I just knew you two belonged together. It was meant to be."

"And here we are now."

"Here we are."

"You know what the hardest part of this is?"
"The people?"
"I'm nervous about that, but that's not the hardest part. It's not seeing her yet."
Tracy smiled. "Oh, Charlie, just you wait. She may have been beautiful before, but you ain't seen nothin' yet."
"I believe it."
Tracy stepped closer to Charlie and put her hands on his shoulders. "I always believed in you two."
He put his arms around her waist. "A real friend is a hard thing to find. I still believe in you, too."
They hugged each other warmly.
She pulled back and looked lovingly into his eyes. "Charlie Jordache. Still the nicest boy I know." She kissed his cheek. "Go get 'em."

Sunday, August 11th, 1985. Charlie walked down the hall and entered the classroom. He pulled out a metal chair and sat down. He remembered when they borrowed these same chairs for a birthday party many years ago. It was the same party when he wished for his dad to come back. It also happened to be the same day that he played with Tracy for the first time. He smiled as he recalled trying to tag her and Lisa. He didn't realize when he turned seven that other wishes would be fulfilled that day and especially the present.

"But that Lisa—she's a keeper. She's a real, true friend. If you never had another friend, you still have the best one in the world. One real friend like that is worth more than a thousand phonies."

His mom was always right. This day was irrefutable proof.

He looked at his watch. Only ten more minutes. He couldn't decide if he couldn't wait for it to start or for it to be over. He closed his eyes and took a deep breath.
"There you are! I've been looking for you!"
He opened his eyes and stood up. "Mom," he said with a smile.
"I can't believe this is finally happening. Look at you! You're so handsome and grown up."
"Nah. You look much better than me."
"You look like your father, that's what it is. Man, if he could see you now."
He nodded. "That's all that's missing."
"Who knew six months ago that you would be wearing a tux again so soon? This is all happening so fast."
"That was when I first told Lisa that I love her. I held that in for thirteen years. For me, this day couldn't come soon enough."

She chuckled. "I can see your point. Still, I just can't get over how this all happened. You have quite an amazing story."

"Should true love be anything less than amazing?"

"Absolutely not. That brings me to something else. I want to give you something."

Charlie already noticed her holding her hand behind her back. She brought it forward and held it out to him.

"This was the watch your dad wore when we got married. The battery died long ago, so he got another watch, the one you were used to seeing him wear. I replaced the battery, and now it works fine."

Charlie looked at the watch and back to her. "This is too much."

"No, it's just right. He would've wanted you to have it."

He took off his watch and put it in his pocket. She began to put his dad's watch on his wrist.

"There's a lesson in this," she stated. "Time stood still for you once." She looked into his eyes. "All you needed was for something inside to change."

A tear came to Charlie's eye. Mom was always right.

She continued, "I've seen such a change in you. It wasn't long ago that you were in this shell. Would hardly talk to anyone, even me. So frustrated and hurt and withdrawn." Tears formed in her eyes as well. "Then came the miracle." She held his hands. "Lisa came back. With the help of that wonderful Mr. Whitfield, you destroyed that shell. She brought the sunshine back into your life again. She brought you the love you needed."

"I know how to love her…" a tear rolled down his cheek, "…because you taught me."

She wiped her own eye. "And now that you're together, there's no stopping you. The two of you will do great things."

"If you love someone, anything's possible."

She put her arms around him as he did the same. "Love changes everything."

"I love you, Mom."

"I love you, Son."

He couldn't wait for it to start.

"Why does it have to take so long?" Lisa sighed with frustration. She paced the floor. Tracy's little sister, Tammy, held the train of Lisa's dress, desperately trying to keep up.

"You're going to trip!" she warned her.

Lisa stopped. "You're right. I just can't sit still."

Tracy walked in. "I just saw Charlie a little bit ago."

Lisa's eyes lit up. "You did? How is he?"

"He looks very handsome. He's nervous, but he's happy. He looks very happy."

Lisa smiled warmly. "I'm so glad to hear that."

"He can't wait to see you."

"I know how he feels."

"Was there ever a more perfect couple?"

They hugged. When Tracy pulled back, Lisa saw tears in her eyes.

"Why are you crying?"

"My two best friends are getting married. These are tears of joy."

Lisa's eyes began to water. "Oh, Tracy. You're going to make me cry, too."

Ilene entered the room. "Could you give us a minute alone?"

"Sure, Mrs. Jordache," Tracy replied as she took Tammy with her.

Ilene stood in front of Lisa. "It's been a busy day already...I almost ran out of time to do this."

"What's that?"

"I have something to give you." She took off her watch. "This is the same watch I wore when I got married."

Lisa shook her head. "I can't take that, Mrs. Jordache. That's too much."

"No, Lisa. It's not nearly enough."

Ilene took Lisa's left hand. She held it out to her as Ilene put the watch on her wrist next to a blue and purple friendship bracelet.

"It's beautiful," Lisa said softly.

"I just gave Charlie his dad's watch. I know you two have your rings, but I wanted to do this, too. I wanted something between us. You and Charlie were separated for years. Different states, different time zones, different everything. But, now you're in the same place at the same time, uniting as one. This is only the beginning of your story. Your past is great, but your future is even better."

"If you love someone, anything's possible."

"I've seen that to be true. You've done so much good already. Your love has made such a difference. There's nothing you can't do."

Lisa's eyes watered again. "You've been the best example."

Ilene put her hands on Lisa's shoulders. "There's something I've wanted to say for a long time." Tears of her own were showing. "Welcome to the family, Lisa."

Lisa swallowed the lump in her throat. "Funny...I thought we were family already."

"I love you...my daughter."

"I love you, Mom."

They held each other tightly as tears of joy overflowed.

Ilene looked into Lisa's eyes. Lisa marveled at the love she saw in them. She knew exactly where Charlie got it from. Ilene said, "I think it's about time."

The sweet strains of Jeremy Allen's violin filled the air. His guitarist friend accompanied him softly. Theresa Allen stood beside them at the microphone. She beautifully sang Noel Paul Stookey's "The Wedding Song (There is Love)." Jeremy harmonized with her at just the right moments. Charlie's heart soared with the most beautiful music he had ever heard. Maid of Honor Tracy walked down the aisle and stood across from Charlie. She gave him a nervous grin that he returned. The ring-bearer took his place by Charlie. Tammy sprinkled flower petals all the way up to her spot by her sister. It never occurred to him in the past that the baby he once held would be his flower girl. A lot of things never occurred to him before. But, some things he knew from the very beginning. The song came to its end. Charlie looked Theresa in the eyes and smiled. "Thank you," he said quietly. "You're welcome," she said while giving him a wink.

The musicians began to play the "Wedding March." Charlie's heart began to beat faster. Everyone in the pews stood up as the bride entered the room. There were other moments in Charlie's life when he saw Lisa for the first time. That summer day in 1972 when a little girl was helped out of a moving truck by her mother, and proceeded to run around the yard without a care… and straight into Charlie's heart. When she came back from vacation one August day in 1975 and ran into his arms. Seven months before this day, when she walked down the halls of the school. It was the first time he had seen her in eight years. She ran into his arms once again, nearly knocking him over. Her beauty always stunned him in those times and every day in between. But, at this moment in time, as she slowly walked the aisle, she was positively breathtaking. She was no longer a little girl. She was a glimpse of Heaven. An angel, so pure and glorious, with love flowing from her smile. He never knew why God had chosen him to have her, but he was more thankful than ever. She approached his side. Her dad removed her hand from his arm and put it on Charlie's. Cal took his place on Charlie's right as his Best Man. They smiled at each other. Charlie looked over to Annie seated in the pew. She blew him a kiss. He put his hand on his heart and smiled. The preacher began to speak. Charlie tried his best to listen, but his heart beat louder and his memories interrupted.

"Thank you, God, for bringing me Lisa. I promise I'll take good care of her."

This was the day that promise would be made again, but this time, he wasn't a little boy kneeling at his bed, whispering for only God to hear. He was going to tell the world.

They exchanged rings and the traditional vows with tears of joy in their eyes. The preacher's reading of Mark 10:7-9 was particularly meaningful to Charlie.

"For this cause shall a man leave his father and mother, and cleave to his wife; and they twain shall be one flesh: so then they are no more twain, but one flesh. What therefore God hath joined together, let not man put asunder."

He realized then more than ever, that his mom would have less of a role in his life. Lisa would be the one who would not only be by his side, but would be a part of him. His mom's words from years gone by still echoed through his mind. They were her memories of her own wedding.

"We became one. We started experiencing everything new all over again in this new chapter of our lives."

Now that he and Lisa were one, there would be no more waiting for the right moments. No more holding back how they felt. They were no longer apart. They were two halves that were always meant to be together, now joined together. They were now whole.

"You may kiss the bride," the preacher said with a smile.

Brother, did they kiss. It would have been even more passionate if not for the onlookers.

"We've Only Just Begun" by The Carpenters played overhead.

Charlie and Lisa looked at each other.

"Mom's idea," he informed her.

"I love it."

They looked straight ahead again, standing hand in hand.

"Ladies and gentlemen, I present to you Mr. and Mrs. Charlie Jordache."

The crowd clapped and cheered. The newlyweds walked down the aisle, quickly observing the smiling faces of their family and friends. The ones who believed in them all along.

The reception flew by in a blur of cake and gifts. Before long, Charlie found himself being pelted with rice on the way to the car. The crowd waved and expressed their well wishes as they buckled up. Charlie started the car. "Do It Again" by The Beach Boys played on the radio. He backed up slowly and got the car into position. He saw his mom waving through the mirror. He and Lisa turned around and waved back one last time. They looked into each other's eyes.

"Ready for an adventure?" Lisa asked with her mischievous smile.

He chuckled slightly and smiled back. "Always."

They made their way to California.

Everything else that follows will get complicated, but as the story of Charlie and Lisa continues, one thing will be easy to see and simple to understand. Love changes everything.

ANOTHER TIME

CHAPTER 2

Chesapeake University, August 1985. Charlie and Lisa approached the building with their hands joined together. He couldn't help but recall a similar moment in time.

"I can't believe how grown up you are!"

"My, how time flies..."

The memories flashed like the cameras Ilene and Annie used that first day of kindergarten. Thirteen years ago was a long time, but still fresh in his mind. He was amused at the thought of how grown up he felt that day compared to the man he was in the present. He didn't know what to expect then as a student, but now they were both on their way to becoming teachers themselves. Lisa didn't have a bow in her hair this time, but a ring on her finger.

She smiled as she looked at him fondly. "Just like the good old days."

He returned her smile and replied, "No..." He brought her hand to his lips and kissed it. "This time, it's better."

Her smile grew bigger.

"Hey, guys!"

They turned their attention to Tracy as she came up behind them and put her arms around their shoulders.

"Hey, Tracy," they said in unison as they let go of their hands and put their arms around her.

"Ready to go be adults?" she asked with a mischievous grin.

"No way," said Charlie.

"Never," said Lisa.

They all laughed.

Tracy replied, "I didn't really think so. But, since we're here..."

They started walking towards the door with their arms still around each other. Charlie opened the door with his free hand.

"Please tell me that you brought pictures from the honeymoon," Tracy said to Lisa.

"Of course."

"Wait till you see the sand castle," Charlie said with a smile.

As they entered their first class, Charlie noticed that a lot of the students kept to themselves. Lisa looked a bit out of her element, being less social than she would like, refraining from greeting everyone as she did when they were younger. As he sat down, a young man walked up to Lisa with a smile. She smiled back, clearly eager to meet someone new.

"Hey there. I couldn't help but notice you when you walked in. I just had to meet you."

He offered his hand to shake. She shook it, but he still held on.

"I'm Lisa."

"Lisa. I like it."

He looked her up and down with a sleazy grin.

"Did you also notice who walked in with me? This is Charlie, my husband."

She pulled her hand away and showed him the ring on her other hand.

"What's your name, Sam Malone?" she said sarcastically.

He chuckled a bit and looked over to Charlie.

"Beat it," he said with a firm glare.

The student scoffed and walked away. Lisa sat down with a sigh.

"Sam Malone?" Charlie asked with a chuckle.

"Well, he was hitting on me like Sam would do. And it sounded like something someone would say in a bar." She started laughing along with Charlie. "It was the first thing that popped in my head."

"I thought I was the one with the TV references."

"Yeah, well, you're rubbing off on me."

Lisa was always kind to everyone, but if there was one thing she wouldn't put up with, it was disrespect.

They excelled in each class that day and all the rest that followed. Charlie remembered Lisa being a fast learner, but was still amazed. Knowing that she was a genius gave a new perspective to the old days, and a consistently surprising and satisfying experience to share their lives together.

One Saturday night, Charlie came home from his job at the restaurant. They had a simple apartment for the time being, but planned to buy a house when they could afford it. Lisa ran up to him and gave him a hug and kiss.

"How was work?"

"Busy. I'm ready to sit down."

He proceeded to do so while Lisa retrieved a record from the stereo.

"Look what Mom got me!"

"The Beach Boys, *Endless Summer*," he said with a smile.

"I couldn't believe it. She found it at a garage sale." She set it down again and sat next to him on the couch. "You're thinking about something. I can tell."

"It just reminded me of something. You know, we were apart from each other for eight years. Now we're married and live together and go to school together... and I just..."

"What are you trying to say?"

"We're still catching up from all those years. We're still getting to know each other in a way. We're still learning about each other."

"That's a good thing... isn't it?"

"Yes. Of course it's a good thing. It's wonderful. I feel like I learn something new about you every day."

"I know what you mean. I didn't know when we were kids that you didn't like mustard."

"And I didn't know that you put chips in your peanut butter and jelly sandwiches."

"Now I've got you doing it," she said with a grin.

"But, I'm still not eating mustard," he said with a laugh.

"I love learning all these things about you."

"So do I. And that's my point. We're a lot alike in a lot of ways, but we're also different in some ways, too... and I wouldn't have it any other way. I want to know everything about you. Because the more I know you, the more I love you."

"Oh, Charlie. I feel the same way. I love everything about you, too. We don't have to learn it all at once, though. We have the rest of our lives. We have all the time in the world."

He nodded. "I agree. But, there is something I want to tell you. It's something about me that I keep private. I don't want to have any secrets between us."

Her face grew serious. "Whatever it is, you can tell me. It won't change anything between us."

He got off the couch and wrung his hands.

"I know it won't make anything worse, but it's still hard for me... I haven't told anyone but my mom and Sam Whitfield, the counselor. I've been keeping it in for too long... and I just want you to be in on it. Maybe I won't feel so much of the weight anymore."

"Charlie, you can tell me everything or you can tell me nothing. I'll still love you. I'm here to help you with that weight."

"Thanks, Lisa. I don't know what I'd do without you. Ok... here goes."

He handed the record to her. He closed his eyes and took a deep breath.

"'Surfin' Safari,' 'Surfer Girl,' 'Catch a Wave,' 'The Warmth of the Sun,' 'Be True to Your School,' 'Surfin' U.S.A.,' 'In My Room,' 'Fun, Fun, Fun,' 'The Girls on the Beach,' 'I Get Around,' 'Little Deuce Coupe,' 'Wendy,' 'Shut Down,' 'Don't Worry, Baby,' 'Help Me, Rhonda,' 'California Girls,' 'Let Him Run Wild,' 'Girl, Don't Tell Me,' 'You're So Good to Me,' 'All Summer Long.'"

He opened his eyes and breathed a nervous sigh of relief.

She smiled. "Wow! You really know your Beach Boys. I'm impressed."

"I've never even heard that album."

"Oh. So you read the back of it?"

"No. I read the 8 track I got you."

"And you remembered all that?"

"Yes."

"Was that supposed to be in order?"

"Well... yeah."

He looked at her quizzically. She giggled.

"You got all the right songs, but it's not in order."

"What? Let me see that."

She handed the record to him with a chuckle. He looked it over with a confused face.

"That was the 8 track order. I have that memorized, too, since I listened to it so much."

"They switched some of the songs around. How dare they do a thing like that."

She laughed. He handed it back to her.

"Well, there's still this. 'All Summer Long,' 'You're So Good to Me,' 'Girl, Don't Tell Me,' 'Let Him Run Wild,' 'California Girls,' 'Help Me, Rhonda,' 'Don't Worry, Baby,' 'Shut Down,' 'Wendy,' 'Little Deuce Coupe,' 'I Get Around,' 'The Girls on the Beach,' 'Fun, Fun, Fun,' 'In My Room,' 'Surfin' U.S.A.,' 'Be True to Your School,' 'The Warmth of the Sun,' 'Catch a Wave,' 'Surfer Girl,' 'Surfin' Safari.'"

"Now, that's just freaky... but in a good way."

"The point is... I remember everything."

"I remember a lot, too."

"I mean *everything*."

"*Everything* everything?"

"'Hi, Charlie! I'm having a lot of fun here, but not as much fun as I would have with you. I still like seeing my grandparents. They are really nice and Grandma's a good cook. This is a picture of the beach we went to today. I wish you could have been here to help me make a sand castle. Mom took a picture of it to show you. Talk to you later, pal!—Lisa.'"

"Holy cow! That was the postcard I sent you! It was..." she looked like she was trying to remember.

"July 7th, 1975. That's when I got it anyway."

"You really do remember everything. I remember most things, but not everything. Why would you want to keep that a secret?"

He sat down.

"Because it's not always a good thing. I remember a lot of painful things."

"Like your dad."

"Yes. And the bullying."

"What bullying?"

"I guess I didn't tell you about that, either. When you moved away, things got worse with Amanda. A lot worse."

"Charlie, I had no idea."

"But, I'm doing better now. Sam really helped me with some things." He looked into her eyes. "*You've* really helped me with some things."

She held his hand. "Just when I thought I couldn't love you more. You have this... this... gift. This thing about you that I never knew that's totally awesome."

"You really think so?"

"Yes! Of course I do! I can't wait to learn more. We can take all those bad memories and overpower them with good ones."

He smiled. "It's already happening."

"There's so much to you... a deepness. I want to spend the rest of my life mining those depths."

"I feel the same way about you."

"So, maybe we can learn these things, and at the same time, have some fun with it."

"What do you have in mind?"

"Something more like a challenge. You know, to keep each other sharp."

"Sounds good to me. What do we do?"

"Well, I was thinking that since you told me something, I should tell you something, too."

She smiled mischievously. He knew that smile. This was going to be good. He laughed.

"I can't wait to hear it. Go for it."

"Yo se espanol. Lo se desde hace anos." ("I know Spanish. I've known it for years.")

He was taken by surprise and laughed. Her smile grew.

"Es un gran lenguaje. Lo conozco bien." ("It's a great language. I know it well.")

She laughed giddily.

"Yeah, I took Spanish, too," he remarked.

Her smile grew more mischievous than he ever saw in his life.

"Parie que vous ne connaissez pas celui-ci."

"Okay... you got me there."

She laughed. "It's French. I said, 'Bet you don't know this one.'"

"How many languages do you know?"

"You'll just have to wait and see. It's all part of the fun."

"Like Tracy told me, 'some secrets are good. Knowing something before you should know it kind of takes the fun out of it.'"

"Exactement."

"Maybe you could teach me."
"I think you already know some of it."
She leaned in and they kissed passionately.

The next morning, Charlie sat in the passenger seat as Lisa drove to an undisclosed location.
"Is it the park?"
"Nope," she answered with a smile.
"Is it..."
"There's no point in asking, because I'm not going to tell you. Kind of takes the fun out of it. Besides, we're almost there."
"You take great delight in watching me not knowing things, don't you?"
"Yes, I do. It was my turn to do it to you anyway."

They got out of the car and walked towards the track.
"It's too chilly to be out here this early with no jacket."
"Don't worry about that. You'll be okay."
"So... are we watching a race?"
"Kind of."
He followed her onto the track.
"You're kidding."
She laughed. "Nope. Not kidding. I used to do this every Sunday before church. Of course, I did it more often at school, but this is when I did it for fun."
"What kind of fun is running?"
"You're about to find out."
She set down the backpack she was carrying and started doing stretches.
"I'll just watch."
"No, Charlie. I'm challenging you to a race."
"A race?! I can't race you! Look at you and your stretching. You're a professional."
"I'm not a professional," she said with a laugh.
"But, you have medals—I've seen them. You're the great 'Sunshine Duvall'—I can't race you."
"Charlie, don't you see? All those years when we were kids, who was it that kept me on my toes?"
"Well, yeah... but..."
"You may be out of practice, but so am I. You had the same experience I did, at least back then. You might be faster than you think."
"I never could keep up with you," he said with a laugh.

"You gave me a run for my money."

"All right. I'll do it. For 'fun'." He emphasized the word, "fun" with air quotes.

She laughed. "I have something for you. I know how you like to do things with music."

She pulled a tape player and headphones from the backpack.

"I have the perfect song to motivate you."

He put them in place.

"Now, don't start playing it till it's time."

"Ok."

They got into position.

"Oh, and there's one other thing that should make us even. My nickname is Sunshine. The song will tell you what yours will be from now on."

"Great," he said with a chuckle.

"On your mark..."

Charlie's heart started to beat faster as they both stared straight ahead.

"Get set..."

She motioned for him to start playing the tape. He did so and immediately started smiling. She acted like she was starting to take off. Charlie followed suit until he saw that it was a trick. She laughed. Knowing that he couldn't hear her over the music, she looked into his eyes and said, "Go."

And they were off. They were running side by side for awhile. When Lisa started going faster, Charlie knew he had to keep up. As they curved around the loop, he started to pass her. His smile was unmissable as he ran to the beat of "Mr. Blue Sky." Charlie was actually having fun. Lisa passed him for just a moment, then Charlie tried harder and overtook her. As they got close to the finish line, he thought, *"I can't believe I'm actually going to win."* Sure enough, he crossed the line right before she did. He stopped the tape.

"Yes!" he exclaimed. Then he quickly sat down and tried to catch his breath.

Lisa handed him a water bottle. She took a drink from hers as he did with his.

"Feel good?"

"Yeah, it kind of does." He panted some more as he handed her his bottle. "I'm hurting all over and my heart is about to burst out of my chest... but it feels good."

"That's good, Mr. Blue Sky."

She put her hand out to help him up.

"I just can't believe I beat you. It doesn't even seem possible."

She gave him that mischievous grin.

"You let me win, didn't you?"

"Kind of like the old days, huh? But, the other way around, of course."

"Why, you sneaky, little..." he laughed.

"And you didn't actually win. That was just the first lap."

"Wait... what?"

"There's a lesson in this. You did too much. Working hard is great, but you tried too hard all at once. You have to learn to pace yourself."

She started jogging in place, still keeping her mischievous grin.

"So, in other words, you're just getting started," he remarked.

"You bet your butt."

"All right, Sunshine. We'll do it your way."

They got into position again.

"On your mark..."

"Get set..." Charlie said as he pushed the play button. "GO!"

He sped off with Lisa laughing as she followed after him. It wasn't long until she passed him. She stayed in the lead for the rest of the race. He didn't know if he would ever in his life be able to keep up with her, but it would always be fun trying.

CHAPTER 3

October 3rd, 1985. Lisa couldn't wait to clock out from work. She normally enjoyed her new job at the mall. But, this wasn't an ordinary night. There were far too many important things on her mind. As she began to drive away, her instincts told her not to go home yet. She went straight to the park.

"The stars are extra bright tonight."

Charlie noticed her as she sat beside him on top of the bench.

"How did you know that I'd be here?"

"How did you know that I would be here on Valentine's Day? We're in each other's hearts."

He nodded and looked up to the sky again.

"I've been doing so much better. Sam helped me to see the truth. I used to think it was my fault. Can you believe that? I thought I did something to make him want to leave."

His eyes teared up. Lisa put her arm around him. She wasn't sure what to say, so she just listened.

"I've moved on. I'm truly happy with you now. I'm not weighed down with this burden like I was before. But, some days..."

His lips trembled. Lisa's eyes watered.

"Some days are harder than others. Some days, it's been twelve years... and I'm just a little boy again. Still praying that same prayer. 'Please, God, bring him back.'"

A tear rolled down his cheek. Lisa wiped it away before doing the same for her own. She had never seen him like this since they were kids. Her heart ached for her husband.

"The hardest part is not knowing. Just no answers at all."

"What cruel irony. Someone with a thirst for knowledge and can remember everything, and yet the one thing that means the most remains the most elusive."

He looked into her eyes.

"I get it, Charlie." She leaned her head on his. "We're one."

He put his arm around her.

"It's different now," she said softly. "The little girl is with you."

They looked into each other's eyes.

"I look out for you, and you look out for me."

"Love changes everything."

They kissed.

"We need to go see your mom."

It was getting late, but Lisa still knew that they needed to visit Ilene. There was still another hurting soul.

They all hugged upon arrival.
"Sorry to get here so late, Mom," Lisa apologized.
"No problem at all," she assured her.
Lisa stood while Charlie and Ilene sat on the couch and held each other's hands.
"How are you doing, Mom?" asked Charlie.
"Oh, I've been better, but I've also been worse. I'm trying not to dwell on the bad memories. I was just thinking about what Mr. Whitfield told me. He told me not to give up. He said that my story's not over yet. He also told me that before there was a Charlie and before there was a Wayne, there was an Ilene. That I had to still be myself."
"That's really good. He was a wise man."
"He said that you never know what will happen in life. We have to live to love."
Lisa took their free hands and held them.
"We can take the bad memories and overpower them with good ones. We can't change the past, but we can make a better future."
"You're absolutely right, Lisa," Ilene said with a smile.
Lisa's heart beat a little faster as she searched for the best way to say it.
"I've been thinking a lot about it. I wasn't sure how to tell you. I wanted it to be just right. But, now I know that this is the right time. With the two of you here, today, this is the best way."
"What are you trying to say, Lisa?" asked Charlie.
"What I'm trying to say is... we had some bad news twelve years ago. Now, it's time for some good news. October 3rd has always meant the day that you lost a dad."
She got choked up as tears surfaced. She put Charlie's and Ilene's hands on her stomach.
"Now, it can be the day when we gained another one."
Ilene gasped. Charlie looked stunned.
"Are you saying what I think you're saying?"
She gazed lovingly into his eyes through her tears of joy.
"Yes, Charlie. We're having a baby."
His eyes teared up.
"I'm going to be a grandma! I can't believe this! This is so amazing!"
Ilene and Charlie stood up and hugged Lisa. Ilene slipped away to let the two of them have a moment.
Lisa whispered in his ear, "I love you, Charlie. I love you so much."
"I love you, too. Love changes everything."
Ilene stood by the record player.
"There's something that we haven't done in the longest time."
Charlie and Lisa let go and turned their attention to Ilene.

“I don’t know if you know this, Lisa, but every Christmas, Charlie and I would dance to the Carpenters song, ‘Merry Christmas, Darling’ in honor of Wayne.”

“No, I didn’t know that. That sounds nice.”

“We didn’t do it last time. Sorry, Mom,” Charlie said regretfully.

“That’s okay, son. I think it is time to move on from that tradition. Now is the time for celebration.” She set the needle in place. “It’s not just the two of us anymore.”

“I Can See Clearly Now” by Johnny Nash began playing. The lyrics and the tune were perfect. She always knew how to pick them. She took Lisa by the hands and started dancing with her. Ilene even lip-synced to the singer. Lisa laughed. She understood why this song was chosen. Not only was Ilene telling her that the pain was going away, but that she was the reason why. The lyrics about it being a “bright, sunshiney day” were unmistakable. When it got to the second verse, Ilene switched to Charlie. He lip-synched along with her as they smiled through their tears of joy. Lisa watched from the side. She was the only other one whom she saw Charlie look at with that kind of love in his eyes. As it got to the bridge, Ilene handed him over to Lisa. Lisa laughed and said, “This is your part.” She was referring to the song’s lyrics about blue skies. They danced and twirled, smiled and cried. The three of them danced as the music filled the room. All that was stronger was the pure love and joy that washed over them. Their hearts soared higher than the sunshine and blue sky. At last, their future was bright. At long last, the pain was gone.

CHAPTER 4

"Thanks for meeting us here. How are you?"

Theresa hugged Charlie.

"Better than ever. How about you?"

"So glad to hear it. I'm doing very well."

She hugged Lisa as Charlie shook Jeremy's hand.

"So, married life is treating you well, eh?"

"Yes, it is. I highly recommend it."

"Hmm. I might have to look into that."

They laughed while Lisa shook his hand and Theresa hugged Ilene. They let go and Theresa asked the group, "Ready for the grand tour?"

November 1985. They all approached the building. Theresa pushed her son up the ramp. Lisa quickly ran up the steps next to it and opened the door.

"Thanks, Lisa," they said in unison.

Theresa led the way.

"The electricity has been shut off for awhile. We came through here earlier with a flashlight and opened the blinds so you can still see it as much as possible."

"Nice, big hallway," noted Ilene.

They entered a classroom.

"Nothing out of the ordinary, but nothing wrong with it, either," Theresa remarked.

They looked it over for a couple of minutes before going to the next room.

"It's about the same in this one. All the desks are still here and some of the supplies," said Theresa.

They started to leave the room.

"Most of the classrooms are pretty identical," Jeremy added. "We could save a little time and just go to the office next."

They all nodded.

"How long has it been closed?" asked Lisa.

"Since last year," Theresa answered. "They put this school here in 1948 to accommodate all the families who lived in the country. It thrived for many years." They entered the office. "But, over time, more businesses were opened in town. The kids who went to this school were growing up and moving to town more often than not. It eventually became far too costly to keep it operating in comparison to the few students still attending. The school board found it more feasible to shut it down than to pay the bills for something hardly being used."

"I'm surprised that they haven't sold it already," Charlie mentioned.

"They've tried. There's not much of a market around here for an old school building outside of town. That is, until now."

"And they're just going to let us have it?" asked Charlie.

"Well, yes and no. When I went to the board about your idea, they liked it. Some even loved it. But, we do have a few things to take care of. It will take some time."

"What is there to take care of?" asked Ilene.

"Most of the building is in good shape. The restrooms need a little work. The cafeteria needs some updates. The kitchen needs a lot of work."

"Most of the school is wheelchair-friendly," added Jeremy, "but there are some areas that can be improved. It shouldn't be too difficult."

"So there needs to be a little remodeling," Charlie stated. "That's to be expected. I thought we would have to build something from scratch. I think this could work a lot better."

"Yes, it is a lot better," Theresa replied. "And there is some work to do. Some things can be put off for awhile, but some will have to be done beforehand. It all takes money. It will take a little time for the board to have enough to put into it. I'm looking into some other options also. The other issue about that is convincing them that it will be worthwhile."

"I thought they liked the idea," Charlie said.

"They do, but ideas are one thing, actions are another."

"We have to have more students here than last time," Lisa remarked.

"Precisely."

"I was away for the past eight years. I'm not as familiar with the community as the four of you are. Do you honestly think that there are enough people who would come to a school like this?"

Ilene answered, "There was a time when Charlie and I had discussions about what we should do with his education."

"I remember those days very well," Theresa added.

Ilene continued, "Nothing was a very good fit. I wonder how many other families are having that same discussion. I wonder if they feel like we did. It's hard to make the right choice when there aren't many options to choose from."

"That's what's lead us here today," Charlie said. "I don't want anyone else to go through the same thing and slip through the cracks."

"This school may be a couple of miles out of town, but it's still considered as Chesapeake," Theresa explained. "If we had this option when Jeremy was a boy, I would have gladly driven those extra miles to give him what he needed."

"Some families are moving miles and miles away so that they can go to another school like this one," Jeremy said. "I've been a substitute teacher for a few years now. I've taught in every one of the schools in town at least once, including this one. I've seen some good things. There have been a few sparks of hope. Most of that came when we started the gifted program. But, I've also seen a lot of inadequacies and just plain ignorance. I've seen some things that as both a teacher and a man with a disability, have made my blood boil. The question was if there would be enough people to come to a school like this. I think the answer is a resounding 'yes.' Because this town hasn't seen a school like this." He looked into Charlie's eyes. "Thanks, my friend. Your little spark of an idea will become a fire. Just watch and see."

"With the help of everyone here, yes, I do think that we can make a difference."

"So... what other actions do we need to take?" asked Lisa.

"I'm glad you asked," Theresa stated. "The board agreed with Charlie's idea of having me as the principal. I'm honored to accept the role."

"I couldn't imagine anyone better," Ilene said.

"Thanks, Ilene. The only other actions are up to Charlie and Lisa. You're still majoring in education, correct?"

"Along with physics, yes," answered Lisa.

"And you still have two years left?"

"I still have four. Charlie has two."

Theresa made a comically frustrated face. "That's still awhile. But, then again, it might take that long anyway. The board went over yours and Charlie's records as well as ours. The work you've been doing with the gifted program has been a good bonus. With some additions to be made to our team, they think that the five of us are the most qualified to teach and oversee this school. But, you still have to be officially qualified."

"We will finish college and lead this school with the knowledge and compassion that these kids deserve," Charlie assured her. Ilene put her arm around him.

"I have no doubt that you will," Theresa said with a loving smile. "*We* will."

"Can you speed it up there a little, Lisa? We want to get this show on the road." They all laughed at Jeremy's joke. It was probably the first time that Lisa was ever told to speed up.

"I'll do the best I can..." Lisa said with a smile. "It might be hard between school, work, and..." she looked down and rubbed her belly.

"You're pregnant?!" Theresa asked with excitement.

"Yes."

"Congratulations!" she enthused while throwing her arms around her.

"That's great news!" Jeremy quipped, "Who's the father?"

They laughed at his disarming sense of humor.

"Jeremy Allen! That's terrible and inappropriate!" his mom rebuked.

"Then why did everyone laugh... including you?"

They laughed again.

He rolled towards Lisa and took her hand.

"In all sincerity, a child born of a woman as wonderful as you... and a man as honorable as this one... gives me hope that the world can have a better future."

"Thank you, Jeremy," Lisa replied with a tear forming in her eye, "that's very sweet of you."

He looked up to his mom and asked, "Better?"

She chuckled. "Much better."

She put her hand on Lisa's and Jeremy's and said, "To the future."

Charlie and Ilene added their hands.

"To the future," they all repeated together.

Charlie looked at the four faces around him. His heart filled with joy as much as he stood with deep respect for them. They were the best and brightest, the most caring and compassionate. The future was in great hands. He tried to overcome the lump in his throat as he said, "Welcome to The Chesapeake School for Special Needs."

CHAPTER 5

Time marched on as Charlie and Lisa enjoyed their life together as one. They continued to excel in school, even racing each other to finish their classroom work first. They helped each other with their homework also, with Lisa testing Charlie's memory at every opportunity. They were each consistently surprised and amazed by their partner's abilities.

For Thanksgiving, the two families got together at Ilene's house as they did in the past. Charlie couldn't recall a time in his life when there was more to be thankful for. They went to the Whitson house on December 22nd to take part in the tenth birthday of Tracy's sister, Tammy. Charlie still remembered Tracy announcing that her mom was pregnant, as well as holding the little bundle of joy. It was hard to believe that ten years had already gone by. Charlie and Lisa celebrated their first Christmas together as newlyweds. After exchanging gifts, they met again with the family, this time at the Duvall house. New Year's was another time for family and fun, with everyone gathered at Charlie's and Lisa's apartment. They all stayed up past midnight to bid farewell to a great year, and welcome a promising new year of happiness in 1986.

February 10th marked the anniversary of the first time they had a date... sort of. They couldn't recreate the events of that night as they wanted to, since Lisa was working at the mall until closing time, and Charlie did as well at the restaurant. But, Valentine's Day had to be special. They had lunch at school as they usually did, but this time, Charlie brought along a surprise—his mom's chocolate chip cookies. Lisa managed to get the night off from work, but Charlie still had to wait tables on a busy night. He served Lisa's parents for the first time. They always ate at this restaurant on Valentine's Day when they lived in town before, just as Charlie remembered when he was there with his mom years ago. They still looked as in love with each other as ever. Lisa came to have dinner with her husband on his lunch break. All of her dresses no longer fit due to her pregnancy, so she wore a new dress that she got from the store she worked in. Charlie was still in awe of her beauty.

When he got off work, he went to the park to meet her again. She sat on the bench this time. As he approached the table, he recalled something his mom said on the first Valentine's Day that they had together.

"We would experience things for the first time together. Everything was new. Our first date, our first kiss, even the little things. The first time we heard a song together... or got ice cream... or saw a rainbow. The first time we watched the sunset. And it all led to this—our wedding day. We became one. We started experiencing everything new all over again in this new chapter of our lives."

"What are you doing here?" Lisa asked.

He sat next to her. He knew that she was slyly repeating what she said a year ago.

"I was about to ask you the same thing."

"I was just thinking."

She looked up to the sky again.

"I come here and do the same thing. What are you thinking about?"

"The future."

"I think that sometimes we need to look back and see where we've been to get a better idea of where we're going."

They held hands and looked into each other's eyes. She quoted him with her next response.

"There's one thing I know. Whatever the future brings, it's better to have a friend by your side."

"I couldn't agree more."

They kissed.

"It's been a year already. I can't believe it," Charlie said.

"Yeah, I know what you mean. Time has just flown by. So much has happened. Even though we've known each other almost our whole lives, it seems like our lives started right here where we're sitting."

"I can't believe I waited so long to say it. I was so afraid of what could go wrong. Look at all the good things that I could have missed. What would it have been like if I never would have told you?"

"I hate to even think about that."

"Three little words changed everything."

"No. It wasn't the words themselves. It was the man who said them. The heart that I saw... the heart that I knew was beating only for me."

"Ready to hear it again?"

"Always," she whispered.

"Lisa Ann Duvall," he caught himself. "Jordache..."

She chuckled.

"I love you. I love everything about you. Not just as a friend. You're the love of my life. I'll never get tired of saying it."

"I'll never get tired of hearing it. I love you, too."

They kissed a little longer this time. Charlie stood up and helped Lisa to her feet. They took a few steps away from the table and held each other.

"The past was great, but the future is better," Charlie said softly. "My heart beats for two now."

They danced slowly in the moonlight. Charlie still couldn't believe how wonderful his life was. He was so afraid that she would break his heart before, but it turned out that she was right. She fixed it.

Charlie and Lisa experienced everything new all over again while spring was in bloom. They couldn't run together anymore, but they went on walks when they could. Lisa may have not have been as fast on her feet for the time being, but she still didn't slow down. She never missed a class nor any time at work, but it did start to get harder. Charlie's nineteenth birthday was May 11th. He still didn't make a wish when he blew out his candles. Instead of his old wish, Charlie would wake up each day and look at his wife. He already had everything he wanted. Their college year ended soon after his birthday. Now, they had more time to spend together just like the old days, yet still new.

CHAPTER 6

The air was filled with excitement. The smell of popcorn and hot dogs. The sounds of children laughing and familiar organ music playing. The sight of pennants and foam fingers waving. Charlie's senses were enchanted. He didn't usually like to be in a big crowd, but this was different. This was baseball. He was a red-blooded American boy in an environment that was synonymous with saluting the flag. If diamonds were a girl's best friend, then a baseball diamond was a boy's. He followed Lisa as they made their way through the stadium with Tracy and Tammy. Annie stood up and waved to get their attention. They came up to the seats that she reserved for them in the front. They set their snacks down to hug Annie.

"Oh, sweetie! I'm so glad you could make it."

"Of course! Gotta cheer on Dad."

"I can barely get my arms around you."

"That won't be a problem much longer."

"I'm so excited! I can't wait to spoil my grandbaby."

They let go. Lisa sat down so Annie could reach Charlie.

"Charlie, my boy! I'm so proud of you."

"Thanks, Annie."

"Call me Mom."

He chuckled. "Mom. I like the sound of that."

She smiled. They let go and Charlie picked up the snacks.

"Hey, girls! So good to see you!" Annie said as she waved to Tracy and Tammy.

"You, too," replied Tracy.

"Hey, come sit by me," Lisa told Tracy.

She squeezed past Charlie to sit between them. Tammy sat on Charlie's right. He was still amazed at how much she looked like her sister.

"There sure are a lot of people here," she said while eating her popcorn.

"Yes, there are. More than usual. That's because this is a very important game."

"Why is it so important?"

"If the Chargers win this one, then they'll go to the championship in Alabama."

"So... will we go down there to see that, too?"

He laughed. "Maybe. I hope so."

The announcer instructed them to rise for the national anthem. When it was over, the game commenced with a hearty, "Play ball!" The crowd roared. Soon after, the announcer introduced Lisa's dad as he waved to the crowd and "Fun, Fun, Fun" by The Beach Boys played.

"Ladies and gentlemen, our coach, Califoooooorrnniiiiaaaa Caaaalll!"

As loud as they cheered, Charlie could hear Lisa above the rest.

"It still cracks me up that they call him that," Annie said with a laugh.

The game moved on with enough thrilling action to keep everyone's attention. The Beach Boys provided much of the soundtrack to the drama played out in front of them.

"I know Lisa's digging all this Beach Boys music that they're playing," Tracy told Charlie, "...but, I've always like Simon and Garfunkel. Why don't they play them?"

He replied with a laugh, "I guess they don't think 'The Sound of Silence' fits a baseball game."

"Hey, 'Mrs. Robinson' talks about Joe DiMaggio."

"Well, ya got me there."

They laughed.

Topics of conversation between the five of them were wildly varied throughout each change of inning.

"Do you have a name for the baby yet?" Tracy asked.

"That's something that we really haven't talked about as much as we should," Charlie informed her as he looked at Lisa for some input.

"Yeah, that's a tough one," she added.

"When is the baby due? It looks like you could pop any day now," said Tracy.

"You're right. It should be sometime around my birthday."

"Then you'd better get on it with this name already!" Tracy said.

"Yeah, Grandma might pick it out for you!" Annie added.

"Lisa, Jr.," Charlie said with a smile.

"Charles, Jr.," Lisa retorted with a smile of her own.

"Nah, that's a terrible name for a girl," Charlie joked. "Besides, it sounds too much like a burger place."

"Maybe you could combine your names," Tracy jokingly suggested. "You know, something like 'Charlisa.'"

Everybody cracked up.

"Or 'Larlie,'" Annie said with a laugh.

Charlie added, "Or 'Chisa.' That way, if we have twins, we can say, 'meet our children, Macaroni and Chisa.'"

They all laughed at his joke, even though it was cheesy.

"Whatever we call this baby needs to be good. They're gonna be stuck with it forever," Lisa stated.

They all thought for a moment while turning their attention to the game.

"Man, all they need is one home run to turn this around," Annie mentioned.

Suddenly, Charlie remembered something. His mom told him something similar that she heard from someone who gave her a baseball.

"What about 'Sam'?" he asked.

"Sam..." Lisa repeated while listening to how it sounded.

"Why Sam?" Tracy asked.

"That was the name of the high school counselor. If it wasn't for him, I don't think I would've had the courage to tell Lisa that I love her."

"Sam... Samuel Jordache... it's not bad," Lisa said.

"You could even call him, 'Sammy,'" Tracy suggested.

"Or, if it's a girl, then you could name her 'Samantha,'" Tammy offered.

Charlie turned to her and smiled. "Yeah... Samantha. Smart kid."

"I got all A's and only one B," she informed him.

"Right on," he said with a high five.

"So, it's Sam?" asked Annie.

Lisa and Charlie looked at each other and smiled. They both nodded and said, "Sam."

The game progressed and the snacks were all used up.

"Charlie," Lisa said. "I could sure use some nachos."

"Again?"

"This one is for the baby."

"Okay."

He stood up.

"And some chocolate, if they have it."

"Anybody else want anything?"

"I'll just eat whatever falls out of her mouth," Tracy joked.

Lisa nudged her and said, "Ewww."

"I'll take some chocolate, too," said Tammy.

He headed towards the concession stand. The crowd became more exuberant. He turned around to see what the fuss was about. A fly ball was coming his way. It was quickly getting closer and closer... to a boy who wasn't watching. He held out his hand in front of the boy's face and caught it. The boy's eyes widened at the ball in front of his nose. He looked up at Charlie.

"Gotta keep your eye on the ball, kid."

He handed it to him and walked away. The crowd cheered.

"I can't believe I caught it," he thought. Just like when he was a kid.

When he returned from his mission, he handed Tammy a box of candy.

"Thank you."

"Here you go," he said to Lisa.

"Thanks. That was some catch."

"I didn't know you could do that," Tracy said.

"Sometimes we don't know what we can do until it's the right time to do it," he quoted Mrs. Allen.

"I like that. I'll have to remember it."

"It was either try to do it or let that kid get a broken nose."

"You still might have missed."

"I would rather try and fail than to fail by not trying."

"You are just full of wisdom, aren't you?"

He laughed. "Sometimes. Full of something, anyway."

The game was in the last inning. The Chargers were making a valiant effort, but they were still behind by one run. The fans were getting concerned.

"I wonder if they would have done better if Robbie was still here," Tracy remarked.

"Do you still talk to him?" asked Lisa.

"Not anymore."

"What happened?"

"We talked on the phone a few times after he moved to Kansas City, but that's been awhile. It's just as well. I need to be a nurse here, and he needs to be a baseball player there. We have different paths."

"He's a jerk," Tammy blurted out.

"Tammy..." Tracy said.

"You can do better than him."

"Why do you say that?" asked Charlie.

"He was kind of preoccupied with baseball," Tracy explained.

"He's full of himself," Tammy stated.

"That doesn't sound like him," Lisa added.

"He was nice at first," Tracy continued. "But... he just didn't care about me as much as he should have. He also didn't like to talk about some things. Like he didn't want to get too close. But, it's okay. He's doing what he needs to do, and I'm doing what I need to do. It just wasn't meant to be. I wish him well."

"Are you okay?" Lisa asked.

"Of course. I'm happy."

She nodded.

They watched as the game came to an end. The Chargers lost 8-7.

"No trip to Alabama, huh?" Tammy asked Charlie.

"I'm afraid not."

“They sure tried hard,” Annie said. Her disappointment was obvious. “It was a good game. They gave their best.”

“What more can you do?” asked Lisa. “Some things just aren’t meant to be.”

CHAPTER 7

Lisa's family and friends were all there for her birthday party on May 25th, 1986. She devoured more chocolate cake than Charlie had ever seen anyone attempt. She said that the baby seemed to enjoy it because he moved several times. Everyone had a gooc time, but also appeared nervous when she would react to the baby. It was like Lisa was a bomb waiting to explode at any moment. That moment wouldn't come until two days later.

Lisa went to work on the morning of the 27th. As much as she tried to do her job, the pain was becoming unbearable. Her co-workers urged her to go home. She eventually gave in. She tried as hard as she could to focus on the road as she made her way home through dizziness. She arrived at the apartment. Her steps were slow and painful as she headed to the door. She entered the building and looked up the stairs leading to their apartment. They looked like a mountain.

"Charlie!" she yelled at the bottom of the stairs.

He came downstairs to find her unconscious.

"Lisa! Come on, wake up!"

He picked her up and carried her out. He put her in the car and sped to the hospital. There was no time to lose.

The labor was intense, but thankfully not too long. Lisa heard the doctor say, "It's a boy" before passing out again. Char ie watched in amazement as the little guy cried upon entry into this strange, new world. It all felt surreal.

A few hours later, Ilene walked into the room quietly to find Charlie sitting by Lisa's bed while holding the baby.

"Has she woken yet?" she whispered.

"She's been asleep the whole time," he whispered back.

"I was going to go with Cal and Annie to get something to eat. Do you want to come with us?"

"I want to be here when she wakes up."

"I understand. Maybe I can bring you something back."

He nodded. She stepped up closer.

"What's going on in that beautiful mind of yours?"

He searched for the right words to say as tears came to his eyes.

"I remember holding Tammy when she was a baby. She was so tiny. I was afraid I might drop her. I saw Lisa holding her, then I was holding her... and for some reason, I thought, *'Lisa would be a good mom.'* Something just felt right even back then. I don't think nine year old boys usually have such thoughts, but I did." His tears increased. "Just as sure as I knew that I wanted to be with Lisa from the moment I saw her... I knew that I wanted to be a dad." She put her hand on his shoulder. "I spent so much of my life being hurt and disappointed. I didn't know that someday it would be like this. I didn't know that all my dreams would come true."

She bent down and put her arm around him. She leaned her head on his. Through her own tears she whispered, "You deserve this. You deserve every bit of this." They looked into each other's eyes. "I love you so much, Charlie." She kissed his cheek. "You're already a great dad."

"What if I'm not? What if I do things wrong? What if I..."

She interrupted him. "You just proved it. No one asks those kind of questions without trying to do their best. You want it more. You love him, don't you?"

"As much as I love you and Lisa."

She smiled. "Then there's nothing to worry about. He's in good hands."

She leaned down to kiss the baby's cheek and then Charlie's.

"They're waiting for me; I'd better go." She started to walk away and paused. She turned to him with a smile. "If you love someone, anything's possible."

He smiled and nodded. His memory was perfect, but sometimes he still needed certain reminders.

CHAPTER 8

"Hey, sleepyhead."

Lisa rubbed her eyes.

"I'm glad you're awake. How do you feel?"

"Like a busted piñata."

"Well, you're going to be okay. The hard part is over."

"Where's Mom?"

"She went with my mom to get something to eat. Did you want anything?"

"I just want to go home."

Lisa had never felt so weak.

"I know. You have to rest, though. You've been through a lot."

"I'm ready to go. I'm tired of hurting. I'm tired of being in this place. I just want it all to end. I want to go home where everything is better."

She knew that it was too soon. There was still more left for her there.

"I want to see him," she said.

"Are you sure?"

"I'm sure."

"Nothing will be the same."

"I'm ready."

"Close your eyes."

She closed them for a few seconds.

When she opened them, she declared, "He's so beautiful!"

"Like a glimpse of Heaven," added Charlie.

Lisa gained a little more energy looking into the eyes of her son.

"I didn't think it could happen twice," said Charlie.

"What's that?"

"Love at first sight."

"I know exactly how you feel."

They smiled as they looked into each other's eyes. He leaned forward and kissed her lips. They both turned their attention to their newborn.

"He has your eyes," she said.

"Let's hope he can see the world the way you do," he replied.

The baby smiled.

"He has your smile," Charlie said.

"Let's hope he can make others happy the way you've made me."

"He's the best of you and the best of me."

"Our little miracle."

Tears of joy began to flow from both parents.

She held the baby closer and kissed him.

"Hi, little Sammy. I'm your mommy, and this is your daddy. We love you very much. We're going to take good care of you. I promise."

Lisa was unaware that Ilene said that about Charlie and that he said that about Lisa the day they met. Some things are just meant to be.

Charlie and Lisa held and kissed their new little miracle. Nothing else mattered. They were a family, and they were in love. Anything was possible.

CHAPTER 9

Charlie woke one night around 2 AM. He was getting used to waking up at random times when the baby cried. He listened, but didn't hear a thing. He turned his head towards Lisa. She slept peacefully. He smiled as he tried to see her face in the dark. He didn't need his eyes to tell him how beautiful she was. He rose from the bed slowly and carefully. He cracked the door open with the same amount of stealth. The light from the hall shone in. He approached the crib. Sammy was sound asleep. He smiled as he admired the little miracle. Charlie tiptoed out the door. He went to the living room and turned on the light. He had far too many thoughts now to ever get back to sleep any time soon.

"They could be a family and they're moving."

"Here's the house."

"We're finally here at our new house in Kansas."

Charlie smiled at the memory of how Lisa would change voices for each doll.

"It sure takes a while to get from California to Kansas."

He remembered adding furniture to the doll house.

"But now I can start my new job."

He realized back then just how much she was telling him through the dolls.

"I hope I can make some new friends."

"Hi, I'm your neighbor. I brought some cookies. Want to be friends?"

"Cookies?! Far out! Of course I want to be friends with you!"

He chuckled.

"TAG! You're it!"

He didn't realize at the time that they would build their own home someday. He looked around the room at the cards from the baby shower, the pictures of Sammy, and the toys lying around.

"Am I beautiful, Charlie?"

"Like a bundle of sunshine. Especially on the inside. That's all that matters anyway."

"Thank you, Charlie."

He sat on the couch.

"God took the best of me and the best of your dad and gave us you. You're our little miracle, Charlie. The same goes for you, Lisa. Your parents have been blessed like I was. And remember, Charlie, as long as you're around, a part of your dad is still here. As you get older, I know that you'll continue to make us happy."

"I'll do my best."

"I know you will. I love you, Charlie, my little Valentine."

"I love you, too."

Tears came to his eyes.

"What are you doing?" Lisa whispered.

Charlie turned his attention to her. She slowly walked towards him.

"I was just thinking."

"About what?"

He stood up and put his arms around her. She did the same. He looked into her eyes as the tears began to roll out.

"I was thinking, *'what did I ever do to deserve all this?'*"

She smiled as tears of her own began to surface.

"I know exactly how you feel."

They kissed and held each other close.

She whispered, "I think about it all the time."

Their moment was interrupted by the sound of Sammy crying.

"There he goes again," she said with a sigh.

They quickly entered the bedroom. Charlie picked him up and held him. "It's my turn," he said.

"Are you sure? I can do it this time, if you want."

"That's ok. It's all a part of the job." He looked into Sammy's eyes. "I love being a dad."

Charlie and Lisa spent their summer break from school enjoying their new roles as parents. They couldn't wait to get home from work each day. Whenever they both had to work at the same time, one of the grandparents was always eager to help. Wherever Sammy was, there was the sound of music and laughter. They would get out the old records and sing along as Sammy bounced and wiggled with delight. Hours would go by with hardly any adult conversation while they played with squeaky toys and rattles. They would wipe away his tears and gently rock him. A full night's sleep was rare, but the supply and demand of diapers was constant. They were tired and sometimes overwhelmed. And, they loved every minute of it.

August 11th crept up rather quickly. Charlie and Lisa spent their anniversary with dinner and a movie while Annie watched Sammy. It was hard to believe that a year had already flown by. There was a saying that Charlie heard when they were little, one that still described his time with Lisa as much as it did then. "Time flies when you're having fun."

CHAPTER 10

"Okay, the diapers are over here. If he really makes a mess, his clothes are in here." She opened the dresser drawer.

Annie laughed. "I know where everything is. How many times have I been here?"

Lisa smiled. "You're right. I just have a thousand things going through my head. I don't want to forget anything."

They headed to the living room.

"OH! I almost forgot!"

She ran to the kitchen and came back with a bottle.

"I filled some bottles for him and have them in the fridge ready to go."

Annie laughed again as Lisa gave the bottle to Sammy.

"Relax, Lisa! I've got this. I know where the fridge is; I know where everything is."

"You're right. I'm sorry," she said with a chuckle. "I've just never been away from him for so long before."

"We're going to be okay, aren't we, Sammy?"

He smiled.

"This is his favorite rattle," Lisa said as she picked it up from the table and set it back down.

"There's nothing to worry about. I have everything under control. You just need to concentrate on having a good day at school."

Lisa took a deep breath and let it out. "Okay."

She smiled at Sammy. "I will see you later, little guy. You be good for Granny Annie, okay?" She kissed his cheek.

"Bye, sweetie," Annie said as she put her free arm around Lisa. "Have a good day."

"I will," she replied as she returned the hug.

She started walking out the door and paused. She turned around and gave Sammy one last wave. Annie picked up his arm and waved back.

Lisa got in the car where Charlie had been waiting. They began driving away.

"I forgot to tell her to call if anything happens!"

"Call the school?" Charlie asked.

"Yes. Maybe we should get one of those beeper things."

Charlie laughed. "It's going to be okay! I promise. Here I thought I was the worrier."

"I've just never been away from him for so long before. I'll only have a little time after school before I have to go to work."

"It's going to be fine. She's an old pro. Look how you turned out. I'll be thinking about Sammy, too, but I know he's in good hands."

"I know he is. I just wish it was easier."

"It's a challenge. It's a new challenge, but we've had those before. And, you know what? We'll have many more new challenges over the years. But, that's okay. That's just the way life works. We can get through anything because we already have. We can do anything together."

She smiled. "You sure sound a lot more confident than you used to."

"I get it from you. Besides, that's the way it's supposed to be. When I'm weak, you're strong, and when you're weak, I'm strong."

"We're a great team."

"We can rise to any challenge. That's what it is, just another challenge."

"Just another manic Monday."

As they approached the school, Tracy came up behind them and put her arms around their shoulders.

"Hey, guys!"

"Hey, Tracy," they said in unison as they put their arms around her.

"Ready for one more year?" she asked Charlie. Then she looked at Lisa and said, "Or three more years?" She playfully stuck her tongue out, which Lisa repeated with a laugh.

"The beginning of the end," said Charlie.

"Or, we've only just begun," said Lisa.

"There's something very familiar about all this," Tracy added.

They all laughed.

School went by without any trouble. Lisa was overjoyed when she got to see Sammy for the short time before she had to go to work. Charlie took care of him until it was time to go to work himself. Ilene took the responsibility from there until they came home. Each day was similar until it was the weekend. Work hours varied between Charlie and Lisa, but at least the only school they had was homework. And Sammy taught them something new every day.

"So, what do you want to read first?" Charlie jokingly asked Sammy.

It was now September 1986. He sat at the kitchen table with the Sunday newspaper as Lisa was making breakfast.

"The business section?"

Sammy seemed unamused.

"I know-- the sports section."

Still no smile.

"I bet I know what you really want. You want the same thing I want-- the comics."

He finally smiled.

"Let's see what's going on with that little round-headed kid today."

He flipped through the pages and stopped at the sports section.

"Huh. What do you know about that? Honey, you have to see this."

Lisa went to the table and looked over his shoulder. Charlie read the news aloud.

"Chesapeake native Robbie Kunkel has signed a seven year contract with the minors. The nineteen-year-old Kansas City College star, who led his team to victory in the June series, is headed for Omaha's greener pastures. 'It's exactly what I hoped would happen,' says Kunkel. 'We won the series, and that caught the eye of the minors. I've had a great time in Kansas City, and now it's time to move on to Omaha. Hopefully, I'll be back here again someday with the majors.' At the current pace he's on, that 'someday' may be sooner rather than later. Adds Kunkel, 'It's like all my dreams are coming true.'"

He looked up to Lisa as they smiled.

"Good for him. That's awesome," he said.

"Yeah, it really is. I'm glad it worked out for him."

"We should put this in the scrapbook."

"We don't have a scrapbook."

"There's a good reason to get one now."

She went back to the food for a moment, but was interrupted by the phone.

"Hello?"

"Lisa! Did you see the paper?"

"Hi, Dad! Yeah, we were just looking at it."

"Did you see the part about Robbie?"

"Yes, we did. It's really something, isn't it?"

"Yeah, that's pretty good! I still think we would've won if he was on the team. Far too late to change that now."

"Yeah, I think you would've won."

"I guess we'll never really know. Oh, well. We'll do it next time." He laughed. "I bet he would've stayed here if you two were still together."

"Eww. Don't even joke about a thing like that," she said with a laugh. "I think things worked out exactly the way they were supposed to."

"So do I. I'm glad you're with Charlie. And I'm glad to have a grandson. That's better than winning some game."

"Couldn't be any better."

"Well, I oughta go. See you at church."

"See you later."

She hung up the phone and sat down at the table. Charlie finished cooking while she was on the phone.

"Did I get the eggs right?"

She glanced at the plate and looked up to him. "Couldn't be any better."

CHAPTER 11

December 21st, 1986. Everyone was gathered together for Tammy's eleventh birthday. Since the 22nd was on a Monday, her parents decided to have it on Sunday to make it easier for everyone. As usual, Christmastime kept most of the kids away, but Tammy was clearly happy with the friends and family who were there. As the kids played, the adults talked about whatever the heck it is that adults talk about. The irony wasn't lost on Charlie. He marveled at the new perspective that came with being one of the grown-ups. Tracy's parents, Lee and Zachary, asked him all kinds of questions about his new role as a dad. Sammy was passed around the room as each of them took turns admiring him and making silly faces. Lisa and Tracy got into a small conversation about the near future.

"So… Robbie called me yesterday," Tracy mentioned.

"He did? What did he say?"

"He told me all about getting a contract with the minors and moving to Omaha. Did you know he dropped out?"

"No, I didn't know that."

"He said that he had to so that he could move and be ready for the season in February."

"I guess that makes sense."

"Well, anyway, he's talking about coming down here for Christmas before he moves next month."

"Oh, really? Is he coming just to see you?"

Tracy squirmed and smiled nervously. "I don't know. Maybe."

Lisa chuckled. "How do you feel about that?"

"I don't know. He might be coming to see his dad, too."

"I thought they didn't get along."

"I don't know… all I know is that he's talking about coming here to see me."

"Do you want to see him?"

"I guess I wouldn't mind. It's just a visit. He can do whatever he wants. If he sees me, fine. If not, fine. It's not that big of a deal."

Lisa smiled and shook her head. "Whatever you say, Tracy."

When it was time for cake, everybody gathered together and sang "Happy Birthday" to Tammy. She blew out the candles after making a wish. She excitedly opened all her presents. The best one from her parents and Tracy was saved for last. She quickly tore the wrapping paper off and screamed.

"MY OWN TAPE PLAYER!!! WITH HEADPHONES AND EVERYTHING!!! RADICAL!!! "

They all laughed.

"There's another one that goes with it," said Zachary as he handed her one last gift.

Her eyes grew even wider. She ripped off the paper in one second. She screamed again as she saw the new cassette tapes to go with her player.

"The Bangles! Michael Jackson! New Kids on the Block? I haven't heard of them, but they're cute."

"They're fairly new, but I have a feeling that they're going to be big," Lee informed her.

Tammy looked at the last tape.

"'Back to the...' (GASP!) I love that movie!"

She got out of her seat and hugged her family.

"Thank you so much!"

"You're welcome."

Charlie turned to his mom. "I never got that excited, did I?"

She laughed. "Not visibly, anyway. But, the girls sure did."

Tammy asked her mom, "Can I play one of my tapes in the stereo so we can all hear it?"

"I think that's a great idea."

She quickly opened one and rushed to the stereo. The house was suddenly filled with the exuberant sound of Huey Lewis and the News as "The Power of Love" played. Tammy and her friends danced to the music as little Sammy giggled and wiggled in Lisa's arms. She looked at Charlie. They smiled at each other and kissed.

Zachary said, "Turn it down a little."

Charlie couldn't resist. He quipped, "Yeah, I'm afraid you're just too darn loud."

A few days later, it was Christmas. Charlie, Lisa, and Sammy spent the day at Ilene's along with Cal and Annie. Everyone loved spoiling the baby with new toys and clothes. The best gift was for Charlie and Lisa. Everyone pitched in and got them a camcorder to record all the special moments that Sammy would bring. Charlie started using it as soon as the battery was charged. The Whitsons came over that night and exchanged more gifts before having dinner. Afterwards, Lisa couldn't help but ask Tracy about Robbie.

"He called last night and said that it snowed a lot. He's not coming now."

"Are you disappointed?"

"Maybe a little," she said with a shrug. "Who knows when he'll ever be around here again?"

"Well, if he's smart, he'll try again before the season starts."

"It's okay. We're just friends anyway."

Lisa wasn't so sure that Tracy's feelings were only platonic.

"Charlie and I were just friends for the longest time."

"Yeah, but you two really have something special. There's no comparison. Just look at Charlie."

They shifted their focus to him as he went around the house recording everyone as if he was making a nature documentary, complete with a British accent. He came up to them and continued his act.

"And now we find a rare beast called a 'Tracy.' She may appear harmless, but she has a ferocious pair of claws."

Tracy didn't miss a beat as she made a cougar noise while demonstrating her "claws."

"Then we have what's known as a 'Lisa.' A creature so fast, she may actually rival a cheetah."

Lisa blinked rapidly for the camera.

"Look at how fast she can blink! Isn't that amazing?!"

They laughed as he moved on to other subjects.

"He's one of a kind," Tracy told Lisa. "Look at how much he's come out of his shell since you two have been together."

"You'll meet the right guy someday. I'm sure of it."

"Maybe I will, maybe I won't. I just hope that if I do, he'll be half as good as Charlie. Maybe it will happen someday."

"Don't worry about it, Tracy. I think your someday is coming."

CHAPTER 12

A new year brought many new changes and challenges for the Jordache family in 1987. No matter what would lie ahead for him each day, Charlie would wake up next to Lisa and smile. He still couldn't get over how good he had it. He would go to school and to work, always giving his best, but still longing to just be home with his family. Whenever he was with Lisa and Sammy, it felt too good to be true, almost like he was living someone else's life. This was his life, though, despite how wonderful it was or how unworthy he felt, he was indeed blessed to live it. So he lived it with all his might. He played with Sammy and read him stories. He recorded tape after tape of Sammy as well as Lisa. The proud parents showed their own parents the footage of Sammy's first time crawling and eventually his first steps. Feeding him was always a test of skill, and bath time wasn't much different. Valentine's Day came and they celebrated their love more than ever. Whatever happened each day, whether usual or unexpected, Charlie still felt like the happiest man alive.

One Sunday afternoon, Lisa called for Charlie to come to the kitchen. He wasn't sure what to expect based on the serious look on her face.

"Is something wrong?"

"No, I just have something I need to tell you."

"It seems pretty serious. Are you sure you're okay?"

"Yes. There's just something I've been thinking about a lot, and I think it's time I finally told you. I just didn't know the best way to do it."

He took her hands. "It's okay. You can tell me anything."

"It's something about me that I keep secret... like the way you have a perfect memory. I've been afraid to say anything because I didn't know how you'd react."

He took her in his arms. "I love you no matter what. There's nothing you can say or do that will ever change that."

She slowly pulled away. They looked into each other's eyes.

"I promise," he whispered.

She took a deep breath.

"Okay. Here goes."

Charlie's anticipation soared. He had a feeling that no matter what she said, it would only make him love her more.

She took another breath.

"I can move things with my mind."

Charlie was taken aback. "W-what?"

"I can move things with my mind."

He smiled. "No way."

"I knew you wouldn't believe me," she said as she started walking away.

"Wait a minute! Are you serious? You can't really do that… can you?"

"Why would I make that up?"

"It does sound pretty unbelievable."

"You're the one who can remember everything."

"Yeah, so?"

"So, you can remember everything because you have a 180 IQ. Mine is 185. Our brains aren't the same as others. They can do things that may seem impossible to anyone else."

"That's true, but…"

"I've never even told anybody before. I don't want to be treated like a freak."

Charlie understood where she was coming from. He saw himself in her eyes.

"I'm sorry I doubted you."

"I'll prove it."

"You don't even have to prove it. I believe you."

"I still want to share it with you. No secrets." Her eyes scanned the room. "I just need something to use… something that's not too big. I haven't done this in a long time." She walked towards the table. "Aha! This should work."

She stared intently at the water bottle. Charlie started to feel a little more skeptical again.

"It's been too long," she explained. "I have to concentrate harder."

She closed her eyes and put her hands on her temples. She took a few deep breaths.

"Is it working?" she asked with her eyes still shut.

"No," he replied. His skepticism began fading away as he observed her conviction.

She tightened her face more. She gritted her teeth and groaned.

"Is it working yet?"

"No."

"Not even a little?"

"No."

She stopped and opened her eyes.

"Maybe it needs to be closer."

She picked up the bottle and placed it in the palm of her left hand. She concentrated till it looked like she was about to break a sweat. Charlie's anticipation grew. He knew that such things were impossible, but his whole life was filled with such improbabilities that his mind began to accept that Lisa may just pull it off.

"You can do it, Lisa," he whispered as encouragement.

"I held back for so long... I... I don't know anymore."

She strained and groaned and appeared very frustrated. She opened her eyes.

"Maybe this is still too much. I need something lighter. I know!" she loosened the cap with her right hand. "If I can't make this little cap move, then I give up."

She closed her eyes again and concentrated on the cap. Charlie watched closely for any sign of the slightest movement. Lisa always showed him that if you love someone, anything's possible. Surely, this would be easy for someone who changed his life.

"Is it moving yet?" she asked with her eyes tightly clinched.

"Not yet."

"Are you watching closely?"

"I'm watching closely."

"I feel like it's happening! Look close! Look close!"

He got two inches away from it and watched it like a hawk.

"Is it moving?" she asked, nearly shouting in desperation.

"Not yet," he answered. "Come on, come on," he whispered as his nerves could hardly take any more.

"Here it comes!" she exclaimed with nervous excitement.

Charlie kept his focus.

And then the cap along with the water flew into his face while Lisa squeezed the bottle.

"HAHAHAHAHAHAHAHAHA!!!!" Lisa laughed hysterically as a startled Charlie wiped his face with his sleeve.

"I can't believe you fell for that!!" Lisa said as she doubled over in laughter.

"You really got me. I can't believe I believed you!"

"You should see your face! 'You can do it, Lisa!' I almost lost it when you said that! HAHAHAHAHA!!!" She flopped down to the floor.

"You were very convincing." He started to laugh. "I didn't know you could act."

"I didn't know you were so gullible! HAHAHAHAHA!!!"

"That's right, yuk it up. One of these days, you'll get yours."

He walked over to the sink.

"It will take awhile before you can come up with anything that could top that," she said.

"Maybe," he said with a shrug. "It will happen one of these days. Maybe even right NOW!"

He sprayed her with the hose from the sink. She screamed with surprise as he laughed along with her.

He stopped and said, "Hey, stop screaming. You're going to wake the baby."

She got off the floor quickly and said, "I'll give you something to scream about!"

She tried to get the hose from him. He let go and ran with her chasing after him. He ran into the bathroom, but couldn't shut the door fast enough.

"So, you think you can outrun the great 'Sunshine Duvall,' eh?"

She had a menacing look on her face. He kept stepping backwards as she kept moving towards him. He was stopped by the wall. She kept her icy glare focused on his eyes and stood directly in front of him. Without even a blink, she grabbed the bottom of her shirt and wrung the water onto his feet. He looked down and back to her.

"I hate wet socks," he grumbled.

She tried to hold back a smile.

"Hey, you started it!" he reminded her.

"And I'm going to finish it."

She swiftly nabbed the shower hose and pointed it at him.

He held his hands out and said, "You wouldn't."

She reached for the faucet.

"Think of the mess it will make!" he pleaded.

She ignored his pleas and turned on the water works. They laughed hysterically.

"WORTH IT!!!" she enthused.

The baby started crying. She turned off the water.

"Now look what you've done," Charlie teased.

"It's your turn," she retorted.

"As I said before, think of the mess it will make. You don't want me getting all this water in the bedroom, do ya?"

She scrunched up her face and said, "Fine!"

She playfully stormed off as Charlie got out the towels with a laugh. This was one of those times when everyone was a winner.

Charlie's twentieth birthday was another good time with family and friends, as was Mother's Day. But, May was also the time of another event that was long-awaited.

His name was called by the Dean, "Charles Allen Jordache."

Charlie's family and friends cheered him on while he accepted his degree. After a few minutes, they cheered for another graduate.

"Tracy Aiko Whitson."

When the ceremony was nearly over, the Valedictorian gave a speech. Charlie had never been so nervous in all his life.

They all gathered together outside taking turns congratulating the graduates.

“Hey, Mr. Valedictorian! How does it feel?” asked Jeremy Allen.

“Pretty darn good,” Charlie answered with a laugh. “I’m just glad to get that speech out of the way.”

“You were great. Now we’re one big step closer to starting our school.”

“I can’t wait.”

“Charlie, I’m so proud of you!” Theresa exclaimed as she gave him a hug.

“Thanks, Mrs. Allen. I wouldn’t be here without you.”

They let go.

“Well done, young man,” Glenn Allen said with a handshake.

“Thanks, Mr. Allen,” Charlie said.

The Jordaches, Duvalls, Whitsons, and Allens hugged, talked, joked, and laughed. They finally remembered that they needed to take pictures. Charlie and Tracy stood next to each other. Lisa ran up and got in between them.

“Just like high school,” she said.

“CHEEESE!!” they said in unison.

The cameras flashed and they laughed.

“Okay, just you two,” Lisa said as she got out of the shot.

Tracy and Charlie put their arms around each other and smiled for the cameras.

When they were done, Tracy smiled at him and said, “We did it.”

Charlie smiled back and said, “I kept believing in you, and you kept believing in me.”

Tracy smiled even bigger. “You remember that?”

“Of course I do,” he chuckled. “I remember all the important things. How could I forget when it comes to you? You’re a real friend, and...”

She said with him, “...that’s a hard thing to find.”

They held each other close.

“I love you, Charlie--as a friend.”

“I love you, too--as a friend.”

The more things changed, the more some things stayed the same. For that, Charlie couldn’t be more thankful.

Lisa’s birthday came soon thereafter and was another joyful occasion with loved ones. The greater joy came a couple of days later when they all got together again for something that seemed too soon to be possible.

Theresa Allen gently played the keyboard she brought to the Duvall house. She smiled as she sang the opening lines to “(They Long to Be) Close to You” by The Carpenters. Jeremy added his violin and voice to the next part. Annie and Ilene took the chorus as they gathered around little Sammy, who was dancing in Lisa's arms. Tracy, Tammy, and Lee sang the background harmony and swayed back and forth. The trumpet solo was replaced by a harmonica this time.

"I didn't know your dad could play the harmonica," Charlie said quietly to Lisa.

"He's versatile. Here comes our part."

Lisa and Charlie sang the chorus together as Sammy's smile grew even bigger. Lisa took the lead for the rest of the song as everyone else sang harmonies and swayed and danced. Sammy clearly loved every bit of it. Charlie wrapped his arms around Lisa and Sammy and kissed Lisa's lips. They each kissed Sammy's cheeks.

She said softly, "Happy birthday, little man."

Summer break was more fun than ever for Charlie. He got to spend more time with his family and enjoy the outdoors. One Thursday night, he was off work. He took Sammy to his mom's house and waited for Lisa to come home from work. Everything had to be just right.

"Man, it was crazy at work. I'm so glad that's over."

She plopped down on the couch and kicked her shoes off.

Charlie stood by the door.

"Where's Sammy?" she asked.

"At Mom's. Tonight's a special occasion."

"Oh, yeah? We've already had birthdays, graduation, holidays, and our anniversary isn't until August. What's left?"

"First, a gift."

He handed her a plate of cookies that was hidden on the top shelf.

"Mom's chocolate chip!"

She quickly devoured one and let out an almost unintelligible, "Thank you."

He smiled and walked back to the door.

"I heard a noise one day. It was coming from outside. It sounded like a big truck."

"Probably the garbage man."

He chuckled and shook his head. "No, this wasn't recent. I ran to the door to see what it was." He opened the door. "I looked through the screen door, but I didn't open it so that I wouldn't let all the cold air out." He looked through the screen door. "And there it was-- a big truck. This nice-looking lady got out and let a little girl down. She was wearing a dress that twirled as she ran around the yard. She was the most beautiful thing I've ever seen. Mom came up behind me and said, 'She's a pretty little girl. Looks like she's your age, too.'" He shut the door and turned to her.

"That little girl was me, wasn't it?" she said with a big smile and a touch of sarcasm.

He laughed. "Yes, it was. But, do you know when it was?"

"1972."

"June 25th, 1972."

"You really do remember everything."

"It was fifteen years ago today."

"That long?"

He nodded his head. "How could I ever forget?" He sat next to her and held her hand. "It wasn't just a little girl I saw that day. I knew then as I still know today. It was a glimpse of the rest of my life."

He reached under the couch and pulled out a scrapbook.

"What in the world?" she asked with a smile.

"This is our story."

They set it on the table and opened it. They laughed and reminisced as they looked at all the old photos.

"Wow! Look how young we are! First day of kindergarten! That really takes me back!"

"Wait till you see what's next."

"The watch I gave you for your sixth birthday! You still have it!"

"Of course! Just like you and your friendship bracelet."

"That's the card you made me when I was sick! How did you get that?"

"Your mom had it. She gave me some of the other things, too."

"There's the one with Tracy! I always loved this picture!"

"Yeah, I think it's my favorite."

"And there's the postcard I sent you! And the one you sent me!"

Her eyes lit up every time. There were birthday and Christmas cards and little notes throughout.

"The picture with the house in California... and the school picture... how much is in here?"

"You'll see."

She laughed. "You actually have my track pictures in here!"

"It was the first time I ever saw them."

"Here's you... I've never seen this before."

"That's right. I included some things from when we weren't even together. We were still in each other's hearts."

She eventually came to the high school graduation picture.

"There ya go. The original Three Amigos. What's this?"

"That's a receipt from the mall. That's when we got hot fudge sundaes."

"Our first date."

"Kinda."

"Here's a doozy-- our engagement announcement in the paper... and the wedding announcement. And the wedding invitation!"

"And more receipts and ticket stubs from our honeymoon."

Lisa started to tear up. "Sammy."

"Look how much he's grown in just a year."

"Aww... the hair from his first haircut."

"Time flies."

"What's this?"

"That would be the magical flying bottle cap of trickery."

She laughed. "I can't believe you kept that. That's hilarious."

"It was a good memory. Recent and quite moist, but still a good memory."

"Of course, there's graduation."

"And still room for more."

She started to tear up again and looked him in the eyes.

"This is the most romantic thing I've ever seen."

"Imagine if you hadn't moved in next door. How much different would life be? But, we were meant to be together. The outgoing California girl and the shy Kansas boy. Sunshine and Mr. Blue Sky. Only God could have brought us together. And together, we're so much better. Together, we have a son. Look at what we've done in fifteen years. It may seem like a long time, but we're just getting started."

"We've only just begun." A tear rolled down her cheek. "Forever means forever."

Charlie got off the couch and took her hands. She stood and followed him to the stereo.

"There's a song that I never really paid much attention to until I heard it on the radio the other day. I had to track it down. Not all of the lyrics match, but a lot of them do. I think you'll understand."

He played the tape. They started to dance to "I Love You" by The Climax Blues Band. They held each other close as tears of joy flooded their eyes. The memories came flooding, too. Playing tag and hide and seek. Falling asleep while coloring after school. Holding hands in the car. The group hug when finding out about his dad. Their sad farewell as she moved away. The big hug when they were reunited. Throwing pennies in the fountain. Confessing their love for each other at the park. Their wedding. Their honeymoon in California. The birth of Sammy. It was only fifteen years, but it was the love of a lifetime. Charlie looked into Lisa's eyes and straight into her soul. He knew they were thinking the same thoughts and feeling the same things. They were one. As the song reached the end, they kissed passionately. They couldn't stop, nor did they have any reason to. They kept kissing as they made their way to the bedroom and shut the door.

The summer days finally came to an end when Charlie began his new job in August 1987. He was the new physics professor of Chesapeake University, a role which gave this twenty-year-old the distinction of being the youngest professor in the school's history. The transition of student to teacher was fairly easy since he was so well-prepared, especially considering his experience with the gifted program. Some of his students were older than him, and scoffed at the sight of his youth. It didn't take too long for his knowledge to convince them. He enjoyed his work, even if it did have its challenges. He always remembered to stay professional and authoritative, never showing a glimpse of his personal feelings and anxieties, however minimized they had become. He was the "man with a plan," living out his plans at long last. It still struck him funny at times, but he did grow to appreciate the title of professor, or "Professor Jordache."

Charlie's new career paid very well, so he cut back his time at the restaurant, only keeping that job just to have a little extra income. His intention was to get financially secure enough to free Lisa to quit her job at the mall and just concentrate on school and motherhood. It was a good plan, and good timing, too. One Saturday morning, Charlie sat at the table with the newspaper.

"I've been thinking," Lisa stated.

"There's my cue to run," Charlie joked.

"Ha-ha, very funny. Seriously, I think that we should start looking for a house."

"A house? What makes you think that?"

"Well, you make more money now, and Sammy's getting bigger and starting to run around more. Besides, we might need more room soon."

"What do you mean?"

She put his hand on her belly. "This is what I mean."

His eyes widened. "Another one?" he said with a smile.

She smiled and nodded. "We're having another baby."

"Did you hear that, Sammy?" he looked over to his son in the highchair. "You're going to have a little brother or sister!"

He smiled.

"When did you find out?" Charlie asked Lisa.

"Just this morning."

He put his hand on her cheek and she closed her eyes.

"I love you so much," he said softly.

"I love you, too."

They kissed. They looked into each other's eyes and took a deep breath as they started to realize the adventure they were about to get into.

"About that house..." Charlie quipped as he turned to the classifieds. "I've already circled a few good ones."

"I bet you have."

It wasn't long until they moved into their new house. It wasn't the fanciest, but it did have its charms. It was a two-story with four bedrooms and a fairly large living room. It was exactly what they wanted. Each kid would have their own room and there was still one left over to use as a study. There was plenty of room to run around and play. It was not only a house for the growing Jordache family, it was their home.

The rest of the year brought many more wonderful memories. No matter what would lie ahead for him each day, Charlie would wake up next to Lisa and smile. He still couldn't get over how good he had it. Every night before bed, he would pray this prayer, sometimes getting down on his knees like he did as a little boy.

"Thank you, God, for my family. I promise I'll take good care of them."

CHAPTER 13

"Lisa! Just look at you! You're ready to pop!"

Ilene threw her arms around her as she entered the house.

"I feel ready to pop, too. I can't wait to get this baby out of me. I'm tired of going up and down the stairs. It's really giving my swollen ankles a workout."

"Hey, big guy!" Ilene said to Sammy as she picked him up.

"Can you say, 'Hi, Grandma Ilene'?" Lisa asked.

He tried, but couldn't quite say it. They laughed and sat on the couch.

"Couldn't you switch the master bedroom with the study so you can stay downstairs, at least for awhile?"

"Yeah, I guess we could do that. That's still too far from Sammy's room, though."

"He'll be okay. Charlie will just have to get more of a workout is all. Speaking of which, is he at work?"

"Yes. He gets off at nine."

"I don't know how he does it."

"Neither do I. I have a hard enough time as it is with school and being a mom. It was worse when I worked at the store. I'm so glad I don't have to keep doing that with the baby. I've always wondered-- how did you do it?"

"You mean with Charlie?"

"Yeah. Weren't you still in school?"

"Yes, I was. Wayne and I got married right before school started. It was just like it was with you and Charlie. We were engaged by the end of high school and got married as soon as we could. We just couldn't wait. That was 1966."

Lisa smiled.

"I was pregnant all through freshman year." She laughed. "It wasn't easy, but I made it. We couldn't afford for both of us to go to school, so Wayne gave up his chance so that I could still go."

"Wow. That was a very honorable thing to do."

"He worked all day to make sure we could get by. After having Charlie, he worked nights and stayed home with him during the day while I went to school. For four years, we did that. Then I started teaching in '70 instead of being the student. Wayne still stayed home with Charlie. But, the plant closed, and we needed more money. So, he took whatever work he could find. He became a janitor at night, and after awhile, started doing it in the daytime, too."

"Who watched Charlie then?"

"We had to start taking him to a daycare. He didn't really like it, and it didn't last too long. That was before summer break, and then he went to kindergarten. Charlie would've had to keep going to daycare if it wasn't for your mom watching him."

"I'm sorry if this is a sore subject, but I'm curious. Was there no family to help?"

She shook her head. "I lost my parents when Charlie was still a baby."

"I remember you telling me that before. I'm sorry, Mom."

"It's okay. I'm just glad that they got to see him. Charlie may have a perfect memory, but there's no way he can remember that. He was far too young."

"I didn't mean to bring up any bad memories, I just didn't know if there was anyone else, like maybe Dad's parents."

"No, I couldn't ask them. We didn't get along."

"It's hard to imagine anyone not getting along with you. You're the kindest person in the world."

"Thanks, but they didn't see me that way."

"What could be so wrong with you?"

"They thought we rushed into things, didn't like him giving up school, things like that. Never even gave me a chance. Never even tried to see Charlie. They can just stay away for all I care."

Trying to put a more positive spin on it, Lisa said, "It's their loss. Clearly you two were meant to be together. I wish I would have known him better. He sounds like a really wonderful man."

"He loved you. He was so happy that you and Charlie were friends. He was so proud of Charlie. He always bragged on him to everyone. If camcorders would've been invented back then, he would've done just what Charlie does."

Lisa laughed. "Like father, like son."

"Charlie really is a lot like him."

"He did spend a lot of time with him in his formative years. Some of it may be learned, and some of it may be nature."

"I guess we'll never really know which. I'm just proud of the man he's become. You have a lot to do with that, too."

"I think it's more from you than anyone. I just hope can be a mom like you."

She held her hand. "You already are. I'm so proud of you, daughter."

Later that night, Lisa put Sammy to bed. The house was silent as she waited for Charlie to come home. Her mind, however, was busy with a thousand thoughts. She got out the scrapbook and thought back to the old days.

"It looks like you had a good time with Charlie. What do you think about your new friend?"

"He's kind of shy, but he's really nice. I like him. I like him a lot."

"So do I. I really like his mom, too."

"Yeah, she's pretty nice. Anyone who makes me cookies is okay in my book."

She chuckled.

"See? Moving here isn't so bad after all. I think we're all going to get along just fine."

Her memory wasn't as perfect as Charlie's, but she still remembered every detail of the most important moments.

"That was a good first day of school, wasn't it, Charlie?"

"Yes, it was. It was a lot better than I expected."

"Mrs. Allen is really nice, isn't she?"

"Yeah. She's a really good teacher."

"She's really smart, too. And she's pretty. Do you think she's pretty, Charlie?"

"Yeah, I-I guess so, for a teacher."

"Well, I think she's beautiful, for a teacher or anybody. Especially on the inside. The inside is all that really matters anyway, you know."

"I agree."

"I wonder what she said to everybody. You know? When she was taking attendance? I've never seen a teacher do that before. I wonder what she said. What did she say to you?"

"She said that my mom told her about me and that she was sorry about my dad."

"I'm sorry—we don't have to talk about it. I know it still hurts."

"It's okay. She told me not to worry, and that she was going to take good care of me. Then, she said, 'welcome to my class.' What did she say to you?"

"She also said, 'welcome to my class.' She said that your mom told her that I was one of her best students, and that I was smart, and nice, and like a bundle of sunshine."

She remembered how nervous she was, more than she ever was up to that point in time.

"She also said that I was beautiful. Am I beautiful, Charlie?"

"Like a bundle of sunshine."

She started smiling a little as she fiddled with her friendship bracelet. Her smile grew as big as could be after he told her the rest. Just the same as back then.

"Especially on the inside. That's all that matters anyway."

"Thank you, Charlie."

She laughed as she remembered him falling asleep and putting her arm around him.

"Poor, sleepy Charlie. I think you're beautiful, too."

She reminisced until Charlie came home.

"Man, I'm tired. I couldn't wait to get here," he said as he walked in.

She got off the couch and held him as close as she could with a pregnant belly.

He chuckled a bit and returned the hug.

"You really know how to make a guy feel welcome."

She kissed him slowly and tenderly.

"Wow. What was that for?"

"I just love you is all. You're a beautiful man, Charlie."

"Well, I did shave," he said with a smile.

She smiled back. "That's not what I meant."

"I know what you meant. I love you, too, my bundle of sunshine."

They kissed again.

The time had finally come. Lisa gave birth to Elijah Charles Jordache on March 30th, 1988. It was love at first sight all over again. Charlie recorded as much as he could that day and all the others after that. Lisa missed the boys tremendously when she went back to school, but made the most of it when she was home. She read stories to Sammy at night and sang little Elijah to sleep. It was also around this time when Sammy began to use real words. He started out with "Mommy," "Daddy," and "baby," but it didn't take long until he started forming sentences. When Charlie had summer break from school, he still worked at the restaurant to have more income. Lisa watched the kids throughout the day, sometimes having help from their parents, Tracy, or Tammy. She loved every moment. When it came time for school again, she hated to give it up. *"Just one more year,"* she would tell herself. *"Mom did it, and so can I."*

CHAPTER 14

It was September 1988. Charlie and Lisa were doing their best to juggle all their responsibilities. The newspaper was keeping track of Robbie's career in the minors. Charlie always saved the articles in the scrapbook. The championship series was televised on one of the cable channels, and Charlie watched and recorded as many of the games as he could.

"Why do you keep watching him? Isn't it weird to you that I used to date him?" asked Lisa.

"A little, but I still ended up with you, so I'm over it. Besides, I think it's cool that someone from here is making it big."

"Is he really that big?"

"The series is tied 3-3. Let's just say that if they win this game, he will probably make it to the majors."

"You don't say."

"I do say."

She sat next to him. It had been quite some time since she saw Robbie play. She almost forgot how good he really was. They cheered each time he hit the ball or threw a runner out at second base. He was strong and quick with no sign of slowing down. He was clearly the star of the game. Lisa paid attention as much as she could, but had to deal with the baby sometimes. She was just finishing up with a diaper change when she heard Charlie say, "Is that Tracy?!"

She ran into the room.

"Where?"

"Too late. Now it's a commercial."

"Are you recording it?"

He rewound it to show her the shot of the crowd.

"That's her, all right," he said.

"She said that Robbie invited her to go to the game, but I didn't know she actually went up there. Maybe she's getting more serious about him."

"Maybe so."

They watched as the game continued. Robbie was guarding second base with a runner on first waiting to pounce. The batter drove the ball close to third base. As the batter ran towards first, the third baseman threw the ball towards Robbie to tag out the other runner. Robbie's legs were spread with his right foot on the base as he tried to catch the ball.

The announcer bellowed, "Fredericks is sliding to second... Whoa! He's knocked over Kunkel!"

Lisa gasped. They watched in disbelief as Robbie fell back and sideways.

"Fredericks is getting up and running to third! But, Kunkel is still down! This doesn't look good."

"It's his knee," observed Charlie.

They watched the stretcher take him away. Another commercial started.

"Play it back," Lisa said.

Charlie rewound the tape.

"There! Did you see that?" she asked as she pointed at the screen.

He played it back again.

"He did it on purpose," Charlie declared.

"Now, why would he do that?"

"To win at any cost."

Lisa shook her head. "Poor Robbie."

"They called it a malicious slide."

Tracy explained the situation to Lisa and Charlie a few days later at their house.

"The other team wanted to win so badly that they thought the best way to do that was to cheat and injure the best player. I don't know if Tyson Fredericks came up with the idea or if it was the manager. I'm not even sure if they thought it would injure him as much as it did. All I know is that they got their way and Robbie had to pay the price."

"How bad is it?" asked Charlie.

"His ACL and meniscus are torn. They let me look at his charts. He'll have to have surgery."

"He'll bounce back, though... right?" asked Lisa.

"Eventually. He has to heal from the surgery, then he has physical therapy. It's going to take weeks, probably a few months. Even then, his knee may not be what it once was."

"But, there's still a chance that he can play ball again, right?" Charlie asked.

"There's a chance, but here's the thing-- the timing is terrible. There's a thirty day disabled list. He's going to be out longer than that. Even if Omaha decides to still keep him on, he may not make it to spring training. And the majors start recruiting in June. All he could talk about was wanting to play for Kansas City. It's been his dream for so long, but now he might miss his shot. I could tell that he was really worried about that. What he would talk about the most in the hospital, though, was Fredericks. He had all kinds of choice words for him. I think he was inventing new cuss words."

"Do you think he would move back here?" asked Charlie.

"Probably not. There's nothing for him here."

"What about you?" Lisa asked.

"Me? He wouldn't move here for me. No, we'll never be more than friends. He's too obsessed with his baseball career to really have a serious relationship."

"But, you said that it might be over," noted Charlie.

"It will never be over for him," Tracy replied. Her tone grew more serious than it already was. "There was something about the way he said things. That look in his eyes. This has changed him. Without baseball, he's going to lose all of his sense of purpose. I saw something change in you, Charlie."

"What do you mean?"

"When Lisa moved away, a part of you died. As the years went by, you became more and more withdrawn and even bitter. Remember those days?"

He nodded. "I remember. Unfortunately."

"It was like we weren't even friends anymore. I finally got so tired of it that I had to start reaching out to you."

"I'm glad you did. I'm sorry for all that."

"Ancient history. I'm just thankful you moved back," she said to Lisa.

"So am I. We were both lost without each other."

"Do you see what I'm saying?" asked Tracy. "You lost your dream, at least temporarily. It all worked out in the end, and I'm so happy for you both. You changed for the better. But, Robbie... his dream may never come true. What's that gonna do to him?"

CHAPTER 15

The year was 1989. Tracy kept Charlie and Lisa informed of Robbie's situation as much as possible. For everyone else, the year was monumental. Elijah had his first birthday in March, and Sammy had his third in May. Charlie and Lisa turned twenty-two in May, and another event took place that month-- Lisa finally became a college graduate. Once again, family and friends gathered together to celebrate, taking pictures by the dozens. It was the end of an era of preparation, and the beginning of a new adventure.

"I have some good news!" Theresa said as the cameras started cooling off.

"It's the perfect day for it!" Lisa remarked.

"I finally, finally, FINALLY got the call yesterday. We got the IDEA grant!"

"YES!" Lisa exclaimed.

"I knew it would happen!" Charlie enthused.

"What's an IDEA grant?" Tracy asked.

Theresa explained, "IDEA stands for Individuals with Disabilities Education Act. It basically means that the school will have the government funding that we've been waiting for."

"Now that you're officially qualified to be a teacher, there's nothing to stop us," Jeremy stated.

"I can't wait," Lisa said with a smile.

"I know some of the work has been done already, but do you really think we can get the rest of the building ready by fall?" asked Ilene.

"We have almost three months," Theresa answered. "I think if everyone pitches in, we can make it."

"I'll help as much as I can," Tracy replied.

"Thanks, Tracy."

"I'm off for the summer," Cal added. "I used to do a little construction work back in the day. I'm in."

"Me, too," said Annie.

Everyone else affirmed their commitment to help.

"I also have a few more teachers in mind to bring aboard," said Theresa. "Now we just need to get the word out so we have enough students enrolled."

"I think that will be the easy part," Jeremy said. "I've been talking to people about this for a long time. There's a strong buzz. We'll have the kids from the gifted program for sure. Like that new movie, 'Field of Dreams,' 'if you build it, they will come.'"

"I think you're right," Charlie said with a smile. "This dream is about to come true."

They went to work the following weekend and throughout the summer. They cleaned, painted, and fixed many problems, unless outside help was required. It was soon decided that they needed to start the enrollment process to know just how many students they would have and what kind of curriculum would be the most suitable. They advertised on the radio and hung flyers throughout the city. One Saturday, Charlie arrived at the school cafeteria with a newspaper... and doughnuts.

"I haven't looked through it yet, but the ad for the school should be here."

He held the paper up and turned it to the back. The group selected their doughnuts and gathered around.

"There it is-- The Chesapeake School for Special Needs on the whole back page. A lot of people will see this."

"Looks good," said Lisa.

"Hey, I was there!" Tammy exclaimed.

"What are you talking about?" asked Lisa.

"On the front page. It says that a girl was saved from drowning. I was there at the pool. It was pretty scary."

He handed the paper to her. "Is she going to be all right?"

"It says that she almost died, but they saved her just in time. She's only ten. Just a few years younger than me."

"Whoa! Now this I didn't see coming!" Cal declared.

Everyone turned to him as he read the headline from the sports section.

"'Kunkel Fired for DUI.'"

"What?!" Lisa asked in disbelief.

"Yeah, it says that he got pulled over for driving under the influence and went to jail. Omaha kept him on 'til he could heal up, but now that he's broken the rules and embarrassed the team, they've canned him."

"Wow, I never would've thought..."

"That's really too bad. I'm surprised that he did that," Annie remarked.

Tracy shook her head, but didn't look as surprised as the rest.

"I tell you what, Lisa," her dad said, "I'm sure glad you married Charlie instead of that bonehead. Someone who's actually helping people instead of endangering lives." He tossed the paper down on the counter and scoffed. "Idiot."

Charlie picked it up and looked it over.

"But, let's not forget the good news," Ilene reminded everyone as she held up the back page. "The school is happening, and we're on the edge of something special."

"That's right, Dorothy," Annie said with a wink. "We even made the paper."

"Let's get back to work then," Cal said as he walked away. The rest followed, except for Charlie, Lisa, and Tracy.

Tracy said to them, "You know those anti-drug ads about the egg and the frying pan?"

They nodded their heads and said, "Yeah."

She held up a doughnut.

"This is Robbie."

She pointed at the hole.

"This is Robbie without baseball. Any questions?"

She took a bite and walked away. Charlie and Lisa looked at each other.

"I feel bad for him. It didn't have to be this way," Charlie said.

"No, it didn't. What happened to him isn't his fault. But, this? A DUI? That's absolutely his fault. He chose that path. He did the crime, he has to do the time. I hope he learns his lesson."

They continued their work throughout the summer. Slowly but surely, the old building was transforming into what Charlie envisioned. As much as he thought about the future, however, there were still echoes of the past to be discovered.

"Charlie, Mom, come with me," Lisa said. "You're not going to believe this!"

They followed her down the hall. She looked excited and surprised. Charlie wondered what it could possibly be. They ended up in Theresa's office.

"I have a big surprise for you both. You might want to sit down for this," Theresa said.

She smiled as much as Lisa. Charlie's curiosity intensified as they followed her suggestion.

"Sometimes when you're going through old stuff, you find something valuable. I just found a priceless treasure."

"What could it be?" Ilene asked with a smile of her own.

Theresa handed her a class picture. Ilene held it for Charlie to see with her. Ilene looked a bit puzzled for a second until it dawned on her. She gasped.

"What is it?" asked Charlie.

"You see that little boy right there?"

"Yeah..."

"That's your dad."

Charlie hardly knew what to say. "I... I've never seen a picture of him as a kid before."

"I've only seen a couple of them."

"How did you know it was him?" he asked Theresa.

"Someone wrote all the names on the back. The name 'Jordache' caught my eye. I almost didn't see it."

Ilene turned it over. There it was.

"There's more," Lisa said.

She handed Charlie a stack of other class pictures while Theresa set a stack of yearbooks on the desk and handed one to Ilene.

Charlie asked his mom, "Did you know that he came to this school?"

"We didn't grow up together like you two did. We didn't meet until high school. I think he might have mentioned it once, but I completely forgot."

Charlie began looking through the pictures. Lisa sat beside him and put her arm around him. Ilene turned the pages of the yearbook to find Wayne.

"There he is," she said as she gently caressed the page. "I never realized just how much Sammy looks like him."

She started to cry. Theresa handed her a tissue.

"See, Charlie?" she asked her son. "Why this school? Of all the ideas you could have, of all the places it could be... this one. This is the one."

Tears of his own surfaced as he said, "Walking the same halls... sitting in the same seats."

"There's a reason for it, Charlie. There's a reason for all of it. There's always a reason." She looked to Theresa. "Thank you so much for this."

"You're so welcome. Take anything you want," she responded.

"I have an idea," Charlie stated. "We're starting something new with this school, something this town hasn't had. But, there's a history with this old school. Generations that grew up here. Others in these pictures... parents, grandparents. The future is bright, but the past should still be honored."

"What are you suggesting?" asked Theresa.

"I think there should be a place set aside, a display of some kind, maybe a wall... something with pictures like these. Something that shows what was here before... so Chesapeake never forgets."

"I think that's a terrific idea," Theresa enthused.

"I like it," Ilene said as she patted his leg.

"Me, too," Lisa said before kissing his cheek.

"We'll do it. I don't think it should be too hard. Well done, Charlie," Theresa said.

As Charlie walked the halls later with Elijah in his arms, he couldn't help but remember what his mom told him long ago.

"And remember, Charlie, as long as you're around, a part of your dad is still here. As you get older, I know that you'll continue to make us happy."

He thought back to high school and what he said to his dad, if only he could hear him.

"Help me to be more like you."

He kissed his son's cheek.

They carried on with their mission with an increasing sense of excitement as the time grew closer. They received phone calls and letters from several interested families, adding more determination to their work. Then one day came another unexpected surprise.

"Guys! Guys! You have to see this!" Tammy motioned for Charlie and Lisa to follow her. "Hurry!"

They ran after her, completely unprepared for what they were about to see in the cafeteria. Ilene was laughing as she watched Sammy dance and sing.

"Grandma Ilene, oh I help her clean
At this school, we clean everything
It's a big mess, but we'll make it less
Cuz it's dirty
Grandma Ilene."

They laughed and watched him in awe.

"He's only three, right?" asked Tammy.

"Yes," Lisa answered.

"You know that tape Sam left at the house?" asked Ilene. "I guess I've played that for him more than I thought."

"Grandma
Ilene ta doo dah day
Grandma
Ilene ta doo dah day
Now's a good day
Now it's okay
Whoooaa Ilene."

They couldn't be more amazed.

Lisa asked Charlie, "Are you thinking what I'm thinking?"

"Yeah," he said with a chuckle. He paused for a second, realizing the importance of what he was about to say. "Our boy's a genius."

"A genius?!" Tammy exclaimed.

"I knew it!" Lisa said without missing a beat, recalling a similar moment from years ago. Charlie said along with her, "Somehow I just knew it!"

It was now August. The repairs and remodeling were complete. All the schoolbooks and supplies were in place. The building was now open for enrollment. Theresa and Jeremy led the Jordache family to the wall next to the front door. There was a double enclosed bulletin board. The left side said, "Honoring the Past." There were pictures of Prairieside Elementary, including some with Wayne. The right side said, "Preparing the Future." The only picture in it was one that Theresa took of everyone who helped over the summer.

She said, "There's plenty of room for new memories."

"This is great," Charlie said.

"Thank you," Ilene said.

Jeremy said, "We have one other surprise."

He pointed to a plaque on the right of the display. There was a picture of Wayne with Ilene and little Charlie.

"I found this picture. I thought it was appropriate," Lisa informed them.

Charlie held Sammy up closer to the picture.

"That's Grandma, and that's me when I was little, and that's your Grandpa."

He smiled. "What does it say?"

Ilene read it aloud with tears in her eyes. "This school is dedicated to the loving memory of Wayne Jordache. May we always teach what we learned from him-- 'If you love someone, anything's possible.'" She turned to Theresa. "It's beautiful. Thank you."

"The very least I could do."

They hugged each other while Lisa put her arm around Charlie and held Elijah in the other arm.

"I hear a car door," Jeremy said. "Looks like it's time for the legacy to continue. We built it, now here they come."

Many parents and children came through the doors that day. When there were a lot at once, they split into different classrooms. One girl in particular stood out. Charlie and Lisa shook hands with her and her mom and introduced themselves.

"I'm Maria, and this is Adriana."

They sat at the desks while Charlie and Lisa stood in front of the teacher's desk. Adriana never said a word and didn't look very happy.

"I'm so glad you guys are starting this school. We haven't had a very good time with the one she's been going to."

"What's the matter?" Charlie asked.

"Well, she's deaf. The teachers don't know how to communicate with her and she can't talk to them, either. She's a smart girl and gets good grades for the most part, but I know it could be better if she could actually be taught by someone who knows what to do with her. And, that's not the worst part. Some of the kids make fun of her. I'm so tired of my baby girl coming home crying."

Charlie's heart broke for her.

"Kids can be cruel sometimes. I know what that's like. That's one of the reasons why we started this school. Being different isn't something we make fun of around here. Those are the kind of people we love the most."

"So, you can help her?"

"We have some who are paralyzed, some have muscular dystrophy, cerebral palsy, learning disorders, and some who are at genius-level intellect. We can and will most certainly help Adriana. My only concern is how we can communicate with her."

Lisa lifted Adriana's chin up. They looked into each other's eyes.

"Hi," Lisa said as she made a sign. "What is your name?"

Her eyes lit up. She spelled out her name in sign language as her mom interpreted aloud, "Adriana."

"Adriana," Lisa repeated the spelling and her special name sign. She continued to sign as she spoke, "that is a beautiful name. My name is Lisa, and this is my husband, Charlie." She made name signs for the both of them. Adriana giggled. "How old are you?"

"Seven."

"Seven? I thought you were ten."

She laughed. "Are you deaf, too?"

"No."

"How do you know how to sign?"

Charlie said, "I was wondering the same thing."

Lisa said, "I went to school with a girl who was deaf. She taught me. It's my favorite language. You remind me of her."

"Because I am deaf?"

"No. Because you are beautiful."

She smiled and blushed. Then, she asked, "Will you be my teacher?"

Lisa's smile grew. "I would be honored to be your teacher."

She got out of her seat and tightly wrapped her arms around Lisa. She held her back.

"I don't even know what to say," Maria said. "I've never seen anything like it."

"She constantly amazes me, too," Charlie said. "She's the absolute best."

"So, I take it we're in."

"There are still some papers to fill out, but yes." He handed them to her.

Adriana looked up to Lisa. There were tears of joy in her eyes. Lisa's eyes were starting to water also. She wiped Adriana's tears and they both smiled.

Adriana let go and signed, "Does Charlie know how to sign?"

"We can teach him."

She smiled.

When Adriana and Maria left, Lisa said, "Did you see how her eyes lit up when she saw me sign?"

"Yeah, mine did, too. I had no idea you could do that. You did say that you knew other languages."

"That sweet little girl. I can't believe someone would ever hurt her. Man, this feels good. So good, and so right. I could just cry. This is what it's all about. We're really going to make a difference here."

"You already have."

They put their arms around each other.

"One thing I wonder, though," Charlie mused.

"Oh? What's that?"

"When you made the sign for my name, she laughed. What was so funny?"

They let go.

"Well, you see, when you say your name, you spell it out, and then you have your own name sign that is given to you. You can just use that instead of spelling it when someone knows it. This is mine."

She spelled out her name and then crossed her arms in front of her chest with her right hand making an 'L'.

"That's the sign for love. It included the L for Lisa, so my name is associated with love."

He repeated her actions.

"That's really nice. What's so funny about mine?"

She chuckled. "This is how to spell yours. I didn't have a sign for your name yet, so I just had to come up with one on the spot."

She spelled it and then made a 'C' that she waved twice in front of her face. He repeated it.

"So, what does that mean?"

"It's similar to cartoon."

She laughed and started to walk away.

"How is she supposed to take me seriously now?"

"I think it fits."
"Why?"
"Because you watch cartoons, of course!"
"I watch them with the kids. There's a difference."
"You were still watching when they already left the room."
"It was a mystery! I had to find out what happened!"
"Ha! A mystery solved by chipmunk detectives."
"Hey, that's a good show."
"It's as silly as the one with the ducks," she said as she started to exit.
"You were singing the theme song in the shower and we both know it!"
He laughed. He also knew that she was only putting up a front. She knew darn well what those shows were called and that they were good.
"Man, I love that woman."

The day had come for The Chesapeake School for Special Needs to officially open its doors to the students. The faculty gathered together in Theresa's office for a quick meeting and a prayer. Just as they were exiting, Theresa and Ilene stopped Charlie and Lisa.
"We are so proud of you two," Ilene said. "Everything you already accomplished, all your hard work, and now, we really get to see you shine."
"It's been a pleasure to watch you two grow and become such a positive influence as adults," Theresa added. "So, we wanted to give you each a little something to show just a small bit of our appreciation."
"You didn't have to do anything," Lisa replied.
"Really. It's an honor to work with you," Charlie said.
"Well, we wanted to," Ilene said. "So, ladies first." She handed a small box to Lisa. "Since it's your first day as a teacher, we wanted to do a little extra."
Lisa opened it. "Oh, wow! It's beautiful." She took out the sun necklace.
Theresa said, "We may call you 'Mrs. Jordache' now, but you'll always be 'Sunshine' to us."
"You've always been the brightest part of our lives," Ilene added.
"Thank you so much," Lisa said as she gave each of them hugs.
"As for you, Charlie," Theresa said as she handed him a similar box, "we wouldn't be here if it wasn't for you."
He smiled as he took a flame-shaped tie pin out of the box.
"Remember the song?" she asked. "The little spark has become a fire. 'The light that shines so bright is the love that burns in me.'"
Ilene continued the train of thought, "Both of you have always had that light. Even in the hard times, that light could never be

extinguished. The love that you two have in your hearts isn't just for each other, it's for everyone. It's the kind of love that changes things."

"And now, we get to see that love spread like a fire," Theresa said. "Just as we always knew it would."

"Thank you," Charlie said with a tear in his eye. "I've learned from the three of you. I was taught by the best."

He hugged each of them as they all grew teary in return.

Theresa declared, "Well, this is all wonderful, but we really do need to get ready. It's almost time."

As they headed out the door, Ilene said, "Time to shine."

The students arrived soon after that. They were all greeted at the door and directed to the gym. When Adriana came in, she ran up to Lisa and hugged her. She took her by the hand and led her to the gym. Fold-up chairs were gathered in a large circle on the floor to accommodate the many who couldn't use the bleachers. Even those who could were in the chairs instead. When everyone was there, Theresa stood in the middle with the rest of the teachers.

"Hello, everyone. My name is Mrs. Allen. We're so glad that all of you are here. What an exciting day! We've been looking forward to this day for the past four years. When Mr. Jordache first told me that he had an idea that would need my help, I agreed before even knowing what it would be. That's how much I believe in him. His vision is what led us here today. Rest assured, this young man and the rest of the teachers here are not only the smartest people I know, they're the most compassionate. I believe in them. You will not only receive the best education possible, you will be treated with the utmost respect and dignity. We're here not because I believe in the teachers, but because the teachers believe in you. Every single one of you is important."

It had been fifteen years since Charlie first saw Mrs. Allen teach. He always marveled at her ability to hold the class's attention. He knew that it wasn't just her striking beauty, nor her eloquence. Her heart was in everything she did, every word she spoke, and it was irresistibly magnetic. She truly was the best. He already realized that she played a big part in why he became a teacher. But in this moment, it occurred to him that she not only still had her gifts after all these years, but those years were preparing her for her greatest use of those gifts. She was just getting started.

"Today, we're going to get to know each other a bit before we break into classes," she continued. "There's something that I've done every year on the first day of my previous school. I'm going to continue that tradition here, but this time, I'll have some help. Welcome to The Chesapeake School for Special Needs."

All of the teachers split up and began talking to each student. Charlie walked up to Adriana first and bent down to her level. They exchanged smiles.

"Hello, Charlie," she signed.

"Hello, Adriana," he said as he signed back. But, he didn't stop there. He kept signing as he said, "Guess who's been learning how to sign?"

Her eyes lit up as she smiled as big as could be. Lisa glanced over and smiled, too.

"I'm still learning. Forgive me if I stutter," he joked.

She laughed and held her hands up and waved them. Charlie didn't realize at the time that it was the way someone deaf would clap.

He continued, "We can laugh, but we won't laugh at you. We will all learn how to sign. You can teach us."

"Really?"

He nodded his head.

Her eyes began to water. "I won't be different?"

"We're all different. That's what makes us the same." He started to tear up as well. He was just like her fifteen years ago. "Don't worry, Adriana. We're going to take good care of you. We love you, Adriana. My special friend. Welcome to our school."

"I love you, Charlie."

She threw her arms around him. They held each other close, both of them with tears running down their faces. Charlie glanced over to Lisa and gave her a thumbs up. She did the same with a tear in her own eye.

Charlie noticed Jeremy approaching a teenage boy in a wheelchair.

"Nice wheels," he said as he held out his hand. "Mr. Allen."

"Andrew."

"Know any tricks?"

"Tricks?"

"With the chair. Can you pop a wheelie?"

He laughed. "You want me to do that here?"

"Yeah, why not? It's a gym."

Andrew rolled back a bit and popped a wheelie.

"That's pretty good," Jeremy said.

"Watch this." He did some quick spins.

"That's great. You're pretty athletic. I used to be, but I'm getting a little old. See Lisa over there? She was a track star. She quit when she found out that she couldn't outrun me."

Andrew laughed. "That's not right, man."

"What?"

"Making fun of people in wheelchairs, man. That's just not right." He laughed again.

"Then why are you laughing? Hey, man, I don't make fun of anybody. If I make fun of anyone, it's myself. If you can't laugh at yourself, then what good is life? Besides, I'm thinking of starting a basketball team. Want in?"

He laughed. "Dude, you're some kind of crazy. I can't play no basketball."

"I didn't ask if you could, I asked if you wanted to."

He stumbled for a response as he looked down to his legs.

Jeremy continued, "I saw you looking up at the hoop earlier, and you're wearing a Michael Jordan shirt. You like basketball, don't you?"

"Yeah, it's all right."

"Let me uncomplicate this. Can you hold a ball?"

"Yeah."

"Can you throw a ball?"

"Yeah."

"Then I don't see any reason why you can't play basketball if you want to."

He chuckled. "You serious?"

"Once in awhile... if I have to be. And... yeah, I'm serious about this. I'm going to start a team and you're welcome to play if you want to."

Andrew looked down again.

Jeremy said, "Hold your head up, son."

He looked him in the eyes. Jeremy pointed at the hoop.

"How else are you ever going to see your goals in life? Don't let anyone tell you that you can't do something. Especially not yourself."

He smiled and nodded. "You're all right, Teach."

"Welcome to our school."

Every student was greeted in a manner that they would later refer to as the "Allen Welcome." Afterwards, they separated into classes. Each teacher had a card on their desk from Mrs. Allen. Lisa was a bit nervous about teaching for the first time, but as with everything else she tried, she excelled. She was a natural. A reporter took notes as a photographer took pictures throughout the day. When the day was over, the reporter met with Charlie and Lisa.

"I hope we weren't too distracting," he said. "Louis Lane, *Chesapeake Times*."

He shook hands with them.

"You were fine. We knew you were coming. Charlie Jordache."

"Lisa Jordache."

"Are you related?"

"We're married," they said together.

"Huh. That just made the story even more interesting. I knew that you were Ilene's son, but she didn't mention that you two were married. Guess I need to start asking better questions."

"I'm sure she just had a lot on her mind. It's a big day for all of us," Lisa reassured him.

"Yes, I understand. I didn't want to interfere too much. I must say that I'm very impressed. The way everyone treats the students is remarkable. Do you have kids?"

"We have two boys," Charlie said.

"I have a ten-year-old daughter. She wouldn't quite qualify as special needs, but she is pretty special. As a parent, I can appreciate how much care is shown to the kids. You two look so young. How long have you been teaching?"

Charlie said, "Two years. I'm the physics professor at Chesapeake University."

"Are you doing both?"

"Yes. I'll be scaling back my time at CU. We have a plan for the couple of times throughout the week when I'm not here."

"And what about you?" he asked Lisa.

"This is my first day," she said with a smile.

His eyes widened. "First day?"

"I graduated from CU this year."

"You certainly seem like you know what you're doing. You must be a born teacher."

"Thank you. I've always been a fast learner. Plus, I've prepared for this for awhile, not only with school, but helping with the gifted program. I'm where I need to be."

"I would say so." He turned to Charlie. "They say that this whole thing was your idea. What made you want to start a school like this?"

"It all started when I was Theresa's student in the second grade. She put me through gifted testing. I passed everything and had an I.Q. of 180. Mom and I talked about our options. The only gifted program or special schools at the time were too far away. We didn't want to move. I could've skipped grades, but I didn't want to do that, either. We decided to just keep going the way it was, but with a little extra work along the way. The problem was, I would get done with work faster than the other kids and get bored. It also wasn't very challenging for me. By the time I was a senior, Mom and Theresa started the gifted program. It was too late for me, but it was still needed for others."

Lisa added, "I moved back to California for awhile and came back for senior year. I was in the gifted program over there. Let me tell you, I never got bored. I know that I would have if I didn't have that extra part of my education."

"You were two sides of the same coin," noted Louis. "Both gifted, but each had a different experience. Very interesting. I'm curious, why didn't you want to skip grades?"

"Because I wouldn't fit in. I was already having a hard time growing up with a missing father, the last thing I wanted was to be even more of a misfit than I already was. I wanted to just be normal, but that was never going to happen. It's taken a long time to embrace my role in life. By senior year, we realized that there were others who needed more than what was available. There were others who were gifted, but there were also kids with physical conditions that made it more difficult to go through school like everyone else. What about them? I didn't want anyone to slip through the cracks. I know what that's like, and I want to help in any way I can to keep that from happening to anyone else. Everyone deserves a chance. I don't want anyone to go through what I went through."

Louis nodded and said, "You've certainly made a great effort to accomplish that. What I've seen here today is extraordinary. The students here are very lucky to have teachers who care so much about them. I love what you're doing here."

"Thank you," they both said.

"Well, I don't want to keep you for too long; I'm sure you want to get home to your kids. Let me give you my card." He handed one to each of them. "If you ever need any publicity, have some kind of special event, what have ya, just give me a call. I'll make it front page news."

"Thank you very much for that," Lisa said.

"We'll keep that in mind," said Charlie.

They shook hands.

"Nice meeting you. Keep up the good work," Louis said.

"Thanks," they replied.

After he left, Charlie and Lisa held each other.

"We did it, Mrs. Jordache. Off to a flying start."

"Gifts are meant to be shared. Light is meant to be seen." She kissed him. "A new adventure has just begun."

While getting ready for bed that night, Lisa replayed the day's events through her mind. Her dreams were finally coming true. She gently held her sun necklace and admired it. Her thoughts drifted back to when she was ten years old.

"How did school go?"

"It was super! For gifted, we each took turns being the teacher. Everyone was really paying attention to what I said. It was fun."

"I'm glad to hear that."

"Oh! And remember Sheila, that girl who teased me about Charlie last year?"

"Yeah."

"She apologized. Just out of the blue. I'm not even sure why. Now, she wants to be friends. Everyone's been treating me a lot better these days."

"That makes sense. Know why they've been nicer?"

"Why?"

"Because you've been acting like yourself again. You've been happy and everyone can see it."

"I've been happier ever since Dad said that he'd try to get a job in Chesapeake again."

"You've also been in gifted and met some other kids who were more like you. You've had more to look forward to. Hope is a powerful thing, isn't it?"

"Yes, it is. All these other kids want to be friends with me now."

"Because you've been yourself. Being yourself makes you happy. You're not the outsider and you're not sad. You're just Lisa. You're the girl who everyone loves because you have this light that shines so bright. Everyone is drawn to you."

"Some of the girls are kind of copying what I do, like the way I do my hair and stuff like that."

"You might be surprised by this, but they look up to you."

"They do? Why would they look up to me?"

"Because you're smart, you're strong, and you're always kind to everyone. Your light shines in so many ways. Even Charlie looked up to you."

"He did?"

"Of course. I could see it easily. You're the sunshine in our world, Lisa."

"Am I really that important?"

"You're important in ways we haven't even seen yet. You're a natural born leader, Sunshine."

She went to bed and cuddled up with Charlie. They always did seem to fit together perfectly. They were always two sides of the same coin. He kissed her.

"Goodnight, Sunshine," he whispered.

"Goodnight, Mr. Blue Sky."

CHAPTER 16

Lisa, Charlie, and the rest shone their light each day at school, despite the challenges that came with the territory. They learned as much as they taught, and the students became increasingly confident. The Chesapeake School for Special Needs was a tremendous success. Charlie managed to juggle the new school with his work at the college, while Annie watched the kids during the day. Charlie and Lisa still made time to be parents at night. The hectic schedule was a bit overwhelming at first, but it became much easier as the months passed.

It was now March 1990, and the Jordache family had a visitor.

"Aunt Tracy!" enthused Sammy.

He reached up for a hug, and she picked him up.

"I can't believe how big you're getting!" Elijah hugged her leg. "Both of you!"

"I'll be four in two months!"

"You will?"

"Uh huh, on May 11th. And Elijah will be two this month on March 30th."

"Wow! You really know your stuff!"

"Yep, Granny Annie taught me."

"She did? Well, you're a smart kid."

"Can you come play with us?"

"Maybe later, kiddo. Right now, I need to talk to your parents about something."

"Ok," he said begrudgingly.

She set him down. The boys ran into the kitchen.

"He's so smart! He's like a little you!" she said to Charlie.

"Now you know how I always felt when I saw Tammy."

"Do you want any tea?" asked Lisa.

"Not right now, maybe later," Tracy answered. "There's something I need to talk about first."

They sat on the couch while Tracy used the chair across from them. Her face changed to a more serious expression.

"Did you see the news?" she asked.

"We haven't had time yet," said Charlie. "Why? What's going on?"

"It's about Robbie."

"What did he do this time?" Lisa said with a groan.

"Apparently, he found out that the Baltimore team was coming to play Omaha. Remember Tyson Fredericks?"

"He's the guy who hurt Robbie," Charlie said.

Lisa said, "I don't like where this is going."

Tracy continued, "Robbie followed him to a motel..." she paused. Her voice cracked, "...and beat him within an inch of his life."

"What?!" Charlie asked in shock.

Lisa leaned her face on Charlie's shoulder and began to cry.

"They know it was him?" Charlie asked.

"Another one of the players heard him calling out for help. As soon as he showed up, Robbie ran away. It didn't take long for the police to catch up with him. He still had blood on his hands."

Lisa turned to Tracy. "He was a good man once. How could it have gotten this bad?!"

Tracy replied, "The good man we once knew, the friend we once had, he no longer exists. I tried to tell you guys. He died that day when he got hurt. The old Robbie stayed on the baseball field. He was never the same after that. He died that day, and I watched it happen." She held her head and began to cry. "If only I would have tried harder. If only I would have been there for him... I..."

"Don't go there, Tracy," Charlie said. "Don't do that to yourself. There's no way you could have known. It's not your fault. He chose what he did. He made up his mind. Sometimes, when someone has their mind made up, there's nothing you can do to stop them. He was dealt a bad hand, and it changed his course, but he chose the rest of his path."

"Now, he has to pay for what he did," Lisa added.

"I know," she said. "I know it's his fault. I just wish it didn't come to this."

"He lost his hope, like you said," Charlie continued. "Hope is a powerful thing. Like her dad said, 'If a man doesn't have a dream, he has nothing to live for.'"

Tracy nodded and wiped her eye.

Lisa asked, "Is he going to make it? Tyson, I mean."

"He'll make it. It's going to take a while to heal, but he'll make it. I can't imagine all the pain he's in. I know he hurt Robbie, but this is beyond what he did to him. This was just evil. Makes me sick."

"Me, too," Lisa said. "I just want all the hurting to stop."

Life went on for everyone. The boys had their birthdays, the school finished its first year, and Charlie and Lisa celebrated their fifth anniversary. The light was bright in the city of Chesapeake. Only one thing would threaten to dim it-- Robbie Kunkel. The hometown hero was known more across the country for his violent crime than anything he did on the field. As he served a prison sentence, Charlie and Lisa served the school, tirelessly striving to bring light into a world that had grown a little darker.

CHAPTER 17

"Say, 'cheese!'"

"Cheeeese!" Sammy said through an enormous grin. His hair was combed just right, with his shirt tucked into his shorts.

"Now, one more with Elijah," Lisa said.

Elijah stood next to his brother on the steps of the school. There were more cameras flashing this day than when Charlie and Lisa first started kindergarten.

"Time flies by so fast," Ilene said. "I can't believe we're here already."

"I know," Annie added. "It seems like yesterday when we did this last."

"Nineteen years later. Man... a whole new generation. And the kids are now the teachers." Ilene laughed. "We're getting old, Granny Annie!"

"Speak for yourself, Grandma Ilene," she said with a laugh.

They put their arms around each other. It was August 1991.

"All right, Sammy. Ready for school?" asked Charlie.

"Yes!" he exclaimed.

"We'd better get going," Annie said as she held out her hand to Elijah. He took Annie's hand as they headed for the car, waving one more time. The rest of the family headed inside the Chesapeake School for Special Needs. Charlie and Lisa each took Sammy's hands. Charlie began to be overcome with pride and joy. It did seem like yesterday. He said, "Let's see what excitement and adventures await us inside these hallowed halls."

The day flew by as fast as it had arrived. Sammy excelled, just as everyone knew he would. As time passed each day, it became increasingly obvious that he inherited traits from both parents. He read everything he could, and rose to every challenge, just as his dad. He never knew a stranger, always showing kindness and friendliness to everyone, just as his mom. He was more than just a young genius, he was the best of Charlie and the best of Lisa. He was a miracle.

Time still flew by quickly as the Jordache family lived life to the fullest. Not only did their family continue to do well personally, they made a difference for those around them. Adriana became very well-adjusted and quite popular, able to speak with everyone and make friends easily. Her grades improved as well as the rest of the school. Besides teaching his other classes, including music, Jeremy did start a basketball team with Andrew. They played against other similar schools, always drawing an enthusiastic crowd. Louis Lane and the *Chesapeake Times* were always there to cover the story, making the Chesapeake Sparks almost as popular as the Chargers. Tracy still kept in touch as much as possible, and even helped as an additional school nurse when her schedule would allow. The dark shadow that Robbie had cast on the town and in their lives had eventually faded. The Sunshine was too bright to go unnoticed and impossible to resist.

Sunday, February 14th, 1993. Charlie and Lisa were cleaning up a few things around the house. They didn't want to leave a mess for Ilene, who was coming over to watch the kids while they have a Valentine's dinner.

"What's this?" Sammy asked as he took what seemed to be a big book off the shelf.

Lisa replied with a smile, "That's our wedding album."

"Can we look at it?"

"It's the perfect day for it."

She sat on the couch with Sammy and Elijah. Charlie smiled as he remembered a similar moment like it was yesterday. He sat down with them.

"That's you and that's daddy," Elijah said as he pointed at a picture.

"There's Grandpa and Granny Annie and Grandma Ilene. And there's Aunt Tracy," Sammy pointed out.

"Who's that girl?" asked Elijah.

"That's Aunt Tammy," Lisa said. "She was only nine years old there. She's gotten bigger since then, huh?"

"Yeah."

"I don't remember this," Sammy said. "Are we in any of the pictures?"

Lisa and Charlie laughed. He said, "You weren't there, son. You weren't born yet."

"Oh."

"Why did you get married?" asked Elijah.

"Because we loved each other," Charlie said. "We knew we belonged together, and we brought out the best in each other. We still do."

Lisa added, "Do you know what happened after that? God took the best of Dad and the best of me and gave us you. You're our little miracle, Sammy."

She put her arm around Sammy.

"Know what he did next?" asked Charlie. "He did it again."

He put his arm around Elijah. The boys smiled. They all told each other, "I love you."

"Want to see how it all began?" asked Charlie.

"Yeah."

He got off the couch and retrieved the scrapbook. He sat down with them again and showed them the old pictures and items.

"That's us when we were little. We've known each other since we were your age, Elijah," Lisa said.

Charlie explained, "We were best friends. You know Grandma Ilene's house? She lived next to us. We always loved each other, but we never said it for the longest time. It wasn't until Valentine's Day eight years ago. We looked at Grandma's pictures on Valentine's Day when we were little, much like we're doing now. This day has always been special to us."

"Why is there a watch here?" asked Sammy.

"That's what she gave me for my birthday when I was your age. That way, I knew when it was time to play."

"And, he gave me this bracelet," Lisa said as she showed them her friendship bracelet. "It means that we'll always be friends. I've never taken it off."

"Really?" asked Sammy with wide eyes. "That's a long time!"

"Time doesn't matter when you love someone. It just gets better each day," Lisa said. "If you love someone, anything's possible."

They looked at the rest of the scrapbook, and the boys especially enjoyed seeing their baby pictures. Ilene came over to watch the kids after awhile. Charlie and Lisa went to the restaurant where he used to work. They greeted Lisa's parents, who had always made the restaurant their Valentine tradition. Tammy was now their waitress, and they left a generous tip. After dinner, they went back to the park where they first professed their love. They sat on the bench with their arms around each other as they looked at the stars. They reminisced about all the good times in the past and the present. It did get better each day.

The whole school congregated in the back one beautiful April morning. Louis Lane and a photographer were there for the occasion. An odd assortment of items were on a table next to a hole in the ground.

Mrs. Allen addressed them all, "When we first started this school, we made the display that you see in the hall by the front door. On the left, we show the generation that was here before-- 'Honoring the Past.' On the right, we show everyone here as we're 'Preparing the Future.' Most of you were here from the beginning, while the rest of you have joined us over the years. Soon, we'll celebrate the graduation of some of you. As we bring this first chapter of our school's story to an end, we begin a new one. New students will join us in the fall, just as the rest of you will become a little older and wiser. The past will still be honored, and we will still prepare the future. What better time than this to commemorate this moment in time? To celebrate your achievements, while simultaneously preserving so many wonderful memories for generations to come?" She picked up one of the items. "We have toys, books, jewelry..." She started placing them into a large PVC pipe. "...lots of interesting pieces for a time capsule."

The *Times* photographer snapped pictures, just as a lot of the students and teachers did. She got to a cassette tape and player with headphones.

"This has my son written all over it. Mr. Allen, is this yours?"

"No."

"Actually, that was our contribution," said Charlie. "I think tape players are being phased out while CD's are gaining prominence. Another generation will wonder what that is."

She looked closer at the songs written on the insert of the tape.

"These are all wonderful, classic songs, but they're hardly indicative of this generation. It does honor the past, however."

Ilene said, "These songs all have particular meaning for our family. It's dedicated to Wayne... just like this school is."

"Can't argue with that," she said.

"Besides, good music is timeless," Lisa added.

"Amen to that!" Jeremy replied.

The tape and player were added to the time capsule. After the last item was placed, Charlie sealed it. He and Lisa, the scientists of the bunch, constructed it to be as water-resistant and long- asting as they possibly could. The table was moved aside and everyone gathered closer together as Theresa and Charlie held the capsule in front of them, posing for the photographer. They set it in the ground after the pictures were taken.

"Let's dig this up in about thirty years. It's a nice, round number," Theresa said.

Charlie and another teacher shoveled the dirt into the hole and placed a marker on it. Everyone began going back inside. Charlie and Lisa lingered behind to speak with Louis for a moment.

"This is a really cool thing you guys are doing," he said. "Barring some kind of crisis, I think this could be the front page story."

"Really?" asked Lisa.

"Oh, yeah. People love stuff like this. I can see the headline now--'Groundbreaking School Plants Seed for the Future.' Something like that, anyway."

"That would be great," she said. "Another one for the scrapbook. Thanks, Louis."

"Any time, Lisa," he said as they shook hands.

"Another great story from the great Louis Lane," Charlie said as they shook hands. "Can't wait to read all about it."

"You guys always give me such great material," he replied.

Charlie added, "I've got to say, your name still makes me chuckle. You don't have a wife named Lois, do you?"

He laughed. "No, her name is Sarah. My pen name is meant to catch your eye and make you do a double take. We've been friends for awhile; I think it's safe to tell you my real name. It's Silver, Lane Silver."

"You learn something new every day."

When May came along, they celebrated some major milestones. They were there with the rest of the family and the Whitsons to cheer on Tammy as she graduated high school. Shortly after that, the Chesapeake School for Special Needs had their first graduating class. Andrew was among the graduates and was named Valedictorian. Charlie had others graduate from his physics class over the years, but this school was different. It was borne of his own heart, and therefore filled it with greater joy.

Summer flew by and it was time for school again. Everyone gathered at the front steps once more as Elijah started his first day of kindergarten. The usual comments about time's aviation skills were made, along with the ones about increased age. The cameras flashed many pictures, especially of Elijah with his arms around his proud big brother. The coming months seemingly proved what had been suspected for some time-- Elijah wasn't obviously gifted. He did well, but didn't appear to inherit the rest of the family's more enhanced capabilities. It was agreed that it would still be in his best interest to let him attend the school. For a young boy who had been there since he was in diapers, making him go to a different school than the rest of his family would have been unnecessarily harsh and difficult for him to understand. For a family that was already missing a member, it would be better to avoid any further damage. This was where he belonged.

The Jordache and Duvall families gathered at church on a Sunday morning. The pastor spoke about the importance of prayer. Lisa noticed when Ilene held Charlie's hand. She could tell that there was a lot on her mind. She could see it in Charlie also. She took his other hand. *"Please, Lord, help us today,"* she prayed within herself. When church was over, the kids went home with Annie and Cal while Lisa and Charlie went to Ilene's. Lisa made sandwiches and listened as Charlie and Ilene reminisced at the kitchen table.

"Remember that time when you put on your dad's shoes and tried to walk around in them?" Ilene said with a laugh. "They were so big! You almost fell over three times!"

Charlie laughed. "Yes, I remember. Elijah just did that the other day!"

She laughed. "I wish I could've seen that. Man, I wish I would've taken a picture. It was one of the funniest things I've ever seen you do."

"At least we still have our memories," Charlie said.

"Yeah. Good memories. It's funny how every little boy wants to walk in his daddy's shoes," she said, her tone becoming more serious.

"Those are still some big shoes to fill."

Lisa brought the sandwiches over to everyone and sat beside them. October 3, 1993.

"I think you do a good job," Lisa said.

"So do I," Ilene replied. "I wish he could've seen it. He would've been one proud grandpa." Her eyes watered. "Savor it while you can, guys. It all slips by so fast. Twenty years... how could it be that long already?"

Lisa took her hand.

"Sometimes it feels like yesterday," Charlie said.

Ilene continued, "You know you're actually a year older than I was when it happened? 'When it happened.' It sounds like some kind of event took place, when the truth is, nothing happened. He was just here one day, and gone the next. No explanation. Like being on pause. He still might be back any time."

"You don't have closure," Lisa said. "Do you really think he might still be back after all this time?"

"Don't you?"

"Yeah... a part of me believes that."

"That's what we've gone by all this time," said Charlie. "It gets harder to believe it after so long, but we just have to. Didn't we just hear why we need to pray? Some things are just too big for us to handle on our own."

He took a bite of his sandwich.

"I'm not saying that you're wrong," said Lisa, "I guess more than anything I'm just amazed at how much you two have kept your faith this whole time. I know it's not easy."

"Having you around makes it easier," Ilene said. "And, that proves my point. You were gone for eight years and came back. I watched Charlie struggle through that time, but I never saw him give up. I have that same struggle sometimes. Once in a while, I'll forget and turn over in bed to tell him, 'good morning...' but, the reality hits me. I'll hear something funny, and I want to tell him because I want to see his reaction and hear his laugh... but, it's not to be. I'll see Charlie or Sammy or Elijah make one of his facial expressions or say something the way he would have said it. And, I'll wish so bad that he could see what a great legacy he left behind." Her eyes filled with tears. "I have you guys, and I have Annie and Cal, and I have the Whitsons, and I have the Allens, and I have all the wonderful people at the school. I have this beautiful, amazing family all around me every day. I'm so blessed to have all of you in my life, the best people God ever put on this earth... but, at the end of the day, I'm still alone. So, yes, I do struggle sometimes. But, I never give up. Like Sam told me, 'hold on to hope.' He also said that my story's not over yet. What would happen if I gave up hope? Wouldn't that be like telling God that I don't believe he can answer prayers? Wouldn't that be a slap in the face to someone who's answered so many already and blessed me far beyond what I deserve? Look at what he's already done for you two. If you love someone, anything's possible."

Lisa replied, "I'm completely on your side here, I just wonder why there hasn't been anything in twenty years. Why so long with no answers? What if he's truly gone?"

"I don't think he is. Where's the proof? After twenty years, nobody has ever found a body or seen anything to prove that something bad happened."

Charlie added, "That's what makes it so hard, that we don't have any answers, but it also seems more hopeful. We very well may still see him again."

Ilene held Charlie's hand and asked, "Remember what I said that night after we came home after going to her house the first time?"

"Of course."

"There's something special about the two of you. I knew from the beginning that you were meant to be together. There may have been struggles along the way, but the truth never changed. What was meant to be still came to be. I also believe with all my heart that I was meant to be with Wayne. Twenty years, seven years, fifty years, that doesn't matter. If it's meant to be, then it's meant to be. I have seen things that I can't explain. I've seen God's hand working in our lives every day. Just as sure as I was that you two would be together, so sure am I that we'll be reunited someday. I have this feeling, this... I don't even know what to call it. I just know in my gut that someday we're going to see a miracle, and it will be in a way that we don't expect, but it will be at the right time."

Later that night as they were getting ready for bed, Lisa could tell that Charlie was still thinking about the past twenty years.

"Do you really still think that he'll just show up one day?"

"I don't know. A part of me does. I used to pray for that every single night. I think it's possible. I just..."

She put her arms around him. "What is it?"

"I just don't want Mom to get her hopes up. I want her to still have hope, I just don't want her to get hurt."

"I think that having hope is what's keeping her from getting hurt."

"Yeah, I get that, but twenty years is still a long time to believe something that may or may not be true. Trust me, I know. If only we just had something--anything--to go by. If I knew that he wasn't coming back, it would be hard, but I could still accept it in a way. Like she said, it's like being on pause. Not moving forward, but not stopping either."

"We do move forward, though. Look at how much the boys have grown. Look at the school. We move forward. We live and learn and grow."

"Yes, I know all that, it's just that with this particular issue, we're stuck. We're mourning the loss of my dad, yet believing that he's still alive. There just isn't an answer. Mom says that she believes it, and she has this feeling... all I know is that she's always right. Maybe we need to trust what she says."

"Works for me."

She kissed him. They went to bed without any further discussion. Lisa still thought about it, trying to make sense of what the past twenty years were about.

"What's wrong, Lisa? Didn't you have a good time with your slumber party?"

"Yeah, I had a good time, it's just... some of the girls..."

"What did they do?"

"Well... they were teasing me about Charlie. They called him my boyfriend. I told them that we're just friends... but, they wouldn't listen."

"They didn't mean any harm by it. They might even be a little jealous."

"Why would they be jealous? We're just friends."

"They see how good you are together. And, girls will be girls. They're probably developing feelings for boys and don't know how to handle it. But, tell me something, Lisa, why does it bother you so much?"

"Because what they said wasn't true."

"I don't think they were trying to be mean. I don't think they were trying to be untruthful, either. They just got a little carried away."

"No, I mean... it bothers me because it's not true."

"Ohhh. I see what you mean now. You want it to be true. I think you have a crush on Charlie."

"What's that?"

"It's when you really like someone, and you might even feel like you love them, but it usually doesn't last very long."

"Then that's not what it is."

"Are you sure?"

"Yes. Because this has been going on since I met him two years ago... and it keeps getting stronger."

"Oh, Lisa... I didn't know."

"Remember how you told me that when Dad is gone sometimes you miss him a lot and you can't wait to see him?"

"Yeah."

"I do that, too. And, when he had to go last night, I really didn't want him to. I tried to have fun with the girls, but I kept thinking about him. I wish it could've been just me and him."

Lisa started to cry just as she did back then.

"And, when he had to leave early from school... I was so worried about him. I couldn't think about anything else. When we went to his house that night and found out about his dad, it really hurt. I wanted to help him so bad... and I didn't know how. I just kept trying to be his friend. I don't have a crush on him, Mom. I love him with all my heart."

CHAPTER 18

"Hello?"

"Hello. May I speak with Charles Jordache?"

"That's me."

"This is Bill at the First Bank of Chesapeake. How are you today?"

"Pretty good."

"Great. The reason I'm calling is to remind you to renew your rental fee on your safe deposit box."

He was caught off guard. "I don't have a safe deposit box."

"Our records indicate that you do... in fact, I was the one to handle the transaction."

He chuckled nervously. "There must be some mistake. I have no idea what you're talking about. Unless maybe this is about my wife?"

"No, this is only in your name. You did tell me that there was a chance that you wouldn't remember."

He laughed. "See, that's what doesn't add up. I happen to have a great memory, and this is something I don't remember one bit. Do you know what's in the box?"

"For your own privacy, nobody knows what's in the box but yourself."

Charlie was truly puzzled. "When did I allegedly do this?"

"Ten years ago, and I remember it quite well."

"Ten years?! This still doesn't make sense. What happens if I don't pay the fee?"

"The contents of the box will be turned over to the state."

"Shouldn't I have a key?"

"Yes. Two keys were issued to you at the time. One of those keys is here."

"It seems like I should know where the other is. Obviously, there's some kind of mistake."

"You gave me some instructions. I wrote them on a sticky note. I've looked at this thing for ten years now. I can assure you, Mr. Jordache, this is no mistake."

"That's certainly a ringing endorsement for the quality of sticky notes." They both laughed. "What are the instructions?"

"It's about the location of the other key. It's intended to be a clue. I have no idea what it means."

"What's the clue?"

"All it takes is one home run."

"Boy, I didn't make this very easy, did I?"

Bill laughed, "No, not really."

"Well, it looks like I need to find this key. Will you be there tomorrow?"

"Yes, but only until noon since it's Saturday."

"I'll come down there tomorrow morning to straighten this out."

"I'll see you then. Goodbye."

"Goodbye."

He hung up the phone. He sat down and shook his head. He wondered aloud, "Man, this is strange. Who would play a trick like this on me?"

It was January 27th, 1995.

Lisa came home with the kids a little while later.

"You look like there's something wrong. What's going on?"

"I had this weird phone call from the bank. They said that I need to go renew the rental fee on my safe deposit box."

"What's so weird about that?"

"I don't have one."

"Then, there's some kind of mistake."

"It gets weirder. Let's go in here to talk."

"All right, kids, just stay in here. We'll be right back."

They went to the bedroom and shut the door.

"Bill, the guy at the bank, said that I did this ten years ago."

"Ten years ago?"

"There's no way I could've done it. I don't forget anything. Especially not something like this."

"Maybe there's someone else with your name?"

"I thought of that, but I realized that for something with that much security, they're not going to make that kind of mistake. I would have to have an account there already."

"Ten years ago... that would be 1985. Did you have an account there yet?"

"Yes. I was working at the restaurant and had direct deposit."

"Do you think someone stole your identity?"

"I don't know. I can't figure it out. I mean, why would someone pretend to be me just to have a safe deposit box? It doesn't add up."

"But, that has to be what happened. What other explanation is there?"

"There's one other thing. I'm supposed to have a key. This is the strangest thing of all. Bill said that I left him a clue-- 'all it takes is one home run.'"

"That's weird all right."

"That's what Sam told my mom to tell me when he left her with a baseball for me."

He went into the closet and pulled out a shoebox. He took the baseball out.

"What does it mean?" Lisa asked.

"I think it means we need to take the kids to the park tonight."

They arrived at the park soon after. The boys started running around.

"It's too chilly to be out here doing this," Lisa said. "What do you think we're going to accomplish?"

"Call it instinct, call it taking a leap of faith, but I think I need to hit a home run."

She nodded.

"Okay, kids, come here," she called. "We're going to play a little baseball. Remember how Grandpa taught you."

"Yea!" they shouted.

They moved to an open area.

"We don't have enough for a team," Sammy pointed out.

"That's ok, son. We're just going to practice throwing and hitting," his dad replied.

"Let's let them go first," Lisa told him.

"Of course."

They gave Sammy and Elijah turns at bat. Lisa threw enough times to let them hit it. They had a good time, but Charlie still kept in mind the reason for their game. Lisa and Charlie had turns at bat. They each hit the ball, but no home run. Then, Charlie had an idea.

"Let's let Sammy throw this time."

Lisa gave him the ball.

"Lisa, go long."

She smiled and ran.

"All right, Sammy. Show me what you've got."

He threw the ball. Charlie swung and missed. Elijah retrieved the ball and threw it back to his brother.

"Remember what Grandpa always says. 'Give me some pepper.'"

Sammy threw it harder, but he still swung and missed.

"That's good, son, that's really good. But, this time, show me some pepper."

"How about this pepper?"

Like father, like son. He threw it harder yet, and this time, Charlie made contact.

"Whoa! That's a homer!" Sammy exclaimed.

Charlie laughed as he watched his first home run fly towards Lisa. She ran to its direction and carefully positioned her mitt.

"I got it!" she shouted.

They all ran towards each other and met in the middle. They huddled around Lisa, trying to catch their breath. She opened her mitt.

"Whoa! You knocked its guts out!" Sammy enthused.

Charlie's and Lisa's faces grew more serious as they were suddenly reminded of their objective. She handed the ball to Charlie. As Sammy so eloquently implied, the ball was busted open. Charlie reached his fingers in and pulled out a key. The boys gasped.

"Cool!!" Sammy said.

"How did that get there?!" Elijah asked.

Their parents looked each other in the eyes.

Lisa said, "Curiouser and curiouser."

"I'm going to ask the obvious question," Charlie told Lisa privately when they got home. "Why was there a key in my baseball?"

"An even better question-- who put it there?"

"How long has it been there? Who else even knows I have it?"

"Someone went to great lengths to get you this safe deposit box and then hide the key."

"And yet still give me a clue that only I could've figured out. This whole thing is fishy." He sat down on the bed. "It's very unsettling."

She sat down beside him.

"It is a little unsettling, but look at the bright side. Who doesn't love a good mystery? Didn't you feel great when you hit that home run?"

"Yeah," he said with a smile.

"Admit it. It was pretty cool to find that key."

"Yeah, it was cool. Creepy, but still kind of cool."

"We'll get all of the answers tomorrow. Maybe it won't be so bad."

"I hope you're right."

"Try not to worry about it. I know you. You won't get any sleep. Let's just let tomorrow's problems be for tomorrow. Tonight, we solved part of the mystery, you hit a home run, and the boys had a good time. That's a good day in my book."

"How do you do that?" he asked with a laugh.

"Do what?" she said with a big grin. "Turn it into a positive? I'm Sunshine, ya know. I have to brighten up Mr. Blue Sky."

"You always do."

They kissed.

Charlie arrived at the bank the next day with the key in his pocket and a lot of questions in his mind.

"Mr. Jordache! Good to see you again," Bill said as he reached out his hand. Charlie shook it, but still didn't recognize him.

"You, too."

He sat in front of his desk.

"I'm sorry for the confusion," Bill said. "I'm sure we can get all this straightened out for you."

"I think the best way to do that would be to see what's in that box."

He presented the key.

"I was worried for a minute that you wouldn't find it. Well, to have access to the box, you'll have to sign the form, and then I'll compare signatures with the original."

He gave Charlie the paper to sign. After he finished, Bill held it to the original.

"Looks good."

"Mind if I take a look?"

Bill handed the original agreement to him. Charlie was stunned to see that it was a perfect match.

"I may have proof before my eyes, but I still have a hard time believing that I signed this. The date says that it was January 28th, 1985. I was in school that day, and then I went to work. It couldn't be me."

"It is a bit concerning that you don't remember, but as long as the key works, that's the important thing."

"What if it doesn't? Do I still have to pay for something that's not mine? How much does it cost anyway?"

"We have monthly and yearly plans. You'll get a discount as you did before, if you choose to renew. We currently have you at $100 per year."

"That much, huh?"

"When you rented the box before, you paid for ten years at once. I've never seen anyone do that before or since."

"That's $1,000! Why would anyone pay that kind of money upfront?"

"It's none of my business what you choose to do, but if it were me, I would see what's in the box first. With that much money for that long, it must be something very important."

Charlie couldn't agree more.

A security guard led Charlie to the vault. His mind raced with all the possibilities that might await him in the deposit box. For all the ideas that sprung from his imagination, none of it made logical sense to his scientifically inclined brain. The guard brought him to his box and put in the key. Charlie put his key in the other lock and turned it. He halfway expected it not to work. Now that it did, his pulse quickened. He paused for a second and took a deep breath. There was no turning back. He opened the door. A manila envelope lay there inside. He carefully removed it. A typed note was taped to the front. It read, *"Do NOT under any circumstance open this here. Open ONLY at home."* His curiosity only grew stronger. "I'll take this with me," he told the guard. She nodded and shut the door to the box. She led him back to the lobby. Charlie stopped at Bill's desk.

"I won't need to renew the box. I'm taking this with me. Thanks."

He handed him the key.

"Thanks for your business, Mr. Jordache. I am curious-- did you solve the mystery?"

Charlie glanced at the envelope and back to Bill.

"The mystery has only just begun."

Charlie arrived home.

"Did you take care of it?" Lisa asked.

"Yes and no," Charlie answered as he showed her the envelope.

"What's in it?"

"I don't know yet. Read this."

She read the note. "The mystery deepens."

"I want us to open it together."

"Of course." She held his hand. "Always together."

They instructed the kids to keep watching their cartoons while they went to the bedroom. They sat on the bed.

"I've been pondering this since I got the phone call. I can't for the life of me figure out what could be in this envelope, who is responsible, or what is so top secret about it. It's driving me nuts."

"Only one way to find out."

He nodded. He closed his eyes and took a deep breath to calm his nerves. He opened his eyes. Nothing could prepare him for what he was about to discover. He opened the clasp. He took out the contents as Lisa took the envelope and set it aside. There was a notebook with a letter envelope attached to the front. The envelope had a note like the other one. *"Read this first."* He opened that envelope and took out a letter. It was also neatly typed, presumably to not have distinguishable handwriting. He read it aloud.

"I'm sure you have a lot of questions. Those questions could lead to answers. If those answers were known, it could bring great danger."

They looked at each other.

"Is that a threat?" he asked.

"I'm not sure."

He continued, *"It's better to just accept this at face value and take a leap of faith. This book should only be seen by you, and kept secure at all times. You are being entrusted with knowledge that others do not have and the responsibility that comes with it. If this ended up in the wrong hands, the consequences would be disastrous."*

They gave each other a look of concern.

He read further, *"This book contains concepts that may seem impossible. After many years of careful research, along with trial and error, the methods presented in this book are not only accurate, but as of this writing, the only known, effective solution. There is one other person who could be trusted with this knowledge, and that is Lisa."*

They looked at each other.

"What?" she asked. "How does he know me?"

She read the next part aloud, *"This is the only solution, but she may have her own ideas to contribute. Listen to her wisdom and follow her instincts."*

She chuckled. "At least he's smart. Sounds like a team effort."

"I saw the date on the original agreement for the deposit box. It was January 28th, 1985. We weren't even together yet. You'd just moved back."

"For something that says that we shouldn't ask questions, it sure raises a lot of them. What else does it say?"

Charlie concluded the letter, *"Finally, this knowledge should be used only under the most necessary circumstance, and even then, as a last resort. I do not know what that situation would be, but you will know it when you see it. A day may come when you clearly see the need to put this knowledge to use in the service of another. It should only be used for that noble purpose. I pray that need never arises, but if it does, I pray you will have the wisdom to accompany the knowledge given you. If Lisa is with you, I'm sure that won't be a problem. Godspeed, Charlie."*

He set the letter aside as they both looked at the notebook.

"I have a feeling that our lives are about to change," Lisa stated.

"I was just thinking the same thing."

He opened the book. His eyes widened.

"Holy...," he searched for the right word to follow. None of them seemed enough to capture his surprise. "I don't believe it. How? *How?!*"

"What is it, dear?"

He turned the page and chuckled with near madness.

"Do you know what this is?" she asked, still unaware of what he found so alarmingly amusing.

He looked her in the eyes.

"Come with me."

They entered the study upstairs. The desk held the computer and a seemingly unorganized mess of notes. The rest of the room was filled with overflowing bookshelves, file cabinets, and boxes. Charlie reached into one of the boxes and pulled out a notebook. He handed it to Lisa.

"They look alike," she noted.

"Oh, it gets better. Open it to the first page."

She did as Charlie held the other notebook next to it.

"They're identical," she said with surprise.

"Turn the page."

They each turned a page and saw the same thing. Again and again, they turned the pages to reveal two identical books.

"I never showed anybody this book before. Not you, not even Mom. I don't know how this could have happened. I started writing this in high school. I never even finished it."

They finally came to a page that was blank in the one Lisa held. She turned more pages, only to see the same emptiness. Charlie's book, however, was filled out.

"What does it mean?" she asked.

"It means something as important and impossible and dangerous and mind-blowing as the letter suggested. Take a closer look, Lisa. You have a physics degree." She looked it over more closely. "These weren't just scribbles I made because I was bored. It was research, it was ideas, it was hypotheses... it was plans. Plans that I abandoned. These were my notes about..."

She gasped and looked him in the eyes. They said it in unison, "time travel."

Sunday the 29th. Lisa woke to find herself alone. She went upstairs to get the kids ready for church. After getting them up, she opened the door to the study. She found Charlie at the desk, still wearing the same clothes as the day before.

"Have you been up all night reading that book?"

"Yes."

"That's not good, Charlie. You have to take care of yourself."

"Even if I tried to sleep, there's no way I could with this on my mind. I had to know."

"What did you learn?"

"We know that I wrote the beginning of the book, but not the rest."

"Right."

"I looked at the beginning very closely. Side by side, with a magnifying glass... I studied it. Every letter, every number, every stroke of the pencil. Even the parts that I erased and wrote over. It's an exact duplicate. I've never seen anything like it. One hundred percent, completely and totally the same. That in itself is nearly impossible."

"Wow. Someone thought of everything."

"They went above and beyond. When it gets into the rest of the book... it gave me chills."

"What do you mean?"

"You know how we sometimes finish each other's sentences or say things at the same time?"

"Yeah. I love when that happens."

"That's what it feels like. When I read the rest of the book, it was like he was taking the words right out of my mouth. Even though I didn't write it, it was very much like I did. It follows my train of thought."

"For someone to make an exact copy of what you did before, he would have to be pretty smart. Maybe he figured out your way of thinking and took it from there. It isn't inconceivable."

"Lisa, he didn't just make a good guess. The equations, the terminology, the drawings, everything that's in it... this took years. It's exactly the way I would've done it. This wasn't someone 'pretty smart.' This was definitely the work of a genius. He knew what he was talking about." He flipped through the pages. "And as far as I can tell, he got it right."

"But, why the subterfuge? Why go through all these elaborate steps? If he wanted you to have this book so badly, why did he make it so difficult? Why didn't he just hand it to you?"

"Maybe he couldn't. Maybe the risk was too great."

"I know we're not supposed to ask these questions, but I'm sure you already have. Do you know who it is?"

"I thought about it and thought about it. I came up with a few possibilities, but eventually, only one made sense."

She sat on his lap and they held each other.

He continued, "Think about it. No one else has ever seen this book. I was so careful about that. He paid for a safe deposit box for ten years all at once. He did it as me, using my same handwriting. He told Bill that I might not remember doing it. Bill recognized me. Who else could look like me from then till now? He hid the key in an object that very few people knew I had. He made sure that I opened the envelope at home. He knows about you and knows that you can be trusted. He planned all this so carefully. No stone was left unturned. Every detail, down to the minutiae." He chuckled. "I think he even knew that Bill would still be there ten years later. That much planning, that much attention to detail... the contents of the book itself... this was brilliantly executed by someone with superior intellect and intimate knowledge of my life. He was careful about this in the same way I was careful about the book all those years ago and for the same reasons. Frankly, I don't know who else could've even begun to come up with something like this. I don't know exactly how, and I don't know exactly when, and I don't know exactly why, but the only one who makes any logical sense... is me."

She smiled. "I think you're right."

"This book doesn't just have theories about time travel. It tells us exactly how to do it. It's literally instructions on how to build a time machine."

"Really? Holy cow!"

"I think some version of myself from another time actually built it and used it to make sure that we have this book. It sounds far-fetched, but it's the only explanation that makes any sense."

"But, to what end?"

"You know me. I don't do anything without thinking it through. For myself to go through all this trouble, to take such carefully orchestrated measures, to give us the keys to time travel... well, I think this is something that we really need to consider. There must be a good reason. He said that we'll know it when we see it."

"This is all fascinating, and I'm very impressed with... you and you," she said with a laugh. She kissed him. "...but, I need to go check on the boys. We need to get ready for church. Are you coming?"

"I'm pretty tired, but I'm going to try to stay awake."

She got up and headed for the door.

He said, "Something tells me that we're going to need God in our corner now more than ever."

Lisa noticed how Charlie struggled with focusing on the sermon. She nudged him a couple of times to keep him from drifting into sleep. Truth be told, her own mind wandered at times. Not that the pastor was ineffective, but because the idea of time travel was hard to put on the backburner.

"Come on, Lisa, focus," she thought to herself. *"Time travel is cool, but so is Jesus feeding the five thousand. One miracle at a time."*

After church, they had lunch at home. Lisa told the boys to keep the noise to a minimum as Charlie went to bed. Sammy and Elijah played quietly upstairs while Lisa went to the study. She sat down and thumbed through the notebook.

"It makes sense. You did it, Charlie."

She thought back to a difficult time in her youth. It was a part of her life that Charlie never saw. She was sitting on her bed crying after a bad day at school. Her mom sat down beside her and put her arm around her.

"What's wrong, Lisa?"

"I hate this stupid school."

"Why? What happened?"

"I got done with the assignment before anyone else did, so I started drawing. I made some hearts and wrote 'Charlie' in some of them. The girl who sits next to me saw it and started laughing, so I stopped doing it. At recess, she came up to me with two other girls and started teasing me about liking Charlie."

"Girls act like that sometimes. I know it's not nice."

"But, that's not all. There's this other boy in my class named Charlie. She thought it was him. She told him about it and he came up to me and started talking to me like he liked me. I had to tell him that I didn't and all the girls were calling me a liar. I think I even hurt his feelings and I wasn't trying to. Why did we have to move back here? Why couldn't we just stay in Kansas with Charlie? I miss him so much."

Her crying increased and Annie wrapped her arms around her.

"Oh, sweetheart. I know it's hard right now, but it will get better."

"I wish none of this ever happened. I wish we never left. I wish I could go back in time."

The grown-up Lisa wiped a tear from her eye and said quietly, "What are you trying to tell us, Charlie? What's so important?"

CHAPTER 19

As they got back into their busy routine of work, Charlie and Lisa didn't talk much about the notebook. It never strayed far from their minds, however. A couple of weeks went by, and it was February 14th. They went out for a pleasant time of dinner and a movie, then took a final stop at their special spot at the park. They sat on the table with their arms around each other as they looked at the stars.

"All the years we knew each other, the friendship we had, and it all got better ten years ago. Right here in this spot. Three little words that changed everything." They looked into each other's eyes. Charlie continued, "You were worth the wait. I love you more each day."

"I love you, too."

They kissed.

"There's something we haven't done in awhile," Charlie said as he stood up. She followed his lead. He put his hands around her waist, and she put hers around his neck. They danced slowly in the moonlight. Ten years later, and their heartbeats were still enough to dance to. They stopped after a few minutes and passionately kissed.

Charlie said, "I've been thinking a lot about this whole time travel thing over the last two weeks."

"I could tell. So have I."

"I was thinking... life is pretty perfect. We have the kids, the school, music in our hearts, and the stars in the sky. What else do we need?"

"It is pretty perfect."

"Why should we do anything that might mess that up?"

"I agree, but I still wonder. Why did you start writing the book in the first place?"

"I was fascinated with the idea of time travel. I wanted to see if it could actually be done. I had some things in my life that I thought needed fixing. But, like you said ten years ago, 'this is where I fix it.' You did. It was my heart that needed to be fixed."

"But, now you know that time travel can happen. Aren't you at least a little curious about the possibilities?"

"Of course I am. But, why fix something that isn't broken? Aren't you happy?"

"Of course I am. I'm extremely happy. I love our life."

"Then, let's keep living it. From where I stand, it couldn't get any better."

She smiled. "Right now is perfect."

They kissed again.

Time marched on in their wonderful lives. Elijah turned seven, Sammy turned nine, and Charlie and Lisa turned twenty-eight. The school was thriving, and everyone was happy. But, Lisa still had a few questions. One day before school was out for the summer, she had a talk with Charlie.

"There's something I've been thinking a lot about lately. Something I used to think about years ago."

"Oh, yeah? What's that?"

"Some of our students have issues that go way beyond their physical disabilities. Being kind to them helps, but I think it's time to take it a step further."

"What do you have in mind?"

"I want to take a summer class and become a counselor. I would know how to help the kids better, and maybe I could have a little practice on the side. It could help with some extra income in the summer-- in a couple of years anyway."

He smiled widely. "I think that's a great idea. You would make an excellent counselor. You've helped so many already, especially me."

"People have always told me their problems. I think it all started with you. I like to help them, and this way, I could do it better."

"Know what I think? I think it's your calling."

"Really? What about teaching?"

"Why can't it be both? You were given many gifts, Sunshine. Just as the sun can serve more than one purpose, so can you. You already do."

She hugged him. "I'm so glad that I have such a supportive husband."

"And I'm so glad that I have a wife with such a big heart. If the sun is going to shine, who am I to stand in its way?"

"You always did have a way with words."

"Well... yeah... you know."

They laughed and kissed.

"We're in it together," he said.

"Always together."

Lisa did start taking classes over the summer. She was always a fast learner, but this time, she felt like she was finally learning what she needed to know. Her natural abilities were being fine-tuned. Throughout this time, her questions still echoed through her mind. As the weeks and months went by, the answers became clear.

It was August 11th, 1995. Charlie and Lisa went back to the park again for their tenth wedding anniversary. Once again, they sat on top of the bench with their arms around each other.

"One of these days, we need to do something different. We should take a trip somewhere. Ten years should be a good excuse," Charlie said.

"Don't you like coming here anymore?"

"Of course I do. I just want to do more for you."

Lisa couldn't hold back any longer. "Funny you should mention that. I've been thinking the same way."

"Where do you want to go?"

"It's not as much of a 'where' as a 'when.'"

"Time travel?"

She nodded. "Hear me out. I've been thinking a lot about this. If you're the one who gave us the notebook, then there's a really good reason. I've been trying to figure out what that reason could be. I've read the letter over and over. It sounds like you weren't even sure why we might need to do it. But, I think I know why. You said to listen to my wisdom and trust my instincts. You wanted me to figure it out."

"Did you figure it out?"

"Yes. I've been taking this class, and it's reinforced what I already felt. You have been doing so well. You've come a long way these past ten years. You're so much happier and confident. You went from being this shy boy to a leader in the community." Her eyes filled with tears. "And, I'm so proud of you."

"We make a good team."

"Yes, we do. But, despite all the progress you've made, all the lives you've touched, there's still something wrong. I know you better than anyone. There's still a pain that you can't quite get rid of."

"Lisa, we've talked about this. I think it's better to just enjoy the life that we have."

"Charlie, I bet you don't know that you talk in your sleep."

"No, I didn't know that."

"You don't always do it, but sometimes you do. In a couple of months, it's going to get bad again. It's going to be the anniversary, and you're going to do it for a few days. 'Please, God, bring him back.' And sometimes, you'll say things like, 'I'm coming, Dad.' Or, 'Dad, don't go.' Or, 'I'll save you, Dad.'" Tears ran down her face as she sobbed. "And, I can't keep watching you suffer! I love you too much, Charlie. Even in your dreams, you're calling out for a solution that we have in our grasp. And what about your mom? That poor woman has been so patient. I love her as much as I love you. We can fix this, Charlie. We can put an end to this pain."

Charlie said through his tears, "I appreciate it, Lisa, I really do. You really are the best. But, have you ever thought about the consequences? I sure have. We don't even know what happened. All we know is that on October 3rd, 1973, my dad didn't come home. We don't know what happened to him, what time it happened, none of it. No clue. So, that in itself is a problem. We can't fix something without knowing the details. But, let's say that we do figure out the details. Let's say that we're in the right place at the right time, and we prevent… whatever it was that happened from happening. Ok. Sounds good. But, then what? What if we make things worse?"

"How could it be worse? What could be so wrong with having him around?"

"Nothing. But, what if that meant that we don't end up together?"

"Don't you think that we were meant to be together, no matter what?"

"I do, but you have to think about it. This happened when we were six years old. This one event has affected our lives for the past twenty-two years. In many ways, this is what's made me who am. This is at the very foundation of everything that was built after that. If we start chipping away at the foundation, wouldn't everything else crumble? We may be meant to be together, but what if it still didn't happen? It happens all the time. People miss out on their one true love. If we change something so big, so far into our past, it could undo a lot of good things that did happen. What about the kids? Would we lose them?" His tears ran down his cheeks. "That's not a risk I'm willing to take."

"I hadn't thought of it like that."

"I've thought about it every day since we got that book. I want to see my father again. God knows that I do. I want that for Mom. I want that for the boys. And, I know you want that. I know you want to give that to me. And, I love you for it. It would be the greatest gift. But, at what cost?"

"If we could figure out a way that would work, a way that wouldn't ruin everything…"

"I don't know if there is one. We can still think about it some more and discuss it. But, no more for tonight." He held her tight. "Just let me hold you. Let me hold on to what I've got."

The days passed by as Charlie still wrestled with conflicting thoughts and emotions. The possibility of seeing his father again seemed within reach. It was the first such sign of hope in twenty-two years. He looked through the notebook and saw how much the science made sense. He imagined what the reunion would be like and cried each time he thought of it. But, the possible consequences were impossible to ignore. Would he trade one life for another? Would having his dad mean not having Lisa, and still bring just as much pain? He watched

Sammy and Elijah play. He couldn't imagine living a life without them in it. He thought back to what Sam told him, *"It's taken up too much of your life. You have to learn to accept it. I know it's not easy. You'll have your bad days. But, you can't let the past control your life anymore. You can't let it keep you from having a future."* He did accept it and moved on to a happy life. But, could he actually have everything he always wanted? He thought back to his prayer since his seventh birthday, *"Please, God, bring him back."* Could this be the answer to his prayers? Charlie stood before the pictures on the wall of the school. "Honoring the Past." There was his dad, as young as his own kids. "Preparing the Future." His kids were among the many pictures added through the years. Adriana, Andrew, and all the others were there. So was the very first picture of all the family and friends who helped make the dream a reality. The teachers who had found rejuvenated careers and deeper purpose for their calling. All the students whose lives were greatly helped by their service. He gazed upon his dad's plaque. *"This school is dedicated to the loving memory of Wayne Jordache. May we always teach what we learned from him-- 'If you love someone, anything's possible.'"* The possibilities were now certainly more than he ever knew them to be. The past could be altered. But, would the future be better or worse? The questions were too hard to answer. He leaned against the wall and began to weep. Crying turned to sobbing as his heart was torn between the known and unknown, the joy of the present versus the healing that might await him in the past.

"Please, God, don't make me choose."

The struggle was too much to bear. Charlie visited his mom the next day to try to find a solution.

"I have a conundrum."

"Oh, one of those," she said with a laugh. "It must be pretty complex if the great Professor Jordache can't figure it out."

"It is."

They sat on the couch.

"Okay, son, what's on your mind?"

"An opportunity has presented itself."

"A job opportunity?"

"Not quite. It's... well, I probably shouldn't give too many details."

"Is it legal?"

"Of course it is. It's just... well... it's a situation that doesn't have a clear answer."

"Have you talked to Lisa about it?"

"Yes."

"What does she think?"

"She thinks that we should do it."

"We? So, it's something for both of you."

He kicked himself internally for letting that part slip. "Yes."

"Well, you know you've got to do it if Lisa says so," she laughed, "whether you want to or not."

"It's just not that cut and dry. There could be some real consequences."

Her face grew more serious to match her son. "What kind of consequences?"

"The kind that couldn't be undone."

"I see. What are the pros and cons?"

"On the pro side, it could be fun. It could be something so challenging, but with a great reward if it all works out. We might even be the first ones to do it."

"That sounds great. What about the cons?"

"It would take a lot of time and effort, no doubt a lot of money, too. It would take years, with no clear way to know if it will pay off. If it doesn't, people might be hurt."

She nodded her head. "It really is a conundrum. I don't know what you're talking about exactly, but I know that it has to be a big deal for you to be this concerned. I can't tell you what you should do. What does your heart tell you?"

He halfway smiled. "That's what Sam said. To be honest, my heart is torn."

"This seems very familiar. When Lisa moved back, you didn't know what to do. Even though it was what you always wanted, you were afraid to take that step of faith. If you wouldn't have, who knows what would've happened? Look at how wonderful it's been because you took that chance. Some of the greatest things in life have to be achieved by faith. There may not be a way to know what will happen until you try one way or another."

"'For we walk by faith, not by sight.'"

"That's right. Besides, maybe it's not your heart that you should listen to. Maybe it's Lisa's. She has the best instincts I've ever seen."

There was that word again, "instinct." It was hard to argue with her logic. To move forward with the idea of time travel would require a tremendous amount of faith. His own instincts were beginning to point more towards Lisa's.

"You've certainly given me more to think about. I knew you were the right one to turn to."

"What can I say? I'm always right," she said with a chuckle.

"Now, you sound like Lisa."

They laughed and put their arms around each other.

"What I do know is that whatever you decide, I'll support you. And, I know that you'll do the right thing as you always do. Want to know the reason why you always do what's right?"

"Because you showed me how."

"True, but I was thinking of something else. Because you always decide things on what's best for someone else. You always put others first. That's what I admire most about you. I'm so proud of you, son." She kissed his cheek. "I love you, Charlie."

"I love you, too, Mom." He kissed her back. "I'm starting to see things a little clearer."

"You're a genius. You'll figure it out."

"Even a genius needs a mom."

She smiled. "That's still one of the smartest things you've ever said."

They laughed and held each other tighter. It was still one of the truest things he ever said.

Charlie and Lisa each thought about the situation for a couple of days after that. One night before bed, they knew it was time to get it settled.

"I've been thinking a lot about this whole time travel thing," Charlie said.

"Me, too."

"There's something I've never told you before. Remember that time when I named all the songs on the Beach Boys album?"

She smiled. "Yeah. It's a great memory."

"I did that with Mom when I was ten. It was the night before starting the fifth grade."

"I bet she loved it."

"She did. She wanted me to do it a few times. Looking back, she responded the best possible way. But, at the time... well, it was the first time I ever told her about my memory. I didn't feel so good about it."

"It was an enormous weight for a little boy to carry."

He nodded. "I told her how I remembered being bullied. All the name-calling, all the hitting... the pain was always fresh. I told her how I remembered everything about the day that we lost Dad. How it made it harder to deal with when it still felt like it just happened. She tried to convince me that I had a gift. But, all I could see was a curse." His eyes watered. "I told her that I thought I was the reason why Dad left."

"Oh, Charlie." Her eyes teared up as well.

"I cried my little eyes out. She held on to me. She told me that there was a reason why God made me this way. I didn't believe it. I said that there wasn't a reason. But, she wouldn't give up. She told me that I was special, that I was a miracle." The tears overflowed.

She put her hands on his shoulders. "She's an amazing mom."

"She said something that I'll never forget, even if my memory wasn't perfect. She said, 'Someday, you'll figure it out. It doesn't have to be today. But, when that time comes, we'll know. And, I'll say, 'did you see that? Did you see that miracle? That's my son.'"

Lisa's tears increased. "That's beautiful."

"I said, 'What am I gonna do, Mom?' She said, 'I don't know yet. But, I know that you'll be the only one who could do it.'"

"She's a wise woman. She's always right."

"I've been thinking a lot about this lately. This time travel thing has stirred up so many old memories and emotions. Back in those days, I was afraid to admit things about myself. I was so ashamed of who I was. Mom always tried to show me that it was a gift. I was too afraid of being myself. Sam showed me that being myself was the key to winning your heart. I didn't know that you loved me, too, until I took that step of faith and told you that I loved you."

"You didn't know how alike we really were."

"That's exactly right. A whole new door was opened. I became happier and more confident. I finally embraced who I was. I used my gifts to teach at the college, I started the school, I've helped a lot of kids with their own struggles. Best of all, I've been a father to two wonderful, beautiful boys. I've always wondered what it was that I was supposed to do. What was it that Mom could see that I couldn't? What was this miracle? How could I be the only one who could do it? I've asked myself these questions for the past eighteen years. I've thought more about it lately, and now, I finally see the answer." He smiled with tears in his eyes. "I finally know what I have to do."

"What is it?" she asked with an enthusiastic smile of her own.

"I was looking at it all wrong, just as I've done before. When Mom said that I was the only one who could do it, I always took it for what it was. She meant that I was unique and would do something special. Just like you said, I knew that she was always right. But, that's just it. This time she was only half right."

"What do you mean?"

"Don't you see, Lisa?" He put his hands on her shoulders. His eyes were filled with passion and tears of joy. "I'm not the only one who could do it."

She smiled. "Two sides of the same coin."

"Everything I've done, every accomplishment, every shred of happiness... it's all been possible because you've been by my side. I couldn't have done any of it without you. You're my partner, my other half, the one who makes me better. We've done it all together as a team. We're one."

Tears filled her eyes. "That's how I feel about you."

"I've read the letter that came with the notebook over and over. I think you're right. I think that this other me wanted you to figure it out. This other me had the wisdom to know that I don't know everything, that you can contribute much more than I. I need to listen to your wisdom and trust your instincts. You've always been one step ahead of me... and, you're always right."

"You're always right, too. You opened my eyes to the possible consequences. This isn't something that we can jump into lightly. I've been thinking and praying a lot about it, and I still come back to it being the right thing to do. Whether or not we can or should try to change what happened to Dad, I don't know. All I know is that my gut says that we need to start building it. There's a reason why we have the book. There's a reason why we feel these things. It's going to take a lot of time to do it. It's going to be a huge leap of faith. But, I do believe that the reason for it will be clear in the end. Like the letter said, we'll know it when we see it. It will be in the service of another. What greater reason would we need? It will take time, it will take faith, and we'll be the only ones who can do it."

"We already have experience in those areas."

"You have to use all your gifts, and I have to trust your instincts."

"And, you have to use all *your* gifts as I trust *your* instincts."

"We have to work together as one."

"We'll have quite the time together."

"Always together."

They smiled. She put her arms around his neck while he put his arms around her waist.

"Sunshine," he said.

"Mr. Blue Sky."

"Ready for an adventure?"

"Always."

"Let's build a time machine."

She gave her trademark mischievous grin. "Heck yeah! Sounds like fun."

CHAPTER 20

"We need to establish some rules," Charlie said.

"Yes, we do. I thought of a few myself," Lisa replied.

It was the next day after their decision to build the time machine. They were in the study with the notebook on the desk beside them.

"First of all, and the most important," Charlie said, "is that no one can know about this."

Lisa nodded her head.

"Not the kids, not our parents, not our friends-- no one."

"Because the more people who know, the greater the chance of causing a disaster in the space-time continuum."

Charlie smiled.

She continued, "Yeah, I've seen some movies."

"Thattagirl."

"Another important one-- everything we do has to be agreed on."

"That's a good one."

"Any purchase, any modifications, anything. We both need to know what is going on and work together. That's especially important when it comes to how we ultimately use it."

"I couldn't agree more. We're a team." He picked up the notebook. "Also, not only do we need to keep the project a secret, but this book needs to be a secret, too."

"Totally. We need to keep it in a safe when we're not using it, and never have it out when anyone else is around."

"We can't even mention that it exists. Think of what would happen if it ended up in the wrong hands."

"We don't need a Biff situation," she said with a wink.

"Another thing-- we can't tell anyone, but it might be hard to keep it completely secret over time. And, I don't want to lie. It might be okay to admit to our family--maybe even Tracy-- that we're working on some kind of project, just as long as we never tell them what it is."

"And, that's only if we keep getting bombarded with questions."

"Exactly. I did tell Mom that there would be something, but that's it. There won't be anything else, if we can help it. I also think that we should do everything in order."

"You mean the order that's in the book, from front to back?"

"Yes. I think it makes good, logical sense. There's a reason why everything was done the way it was done. If it's the 'only known, effective solution,' then let's not fix it if it isn't broken."

"Other than new ideas that I might come up with," she said with a smile.

"Exactly."

"I have another point to bring up. It's not so much of a rule as a question. Where are we going to build this big, secret contraption?"

"I've thought about that, too. No garage, no shop, no basement... we don't have a lot of places that we could go and still keep it secure."

"Does the book say anything about it?"

"No, I checked. It never says where to do it, just gives the dimensions of it. It's going to take up a lot of space."

"It's odd that you never said anything about it in the book, especially considering all the details that you did include."

He shrugged. "My guess is that I--or he-- just didn't know if it would be possible to do it in the same place as he did it."

"That may be true. May I look at the dimensions?"

He handed the book to her.

"Huh. It is pretty good-sized," she said.

"Big enough to fit both of us inside of it."

"I have an idea. Where's the tape measure?"

After retrieving the tape measure, they used it in the study.

"Just as I thought," Lisa remarked. "This room is a perfect fit."

"You want to do it in the house?"

"Where else could we go with it?"

"What about the kids? They might mess around with it."

"Not if we keep it locked at all times. We could keep the safe with the book in here, too."

"It would be more convenient. We can keep an eye on it better than if we used some other place. That would save on cost, too. Well done, Lisa."

"I have my moments. Speaking of cost, I'd hate to see the electric bill with this thing."

"We only have to use it once," he said with a wink.

"We would still have to run tests."

"That's true. But, we don't have to do it all at once. We can take our time. I mean, if we have a time machine, we have all the time in the world."

"That's another reason why this room would work best. I remember seeing something about solar panels in the book."

They looked up to the ceiling.

She said, "Speaking of cost..."

"Good thing you'll have that extra counseling income."

He gave her a cheesy grin.

"Yeah, and maybe my studies will explain to me what exactly is wrong with us to want to do something so crazy."

"You're not having second thoughts are you? Come on, Lisa, where's your sense of adventure?"

"It's still there. I'm just glad that *some* kind of sense is left."

Charlie felt the need to loosen her up again. He joked, "I have an idea. Why don't we just forget all this nonsense about building this contraption in the house? I have a better idea."

"What?"

He did his best impression of Michael J. Fox. "What if we built a time machine... out of a *DeLorean*?"

She shook her head and tried to stifle a laugh. "You and your movie references."

He laughed.

She teased, "You know, one of these days, I'm just gonna slap you. You'll be surprised, but then you'll remember. You'll remember that you had it coming."

He gave her a mockingly tough glare. "You wouldn't slap me."

Without missing a beat, she attempted to slap him with her right hand, but he blocked it with his left. She tried with her left, but he blocked with his right.

With another impression, he said, "Wax on, wax off."

"Grrrrr!!!"

Later that night, Charlie's thoughts waxed philosophical. As he lie in bed with Lisa, the mental activity was enough to keep them both awake.

"What are you thinking about?" she asked.

"I was wondering how much of a coincidence it was that the machine would fit in the study."

"Do you think it was meant to?"

"I think it was either meant to fit or it already did."

"Huh?"

"If some version of myself built a machine before, then it's possible that he did it in the same room in the same house."

"Possible, but very unlikely. I mean, what are the odds that you bought the same house twice?"

"Exactly. Anything different that we do can change things, even small things that we might not realize or even be aware of. Did I really end up with the same house in two different realities? We may never know. But, it does make me wonder an even better question. Are we really walking by faith, or are we just following some kind of predetermined destiny?"

"I think we've been given a choice. We made that choice together, and we're following through with it. We easily could have chosen differently, and still could at any time. We are in control of our own destinies."

"But, are we really though? I was told about the safe deposit box, so I went to the bank. The book says to build a time machine this specific way, so that's what we're doing. Is it really a choice, or just the illusion of a choice? Are we really doing what we want to do, or just following a path that was already laid out for us?"

"Do you think that we're being manipulated?"

"I don't know. All I know is that someone went to a lot of trouble to give us this information, for better or worse. Is it really another version of myself, or is it just me? Am I going to go back to the past and put the book in the safe deposit box just to start the cycle all over again?"

"I've thought of that myself. I really don't know the answer to that."

"The biggest question is this-- can history change, or does it always repeat itself? If we change something, are we really changing it or is that the way it was always meant to be?"

"Like I said, I think we're in control of our own destinies. Yes, God has a plan for all of us and can intervene, but I think that we are still given free will, and therefore a choice. We choose what we do. Whether right or wrong, we make that choice. That's what's so great about time travel. We can go back and fix it if we made the wrong choice."

"I agree with you, but we can't just go back and fix everything. This shouldn't be used for just undoing things that we got wrong. This is far too complicated and next to impossible. What we do with it has to be worth the time and effort. It has to be for a good cause. Not just righting a wrong, but resolving an injustice. It needs to be noble, heroic... used in the service of another. Whether that's about my dad or some other situation, that's the way it has to be."

"I couldn't agree more. But, it sounds like you're not sure if it can be done."

"I don't know if it can or not. I do believe that we'll be able to travel through time. I just don't know if what we end up doing will fix anything or if it will cause another problem. Let's say that we do change something. Will it change, or will time just course correct?"

"What do you mean by that?"

"I mean... what if some things are meant to be the way they are, and there's nothing you can do to stop it? If we save a life, for instance, will that life be saved, or will it just delay the inevitable? Will it still happen some other time?"

"There's no way to really know. We'll just have to be as wise as we can be and do the best we can."

"That's just it, Lisa. We're not just doing this half-heartedly. We're always careful and think things through. We're a team. Let's face it, we're geniuses. We're two of the smartest people in the world. We have degrees in physics, we're educators, and we know what we're doing. If we put our minds to it, we can accomplish anything. Even if it seems impossible. And yet for all that, there are just some things that we don't know. We possibly will never know. We have this book to work with, and yes, we will still have to take some things by faith. But, the questions will still remain. If we change something, would we even know it? Would we remember? We can do the best we can, but will it ever be enough? We may know how to time travel, but we still have a lot to learn about time itself. And, that's a mystery that I don't think anyone will ever solve."

She put her arm around him and kissed him.

"Maybe we'll figure it out together."

"I don't know, Lisa. This is what's keeping me awake. Are we really in control of our destinies? Can we really change the past and the future? Or, are we in over our heads?"

CHAPTER 21

"Whatcha doin'?"

Lisa and Charlie looked at each other to see who could come up with the best answer for Elijah.

"We need to organize this messy study," she told him.

"Why?"

"Because it's a mess, that's why!" she said as she playfully messed up his hair.

He laughed and said, "Can I help?"

"Sure, buddy," Charlie said.

"Me, too?" asked Sammy as he walked up.

"Of course."

They all started moving the papers, boxes, and other items to accommodate the space that the machine would need.

"It's going to get hard to keep this a secret," Lisa whispered to Charlie.

"It will be okay. They're good kids. If we tell them to stay out and keep the door locked, they'll listen."

"What will happen when they see us bringing random, weird pieces into the house? What about all the cords?"

"We can do it when they're not here. They can go see our parents or someone when we need to do that. The cords... well... we'll come up with something."

"This is going to get interesting."

Sammy started singing his "Grandma Ilene" song. Elijah joined him, followed by Lisa and Charlie. They worked the rest of that Saturday on fixing up the room. Charlie felt a little bad that the boys wouldn't later enjoy the fruit of their efforts. But, it was the way it had to be.

After putting the boys to bed that night, Lisa and Charlie went back to the study.

"Man, this is already taking up a lot of time and energy," she said. "We only have a few weeks till school starts again. I still have my class. This may have to be more of a summertime project than anything."

"I was just thinking that, too. We may be able to squeeze a few things in here and there, but this is quite an undertaking."

"I wonder if you had any help before."

"Huh?"

"I mean the you that did this before. It's almost too much for even two people."

"I don't know, but maybe we should start referring to the other me as a 'him' rather than 'me.' Less confusing that way. Besides, we still don't know 100% that it was me anyway."

"That's true. So, what comes next? Get all the parts for the machine or install the solar panels? Where are we even going to find half of this stuff?"

"We could get the parts and start building it. Then again, the solar panels were next in the book. We could get them and maybe start using some solar energy for the house as well as the machine. We would still need electricity, but it would cut costs."

"Now you're talking."

"As far as where to find this stuff goes, well that's a little more complicated. I'm surprised that he didn't get into the specifics about that in the notebook."

"He must have been concentrating on doing it rather than on where he found everything. Another thing to consider is that he may not have thought at the time that anyone else would ever see the book."

"That's a good point. I'm sure he kept receipts for himself, but he just didn't put them in the book. If it was me, he would've remembered anyway."

"I wonder if something happened to make him want to leave the book for us if that wasn't his original intention."

"Maybe it was a backup plan. Who knows? So, as far as where to find stuff is concerned, we can check the phone book and call around. But, there's also another way..." He turned his gaze to the computer. "I think our next expense will need to be a computer upgrade."

"Already?"

"It has been a few years. Some of the things we'll need to do with the machine is dependent on it. And, we're more likely to find everything we need by looking for it through there."

"This is the '90's, I suppose. If we're going to change something in time, then we have to change *with* the times as well."

He said with a sigh, "Yeah... we do have to adapt a little more. We have to join the World Wide Web."

Lisa finished her class for the year just in time to start teaching again. They did get their new computer. They held onto the old one, thinking that they may need more than one for the task at hand. Lisa would find Charlie using it late at night, caught up in reading all sorts of things. He quipped that it must be the reason why they called it the web. He soon realized that for someone with a perfect memory, it might be information overload. He did, however, become so impressed with its capabilities that he convinced the school board to allow more in the budget to add it to the school. He researched parts for the time machine whenever he could. Their busy lives and lack of funds kept them from doing much more than that for the time being.

The following summer in 1996, they installed the solar panels. Lisa continued her class as Charlie did his best to keep the kids occupied and divert their attention away from the room. They soon realized that they needed another place for Lisa to practice her counselling. When she finished her class, they found a small office space downtown next to Cierra's Hair Salon. The irony of it being a former travel agency made it that much better. There were only two obstacles-- it was more than they could afford, and Cierra wanted the space to expand her growing business. Charlie came up with a solution. Since Lisa would only need it as a part-time, appointment only business, Cierra could move her reception space next door with a walkway in between. The salon area would be expanded in the original space, especially if they also shared the office and bathroom with a door connecting the two businesses. Lisa would let her know ahead of time when she needed the space for a client, and would also pay part of the fee to use the space. Cierra thought it was a great idea. Lisa was soon taking on clients, including people from the salon. She enjoyed her new calling.

The summer of 1997 was now underway. Lisa was able to do a little more counselling while still working on the project with Charlie. After many web searches and phone calls, Charlie found some good news.

He informed Lisa, "I finally found the place that sells what we need for the machine. We'll have to order it. We'll only be able to get it a little at a time."

"That hard to find, huh?"

"No, it's that expensive."

"What's it called again?"

"Aluminum oxynitride. It also comes in pieces no bigger than thirty-five inches."

"How much do we need?"

"A lot more than thirty-five inches... twice."

"For the inner wall and the outer wall."

"Exactly."

"Does it come curved?"

"It can, if that's what we pay for."

"Then, that's what we should do."

It wasn't long until their first order of aluminum oxynitride arrived. It was a little lighter than expected, but not so much when carried upstairs.

“This is heavy,” Charlie said in his best Michael J. Fox voice.

Lisa didn’t miss a beat. “Weight has nothing to do with it.”

In his regular voice, he quipped, “Weight has everything to do with it.”

They took another look at it when they set it down in the study.

“This stuff can really withstand the pressure, right?” Lisa asked.

“Right. It’s used for bulletproof glass. It can definitely stand the pressure of our weight and the energy that will travel through it.”

“About this energy. What exactly is it? I never saw it named in the book. That’s about the only other major thing we need besides the rest of this stuff and some more cords.”

“Part of the energy is the solar power.”

“Of course.”

“But, the rest of it... well, you’re right. He did leave it a bit hazy. There is definitely another power source that works with the sun. Maybe he didn’t want to say what it’s called.”

“Or, maybe he didn’t know what it’s called.”

“Either way, he left detailed instructions for how to use it.”

“Did he get as detailed about where to find it?”

“Yes and no.”

He got the book out of the safe. They sat at the desk and looked at it together.

He said, “Notice how we should build the machine first.”

“Yes, but we could still get a better idea of what we’re doing and plan ahead.”

“That’s true.” He turned another page. “Ah, here it is. See what you make of what he wrote. *‘The energy source is the most vital component of the machine, and therefore the thing that must be kept hidden most of all. It took many years of research to even have the smallest lead of where to find such a powerful object. Only by faith could I have ever discovered it. Printing too many details would make it too easy for the wrong person to find it. What information I leave you will still save many years, however, precautions still need to be taken.’*”

“So, it doesn’t run on batteries,” she joked.

He turned the page.

“This is the part that I tried not to think too much about before. But, maybe it’s time that we put our heads together and figured it out.”

“I remember this. Seems like a bunch of odd, randomly assembled notes.”

He read the first one. “‘FDR becomes 32.’”

“Then there’s this drawing of a cartoon character.”

“That’s Dot, sister of Yakko and Wakko. Do you have no culture, woman?”

She laughed. "Okay, so I know the show. I still don't see the significance yet."

"Well, he definitely time travelled. You can't put a book into a safe deposit box in 1985 and have a drawing of a character that didn't exist until recently without that explanation."

"You never know, he might have went back to it through the years."

"I guess that's possible. Anyway, the next thing is 'a Revolution in red.'"

"I'm starting to think that these are riddles."

"I think you're right. It's like the clue about the key in the baseball."

"Speaking of which, it says, 'Doyle's detective collective.' Obviously, that means Sherlock Holmes."

"Obviously. Not sure what the 'collective' part means, though."

"This is a weird one-- 'physics and education.' It just happens to be what we majored in."

"Oliver Never? Who the heck is Oliver, and why wouldn't he?"

"Your guess is as good as mine," she said with a laugh.

"Then, it goes to another column. There must be a reason why they're separated."

"This looks like a hard one," she said. "'Emperor Trajan invaded Armenia.'"

"Then, another picture of Dot. There has to be a connection, weird as it sounds. Then, it's 'Wilson goes for a second.'"

"'Karen is silenced.'"

"'Physics and education' again."

"And, 'Adam Wheat.'"

They stared at it for a moment.

"What's the connection?" he asked.

"Well, we figured out Sherlock Holmes. We have to really put our deduction skills to work."

"Adam Wheat. That's like Oliver Never. Oliver and Adam..." he said quietly as he stared into space. "Oliver who? Hardy? Twist? Queen? Maybe it's about the last names. Never and Wheat... Never Wheat. I'VE GOT IT!"

"You do?! What?!"

"Never Eat Shredded Wheat. Remember that from when we were kids? North, East, South, and West. Oliver North and Adam West!"

"Very good! I think you're right! And, Adam West played another detective who had to figure out riddles."

"Holy Burt Ward, Lisa! That's amazing!"

She giggled. "This is fun! But, what does it have to do with time travel?" Then it hit her. "Directions! North and West-- they're part of the direction of where to find this power source."

"That makes sense, but what does all the rest of this mean?"
"Let's take it in order."
"'FDR becomes 32.'"
"When is his birthday?"
"He was the 32nd President."
"When was that?"
"1933."
"Do we need to go back to 1933?"
"No, but maybe we're onto something. Maybe this stil has to do with time."
"So why is there a picture of Dot?"
"I'm not sure. Maybe we'll figure out the pattern. 'A Revolution in red.' Why is that capitalized? A Revolution in red...."
"The Russian Revolution?"
"I bet that's what it is."
"When was that?"
"1905."
"We should write this down."
She started writing notes on another paper.
"Doyle's detective collective," he said.
"When was the first Sherlock book?"
"That was *A Study in Scarlet* in 1887."
"That old, huh?"
"Yep."
"So, why does it say, 'collective'?"
Charlie thought for a few seconds. He answered, "That was the first book, but he also wrote short stories. The first book that *collected* the stories was *The Adventures of Sherlock Holmes*, and that was in 1892."
"Elementary, my dear Charlie," she said with a smile. She read her notes aloud, "So far, we have 1933, Dot, 1905, and 1892. These aren't just riddles, they're a code. I'm still not sure what all the years are for. Do we add them together?"
"Well, the next thing in the column is 'physics and education.'"
"You graduated in 1987; I graduated in 1989. Which year do we use?"
"Maybe it's not the year this time."
"Hmm... they're subjects... they're classes... they're degrees... AHA! That's it!"
"Degrees. The next thing is North, so that means 'degrees North.'"
"It's a coordinates!" She read the notes again. "1933, Dot, 1905, 1892, degrees, North."
"Take off the first parts of the years, and you have 33.0592°N."
"Yes! Now we're getting somewhere!"
He turned on the computer.

"I'll look it up when we figure out the rest. Gotta give it time to warm up."

"Right on. So, when did Emperor Trajan invade Armenia?"

"114 AD."

"You really do remember everything."

"Sometimes it comes in handy," he said with a smile.

"So, that makes 114, Dot, then two more years. 'Wilson goes for a second' and 'Karen is silenced.'"

"'Wilson goes for a second,'" he repeated out loud, trying to think of what it could mean. "Brian Wilson?"

"Jackie Wilson? Wilson Pickett?"

"Goes for a second what? Hit song? Too many possibilities with that. Maybe it's similar to another clue."

"FDR becomes 32," she said. "Maybe it's Woodrow Wilson."

"Yes! Wilson had a second term as President in 1917!"

She wrote it down. "Okay, the next one is 'Karen is silenced.'"

"That's easy. If this was really written by me, then it would be referring to the one Karen who had an impact in my life."

They said it together, "Karen Carpenter."

"Her voice was silenced in 1983," he said. "I'll never forget that day."

"That's the one event that we actually lived through," she noted.

"So, what do we have?"

"114.1783°W."

He opened up the web browser and started typing.

"33.0592°N, 114.1783°W."

They both felt butterflies in their stomachs as they awaited the results. Wherever this coordinates was, it would no doubt lead them on a great adventure.

"Here it is..." he said.

"Hull Mine," she read aloud.

"Never heard of it. Sounds like a good place to hide something. It's about forty-two miles from Yuma, Arizona. Of course, we still might have guessed wrong about some of this."

Charlie turned to Lisa to see her expression become serious.

She shook her head and said, "It's not wrong."

"What makes you so sure?"

"When I was a kid, we went to Yuma since it was only a few hours away. You know how my dad likes Westerns. Yuma also happens to be the place that has the most sunshine year-round-- more than anywhere else in the world."

"I didn't know that. Here I thought the most sunshine was sitting next to me."

"We were going to go up to see Hull Mine and the ghost town, but Grandma was getting too hot and wanted to go back home. We never did make it over there." She fiddled with her friendship bracelet and seemed nervous. "There's something I never told anyone until now. I didn't want to sound crazy."

He held her hand. "I'll believe you."

"I felt something."

"Like what?"

"I don't know how to describe it. Like something was urging me. Almost like it was calling for me."

"It had to be what we're looking for."

"Maybe it was moved to the mine after that. Or, maybe it was still close enough to still give me that feeling. I don't know." She looked him in the eyes. Her eyes began to water. "All I know is that this is more than just some treasure hunt. This is something even bigger than time travel." Her lips quivered. "It's destiny."

CHAPTER 22

"How long is it gonna take to get there?" Elijah asked from the back seat.

"About twenty hours without stopping," Lisa answered.

"Twenty hours?!" he said in shock along with Sammy.

"Don't worry; we'll stop along the way. We'll get a motel tonight." Charlie assured them.

"Good, cuz I don't think I can handle twenty hours without going to the bathroom," Elijah said.

Charlie and Lisa took turns driving. They drove as much as they could with minimal stops. Along the way, they talked, played games, and sang along to The Beach Boys, among others. It was a fun time of family bonding-- something that was needed for too long. It was the summer of 1998.

They stopped at a motel in New Mexico. Everyone was very tired from the long journey. It didn't take long for the boys to fall asleep. Charlie got out of the shower to find that Lisa wasn't in the room. The door was cracked open. He quietly went outside to find her there looking at the stars. He put his arms around her from behind. She smiled and put her hands on his.

"It's beautiful out here," she said.

"Yes, it is," he said as he kissed her neck.

"I was thinking back to when we were kids and I moved away. I used to look up there and feel so small. I knew that there was so much more out there. I'm bigger now, and we have kids of our own, but I still feel small in the grand scheme of things."

"You're not so small to me. You've always been my sunshine."

"And, you've always been my world."

"I feel like we've had this conversation before."

She chuckled. "Yes, we have."

"It's still one of my favorites."

She turned around and put her arms around his neck. They looked into each other's eyes.

"Maybe we're not so small anymore," she said. "Our world is getting bigger. I don't know exactly what we're getting ourselves into, but I believe that we're about to find another piece of the puzzle. We're finding where our place is in this world."

"I think you're right. It's not just a power source that we're after. We might find the answers to some questions. But, for now, our place is right here, in the moonlight... in each other's arms."

"Always together."

Their lips embraced with tenderness and passion. Their world was indeed getting bigger, but they would always be the center of each other's universe.

They resumed their journey early in the morning. Charlie tried to enjoy the scenery around him, but his mind was distracting. There was a feeling of familiarity, yet a feeling of being a stranger. He'd been this way before, but circumstances were much different this time. He knew that what he needed to find was something that went beyond what his eyes could see.

They finally reached their destination. The family got out of the car and went to the door. Lisa knocked. The door opened right away.

"Is it Trick or Treat already?"

"I hope you have candy," Lisa said with a laugh.

"No, but I have a hug."

"I'll take it." They held each other close. "I'm so glad to see you, Grandma."

"It's so good to see you, too, Sunshine. You're as pretty as ever."

They let go.

"It's been too long," Charlie said as they hugged.

"Only thirteen years, but who's counting?"

She let go and smiled even bigger when she saw the kids.

"It's so good to finally see you two! The pictures don't do you justice. Look at how tall and handsome you both are!" She hugged them. "You boys don't happen to like chocolate cake, do you?"

"Like it? I love it!" Elijah enthused.

"Good! Maybe you can help me get rid of this one I have in the kitchen. I made way too much for one little old woman to eat all by herself." She winked at Charlie as they started to go inside.

Charlie paused and turned to Lisa.

"It just dawned on me."

"What's that?"

"Your whole affection for chocolate cake started right here in this house, didn't it?"

"That, and cookies, pie, banana nut bread, and... let's see... what else... OH! She's the one who first started calling me Sunshine."

"Huh. After all this time, I'm still learning things about you."

"Would you have it any other way?"

"Nope. I can't imagine anything better."

It was Lisa's hometown, Heatherton, California. The family had their cake and laughed a lot as they told stories. They caught up on the present and reminisced about the good old days of the past. Charlie had never known his grandparents. To Charlie, Lisa's Grandma was his own.

They went to the beach the next morning. The sun shone brightly as they played in the sand and surf. Charlie and Lisa showed the boys how to make a sand castle in the same spot they used on their honeymoon. Grandma joined in as they made a sand castle bigger than any wave. She took a lot of pictures of the family as they had the time of their lives.

That night, they had an extra surprise when they were invited to dinner. Lisa's cousin, Vada, happened to be in town promoting her new memoir entitled *Weeping Willow*. Charlie was amazed by the similarities of the cousins. Both were smart, outgoing, funny, and compassionate. He couldn't wait to read her story of overcoming childhood tragedy to become successful.

The next morning, Charlie and Lisa awoke knowing that they must proceed with the main reason for their trip. After a hearty breakfast from Grandma, they gathered a backpack full of supplies that they would need for their mission.

"You two need to be on your best behavior and listen to Grandma," Lisa told the boys as she hugged them at the front door.

"We will," said Sammy.

"Don't you worry about anything," Grandma replied. "You two go enjoy the rest of your vacation. You deserve it. We're gonna get along just fine."

"I know they're in good hands," Charlie said as he hugged her. "Thanks, Grandma."

"No problem."

Lisa hugged her and said, "It's not goodbye, it's just see you later."

She laughed and said, "You remember that?"

"Of course. You taught me well."

"See ya later, Sunshine."

"See ya later, Grandma. See ya later, boys."

They all waved as they headed for the car.

Charlie smiled and said, "Still learning."

As they drove through the desert, the warm feelings of family became more distant, giving way to feelings of isolation and an underlying fear of the unknown. However, the closer they came to their destination, the more they felt like this was where they needed to be.

Lisa stated, "I'm feeling the same things that I felt when I was a kid."

"Like something is calling you?" Charlie asked. "Like something is waiting just for you?"

"Yes."

"I feel it, too." Charlie took his right hand off the steering wheel and held her hand. "'For we walk by faith, not by sight.'"

When they finally arrived at Hull Mine, the strange feelings were nearly overwhelming. They got out of the car and approached the entrance of the cave. Suddenly, Lisa jumped back and grabbed Charlie's arm. Before he could ask what was wrong, she explained it.

"There's a rattlesnake!"

Charlie's pulse quickened as his eyes spotted the deadly reptile. It blocked the entrance.

"What do we do?" she asked.

"If we get anywhere near it, it would strike. We could wait it out, or... I have an idea."

He slowly backed up as she followed his lead. They got back into the car.

"They don't like noise and vibrations," he said as he turned the ignition.

He started to slowly drive closer to the snake. They watched as it rattled its tail. He parked close to it. He revved the engine and honked the horn. He drove backwards to watch the snake quickly slither away.

Lisa breathed a sigh of relief and said, "At least he didn't go into the cave."

"Boy, we're off to a great start!" Charlie said with sarcastic enthusiasm.

They parked the car once more and resumed their path to the mine. They stepped cautiously with a flashlight in hand and eyes wide open for hidden dangers and buried secrets. Without the light, they would be in utter darkness surrounded by eerie silence. Surely, this would be the last place anyone would ever look for something important. The only thing that reassured them in their quest was the undeniable feeling that they were meant to be there. Minutes felt like an hour, yet it wasn't long until they discovered the wall of crystals that was referenced in the notebook.

"This is when we get out the blacklight," Charlie said. "The book doesn't say why."

Lisa removed a blacklight flashlight from the backpack.

"Want to do the honors?" she asked.

"I've done it before, apparently. It's your turn."

She turned it on.

"Okay... I don't get it," she said.
"Keep shining it on the wall... I guess."
They waited a few seconds. Then came their answer.
"Wow! It's gorgeous!" she exclaimed.
"I'm speechless. I-- I didn't expect anything like this!"
The minerals of the cave wall were turned into a brightly glowing display of colors. Varying shades of red, green, yellow, orange, and blue vividly lit up the hall as well as the expressions on their faces.
"It's the fluorescent and phosphorescent properties responding to the ultraviolet light," Charlie tried to explain. "I've never even considered such a concept before. I don't think anyone has. We may be the only ones who know about this. If anyone else knew, then everybody would be here."
"This is as majestic as the Milky Way... as beautiful as the sunset or a field of butterflies. I don't care what the scientific term could be, all I know is that this had to be painted by God himself." She stepped closer and pointed out a portion of the wall. Tears came to her eyes. "Look at it, Charlie. I don't even know what color this is! This isn't even a known color. This is a huge discovery. We really should take pictures."
"We can't do that. As breathtaking as it is, we can't have evidence of being here. It's all kept secret for a reason."
"You're right," she admitted. "Good thing you have your perfect memory. I still won't forget."
She stepped back to his side and beheld it with awe.
"There has to be more to it," Charlie said.
"More to this? Isn't this more than enough?"
"I mean... there has to be a reason why we're here. It's not just to look at some pretty crystals. The power source is still here somewhere. We just have to look closer."
They looked it over with more scrutiny.
Lisa said, "I don't know... it's all so mesmerizing."
"I think I found something."
"What is it?"
"Look at this one," he said as he pointed to one of the crystals. "It's not lit up."
"Yeah. That is pretty odd."
"My gut tells me that this is all a distraction. It keeps us thrown off the scent of the real thing." He put his hand on the plain crystal. "Unless I'm very wrong..."
He pushed it. A portion of the wall next to it slowly opened. He smiled.
"Whoa. Dude," Lisa said. "This is like next level, adventure book, Harrison Ford kind of stuff."

He chuckled. "Yeah. Pretty awesome, huh?"

She smiled. "Yeah, it is."

They peeked into the darkness, then turned back to each other.

Her face became more serious. "What are we getting ourselves into, Charlie?"

He put his hand on her shoulder and looked into her eyes.

"The adventure of a lifetime."

She smiled again. "Well, when you put it that way..."

"If you really don't want to continue, then we don't have to. I think that whatever we find is going to change everything. There's no going back after this."

"We didn't come this far only to come this far. We'll find what we're looking for."

He smiled and took her hand. "Let's find out together."

They turned off the blacklight and returned to the regular flashlight. They slowly and cautiously stepped into the entrance. Each step was taken carefully. Every inch of their surroundings was fully considered with their flashlight. Their footsteps were the only sound in the darkness. Slowly they made their way forward, compelled by curiosity, driven by the desire for answers. Answers not only to the mysteries of the notebook, but to the strange feelings that urged them. They could almost hear their names being called aloud, practically begging these explorers to press on. It didn't take long until they found something unusual. There was an opening in the roof of the cave that allowed the sun to illuminate a corner of the darkness. They were stunned to see an old native man sitting on the ground in the sunlight. He rose to his feet with a swiftness that was normally reserved for a younger man.

"What is your purpose?" he spit out sternly and without hesitation. His presence was commanding. Although he was unarmed, the look on his face told them that they'd better have a good answer or else face violent consequences.

"I'm sorry to disturb you," Charlie said through his nerves. "We are just as surprised to find you here as you are to find us. I can assure you, we mean no harm."

"That doesn't answer my question. Why are you here? How did you know about this place?"

"We were given instructions. We just knew that we had to come here to find what we were looking for."

"And, what do you seek?"

"There's a source of power..."

The old man's expression grew more intense. He looked like a cobra ready to strike.

"...BUT, it's for a good cause!" Charlie tried to ease the situation.

"I saw you in a dream," Lisa blurted out.

The old man turned his attention towards her.

She continued, "I didn't know you were real."

The old native's expression changed to one of intrigue. He said, "Dreams have a way of telling us things about ourselves that we don't know."

"I think we got off on the wrong foot. Let's start over with the right hand." She extended her hand. "My name is Lisa Jordache. This is my husband, Charlie."

He hesitated for a moment, but then shook her hand. Charlie held his hand out for the same welcome.

"We are not here to steal from you," Charlie said. "We are here for answers more than anything. I think we should discuss the situation peacefully. You look like a man who is usually one of peace."

"I am," he said with a nod. "I hate violence. But, I will fight for what is right. It is my sacred duty."

"I deeply respect that. We feel the same way. We are on the same side, my friend."

He nodded. Then, he turned to Lisa and said, "What was I doing in this dream, Lisa Jordache?"

"You were standing in this same spot. There was water coming up behind you, but it stopped and went back."

"Water? Out here?"

"Yes. It was like a wave."

An old dream Charlie once had suddenly flashed to his mind. Could it really be connected? He ignored it for the time being, choosing to stay focused on the task at hand.

"That is a very interesting dream, Lisa Jordache," said the old man. "There may be more truth in it than you think. I'm sure you wonder why an old man is here in this place. I also wonder why two young people are here. You don't know the reason to either question. I know my purpose. Please, state yours."

Charlie removed his backpack and opened it. He took out the notebook.

"I was given this book. It has instructions for a project that we're working on. One of the things we need, the most important part, actually, is some kind of power source. The coordinates led us here. But, we also feel drawn to it. Like we belong here."

"Hmm. Your book never said what it was, did it?"

"No, Sir. Just walking by faith."

He nodded. "Faith is a powerful thing. More powerful than the object you seek. It can move mountains."

"Our faith is what led us here," added Lisa. "It's what brought us together years ago."

"Where are you from, Charlie and Lisa Jordache?"

"Kansas," they said.

"I'm from California, originally. I had these same feelings when we went to Yuma when I was a kid."

"You've come a long way to find something you can't name in a place you've seen only in a dream. That is either faith, or it's madness."

"Maybe it's a little of both," Charlie joked.

The old man chuckled a bit.

"There's something I just have to ask," Charlie said. "Have I been here before?"

"How can you know where you're going, if you don't know where you've been?"

"It's complicated. I just didn't know if you've ever seen me before, maybe at a different age."

"This sounds like madness. How could you be here without knowing?"

"Someone has been here before to know what to put in this book."

"No. That's not possible."

Charlie realized that it must have happened at another point in the future. He knew that it was time to change subjects.

"How long have you been here?" Charlie asked.

"Many years."

"Don't you ever leave? What about food? Water?"

"I have help. I have a question for you. What do you do when you're not exploring hidden places?"

"We're teachers."

"Hmm. A good purpose. Another sacred duty."

Lisa said, "We work in a school that helps people with disabilities. I'm also a counselor, and he's a physics professor, too."

"You like to help people," he said. "You have compassion."

"Yes," they said.

The old man appeared very contemplative. He didn't say anything for a few seconds. He broke his silence. "This project you speak of, is it meant to help people?"

"Absolutely," she answered. "It's the only way we'll do it."

He turned to Charlie. "Professor. You like to teach. You also like to learn."

"Very much so."

"You are a knowledgeable man. To be entrusted with great power, one must first possess great wisdom. Tell me, Charlie Jordache, are you a wise man?"

"I know that I'll never know everything. I know that I need to trust in her wisdom. I know that knowledge is just what you know, but wisdom is what you do with it. That's why I teach. It's my responsibility--my sacred duty--to share my knowledge with others. It would be unwise to keep to myself that which could help those who need it."

"Hmm. You answer wisely." He nodded his head. "Very wisely indeed."

Lisa took Charlie's hand.

The old man continued, "Now, I will tell you what I do. I have been given the responsibility to protect great power. Many who would learn of its existence would seek to use it for evil. I must not let that happen."

"How long has it been here? Where does it come from?"

"It is much older than I. There are some things that I do not know. I think it has always existed."

He stepped aside to reveal a pillar with two crystals on top of it.

"Tell me, Charlie and Lisa Jordache, which one do you seek?"

The sun shone brightly on the two crystals. One was blue and the other was clear with a white glow. They both glowed in the sunlight almost too brightly to look at safely.

"I feel the white one, like it's calling me," Lisa said.

"Me, too," Charlie added.

"Interesting," the old man said. "I knew that you would say that. The white one is not the one for you. Not yet."

"Why do we feel this connection?" she asked.

"There are those who would use it for evil. When I look at you two, I do not see evil, I see only good. The crystal knows. I knew all along. I'm sorry, but I had to test you. Even evil can appear to be good. I'm known as The Protector. If I give you the crystal, then you would also become Protectors. This is not for just anyone."

"Why would you give it to us?"

"Not everyone can have that connection you feel. You are worthy. My faith in you is strong. You may have the blue crystal to use for the service of another."

It was the same wording as the letter that came with the book.

"How does it work?" asked Charlie.

"That I cannot tell you. I only guard it. I know that it is fed by the sun. Without it, the power would cease."

"I still can't believe that you would just let us have it."

"You said it yourself. It would be unwise to keep that which could be used to help another. This isn't meant to just stay hidden. What is the purpose? What good is the sun if it does not shine? Faith without works is dead. You two have great faith, but you have only just started to see how far it will take you. Mountains will move and be tossed into the sea. Many wonders will be accomplished." He handed the crystal to Charlie. "Not because of a rock, but because you are as strong as a rock." He looked at Lisa. "Not because of the light that is stored within the rock, but because of the light that is within you. This is only a tool. In your hands, it will be used for a noble purpose. You are not just Protectors, you are Changers."

"What is that?" asked Charlie, curious to see how he would answer.

"You will change bad to good and dark to light. This is something that you already do."

"Are there any others?"

"There is one man. He is not one of us, but we are aware of his efforts in a spiritual sense. He, too, knows that there is a higher purpose to his mission. He is also a man of great wisdom and compassion. He wants nothing more than to help others. He is one man who lives many lives. Putting things right that once went wrong."

Charlie looked at the crystal. What had once felt mysterious now took on a deeper meaning. A higher purpose. Something much bigger than two people, yet needed them to fulfill it. They had the means to put right what once went wrong. The ever humble Charlie began to question why it should be so.

He looked The Protector in the eyes and asked, "Why us?"

The Protector smiled. "Even after telling you of your goodness and strength, your wisdom and faith, you still don't know why?"

"It just seems so big. Something that's been here for so long... something so important... and yet..." his eyes began to water. "I'm... I'm just a guy from Kansas. A husband, a father, a teacher... just a man."

"Do you feel this way, too, Lisa?" he asked.

"I do."

He put his hands on their shoulders. "This reason above all is why you can be trusted with the crystal. Others may be wise. Others may be strong. But, mixed with humility is a rare thing indeed. 'Humble yourselves in the sight of the Lord, and he shall lift you up.'"

Lisa asked a question that Charlie was wondering himself, "Are you an angel?"

"No. I'm just a man. Another man who is called to a higher purpose. A man who is humble enough to serve."

"I'm sure this is something you never hear," she said. "Thank you. Thank you for the crystal, but most of all, thank you for what you do."

The Protector put his head down and stepped back to where he first was. It looked like tears were beginning to surface in his dark eyes. Here was a man of quiet strength, who no doubt had sacrificed a more comfortable life, choosing instead to live a solitary existence. A more fascinating man Charlie had never encountered. He knew his purpose and fulfilled it no matter the cost, possibly saving the world in the process. He quietly said, "It is an honor."

"Thank you, friend," Charlie said. "Perhaps we'll meet again someday."

"One never knows what the future will bring."

Charlie and Lisa exchanged glances.

The old man looked to them and said, "I will pray that your mission succeeds. Godspeed, Charlie and Lisa Jordache, my brother and sister. Change the bad to good."

As they started driving back to Heatherton, Lisa said, "So... now that we can talk about it..."

"There's so much to say, and yet I'm speechless."

"When he gave us the crystal, it felt like something was changing, like you said. Like we're starting a whole new life."

"I felt the same way. It was like a missing piece was found."

"But, what about the white one? What was that all about?"

"I don't know. I have a feeling that we'll find out someday. After all, we're Protectors now."

"It's all so big and exciting and mysterious and overwhelming. Like it's meant to be, yet we really don't know what we're getting ourselves into."

Charlie laughed. "You know, the way you described it sounds a lot like becoming parents."

She laughed. "You're right, it does sound a lot like that. Except this little blue bundle of joy has the potential to change the world."

He gave her a knowing glance.

She said, "Right again."

They drove a few more miles until the car started acting up before coming to a stop.

"Now what?!" Charlie asked in frustration. He knew that there was enough gas. He popped the hood and they got out of the car.

"I bet it's the battery," Lisa said.

They looked under the hood.

"I think you're right," he replied. "What do we do now? We're in the middle of nowhere. I guess we have to start walking."

"I have an idea. May I have the keys?" He handed them to her and she opened the trunk. She gave them back to Charlie. "Get in and turn the key when I tell you to."

Charlie did as she said.

She shut the trunk and went under the hood.

"Okay, now."

He turned the key. The car started. Charlie laughed in disbelief. She shut the hood and got back in the car.

"What did you do?"

She held the glowing blue crystal up with a smile. "All I had to do was put it on the battery."

"I wonder what else it can do," he mused.

"It could change the world! We don't even know the possibilities! We're Changers, right?"

"That's true, but it could be weaponized. That's why we're also Protectors."

"We just have to do what we can."

"We can change the world one life at a time."

CHAPTER 23

The Jordache family was back home in Chesapeake after their great adventure. Charlie and Lisa knew that the biggest adventure was still to come. They entered the study with their latest acquisition.

Lisa beheld the boxes of parts before them and remarked, "Some assembly required."

"Batteries not included," Charlie added.

They put the crystal in the place designed for it with the solar panels. They wouldn't have as much sunshine as there was in Arizona, but there would still be plenty during the hot Kansas summer. They went to work on putting the pieces of the machine together. It seemed difficult enough on paper, but in practice, it became obvious that this was going to take a lot of time. They did as much as they could for the rest of the summer whenever they had extra time.

It was back to business as usual when school resumed in the fall. Charlie and Lisa tried to work on the machine whenever they had the opportunity. They knew that it would indeed take years to complete it, not just for acquiring all the parts, but because time was much scarcer with their busy schedules. The irony was not lost on them.

In the meantime, they were also raising two boys. It was a job that was just as complex and rewarding as building a time machine. They were planning on visiting the past, but Sammy and Elijah were the future. Charlie passed by Sammy's room. He heard him playing with his guitar, but sounded like he was struggling to find the right note. He went to talk to him.

"Are you writing a new song?"

"Yeah. I just can't quite get this right. I'm having a hard time concentrating."

Charlie sat on the bed next to him. "What's on your mind, son?"

"There's this girl I like."

"Anyone I know?"

"Adriana."

Charlie smiled. "She's a pretty girl."

"She's really amazing. It's not just about her looks though."

"You're right. She really is amazing. She's a very special girl. Like a daughter to me."

"She's different than everyone else. I just don't know if it will work."

"And, why's that?"

"She's a few years older than me. The way I feel... I just want to write songs for her." He hung his head. "But, she would never hear them."

Charlie put his hand on his shoulder.

"That is a challenge. But, that's all it is-- a challenge. This family doesn't back down from a challenge. We pray and we persevere. And, do you know what happens?"

"What?"

"We're rewarded for it."

Sammy looked into his eyes. "If you love someone, anything's possible."

Charlie smiled. "I've taught you well."

"But, it was different with you and Mom. You're the same age, she lived next door, and you knew her when you were five. It was kind of easy."

Charlie laughed. "Son, it was far from easy. I was also dealing with the loss of my dad and was afraid to get too close. She moved away for eight years. That just killed me. I didn't even know how to react when she did come back. If it wasn't for a counsellor, I don't think I would've even had the guts to tell her that I love her. Imagine that. We still might not have ended up together, no matter how perfect we fit, if I wouldn't have overcome my challenges. I thought so highly of the counsellor that we named you after him."

"I didn't realize it was like that."

"But, that's our story. You have your own."

"These are some big challenges. She might not want to be with someone younger. She'll never get to enjoy what I love so much-- music."

"Don't you see, son? We all have challenges to overcome. If there's anything worth having in life, it's never easy. But, the reward is worth everything. Like your Grandpa says, 'the reward is worth the struggle.' She's older than you. Yes, that could be a problem. You're only twelve now. Suppose she turns eighteen and you're fourteen. You still have to wait a few more years to ever go out with her. Can you be that patient?"

"I would have to be."

"As far as music goes, that's another big one. She lives in a whole different world than you and me. She's used to not hearing music. That would be more of a frustration for yourself. I don't know if you're meant to be with her or not. I'm sure that after we're done talking, I'm going to walk away and feel a heck of a lot older because it will hit me that I'm talking to you about this stuff when just yesterday you were still a baby in my arms."

Sammy smiled.

He continued, "I don't know if she's the one for you or who else it could be or when it will happen. You're still so young. All I know is that music is in your heart and it always has been. But, the love that is in your heart is even bigger. If you just be yourself, then it wouldn't matter if she can hear your words or not. She's deaf, not blind. She will still see the love that's in your heart as much as I do. That's something I've always noticed about her. When she sees it, she responds to it. Just be the best darn Sammy Jordache you can be. Whether it's Adriana or someone else, the right girl will be drawn to you."

"Is that the way it was with you and Mom?"

"That's exactly what it was. That's the way it works. No matter who it is, what year it is, or anything else. If it's meant to be, then it's meant to be. Sometimes you have to be patient, sometimes you have to really work for it. But, if you love someone, and she loves you, too, then that's all that matters."

"I think I'm going to write those songs anyway. My feelings have to go somewhere."

"That's my boy. I knew you were smart."

He got up and started to walk away.

Sammy said, "If I could just find the right note."

"You said that you're having a hard time concentrating. Stop focusing on the problems, and just focus on how you feel about her. It will all come to you. I promise."

"You're right. I know you're right."

"This is your story, your song. I can help as much as I can, but I can't tell you how to write it. That's in your own heart. I can't wait to hear it."

Sammy smiled. "Thanks, Dad. I do feel better."

"You've got this."

He walked away with a smile. His feelings of pride started to give way to the feelings that he already foresaw-- those of getting old. He went downstairs and sat on the couch with Lisa.

"I just had an interesting talk with our eldest son."

"Oh? What did you talk about?"

"We seem to have a lovesick teenager in our midst."

She smiled. "Really? He told you that?"

"Yeah. He has it bad."

"And, you're just now finding out?"

"Wait-- did he tell you already?"

"No, but I have eyes. I see how he is when he's around Adriana."

"You can see that?"

She laughed. "Of course! He's just like you."

"Don't you find it a bit alarming that we're old enough to have a son who's old enough to be in love?"

She laughed again. "What are you talking about? We were only five when we fell in love. He's more than twice that old. You just don't like getting older."

"This is our baby we're talking about. Remember him? The little feller who used to pee on us?"

"Yes, I remember quite well," she said with a laugh. "I remember all the messes and the crying at night. But, he's no baby anymore. No, the real baby of the family is Elijah, and he's no baby, either. I hate to break it to you, but he's already quite girl-crazy."

"Nooo," he replied with a groan.

"Yeppers, and he's not so shy about it."

"Nooo," he groaned a little louder.

"And, the little girls seem to like him right back."

"Nooooohohohoh," he bemoaned as he put his head on her shoulder and acted like he was going to cry.

She leaned her head on his and laughed. "There, there, old man. You knew this would happen. It's all a part of life."

"I'm not ready for all this. I just didn't expect it to happen so fast."

"It won't be that fast. Adriana is still four years older than him. There's still plenty of time."

"Do you think that she feels the same way about him?"

"Not really. I think she hasn't thought of him that way yet. He's too young for her. But, I can see it working out when it's the right time."

"Can't we just skip all this? We are working on a time machine, after all."

"Where's the fun in that?"

They heard the guitar playing a little louder. Charlie sat up straight and listened. A sense of calm came over him as he smiled.

"Looks like he found the right note."

"What are you even worried about, Charlie? I think it's sweet and exciting. This is Adriana we're talking about. Wouldn't it be amazing to have her as our daughter someday?"

He nodded. "Yes, it would. I know you're right."

They stopped and listened to the music.

"A house full of love and music, just as it's always been," said Lisa. "We're just going to share it with more people. What could be better than that?"

"It sounds absolutely perfect."

They kissed.

"He's the best of you and the best of me," she said.

"And, it keeps getting better."

Time marched on, whether Charlie was ready or not. His eyes were now opened to see how much of a little flirt Elijah was. He was befuddled that his own son could be so different in this way-- and at ten years old no less. He also noticed how Sammy acted around Adriana. He was so nervous and happy, scared, yet brave. Charlie had never seen someone get tongue-tied while using sign language before. It was quite humorous to witness. He imagined that he would be the same way if it were himself. The boy was definitely in love. He didn't interfere, deciding to let nature take its course. But, internally, he cheered them on. Although it meant that he and Lisa were getting older, he gave in to the idea that the younger generation was taking their rightful place. It was their turn. It didn't take long for him to actually love what was happening. Like music to his ears.

October 3rd, 1998. It was a milestone anniversary for two generations. It was twenty-five years since the disappearance of Wayne. This realization made it tough to get through the day, but Lisa reminded Charlie and Ilene that it was also the thirteenth anniversary of finding out that she was pregnant with Sammy. The sorrow that was normally associated with the occasion was soothed by the memories of Sammy through the years. A new generation was bringing love and joy into the world. It was hard to deny the truth that Lisa spoke. Even without being a counselor, she was right. For Christmas, Lisa had one of her best ideas. They arrived at Ilene's house, but only Lisa and the boys went to the door.

"Where's Charlie?" his mom asked as they made their way inside.

"He's getting your gift from the car."

"Does he need help?"

"No, it's okay. We have something very special for you this year. Why don't you go ahead and sit down, and we'll give it to you right away. Sammy, get the camera ready."

They all grinned from ear to ear.

Ilene said, "We always let the kids go first. I can wait."

Charlie came in and said, "This one can't wait."

A golden retriever ran up to Ilene and started sniffing her.

Her eyes lit up. "Oh my goodness! Look at you! Hi, little guy! You're so cute!" She petted him and rubbed his ears. "Do you have a name?"

"We thought we'd leave that up to you," said Charlie.

"I know it gets hard for you sometimes," Lisa added. "Nothing can replace Dad, but maybe a little extra companionship wouldn't hurt."

Ilene picked up the puppy and put him on her lap.

"You guys..." she searched for the words. "Thank you. You really outdid yourselves. What a great surprise." She looked at the puppy again as he licked her hands. "He's perfect. Now, what am I going to call you?" She smiled even wider. "I know. Since Wayne was named after John Wayne, I'll call you 'Duke.'"

"I like that," Lisa said.

"That's just right," added Charlie.

She got up and set Duke down on the floor. "Why don't you play with the boys for a minute? I have some hugging to do."

She hugged Lisa and Charlie together. She held on tightly for a moment before looking them in the eyes. Her eyes were wet.

"You gave me grandchildren, you gave me a dog, and you give me love and hope every day. I cannot express how much I love you two."

"Right back atcha," they said at the same time.

"You give me so many blessings. How could I ask for more?"

An eventful year came to an end. 1999 was now underway. The blessings kept coming as the family kept spreading their love. The boys would visit Grandma a little more often to play with Duke. Lisa kept in touch with her own grandma. The school was thriving, their friends were well, and Cal's team was better than ever. On Sammy's thirteenth birthday, his parents had something special for his party. They made a video of some of the things they recorded of him over the years. The whole family and a few friends gathered together to watch it--including Adriana. Smiles never faded as they all witnessed his first crawl, his first steps, and some of his first attempts at singing. There was school and home. There were birthdays and holidays. Playing with his brother and playing the guitar. He was a typical boy, and yet a genius with potential still waiting to fully realize. He was now crossing the threshold from childhood to being a young man. Charlie was still amazed by how fast it all happened. Lisa held Charlie's hand. They looked into each other's eyes. He knew that she felt the same feelings. They were happy and proud, but they also knew that it was the end of an era.

Their thoughts never strayed far from their project, nor from The Protector and the crystals. Their lives would have to be a balancing act between their daily responsibilities as parents and teachers and the broader implications of being Protectors and Changers. Charlie and Lisa got another shipment of aluminum oxynitride and worked on the machine as much as they could during the summer. It was getting increasingly harder to find the time to work on it otherwise, but even harder to keep it a secret. Everyone from their family to Tracy was curious about the strange wires in the living room. The kids were obedient and never tried to discover anything for themselves, but it still almost felt like they were lying to them.

The school celebrated its tenth anniversary in August. They held a special event one Saturday night to commemorate the occasion. Of course, Louis Lane was there to make it front page news. The gym was filled to capacity as students and their families past and present heard stories and watched a video projection of the school's many accomplishments. From the students' improved grades to the time capsule to the success of the Sparks basketball team and everything in between, there was a lot to be thankful for. The Chesapeake School for Special Needs was singularly responsible for bringing an increased community awareness to the needs of the disabled. Their efforts reached beyond their own school and made an impact on other schools as well, and even carried over into the workforce. The *Times'* annual reader's poll chose them as the best school in town every single year. Louis presented Theresa with a plaque to honor their distinction as the first school to have a ten-year winning streak in the paper's history. They were known throughout the state for their achievements in the classroom as well as the basketball court. But, they had also recently drawn the attention of the global spotlight. With tears of joy, Jeremy Allen introduced their special guest. It was the highlight of the evening as Andrew Lolar spoke of his background before the school started and how Jeremy taught him to never "let anyone tell you that you can't do something. Especially not yourself." He showed them his gold medal that he recently won in the Special Olympics World Summer Games. There wasn't a dry eye in the building.

The year continued with more success stories at the school and in Lisa's counseling. All would have been well for the rest of the year if not for the fears of the dreaded Y2K bug. Charlie and Lisa didn't believe that there would be a problem, and even laughed at the situation. As the clock struck midnight on New Year's, their suspicions were confirmed and all was fine for the year 2000. Charlie had always thought of a new millennium as something so distant when he was a kid, hardly imagining that he would live to see it become a reality. Ready or not, time did move forward... even without a completed time machine. As prosperous as his life was, he found it more difficult to see the need for changing the past. If everything kept going on the course it was on, the future remained exceptionally bright. Still, he pressed on with Lisa, working on the machine whenever time would allow, never forgetting that there was still a reason for receiving the notebook. Faith brought them this far, and faith would still be the path that they would travel.

Fifteen years had now passed since Charlie and Lisa first expressed their love for each other. Sammy turned fourteen, Elijah turned twelve, and they both turned thirty-three. When the school came to the end of its first ten years, they gathered once more in the gym for another big celebration-- graduation. It came time for the Valedictorian to give a speech. Lisa stood nearby to interpret as Adriana stepped up to the podium.

"When I first came to this school, I was a little girl who only knew one thing about school. It was a place that would hurt me. I wanted to learn and do what everyone else did, but other kids would laugh at me. I couldn't hear them, but I could see their faces. I could read their lips and knew what they said about me. I'm sure a lot of you have been through these same situations. I was different. I didn't fit in. But, when my mom and I came to see what this new school was all about, I found something different." She looked over to Lisa and began to tear up. "I found someone who could speak my language. I found people who wanted to help. I found open arms." A tear ran down her cheek. "I found my voice." Others began wiping tears from their eyes. "Charlie told me that everyone would learn my language. You did it, just as he said. I couldn't believe it when he told me. It made me cry. I asked, 'I won't be different?' He said something that I'll never forget. 'We're all different. That's what makes us the same.' I came here as a sad little girl with no friends. I stand here now as a confident woman who found something even better than friends. I found a family. A second mom." She looked over to Lisa, who was overflowing with tears. They continued, "A second dad." She looked over to Charlie, sitting nearby wiping his tears. "I found love at this school. I have learned so much from all of you here. You have given me the strength and courage to face the next chapter of my life. College will be a challenge, but I can do anything. I was taught here that if you love someone, anything's possible. I love you all very much, and I will never forget you."

The crowd gave her a standing ovation-- with hands waving instead of clapping. She tightly wrapped her arms around Lisa. They held on for a moment, and then looked into each other's eyes. Lisa knew that she could read her lips as she said, "I'm so proud of you." Adriana kissed her cheek and Lisa did the same. Then, she went to Charlie for another hug and kiss. She was once an outsider, but became someone who wasn't so different. Charlie knew that there were still qualities that did set her apart, however, and it wasn't a disability in the slightest. As Sammy once said, "she's different than everyone else."

As time went by, they continued to change the world one life at a time. They taught and counseled, loved and encouraged. Even Charlie started taking classes in counseling. Each summer, they ordered more aluminum oxynitride and worked at putting all the pieces together. In 2003, they had almost everything they needed. What they needed the most was a little more time.

October 3rd was approaching. Lisa prepared herself for the worst. She didn't want to bring it up and possibly make things worse, so she waited to see what would happen and be there to handle it. The night before, she woke from her sleep to the sounds of her husband.

"Dad! Dad! Where are you? Why don't you come back?"

She put her arms around him. "Wake up, Charlie. You're having a bad dream."

"Dad! Dad! I miss you! Don't you love me anymore?"

"Come on, Charlie, wake up. It's just a dream. I've got you. You're going to be okay. I'm still here."

It had been a few years since this happened last. He did so well for so long, but this was one of those times when it was almost inevitable. He woke up and looked at Lisa.

She said, "You're going to be okay, baby. I'm here."

He put his head on her chest and started crying uncontrollably. "Thirty years."

"I know," she said as she held him with one arm and ran her other fingers through his hair to try to relax him. "I know. We're gonna get through this together."

She always tried to be his rock when he felt weak. This time was more difficult to stay strong when her own heart was breaking. She couldn't hold back her tears, but tried not to let it show too much.

She whispered, "Always together."

The following day was tough, but they managed to get through it. They met at Ilene's house that night and tried to focus on the positive. Elijah stayed the night there. When they got home, Sammy went to bed because he had work early in the morning. They hugged good-night, and went to bed not long after. Charlie surprisingly went to sleep easily. Maybe he was worn out from the stress of the day and the night before. Lisa, however, was wide awake. She couldn't shut her mind off. Her memories from childhood came flooding back.

"How did I do on the testing, Mom?"

"Man, this feels familiar. Okay, here it is... you passed everything with flying colors!"

"Yes!"

"I knew you would, baby girl. Way to go, Sunshine!"

"Does this mean that I could go to the gifted program?"

"If that's what you want."

"Don't tell Charlie. I don't want him to be jealous."

She couldn't believe that she would ever think that he would be jealous.

"You know what they said about you? They said that you were the sweetest girl they've ever seen. They also said that whenever you have a challenge, you don't give up."

"Some of it was kind of hard, but I figured it out. I kept trying, just like you and Dad taught me."

"I'm very proud of you. They said that you were a fast learner, which I already knew. What I didn't know was how high your IQ was. Wasn't Charlie's 180?"

"Yeah. Don't tell me it's almost as high as his."

"Yours is 185."

"Are you serious?"

"Yes, I'm serious."

"Definitely don't tell Charlie about that."

"I won't. You know what this means, right? If Charlie is considered one of the smartest people in the world, then you are, too. You're a genius, Sunshine."

"I didn't realize that I was. I thought geniuses were quieter like Charlie."

"Not everyone is the same. You're an extrovert and he's an introvert. I think it's pretty amazing. They said that because you're so smart and can pick up on things so fast, that you could do anything. If you wanted to be a doctor, you could be a doctor. If you wanted to be a teacher, you could be a teacher. If you wanted to be the President, you could be the President. If you put your mind to it, you could accomplish anything."

"I think that whatever I do, I want to do something that helps people. God made me this way for a reason. I should do something really good."

"That's the best thing I've heard yet. I really believe that you will."

"I was thinking... if I'm a genius and Charlie's a genius... maybe we really are meant to be together. Maybe there's something that we need to do together."

"Anything's possible. You might just change the world."

She got out of bed quietly. She tiptoed across the house and up the stairs. She unlocked the study and went in. She looked at the machine that they'd spent so many years on. More memories came back.

"It would be unwise to keep that which could be used to help another. This isn't meant to just stay hidden. What is the purpose? What good is the sun if it does not shine? Faith without works is dead. You two have great faith, but you have only just started to see how far it will take you. Mountains will move and be tossed into the sea. Many wonders will be accomplished."

She looked up at the crystal.

"Not because of a rock, but because you are as strong as a rock. Not because of the light that is stored within the rock, but because of the light that is within you. This is only a tool. In your hands, it will be used for a noble purpose. You are not just Protectors, you are Changers."

She got out the notebook and looked at the letter.

"You will know it when you see it."

Tears came to her eyes as she thought of her husband's thirty years of suffering. She looked at the machine again. They were so close to finishing it. She said aloud, "I see it every day."

CHAPTER 24

Charlie awoke to the smell of bacon. He breathed deep through his nostrils. There were eggs, too. He smiled and sat up. He heard the sound of the oven open as he headed for the door. Ahh... biscuits.

"What's the occasion?" he asked Lisa. Their busy lives usually kept them from having a home-cooked breakfast. Granola bars while driving to work had become the routine.

"We need the energy," she answered as she stirred the gravy.

"For what?"

"Both of the kids are gone and we have nothing else planned, so today, we work."

"What kind of work do you have in mind?"

"The kind of work that should be done by now."

"You mean on the you-know-what?"

"Yes, the you-know-what. It's okay to call it a time machine when the kids aren't around."

"Why the sudden determination?"

"It's been almost nine years since this all started. It's hardly sudden."

"Good point."

He put the biscuits on the plates next to the hash browns. She added the gravy. They put their food on the table and sat down.

"You look like you didn't sleep much," Charlie noted.

"I didn't. Had too much on my mind."

"You think that you can do the work in this condition?"

"It's the only way I can settle my mind."

"You're right. It's time to finish this."

For the rest of the day, Charlie and Lisa strived on the machine. He noticed that she didn't make her usual jokes. She kept a serious focus and strong will to keep going. They kept at it all day and into the night. Sammy and Elijah had already come home early in the evening, but Lisa pushed forward while Charlie took care of supper. It was late at night when Lisa's attention began to fade and she grew noticeably tired. She sat on the floor and started nodding off.

"Lisa, wake up for a minute. There's something I want to show you."

He held out his hands and she took them.

"Sorry, I started drifting off there. I won't let it happen again. We need to keep working."

He chuckled as he helped her up gently.

"You really need your sleep. But, I want to show you this one thing first."

"What is it?"

He stood behind her and wrapped his arms around her.

"I'd tell you to close your eyes, but that won't work under the circumstances. Take a good look at the machine."

"I don't get it."

"You really are tired," he said with a laugh. "Look again, honey. Soak it in." He whispered in her ear, "You did it."

She gasped and perked up. "What?"

"You did it. You wouldn't give up. You started falling asleep as soon as you finished."

She laughed. "It really is done. All this time... all these years... it's finally done."

"I'd turn it on, but it would wake the kids."

She turned around as they looked into each other's teary eyes.

He said, "You did it."

"No, *we* did it." She kissed him. "We did it together. Always together."

They held each other tightly.

"Too bad we can't tell anyone," he stated.

"That's okay. It's a personal victory. Now, we just have to test it."

"Not tonight. We need to rest. You can finally settle your mind. This day will be the day that we'll remember. The day when we made history. October 4th, 2003... 10-04. It's the date of a new beginning."

"A brighter future."

The next day after church, the boys went to see friends, leaving Charlie and Lisa with the house to themselves again. The curiosity was too strong to resist.

"What do you say, Mr. Blue Sky? Want to wake the sleeping giant?"

They started walking up the stairs.

Charlie quipped, "You know, it used to be that when we had the place to ourselves, it was a different kind of turn on."

She laughed and replied, "The day's not over yet."

They opened the door to the study and walked in. Through the eyes of a new day, the machine had become an awe-inspiring sight to behold.

"I still can't believe it's done," Lisa said as she felt the smooth surface.

Charlie powered on the computers. "And now, without further ado..." He pushed a few more buttons. The machine hummed to life.

Lisa laughed with glee. "It really works!"

"Now to see what the crystal can do."

"Let's not use up all the energy," she cautioned.

"I won't. We still need to make sure that it does what we think it will. So, I'll just get it started."

"Wait! We still need to move it to the bottom of the machine."

"You're right. It's only up there to absorb the solar energy. We have to move it closer to the wires, like it says in the book."

She climbed up the ladder and removed it, then put it in its place at the bottom of the sphere. He pushed a few buttons on the laptop. There were a few notable moments in Charlie's life when he felt that years of hard work had paid off. Those times always involved his family or school in some way. But, as he watched the blue energy rise from the crystal and circle the walls of the sphere, he felt a new sense of achievement. He exchanged smiles with Lisa as he put his free arm around her shoulder. They just made the impossible possible. The energy spun faster around the orb. He looked at the laptop. The word, "SYNCED" appeared on screen.

"That's funny," Charlie said.

"What is it?" Lisa asked.

He showed her. "How did that get there?"

"Synced to what?" she asked.

A set of numbers suddenly appeared under "SYNCED."

"Write that down," he instructed.

She went to the desk and did as he said. The energy kept speeding up.

"Okay, we know it works. Let's shut it down."

He pushed a few more buttons on the laptop and the desktop computers to end the test.

"I still need to make that remote that the book talked about."

"Well, Charlie, it was a success. But, now we have a new mystery."

As the machine slowed to a complete stop, Lisa typed the numbers into the computer's search engine.

"It's new coordinates, isn't it?"

"Yep."

"Down the rabbit hole we go again."

The map showed where the location was.

"Huh. No grand adventure this time. That's just on the outskirts of town."

He quipped, "Well, it's a different kind of outskirts than what we had in mind..."

She chuckled, "But, it's still exciting. Ready to go see what new complication we've encountered?"

"Boy, am I ever. Don't you know that I just live for complications?"

She laughed. "That's the spirit. I'll bring the snake repellant."

They parked the car next to a field. They got out and started walking through the tall grass.

"It's still a bit disappointing and surprising that whatever we're looking for is out here instead of another cave or some other exotic location," Lisa mused.

"Look around you, Lisa. What do you see?"

"Not much. A lot of grass, a few trees here and there."

"Exactly. Just the plain, old countryside of Kansas. We're literally in the middle of nowhere."

"That does make sense when you put it that way. Instead of hidden underground, it's hidden in plain sight-- only no one is looking out here. But, what exactly are we looking for?"

Charlie took her hands and they stood in front of each other.

"Close your eyes," he said. "Listen. Don't you feel it, too?"

She closed her eyes. "I do," she said with a smile. "I've gotten so used to it from the study. It feels the same out here. Just like it was in Hull Mine."

"There must be another crystal."

"How could there be? And if there is, why couldn't we just come here in the first place instead of going all the way to Arizona?"

"I don't know. Maybe we'll find the answer soon enough."

She nodded and they proceeded to walk.

"I wonder if the kids ever feel it at home," she said.

"I never thought of that. They've never said anything about it. Maybe we should ask... or maybe we'll just never know."

"Check this out," she said, pointing at a big rock. "Looks like it's been here awhile."

"Yeah, but rocks like that don't just appear out here in a field."

"Maybe we should've brought the blacklight."

They bent down to examine it closer.

"There's a hole here. Looks like maybe something metal is in it?" Lisa noted.

He knocked on the rock and smiled. He knocked again.

"It's hollow. Let's tip it over."

They grunted as they struggled to push it back.

"This is heavy," she said.

"There's that word again, 'heavy,'" he joked.

They succeeded to turn it over.

"Ewwwww," Lisa complained at the sight of the worms and bugs that were revealed.

"Yuck," Charlie added. "There always has to be something, doesn't there?"

"There's definitely something inside this," she said as she pointed at the sheet at the bottom.

"PVC, just like we used for the time capsule. Someone knew what he was doing. This was meant to be here for awhile."

They both grabbed it and started pulling. It eventually broke loose.

"What's that?" she asked.

He pulled a strange device out of the rock.

"An antenna. That's what that metal thing was," she said.

"It looks like some kind of homemade receiver."

"If it's a receiver, then there must be a transmitter."

They looked at each other and said, "The machine!"

Charlie said, "This must be what it synced with. But, was this already on, or did it turn on when we turned the machine on?"

"It's been here for a long time. Does it have batteries? There's no way they could last that long, I don't care what that pink rabbit says."

He looked it over. "I don't see any place for them. We might have to open it up at home and take a better look."

"Agreed." She then had a look on her face that indicated an idea. Charlie always loved when that happened. "Remember when the car died on our trip?"

"Of course." He smiled. "Do you think there's a crystal inside this?"

"No, but I think it's close by."

They turned towards two trees that stood several yards apart.

"You take the one on the left, and I'll take the one on the right."

She nodded. They approached their respective trees. They looked them over carefully for any mysterious knot or hole. When none were found, Charlie looked at the branches. Right where there was a fork at the trunk, he saw something blue.

"Found it!"

"So did I!" she yelled in response.

Surprised, he took it from its crevice and headed towards Lisa.

"How can there be two more?" he asked.

"I have no idea. I thought we had the only one."

A deep thought occurred to him. "How many times did he do it?"

"That brings up some big implications. I don't know the answer to that. Maybe we'll never know."

"What's this thing that they're in?"

She answered as soon as he realized it for himself. "Aluminum oxynitride."

"This is a lot to process. So many questions are raised, just when we thought we were at the end."

"Maybe we should take it all home, get out the notebook, and try to piece it all together."

"Good idea."

They started walking back to the car. They stopped at the rock.

Charlie said, "Let's not leave any stone unturned."

"Good one," she said with a laugh. They turned the rock back over.

"One thing is pretty clear to me," Charlie remarked.

"Oh? What's that?"

"The book said that when we actually use the machine, that we should have it send us to a safe spot. We don't want to end up inside a wall or a tree that may or may not have been there before. It also has to be where no one will see us appear out of nowhere. It has to be just as secretive as the machine itself. It has to be a place that has remained unchanged from our time to the time we travel back to." He held out his arms. "I think we found our destination."

"I totally agree. We found the 'where,' now we just need to find the 'when.'"

He looked at the crystal. "I think we need to solve this mystery first."

They returned to the study with their newfound pieces of a puzzle.

"Looks like this study is really going to be used for studying this time," Charlie quipped.

Lisa opened up the notebook and skimmed through its pages.

"I don't see anything about this in here. The closest thing is the part that talks about the computer codes. Now we know what some of that meant."

"So, if the machine acts as a transmitter and is synced with the receiver, it stands to reason that there must be something that's meant to be sent as a signal. It's not just a time machine."

"Let's crack it open and take a look."

They opened the receiver.

"Nothing appears out of the ordinary, except for this extra tubular plastic piece," Charlie said as he removed it. He peered into it. "There's something in here." He shook it until a rolled up piece of paper fell out.

"I've got to say, this is the greatest scavenger hunt I've ever been a part of," Lisa joked. She picked it up and read what it said, *"If you've come this far, then you have no doubt completed the project. You could proceed with whatever mission you have planned. However, if you have a need or desire to take it further, these are the tools that could help you accomplish your task."* She looked at Charlie.

"Take it further?" asked Charlie. "What could be further than time travel?"

"I don't know," she said with a shrug. She continued reading, *"I only have a vague idea for how to fully execute this. I'm sorry. I had a better idea once, but my memory isn't what it used to be. I also lack the time to solve it myself. I know that the two of you can put your minds together and do what I never could. Remember to always listen to her wisdom and trust her instincts. You are together for a reason."*

"What do you think, Lisa? We have a receiver, two more crystals, both contained in the same material used to make the machine, and a note written by an absent-minded professor. What does it all mean?"

She thought for a moment. "Let's fire up the machine again and see what it does."

Charlie and Lisa watched as the machine roared to life again. He turned his focus to the laptop while Lisa kept an eye on the receiver and the crystals on the floor.

"We're getting closer," he said. "SYNCED" appeared on the screen again. "There it is."

"Look, Charlie!"

The crystals lit up brilliantly.

"Of course. Why am I not surprised?" he said with a smile. He looked at the laptop again. "We have new coordinates."

Lisa typed the numbers into the desktop computer. "Just as I thought. The location is right here."

"Let's shut it down."

They each pushed a few buttons and brought the machine down to a halt. The crystals stopped glowing.

"Does it send a signal to the antenna first, or do the crystals communicate with each other and then send it to the antenna?" Charlie asked.

"I think the crystals enhance the signal."

"I don't know why it would need to be enhanced. It doesn't have to travel that far..." he paused and smiled. "...unless it's travelling through time."

Lisa pointed her finger at him. "Exactly! If it's enough power to send us through time, then why not a signal?"

"What is this signal? Radio waves. The antenna built into the machine sends the waves out, the receiver... well, receives them. But, why would it need to go back in time? The machine doesn't need it to do that to work; the note even said so."

They thought for a moment. Charlie picked up the receiver and moved the antenna around. Lisa picked up one of the crystals and looked it over.

"The crystal in the machine is more than enough to send the signal back in time," she stated. "Why would we need not only one, but two more?"

"If we send the signal back to any time that the crystals were there in the field, it would work. Only we wouldn't know it." His eyes lit up. "Unless the signal goes both ways!"

She gasped. "Yes! But, that means that we would need a transmitter to go with it."

"A transceiver! It sends and receives signals in the same device! I think our benefactor had the right idea, just not the whole idea. It's time for an upgrade."

"I think we're still missing something. Why two more crystals? Why are they in the aluminum oxynitride? To protect them?"

"Possibly. I still think there's another reason."

He set the receiver down and went back to the notebook on the desk.

"I've read through this from cover to cover just as you have. Even though I have it memorized, I still read parts of it again. There's one thing I've wondered, one question that I've still asked, that I can't find an answer to satisfy."

"What could that be?"

"Look through the book, Lisa. Read between the lines. This tells us everything we need to know to build the machine and how it works. Yet, for all that information, all the details, down to what kind of screws to use, there's a major detail left out. I think it's left out because it's not a part of it. After we go back in time and do whatever it is that we need to do, tell me, Lisa, how do we get back?"

She searched for the words. "I-- I don't have the answer to that."

"This is one of the reasons why I've been a little hesitant at times in following through with this. I've thought a lot about it. It's kept me awake a few times. The only answer I can come up with is that there is no answer. It's a one-way ticket. There is no going back. That's why whatever we do had better count. It has to be worth risking everything."

"But, if we change the past, wouldn't everything work out? In other words, if we go back and fix something, then there would be no reason to build the machine in the first place and everything would adjust around it."

"That's a good theory, and that's the way I think about it, but what if we're wrong? How could we possibly know? I think if it's a major change, it would all adjust, but if it's something that doesn't affect us as much, we might be stuck there."

"So what do we do?"

He put his hand on hers as she still held the crystal.

"Think about it. 'A need or desire to take it further.'"

"To do what he never could." She looked down at the crystal and back to him. "One for each of us."

"If we can send the signal both ways..."

"...then why not us?"

They smiled. They knew that they were thinking the same thing.

Charlie said, "He's giving us a way back."

"We just have to get the details right. You can work on the transceiver and the remote." She held up the crystal. "I'm getting an idea about this."

He smiled wider. "He said that you might have some ideas of your own."

"I'm going to think it through some more and do some research. If what I'm picturing will work, then it's really going to change the game."

"I trust your instincts. I can't wait to see what you come up with."

She gave her trademark mischievous grin. "Hang in there, Mr. Blue Sky. The Sunshine is just getting brighter."

The duo researched and worked on their projects as much as time would allow. October became November, and holidays started taking priority. It quickly became 2004. They began to give Elijah driving lessons, and he received his license on his birthday in March. He soon got a part time job to buy his own car. Just before his eighteenth birthday in May, Sammy graduated high school. The times were certainly changing all on their own.

Now that Sammy was headed for college and Elijah was working more hours, Charlie and Lisa had more time to themselves between counselling. They gathered in the study to continue their work.

"I have it all set up to send the signal from the machine to the transceiver and back again," Charlie stated.

"How will we know if it really went through time?" Lisa asked. "What kind of signal is it?"

"I've thought a lot about that. I think that using something too simple won't really tell us much. We need real proof. Something more tangible. But, then I realized that we can still do that with the signal."

"Oh? What did you come up with?"

"Music. Just like a radio station sends music through the radio waves, we can do it, too, only ours would go through time as well."

She smiled and giggled. "I love it! Something we couldn't touch, but we could still sense and know that it worked. Absolutely brilliant."

"Thank you. There's still one thing I haven't quite figured out, however. Maybe you can help me."

"Go for it."

"If we send it back in time, we almost need a way to record it to know that it worked."

"But, if we had a recording device of some kind, it still might not work or it might be ruined if it's there too long."

"Exactly. Even if we did it today and sent the song back to yesterday, we still wouldn't know. It could start playing a song while we're here talking about it or when we're not even here to witness it. We have to really plan this to a tee."

"Yeah, this time stuff can get really confusing. Maybe there's another way that we're not thinking about."

They thought for a moment. Then, Charlie's eyes lit up.

"Of course! There is another way! We don't send it back in time at all!"

She laughed. "What are you talking about? What would be the point?"

"We don't send it back... we send it *forward*."

Her eyes widened. "The future!"

"All we have to do is send the signal from the machine's antenna to the transceiver out in the field in the past. But, we also program it to send it back to the machine in the future. We can have the song go to the field yesterday and come back here to this time tomorrow. That way, it will have travelled back one day and forward two days, proving beyond a doubt that it worked!"

"That's a great idea! One question, though. How will we make it go to the future when everything we've done has been built around it going to the past?"

"It's actually simple." He walked up to the machine and made motions with his hands as he described it. Lisa couldn't help but be reminded of Doc Brown. "As we both know, to achieve time travel, we have to have two things: an incredible amount of power and an incredible rate of speed. The electricity gives us that speed, but the energy from the crystal gives us the power and enhances it. They unite and travel through the walls of the sphere, eventually surpassing the speed of light. All this is done backwards to send us back. That's not the natural flow. We made it do that, and all we have to do is reverse it. Think about it. Going to the future should actually be easier than going to the past because we're already travelling that way anyway."

"You really think we can make the machine do both?"

"No doubt in my mind."

"I was actually kind of counting on that for my other idea. I realized that we would need to go forward for it to bring us back. Now, it's all becoming clear."

"Great!"

"But, one thing at a time. Let's try this music thing out first."

"Right as always."

They headed for the computers.

"You know, we really should come up with names for things," Lisa mentioned. "We keep saying, 'blue energy,' 'the machine,' 'the blue crystal,' and so on. It's all kind of bland. We have nicknames for each other, why not for these things?"

"Hmm. That's a good point. Maybe we should come up with something. For the blue energy, we could call it, 'Crystal Blue Persuasion.'"

"Too long. But, not bad. We'll figure it out. Ok, Mr. Blue Sky, do you have a song? And, how do we do this exactly?"

"I'll use my MP3 player. And, yes, I do have a song."

"What is it?"

He smiled. "Some secrets are good. Knowing something before you should know it kind of takes the fun out of it."

She mildly punched his arm. "Fine. Be that way. I just hope it's something good."

"It is. Trust me."

"'Crystal Blue Persuasion'?"

"Nope. Nice try."

They finished typing all their commands.

"Ready?" Charlie asked.

"I was born ready," she replied with a smile.

The machine hummed to life.

"Let's make history."

The energy spun faster and faster through the machine.

"There goes the song!" Charlie enthused.

A blinding flash of blue light topped off the spectacle before them. The machine began to slow down and soon came to a stop.

"Now, we wait," Lisa said.

The next day, they met in the study again around the same time as the day before. Butterflies flew like hummingbirds in their stomachs as they awaited the end result of their test.

"What song did you use?"

"You'll find out soon."

"Please tell me that it's not 'Weird Al'."

He smiled.

She started to become slightly exasperated. "Please tell me that the first thing to time travel is not a 'Weird Al' song."

"What? Don't you like him?"

"Yes, but it's hardly appropriate under the circumstances."

He laughed. "It's not 'Weird Al'. Just trust me."

The blue energy grew brighter as it spun faster.

"We really should be wearing protection for our eyes," Lisa said.

"Next time," he replied.

They averted their gaze towards the laptop. Everything was running according to plan. Faster and faster the light coursed through the walls of the sphere. The time calculated on the screen stood still.

"It's coming! We're almost there!" Charlie shouted over the noise with excitement.

"I have goosebumps!" Lisa added with delight.

They squinted as they watched the machine. One last glance at the laptop told them that success was imminent. Charlie set it aside and held Lisa's hand. She was trembling as much as he was.

"Ready, Sunshine?"

"Rock and roll."

The room was ignited with the sounds of guitars and drums.

She gasped. They both started laughing with glee. She jumped into his arms with her legs wrapped around him as he spun her in circles.

"It worked!!! It really worked!!! We did it!!!" she exclaimed.

"I never had any doubt."

"And the song is perfect! You always knew how to pick the right one."

"You always inspire me."

She gave him a big kiss. She got back on her feet and they proceeded to dance and sing along to Foreigner's "Feels Like the First Time."

After the song was over, Charlie declared, "June 1st, 2004. The date that we successfully achieved time travel."

"Now we have to test it on something physical."

"Yes, an inanimate object. But, what should we use?"

"I have an idea." Lisa took a piece of paper from the desk. "I'll write something on this piece of paper and send it back in time."

"How will we know if it went back? If you send it to yesterday, we wouldn't know that you did that today." He made a quizzical face and laughed. "I hope that's not too confusing."

"Yes, I get what you're saying. That's why I'll write part of it now and send it forward. Then, I'll just write more on it in the future and send it back a minute after sending the first one."

"You know, that actually makes sense. Great idea, Sunshine. Let's do it."

She grinned slyly and wrote on the paper.

"What did you write?" he asked.

"It's my turn to surprise you."

"Fair enough."

She put it inside the machine and shut the door. They ran the computers again.

“Let’s just send it to the machine instead of the field in case it rains or the wind blows it away,” Charlie suggested.

“Perfect. I’m glad you thought of that.”

The machine went into action again.

“On second thought, maybe I should tell you what I wrote today and leave the second part as a surprise,” she said.

“Okay, what was it?”

“‘I love you.’”

He smiled. “First words on paper sent through time. It couldn’t be more perfect.”

“Just wait. It will get better.”

The paper disappeared in a flash.

“We have one minute until it shows up again,” she said.

“How far did you send it?”

“Instead of doing it tomorrow, I thought we could stretch this a little further. I sent it to a week from now.”

“A week? I guess that would work, as long as you remember to do it.”

“Of course I will. There’s no way you would let me forget.”

He laughed. “That’s true.”

They looked at their watches. Why did that minute have to take so long?

Charlie interjected, “We still have to test the remote. Plus, we need to figure out a way to send things to the field and know that it worked.”

“Very true. Perhaps we can figure that out within the coming week and test it out after sending the paper back.”

“Good plan.”

As it grew closer to the minute, Lisa became a bit concerned.

“Why hasn’t the machine come on?”

“It doesn’t have to. The machine is only the destination this time, just like the field. We only had it come on for the song because I programmed it to play it when it came.”

“Okay, that makes sense. So when we get this in the future, we shouldn’t expect it to come on. All we have to do is open the door at the right time.”

“Exactement.”

She smiled at his French. “Okay, it’s almost time.”

When the full minute was up, Lisa opened the door. She motioned to Charlie. “Go ahead and see what it says.”

He smiled and picked up the paper. He read it aloud, ‘I love you! 555-4823.’” He laughed along with her. “Just like Jennifer. It really is perfect.”

She put her arms around him and said, “That’s the power of love.”

They kissed.

As the week progressed, Lisa finalized her research for her idea about the crystals. They met together in the study on June 8th.

"Okay, it's almost time for the paper to get here," Charlie stated as he looked at his watch.

"This is so exciting!" Lisa said. "I'm literally writing the future."

"You could even change what it says. After all, the future isn't written yet."

"True, but I think I should stick with the original plan. No sense in confusing our past selves."

"I agree." He looked at his watch again. "It's time."

Lisa opened the door to the machine.

"Right on schedule."

She took it out and wrote the phone number on it. She put it back inside and they started it up.

"Let's try out the remote," Charlie said.

They let it run for a bit before he pushed the button. The machine slowed down and came to a stop.

"Now we know that it works," he said.

"Can we start it again with the remote?"

"No. It would take a lot more time to get it to do that. Maybe some other time. For now, this is just to use in case of emergencies."

She nodded. "Okay, let's do it again."

They started the machine and put on sunglasses this time. The energy spun through the machine until the paper was sent back in time. They opened the door to confirm that it was gone. They walked over to the safe and took out the paper as they received it a week earlier.

"This is so weird," Charlie said with a laugh. "Weird, but cool."

"It's totally amazing. This time travel thing is actually working."

"I was just thinking about this whole naming business, also."

"Okay, what did you come up with?"

"Something like 'machine' or 'sphere' or 'ball' is still too bland. I got to thinking about the different things we could do with it. The possibilities are endless. Then, it hit me-- the Possibility Pod."

"Hmm. Not bad. Still kind of a mouthful."

"Maybe so. Okay, so let's look at it this way-- we're Protectors, we're Changers... this is used to change things... the Changing Station."

"That sounds like something for diapers."

"Yeah, you're right. What are other words for change?"

"Transform, convert, mutate, shift..."

"Aha! That's it! The Shifter!"

"Shifter." She rubbed her chin. "Shifter. I can live with that."

"We just need names for the crystal and the energy. But, hey, what about this research you've been doing? Are you going to let me in on it?"

"Yes, of course! I think I have it figured out. Tell me what you think."

They went to the computer.

"I realized that we need something more than just the crystals in the orb things." She caught herself. "Or, little Shifters." She took out a pad and showed him her sketches. "These things are almost time machines in themselves. We can't very well just hold them in our hands because they might get too hot or something that we're not prepared for. So, I wanted something hands-free, and yet, still strong enough to withstand everything that we might throw at it."

She showed him what she found online.

"Kevlar?" he asked.

"We need something that we can wear. Since the Shifter is made of bulletproof material, shouldn't this be, too? Why not have bulletproof vests?"

He smiled. "That's a brilliant idea! What do we do, put the crystal in the center?"

"Exactly." She showed him her sketches. "The bigger crystal used for the Shifter is always outside. These smaller ones would be on the inside instead, just as they are now. All we have to do is remove part of the shell to attach it to the vest. The vest would serve as the other part of the shell. The electrical components inside will be activated when the Shifter sends the signal to the transceiver, then to these crystals, and voila. The energy travels through the vest quickly and sends us back to where we belong."

"I am very impressed. I think that might actually work."

"Only one way to find out."

"Okay. Let's order it." He looked at the price. "Are we sure?"

She laughed. "Quite sure."

"Okay. We have to do what we have to do."

She went through the ordering process for the vests.

"They should arrive in a couple of weeks. What should we do until then?"

"We still need to test it on something living."

"Not the kids and not Duke!" she said adamantly.

"Of course not! But, I'm still not sure who it will be."

"What if it's not a who, but a what?"

He looked confused. "What do you mean?"

She grinned. "I have an idea. You're going to love this."

A short time later, they stepped into the flower shop downtown. An elderly lady greeted them.

"Hello, my name is Rose. Can I help you find something?"

"You're kidding me. Your name is Rose?" asked an amused Lisa. Charlie gently elbowed her.

Rose laughed. "Yes, it really is my name. I suppose it was some sort of destiny to work in a flower shop. I could've had any other name, like Lily or Daisy or Iris. At least my last name isn't Thorn."

They laughed.

"My name is Charlie, and this is my wife, Lisa."

"Charlie, nickname of Charles. It means 'free man.' Lisa means 'light.'"

"Wow, I'm impressed," he said. "How do you know all that?"

"When you work with flowers and plants, they have these fancy Latin names. I made it a hobby to learn all the names and what they mean. That carried over to people names. These young kids who come work here in the summer don't always care about that. Some of them hardly know the difference between a lily and a lilac. Anyways, that's neither here nor there. What can I help you find, Charlie and Lisa? A gift for a loved one?"

Charlie looked to Lisa for the answer.

"I remember reading about this plant that only blooms once a year."

"Oh, yes. That's the Epiphyllum oxypetalum, better known as the 'Queen of the Night.'" She walked them over to a plant with white flowers. "I have one of these at home. It only blooms once a year, and only late at night. It withers away before dawn. I have an old friend who comes over every year and we stay up late and watch it. I always refer to it as 'Her Royal Majesty paying us a visit.' It's truly one of the most beautiful things I've ever seen. Like seeing a baby born. You ever see anything like that?"

"Yes, we've been blessed to have a few experiences like that," said Charlie. He held Lisa's hand as he thought of the wall of crystals, their newborn sons, and especially seeing her for the first time.

"It's one of life's greatest gifts, isn't it?" Rose continued. "Something that makes it all worthwhile. One of those things where God really came up with something special. When it blooms, there's this fragrance that's downright intoxicating."

"It sounds really wonderful," he said. "Is this what you had in mind, Lisa?"

"When is it due to bloom?"

"You couldn't have come at a better time. Her Majesty is due to arrive this Saturday night."

"Is this one going to do it at the same time as yours?"

"Oh, yes. I've tended to them in the same way to give them the same conditions."

Lisa smiled. "Do you have two?"

They set their new plants on the floor in the study.

"So, here's my idea," said Lisa. "We send them to different times."

She got out two index cards and a marker.

"We'll call them 'Queen A and Queen B'."

She wrote the names down and taped the cards to the pots.

"I like this so far," he said.

She continued, "We know that we have four days until they bloom. We wait until Thursday and send Queen A back two days, which would be today. The plant won't know the difference. We leave it alone in the field and watch it bloom Thursday night."

"Don't we have to water it?"

"No. It's in the cactus family and doesn't have to be watered every day."

"I see. So, we send it back two days and basically trick it into thinking that Thursday is Saturday?"

"Exactamente," Lisa replied in Spanish.

"Very good, Lisa! We would have scientific proof that it time travelled. That is, if Rose is correct about the timing."

"I would consider her an expert on the subject. We can also call her on Monday morning and confirm that her own Queen bloomed on Saturday."

"You were right-- I love this plan. What do you have in mind for Queen B? The future?"

She used the sign for "exact." "We wait until Thursday. Then, we send Queen B ahead one week. Two days later, it should still bloom on schedule."

Charlie smiled. "If we weren't already married, I'd ask you to marry me right now."

She laughed.

He continued, "Seriously, that is a brilliant plan! You must be some kind of genius."

"Well, you know... there's been some suspicion."

They laughed as they wrapped their arms around each other.

"This gives me another idea," he said.

"Oh, yeah? What could it be?"

"My turn to surprise you. Hopefully, I can get it done by the time the vests get here."

"We always did have a way of keeping each other sharp. It feels like the old days when we first got married."

He looked lovingly into her eyes. "Like turning back time."

Thursday, June 10th couldn't come soon enough. Lisa placed Queen A into the Shifter. They set the machine into motion and soon watched the plant vanish. When it came to a stop, Lisa put Queen B inside. They repeated the process, only in reverse. The second plant was quickly propelled to the future. No matter how many times they did it, the spectacle was still astounding.

"I can't wait until tonight," Charlie said with a smile.

"I know what you mean. The suspense is killing me."

"It's not every day that royalty comes to visit."

"Especially not one that came from so far."

"Should we go to the field now just to see it?"

"Nah. Let's wait it out and go there just tonight. Let's not take the fun out of it."

He chuckled. "I've always had to be patient with you."

They arrived at the field that night with a flashlight to guide their path. They reached the spot near the rock.

"There it is!" Lisa enthused.

"This is so amazing. We've sent a living object through time and it appears to be unharmed."

"The true test will be if it blooms."

"How much longer?"

"Any minute now."

They turned their attention to Queen A.

"I think it's starting!" Lisa exclaimed.

The plant began to open its petals. Charlie shifted his attention between it and Lisa. This wonder of nature was truly a remarkably beautiful sight to behold, but to Charlie, watching the joyful expression on her face was a marvel that could never be rivaled. The Sunshine would always be more glorious than the Queen of the Night.

She turned to Charlie and said with tears in her eyes, "It worked."

"I knew it would."

He wished that he brought a camera, but he knew that he would never forget this moment.

"Rose was right about the smell, too," she said.

They took a deep breath through their noses as they inhaled the tantalizing aroma.

"It's kind of an aphrodisiac," she said as she put her arms around his neck.

He put his arms around her and kissed his Queen.

"Let's go home and celebrate," he whispered.

As they awaited the arrival of Queen B, Charlie tinkered on his surprise project. All of this tinkering with time itself brought back memories of his mom giving him his dad's watch on his wedding day.

"Time stood still for you once. All you needed was for something inside to change."

He smiled.

"I know how to love her... because you taught me."

"And now that you're together, there's no stopping you. The two of you will do great things."

"If you love someone, anything's possible."

"Love changes everything."

In light of their current situation, he knew something that was always obvious-- Mom was always right.

Tuesday, June 15th. The vests finally arrived.

"Great! Now we can get these ready," said Lisa.

"I've been waiting for those to see if my extra modification would work also."

"Oh, so you want to modify them even more? Hmm. What do you have in mind?"

"I'll show you."

They went upstairs to the study.

"I got to thinking that we might need to know precisely when and where we are when we use these."

"Wouldn't we already program that information into the Shifter?"

"Yes, but it's one thing to send objects through time for a couple of days or for a week. It would be another thing for us to go back for years, possibly decades. It would be good to know if it was accurate without having to find a newspaper to verify it or find out the hard way that we were off."

"That's a good point. So, what did you come up with?"

He showed her his devices.

"I have these atomic clocks. They're synced with the NIST-F1, the world clock in Boulder, Colorado. The time should always be accurate. My idea is to program the Shifter to send out a frequency to the NIST-F1 immediately after sending the other signal. I want to modify the clocks to fit the vests right above the crystals. If all goes according to plan, we'll get not only the time, but the date as well. It might take a minute to adjust, but it should give us an accurate reading on the vests."

She smiled. "I love it. Way to go, Mr. Blue Sky!"

"Hopefully it works. It would sure remove the guesswork."

"And in another few days, we can see if Queen B works out."
"Until then, let's get to work."

They spent the next two days working on the vests. On Thursday, they knew that Queen B should be in the field.
"Let's not leave it out there and wait to see what happens," Charlie said.
They found it in the field where the other one was before. They decided to take it home to watch it bloom on Saturday. On Friday the 18th, they were finished with the vests. They looked at their twin plants that night. Unlike human twins, they were different in appearance and identical on the inside. One more day and time would catch up. Charlie had the video camera ready this time as they waited for Queen B to bloom that Saturday night.
"There it goes!" Lisa exclaimed. "I can't believe we get to witness this twice."
"And, that's not even because of time travel. We could even go back and do it again if we wanted to. At least I have it recorded this time."
"It also proves that time travel won't affect the object going through time, it's only a change in surroundings."
"Other than the fatigue that the notebook talked about."
"Right. That could have been relative to the amount of time that is travelled. The plants don't appear to be any worse for the wear."
"Then I'd say that this has been a complete success. We've sent living objects into the past and the future without any harmful effects. All we have to do now is to test the vests." Charlie shut off the camera. "But, let's wait until tomorrow when we have daylight. It will give the crystal more time to recharge a bit, too."
"Tonight, we celebrate. This time, it's my turn to pick the song."
She started programming the computers.
"You're going to send it through time?"
"Why not? This is the best stereo in the house."
She finished typing her commands.
"There. I just sent it a minute into the future."
Charlie smiled. "What will we do with the next minute?"
She smiled back. "Whatever we want. Anything is possible."
He took her into his arms and kissed her. He knew that with her, the possibilities were endless.
The minute went by and the music began to play. They danced as The Beach Boys played "Kokomo." The couple started out slowly, then more energetic as they laughed and sang along. In a few days, it would be thirty-two years since Charlie first laid eyes on Lisa. He could still see

that little girl in her, no matter how much older and wiser they had become. In many ways, it felt like they were still just getting started.

Sunday the 20th. They made sure that Elijah spent some time with friends that afternoon so that they would have the house to themselves. After having lunch, they took the camera to the field and set it on the tripod. They checked their watches.

"We'll have to hurry before the battery dies," Charlie informed her.

"There should be plenty of time."

They started recording when the time was 1:30.

When they got home, they patiently waited a bit. When the time was closer, they got started.

"Okay, Your Majesty," Charlie addressed Queen A as he put the vest around the pot. "It's time to try a new trick."

He put the plant into the Shifter and shut the door. He and Lisa typed some commands into the computers.

"Half an hour back, an hour there, and then it will be back here again," Lisa stated. "That's if everything goes right."

The Shifter went to work. Charlie watched the time as it moved faster.

"There it goes!" he said as it vanished. "2:00-- right on schedule."

"We still have half an hour to kill before it comes back. Maybe we should go ahead and send Queen B to the future to test out the other vest."

"We won't have the camera there, but okay. That's worth trying."

They put the vest on the other plant and sent it forward one day into the future.

"Now, we wait," said Charlie. "2:30 for Queen A and 2:31 for Queen B."

It didn't take long before that time came.

"2:30, right on the dot," said Lisa with a laugh. "Or should I say with pun fully intended, 'right on time.'"

"This really is a breakthrough, Lisa. We actually sent it back in time and brought it back with clockwork accuracy. Your idea was pure brilliance. I'm so proud of you."

"Now we just need to check the tape to make absolutely sure it went to the right place."

"I'm sure it did." He looked at this watch. "It's almost time for Her Royal Majesty's arrival from tomorrow."

Lisa laughed. "That statement would sound really strange if we didn't understand it."

"Here she comes... any second now..."

At precisely 2:31, Queen B arrived.

"Look at the clock!" Lisa said. "It still has tomorrow's date!"

"That's very convenient. Now, we can see how long it takes to adjust to the correct date."

Within a few seconds, the date on the clock went from the 21st to the 20th.

"That's faster than I expected," Charlie noted.

"It might be relative to the length of time, also," Lisa pointed out.

"True. Let's go get that camera."

A short time later, Charlie and Lisa gathered in front of the TV. Charlie put the tape into the VCR and rewound it. They soon played it back.

"There it is, right after we walked away," Lisa said as she pointed at the plant onscreen.

Charlie zoomed in.

"Look at the clock."

They watched as the time went from 2:00 to 1:30.

"That is so awesome," Lisa said.

Charlie fast-forwarded the tape through the next hour of footage. They watched as the crystal in the vest lit up and the plant disappeared. They turned to each other and smiled.

"And the rest was history," he said.

Her smile grew mischievous and she flashed her eyebrows. "Follow me," she said as she ran up the stairs. Charlie followed after her. As he entered the study, he saw her grab one of the vests and proceed to put it on.

"What are you doing?" he asked with slight exasperation.

"What do you think I'm doing? It's time to test it out ourselves."

"Are you crazy? We're only supposed to use it for a noble purpose."

"Doesn't mean that we can't and shouldn't test it. You know that. We've tested it on inanimate objects and living plants. We've sent them to the past and the future and brought them back with precision. We have proof after proof after proof that this works exactly like we programmed it to, and it's as safe as safe can be." She handed him the other vest. "This is the next logical step."

"It's logical, but I just don't know..."

"Don't know what?"

"Don't know if I'm ready."

She put her hand on his shoulder. "It still needs to be done. All these years, all this hard work, it's built up to this moment. This is what it's been all about-- the two of us travelling through time. We know that it works. We've done every test that we can think of and they've all been successful. The only test left is on us. As scientists, we have to do it. As a part of this whole mysterious quest that this notebook has brought into our lives, we have to do it. We owe it to the one who wrote it, to the Protector, and to ourselves." She opened the door to the Shifter. "It's time. No pun intended. It's just time."

"I-- I just didn't expect to do it today. I'm not mentally prepared."

"I still want to do it."

"We always do things together. Would you really go without me?"

"I don't really want to do it alone, but if that's what it takes, then I will. This is bigger than us, Charlie. There is a reason for all this."

Charlie's phone rang.

"Who could that be?" he asked as he took it out of his pocket. His eyebrows raised as he saw who was on the other end. "It's you."

"What? That's not possible." She took her silent phone out of her pocket.

He answered it. "Hello?"

"Charlie, this is Lisa. Put me on speaker."

They gave each other a quizzical look and he complied.

"Hi, Lisa!" the voice on the phone said.

"Hi... me..." Lisa replied. "This is really weird. What's happening?"

She laughed. "I know this is weird, but I can explain. I know who wins this argument. Charlie, you stay behind to make sure that everything goes okay. That's fine. But, let me tell you, it does work. Here's your proof."

"So you're the Lisa who's with me right now... but you went back and you're calling me from the field?"

"Bingo, Mr. Blue Sky. There's just one problem."

They looked at each other again. "Problem? What problem? Are you okay?"

"Oh, I'm just peachy. See, you two go back and forth about this for awhile. Should we? Should we not? Should it be one of us or both of us? What about the philosophy of time travel? On and on and on it goes until 4:00. Then, you send me back to a different part of the field at 2:00. I'm supposed to be brought back with the vest around 4:05. It's almost 3 now. I have been out here in this field for an hour with nothing to do but get sunburnt. I'm not a member of the cactus family. I need water. I also need to pee, ironically, but I don't want to do it out here. I thought about walking to town, but you know, still hot out. Plus, if I disappear in front of people, it's going to raise some eyebrows. This could have been thought through a little better. I don't want to wait out here for another hour. I'm already bored out of my mind. I've started talking to a grasshopper."

Charlie said, "It's really you alright."

The Lisa still in the study said, "So this works, but we need to come up with a better plan."

The Lisa in the field said, "Yes, please come up with a better plan. Send me back to an hour ago if you want, but don't make me stay for any longer than a minute tops."

"Okay. That's what we'll do then," Charlie said. "Sorry, Lisa. We'll fix it."

"That's okay. That's what tests are for, you know? No real damage done. If you get it right soon, then none of us will even remember it. It will have never happened."

They looked at each other quizzically and then said at the same time, "I think she's right."

"Yeah, I've been thinking about it. I think when you do something different than what I did, that would change what happens to me. If you go back sooner than I did, then I wouldn't be here."

"So what happens to you?" asked the Lisa in the study.

"I don't know. I just... cease to exist I guess. It will never happen."

"That was the sense that I got from reading the notebook," Charlie said. "It was a one-way ticket. That's why we're making a way to come back. As long as we're not changing something major from our own lives, we should be able to come back unscathed. It still seems kind of sad for you."

"Nah, I'll get over it. I'll just become a better, less sunburnt version of myself. One who thought to go to the bathroom before leaving."

They chuckled.

"At least you'll have the grasshopper to keep you company," joked the present day Lisa.

"I will say this while I still can," Lisa said. "Although this hasn't been perfect, this has been an amazing experience. Don't put it off any longer. There's no time like the present." She laughed. "Whether or not I intended that pun is up for you to decide."

Charlie said, "Thanks for the eye-opener. It really helps."

"Yeah, it's been... surreal," Lisa told her counterpart.

"I wish there was another way. It seems bittersweet at best," Charlie told the Lisa on the phone.

"It's okay, my love. I'm still right beside you."

He looked at Lisa and they smiled.

He replied, "See ya later."

There was no response.

"Lisa?" Charlie asked.

"We've already changed it," Lisa said. "It never happened. We're going to forget any second now. So before I take this trip, I'm going to the bathroom."

Charlie nodded as she walked away. He looked at his phone. No calls for the day. He wasn't sure why he had it in his hand. He shrugged and put it in his pocket. He looked at the vest in his other hand and then at the Shifter. Years of hard work were finally over. Time travel was possible and just waiting to be experienced. What noble purpose should ultimately be realized, he wasn't sure yet. All he knew was that Lisa was right as usual. It still needed to be tested by humans before going any further. He went to the computers and started the sequence. He thought this time that he would try a different part of the field and only send her an hour back. His thoughts drifted back to another period in his life when he went through testing.

"What's wrong? Are you worried again?"

"Yeah. I have a bad feeling about this."

"Why? You've already done the tests. The worst is over."

"I just have a feeling that something is gonna change."

"Nah, they're just talking about your good work and how you passed all the tests."

"I don't know..."

"I'm sure that everything's okay. You have to loosen up a little. Come on, let's play!"

"Maybe you're right... I mean of course you're right!"

Charlie worried too much and Lisa saw the bright side. Some things never changed.

Charlie smiled as Lisa walked in.

"It's all ready for you," he told her. "I'll stay behind this time in case of any issues."

She smiled. "Really? You're not going to put up a fight?"

"I trust you. If you say that it's time, then it's time."

He got out of his chair and they hugged.

"I'm so excited, but I'm also kind of nervous," she said.

"That's what the song is for. Remember to focus on that and breathe calmly. When it gets towards the end, put your hands on the walls."

They pulled away and held hands.

"Okay, I remember," she said with a nervous nod.

"It's about 3 now. I'm sending you back an hour, and then the vest will bring you back a minute later. I hope that's not too much too quickly."

"Only one way to find out."

"Okay. I'm going to try not to worry the whole time."

"Relax-- we've got this. Easy peasy mac and cheesy."

"Easy peasy George and Weezy."

She laughed. "That's a good one." She stepped into the Shifter. "That's one small step for woman..."

"One giant leap for womankind."

"I'll see you in a minute," she said with a loving smile.

He returned her smile. "I can't wait."

He shut the door and pushed the last of the buttons. The machine hummed to life along with "The Warmth of the Sun" by The Beach Boys. Lisa closed her eyes and held her head back. Charlie noticed her lip syncing with the song. He was thoroughly impressed with her ability to remain calm and brave. His thoughts turned to some of his favorite memories of her.

"That's what friends do for each other, huh, Charlie? I look out for you, and you look out for me. Like when you made me that card when I was sick. That was a best friend kind of thing to do."

"Yeah, I'll always look out for you. You're the best friend I could ever have."

"The point is... what I'm trying to say... Lisa Ann Duvall, I love you. I love everything about you. Not just as a friend. You're the love of my life."

"Where are you going? Why are you leaving?"

"Because this is where you break my heart."

"No, Charlie. Not this time. This is where I fix it. I've waited... I've waited the longest time to hear you say that... because I couldn't wait to say it right back. Charlie, I love you. I've always loved you. I love everything about you, too."

"We have the rest of our lives. We have all the time in the world."

"Ready for an adventure?"

"Always."

As the song reached its climax, she held her arms out and touched the walls. The energy immersed her entire being. She looked over to Charlie and simply said, "I love you." And with that, she was gone. As the machine slowed down, Charlie sat down and reminisced some more, trying to keep his mind from worrying.

"Are you saying what I think you're saying?"

"Yes, Charlie. We're having a baby."

"Gifts are meant to be shared. Light is meant to be seen. A new adventure has just begun."

"It wasn't just a little girl I saw that day. I knew then as I still know today. It was a glimpse of the rest of my life."

"I'm so glad that I have such a supportive husband."

"And I'm so glad that I have a wife with such a big heart. If the sun is going to shine, who am I to stand in its way?"

They already had a lifetime together full of love and laughter. Each day was a new adventure with even bigger ones to come. They weren't just partners in this crazy life, she was the love of his life, his better half, the one who gave it all meaning.

He wiped a tear from his eye and said, "Being away from you for one minute feels like eternity."

And then, she was back.

"Are you okay? How do you feel?" he asked as he ran up to her.

"I feel great! Maybe some slight dizziness, but otherwise, I'm fine." She held out her phone. "There's something I want to show you."

She played a video.

"Look, Charlie," she said as the phone's view turned to her surroundings and then back to herself. "I'm in the field. It worked! This is AWESOME!! Look at the vest. It says three o'clock. It should turn to two any second now." The time changed to two. "See that? It's official. I just time travelled! No one else can hear me, so I'm going to do it. I JUST TIME TRAVELLED!! WOOHOO!!!"

They laughed.

"I went back in time one hour, and I'm going forward again really soon. I feel great, I feel amazing, and I highly recommend this experience. Come on in, Charlie, the water is fine. Oh, look-- a grasshopper." The view turned to the grasshopper and then back to her again. The crystal was glowing. "Well, it looks like my ride is here. The only thing that could've made this better was having you with me. See ya on the other side."

"What do you say, Mr. Blue Sky?" asked Lisa. "Ready to take it for a spin?"

He smiled slyly and went to grab the other vest. Lisa began to enter the commands into the computers.

"Are we going back an hour?" Charlie asked as he put on the vest.

"I have something else in mind."

"And what would that be?"

"Of all the times that you've surprised me with romantic gestures, it's my turn to do it for you. I even have the right song."

"Okay. I trust you."

They took each other by the hand and stepped into the Shifter. They closed the door. The machine began to work as "You Make Me Feel Brand New" began to play.

"It's the new version by Simply Red," she said.

"Good choice."
"Are you nervous?"
"A little bit."
She put her arms around him and whispered in his ear, "Block out everything else. It's just you and me and the song."
He held her in return and closed his eyes. His anxiety faded away. *"How does she do it?"* he thought to himself. The crystal's energy spun faster and faster through the walls of the Shifter, yet Charlie and Lisa were already in another place. Before long, Lisa put her arms to the side and Charlie followed her lead. They looked into each other's eyes.
"You've always been my Sunshine."
"And you've always been my world."
They put their hands on the walls of the Shifter. The energy enveloped them and sent them to another time.

"Whoa! It worked!"
"Of course it worked!" Lisa said with a laugh.
He looked at his surroundings.
"The beach?" he asked with surprise. "When is this?"
"Check out the clock on the vest."
"1998?! That was six years ago!"
"The farthest we've travelled through time or space. Don't worry, this was right after we left when we were here last with Grandma. No one else was here at this time. We have it all to ourselves."
"I can't believe it!" he said as he reached down for a handful of sand. He watched it fall through his fingers. "We did it! We really did it!"
"Look over there!"
They turned their attention closer to the ocean.
"That's the sand castle we built!" he said with a laugh. "How much time do we have?"
"Just a few more minutes. Not enough time to build another one."
"We don't need another one. We have the beach, the ocean, and the most beautiful girl of all time. What more could a boy want?"
"How about a dance?"
They tried to dance up close, but the vests made it awkward. They tried other ways instead. When their time was drawing to a close, the vests lit up. They held each other and kissed.

They arrived in the study once more.
"Quite a trip, isn't it?" she asked with a grin. She took her shoes off and shook the sand out of them.
"Yeah! We could really have some fun with this."

"As tempting as that is, we still need to remember the purpose of the machine."

"You're right. You're absolutely right. It needs to be used for a noble purpose. No more testing. We know that it works. We just have to figure out what that noble purpose is."

"I'm sure we'll figure it out in time," she said as she removed her vest.

"I have a feeling that it won't be long. There's a reason why we're done with it now. There's always a reason."

She casually looked at his watch... the one that used to belong to his father.

"We just have to keep our eyes open," he said as he took off his vest.

"We'll know it when we see it," she reminded him.

"If we're going to be taking a trip, as it were, we need to be properly prepared," said Charlie a few days later.

"Like stocking up on sunblock and snake repellant?" Lisa joked.

"Something like that. I mean that we need to find things that we can use for the proper time period."

"We're not even sure when that will be yet."

"True. Which is why we need to start getting prepared."

"Where do we start?"

"We start with the first thing anyone will notice when they see us. We need the right clothes."

"Charlie Jordache wants to go clothes shopping? Now I've seen it all."

They went to the thrift store in search of garments that would not only fit, but fit in with the times. With the timing being unclear, that would mean trying on a wide variety from the past few decades. Some of these styles looked so appalling that it brought hesitance at first, then acceptance of the fact that they would need to try them anyway. Scoffs quickly became giggles, and disgusted expressions became enthusiastic bursts of laughter. Nothing was off limits. Bell bottoms, tie dyed t-shirts, leisure suits, jumpsuits, peasant dresses, baggy jeans, skinny jeans, spandex, stone-washed denim jackets, windbreakers, flannel shirts, and many more diverse items of apparel were up for grabs. From paisley to neon, polyester to wool, Charlie and Lisa modelled their peculiar fashion choices for each other each time they stepped out of the dressing room. They soon realized that they also needed the proper accessories. Ties, scarves, hats, sunglasses, and even a few wigs were added to the fun. Other customers couldn't help but add their own laughs to theirs. Then the moment came. Charlie found the perfect outfit for a time traveler. He knew that he probably couldn't actually use it, but he just had to try it on. He smiled from ear to ear. Lisa smiled and shook her head. Charlie nodded. She rolled her eyes and said, "Okay." A couple of minutes later, the door to the dressing room opened. White sneakers with red swooshes. Blue jeans. Red t-shirt underneath a halfway unbuttoned black and white checkered shirt. Denim jacket. Orange vest. Charlie pulled his sunglasses up to his forehead and looked at his watch.

Without missing a beat, Lisa quipped, "The look of density."

He laughed.

"My turn," she said.

She soon emerged from the dressing room with her own time-tested wardrobe. Light gray high-tops. Pink floral pants. White collared, long-sleeved shirt. Blue vest.

"How about a ride, mister?"

"You're a sight for sore eyes," he said with a wink and a smile. "I'd go anywhere with you."

They put their arms around each other.

"Anywhere. Any time," he said before they kissed.

June 24th. Lisa's thoughts kept her awake. She knew that the next day was the anniversary of the first time Charlie saw her moving in next door. She wondered if certain dates had a bigger significance, perhaps even some sort of destiny. Looking back on some of their life moments, a strong case could be made. So many birthdays were close together, including theirs. Was it all a coincidence, or was there a deeper meaning? They had free will, she reasoned. They were in control of their actions.

"Are we really walking by faith, or are we just following some kind of predetermined destiny?"

"I think we've been given a choice. We made that choice together, and we're following through with it. We easily could have chosen differently, and still could at any time. We are in control of our own destinies."

She headed up the stairs.

"I don't know how to describe it. Like something was urging me. Almost like it was calling for me."

Her words came back to her conscience as she felt that urge again. She quietly opened the study door. There it was. The time machine. The thing that took so many years to build and so much faith to do so. She knew beyond any doubt that it worked exactly as it should. The Protector had given them a heavy responsibility in giving them the crystal. Now that they could go anywhere they wanted in time, that responsibility was intensified. There was a reason why it was them. As

Charlie wisely said, "there's always a reason." She knew with everything in her being that the time was imminent.

"We'll know it when we see it," she stammered aloud.

"I will pray that your mission succeeds. Godspeed, Charlie and Lisa Jordache, my brother and sister. Change the bad to good."

The wise old Protector's voice echoed in her mind as clearly as if he were in the same room. She knew exactly what she wanted to change.

"This is at the very foundation of everything that was built after that. If we start chipping away at the foundation, wouldn't everything else crumble?"

Charlie was also wise. His words still gave her a reason to question her motives, no matter how sincere and selfless they were. She knelt down with her head bowed and began to cry.

"Listen to her wisdom and follow her instincts."

"Please, Lord. Please give me the wisdom that I need. Give us both the wisdom to do what is right. My heart is torn. Show me. Show us both. Let it be in the service of another. Help us to know it when we see it."

She looked at the crystal.

"To put right what once went wrong."

CHAPTER 25

The 25th came and went. Charlie and Lisa had a good anniversary, but nothing else stood out as exceptional. The 26th also went by without anything unusual happening. And the 27th. Whatever their strong feelings about some sort of time-travelling destiny were, it clearly wasn't going to become obvious whenever they were on guard.

Monday, June 28th. Lisa was getting the food out of the oven while Charlie watched TV. There was a knock at the door. They didn't get many visitors, so Charlie was curious. "I'll get it," he informed Lisa. He turned off the TV and went to answer it. Nothing could prepare him for what happened next. He opened the door and went speechless for a moment. He finally uttered the name of his visitor.

"Robbie."

"Hello, old friend. Haven't seen you in the longest time."

He searched for the proper response, but nothing came to mind. Charlie was dumbfounded.

"Mind if I come in?"

Against his better judgment, Charlie stood back and let his unexpected guest enter his home. Perhaps he had changed for the better over the years. Robbie surveyed the living room with a mild sense of awe apparent.

"Nice place you got here. Lots of space. What's with the wires up there? Got some kind of fancy stereo upstairs?"

"Something like that."

"Can I see it?"

"It's a mess right now... we weren't exactly expecting company."

"Fair enough. Where's the better half?"

Before Charlie could answer, Lisa walked in. Her eyes grew as big as saucers.

"Robbie!"

He smiled. "Hi, Lisa. You haven't aged a bit."

"Thanks. You look good, too."

"I stay in shape."

He did indeed look just as athletic as he did in his prime, perhaps even more so. Charlie remembered seeing prisoners lifting weights on TV.

"You look like a deer in the headlights," Robbie said with a laugh. "You should've seen his face when he opened the door."

"Sorry, Robbie, you're just the last person we would've expected to see," Charlie replied.

His friendliness was certainly surprising. However, the mere fact that he was there was enough to keep Charlie and Lisa on edge. There was an underlying creepiness to his demeanor. Something didn't feel right.

"I guess no one is ever ready to see a ghost from their past," Robbie said with a sly grin.

"The last we knew, you were in prison," Charlie said, unsure if he should bring up the elephant in the room.

"Did you get out early?" asked Lisa.

"Something like that."

Not exactly a reassuring answer.

"Would you like some coffee?" asked the ever hospitable Lisa.

"No, thanks. I don't plan on staying long. Just a quick visit."

He walked over to the bookshelf. He picked up an old picture.

"Now here's a blast from the past-- the three amigos. Charlie, Lisa, and Tracy. Those were the good old days, am I right?"

"Yes, Robbie. A lot of good memories," Charlie said.

He looked at it for a few more seconds before putting it back. He looked at the next picture on the shelf. He turned to them and asked, "Is this your boy?"

"Yeah, that's our oldest. He's about to start college."

"Oh, really? That old already?"

He looked at the picture next to it.

"You have another one?"

"Yes, he's going to be a senior."

"Are they here?"

"Uh, no, they're at work."

"Aw, that's too bad. Good-looking kids. They grow up so fast, don't they? Like they say, 'time flies when you're having fun.'"

"That's definitely true," Lisa said.

His face became more serious. "What happens when you're not having fun?"

"I-- I don't know."

"Time ticks by slowly. Tick... tock... tick... tock." His face hardened. "For fourteen years." He stepped closer to them. "When you're locked up for that long, there's not much you can do... but think. And think. And think... and think. Then, I started reading. I read the paper. I read all about your dad making the Chargers a big success." He smiled slightly. "'California Cal'... has a nice ring to it. I read all about that till I couldn't stomach it anymore. I was surprised to see you guys make the news a few times. How you started that school for all the cripples and retards."

"That kind of terminology..."

"I don't care. You guys became do-gooders. Heroes of the community." He paused. "I was the local hero once. I used to make the paper."

"We were really proud of you, too. Weren't we, Charlie?"

"Yeah, we kept a scrapbook."

"The headlines changed, didn't they? Weren't so proud of me anymore, I bet."

"We were shocked and felt terrible for you."

"Oh, yeah? Felt terrible for me? Did you ever come visit? Did you check to see how I was doing?"

"No, we didn't," Charlie replied. "I'm sorry, Robbie. That was our mistake. We should've been better friends to you."

"You just kept on going like I didn't exist. You just kept on living your perfect little lives with your perfect kids and perfect jobs in this perfect house without a care in the world."

Charlie answered, "Do you really think that we never have any problems? Do you really think that life is perfect? We have worked hard to get where we are and overcame obstacles that you don't know about."

"I worked hard, too! Baseball was my life! All it took was that cheater Tyson Fredericks to ruin everything. It was all downhill from there."

Lisa said, "We're really sorry that he hurt you, and it isn't fair, but everything you did after that was your own fault. You chose to drive drunk. You chose to attack Tyson. Actions have consequences, and your actions rightfully put you in prison."

"Well, see, that's just it. I did a lot of thinking about that. Sometimes it's not your own actions that have consequences. Like Tyson..." he turned to Charlie. "... or you."

"What do you mean by that?"

"This perfect life you have, the one where you're married to Lisa... you're living the life that I was meant to have." He gritted his teeth. "You stole her from me."

"Nobody stole anyone. Charlie and I were meant to be together," Lisa interjected.

"Then why did everything get worse without you? You hurt me more than you think. I had fourteen years to think about it, and another five before that. Almost twenty years of hurt and disappointments and anger and hate! *Twenty years!* A wasted life! Well, I'm tired of wasting time and never having things work out the way I want it to. It's time I started taking control of my life again. It's time I started having fun again."

"You're scaring me, Robbie."

"I think it's time for you to leave," Charlie said firmly.

"Don't worry; this won't take long."

"Lisa, call the police."

"I'm not afraid of the police. My future is already set. Why do you think I escaped? They'll eventually catch up with me and I'll be locked up for the rest of my life. Might as well go back knowing that I accomplished something for once."

"It doesn't have to be this way. You can--"

"Oh, but it does. It has to be this way. It will be very satisfying. I already had a warmup. She was too easy. The two of you will be more fun."

"Who are you talking about?"

"Who do you think?"

"Tracy?!"

Robbie made an evil grin.

"What did you do?!"

"Relax. I held back a little."

"What did you do?!"

Lisa said, "Charlie, look at his sleeve... there's blood."

Charlie couldn't hold back his rage. He punched Robbie so hard that he fell to the floor. Lisa gasped and grabbed Charlie by the arm.

Robbie felt his jaw. "Whoa! Nice one, nerd! I didn't know you had it in you. I'm a little proud of you." He stood up and took a gun out of his pocket and pointed it at Charlie. "But, you really shouldn't have done that."

Charlie pushed Lisa to the side to keep her out of the line of fire. Their hearts pounded like drums.

Charlie held out his hands. "Easy, Robbie. Let's slow down. It doesn't have to be this way. You can just leave here now and we won't call the police. We'll act like nothing ever happened."

"Aww. Where's the fun in that?"

Lisa kicked Robbie in the armpit, causing him to drop the gun. He turned to her and she said, "Did I ever mention that I'm a black belt in Tae Kwon Do?"

"Aren't you just full of surprises?" he quipped as he walked toward her.

"Don't you dare touch her!" Charlie yelled.

"What are you gonna do about it?" Robbie asked with a chuckle. He turned around to see Charlie pointing the gun at him. "Oh. I see."

Charlie had never held a gun before, nor was he a violent person by any stretch of the imagination. Even when he was bullied and attacked by Amanda as a kid, he never fought back. No matter how angry it made him, no matter how many other challenges came up in his life, Charlie tried very hard to obey the Biblical teachings of turning the other cheek. This time was different. A man escaped prison for the sole purpose of doing them harm, possibly of a permanent nature. This was far worse than anything Amanda could dish out. It was one thing for his life to be threatened, but coming after his wife?

"You wouldn't shoot me," Robbie said.

"Don't give me a reason to."

He stepped closer to him. "It's one thing to throw a punch, but I don't think you're capable of shooting me."

"Don't underestimate what I'm capable of."

Robbie took another step towards him.

Charlie said, "I'm going to give you another chance to leave."

"I can't do that," Robbie said.

"Then, you give me no choice."

"Do you think I have anything left to lose? Bring it on, Professor!"

Lisa broke a vase on the back of Robbie's head, stunning everyone. She was surprised that it didn't knock him out.

"Why didn't that work? It always works in the movies!"

"I've always been hardheaded."

He started to lunge towards Lisa, but stopped. He quickly turned to Charlie to wrest the gun from his hand. Robbie punched Charlie in the jaw with his free hand.

"How does that feel? Huh?!"

The two men still held a firm grip on the gun pointed upward.

Lisa chopped Robbie in the neck.

"AAAHHH!!" he cried out.

She kicked his knee, causing him to lose his balance. He and Charlie fell over. The gun fired. Lisa screamed.

"Stay back, Lisa!!" Charlie warned her.

She tried to think of what else she could do to help as she watched them grapple on the floor. Robbie was on top, but Charlie put up a good fight. Each of them took turns hitting each other with their free hands. She went to the kitchen.

"You really think you're something, don't you?" Robbie taunted Charlie. "You say that you worked for everything, but I think you're spoiled. You haven't had your dreams taken away from you."

"I don't go around blaming everyone else for my problems. I conquer them." He punched his side again.

Lisa came back and Charlie said, "Lisa! I have an idea!"

She got closer. He motioned with his eyes towards the gun.

"Pretend there's a spider."

"What are you talking about?" Robbie asked.

She stomped his hand. Both of them groaned from the pain.

"Do it again!" Charlie said.

"But, it hurts you!"

"Just do it!"

She did it again and both men loosened their grip. She took the gun and pointed it at Robbie.

"Get up."

"I'd listen to her if I were you," Charlie told Robbie.

"You wouldn't shoot me," he said as he got up. Charlie rose to his feet as well.

"Like you said, I'm full of surprises."

Charlie added, "Trust me, she's not kidding."

Robbie laughed. "I just fought him over that gun. You really think I can't get it out of your hands? I'm twice your size."

"Is this what you used on Tracy?"

"Didn't need to," he said with a smirk. "But, you guys have me outnumbered. She wasn't the scrapper that you are."

She tried to hold back tears. She wasn't going to let him see her cry. "Move away from the door," she ordered.

Robbie and Charlie moved away as Lisa moved towards the door. Robbie kept his hands out while Charlie kept a close eye on him from behind.

"You were a good man once," she lamented. "I used to care about you. How could you do this?"

"I tried to be a good man. It just wasn't the life I was given. So I accepted my role. And now, I have to finish what I started."

She opened the door and threw the gun out. "I'm tired of that thing," she stated as she shut the door.

Charlie hoped she had a plan. She did, just not the way he expected.

She moved further into the living room. She positioned herself into a long stance with her fists closed. She stared Robbie down with fire in her eyes and said, "Come at me." Charlie smiled.

Robbie barreled toward her with his fist flying, but was met with a rapid series of punches and kicks that left him stunned before he could even come close to making contact. He took a couple of steps back. Charlie tapped him on the shoulder. He turned around only to receive a mean right hook from Charlie. Robbie was truly dazed. He fumbled and fell face first on the coffee table.

"Nice work, Rocky!" Lisa exclaimed to Charlie.

"That's nothing compared to you, Bruce Lee!"

Robbie growled and got up. He picked up the coffee table and started to swing it like a bat towards Lisa. She got into a stance once again.

"Oh, no you don't!" said Charlie. He grabbed the table from behind Robbie and pulled it towards him to hit him in the head. It worked, but they both fell down backwards with the table.

Lisa gasped. "Are you okay?"

"Yeah, I'm all right." He stood up. "I've gotta say though, that's one high quality coffee table we have there. It holds up way better than they do in the movies."

Lisa quipped, "Well, we *are* more sci-fi than action."

Robbie started to get up. "That's it. No more playing around. You two are dead."

Lisa ran towards the couch and quickly jumped onto the edge and back off with a flying kick to Robbie's face. He fell over as she was landing on her feet.

"Sometimes I really can't believe I'm married to you," Charlie said with a smile. "That was spectacular!"

Robbie was angrier than ever. He started to get up again.

"I can kick your butt all night," Lisa taunted. "But, if it makes you feel more like a man, why don't you go get your gun?"

"Are you serious?" Robbie scoffed.

"Yeah, we'll wait."

"Are you crazy?!" Charlie nearly shouted.

Lisa said, "A little bit."

Robbie chuckled. "Stupid is more like it. I'll be right back."

As he went outside, Charlie looked at Lisa and asked, "Have you completely lost your mind?"

"Wait for it..."

They watched from the cracked door as he picked up the gun. Suddenly, red and blue lights flashed and sirens blared.

"About time," she said. "I called them when you two were wrestling over the gun."

They hugged.

"DROP YOUR WEAPON AND PUT YOUR HANDS ON YOUR HEAD!" an officer commanded.

Robbie complied. Charlie and Lisa went outside, knowing that they would need to give them a statement. As Charlie began to explain what happened to an officer, Lisa had a phone call.

"I have to take this; I think it's related."

The officer nodded.

"Tammy! What's going on?"

"Something happened to Tracy. We're in the ER now. She said Robbie did it. You guys might be in trouble, too."

"We just had a tussle with him ourselves."

"Oh, no! Are you okay?!"

"We outnumbered him. Don't worry-- they just cuffed him and put him in the police car."

"Thank God. I was scared for you guys." She sniffled. "I'm still scared for Tracy. He really did some damage."

"We'll be there as soon as we can. Hang in there, sweetheart."

"Okay." She started to cry. "I'll see you later."

Lisa told the officer, "That was confirmation from Tammy Whitson that he assaulted her sister Tracy. She's in the ER. They knew that he was coming after us next. He was out to kill us."

"We'll make sure to get a statement from them as well," the officer replied. "That does help to know. The gun also matches the one reported by a pawn shop as stolen earlier." He looked over at Charlie again and asked, "Do you need a doctor? Looks like he got a few good pokes in."

He rubbed his jaw, "Naw, I'll be okay. Maybe a dentist later. Don't worry-- the two of us gave him worse."

"Glad to hear that. I won't keep you much longer. Just a few more questions."

Lisa said, "Just make sure that he doesn't hurt anyone else again."

"You got it, Ma'am. You have my personal guarantee."

When they arrived at the hospital, Zachary and Lee hugged them in the waiting room.

"How could anyone do this to our sweet girl?" Lee asked. "She would never hurt anyone. She has devoted her life to helping people. She's an angel." She began to cry. Lisa held her tighter.

"Something in him just snapped," Charlie replied. "He was out to kill us. As soon as he mentioned hurting Tracy, I busted him in the jaw."

"Good job, son," said Zachary. "I wish I could've seen that."

"We fought back," added Lisa. "The police have him now. He won't do this again."

"Why did he do it at all?" Zachary asked.

"We haven't really had time to process it yet," answered Charlie. "From what we gathered from him, in his mind, we were all to blame for all the bad things he went through and he wanted revenge."

"He just went nuts," Lisa succinctly summarized it.

Tammy walked in. She hugged Charlie and said, "Told you he was no good."

"You always were a smart kid."

She looked up to him with tears in her eyes and said, "I'm so glad you're okay."

"You should've seen him when we got done with him."

She smiled. "Right on."

He kissed her cheek. They let go and she hugged Lisa.

"Where are the boys?"

"They're staying with Grandma tonight when they get off work."
They let go.
"It's time to go see her," Lisa said.
"Be prepared. She's tough to look at."
"Thanks for the heads up."

As they entered Tracy's room, they saw what Tammy meant. Her left arm and leg were both in casts. Her left eye was swollen shut and bruised. Her lip was also swollen. It was hard to see someone they loved in so much pain.

"Don't try to hug me," she said with a weak voice. "Two of my ribs are broken, too."

"Holy cow, Tracy," Lisa said as she held her right hand. "How could he do this to you?"

"He gave up on a future, so he's still living in the past. We moved on, but he didn't."

Charlie said, "You're lucky he didn't use the gun."

"What? He had a gun? Did he shoot you?"

"He would have, but we got it away from him. He was going to kill us."

"He was no match for Charlie's right hook," Lisa said.

"Or, Lisa's Tae Kwon Do. You should've seen her. She was like Bruce Lee and Jackie Chan rolled into one."

Tracy smiled. "That's good. Serves him right."

Charlie put his left hand on hers. "The good guys won tonight. He's not going to hurt anyone ever again."

She nodded. They stayed silent for a few seconds just holding hands. Then, Tracy said, "You still have that bracelet on."

"I've never taken it off," Lisa said.

"Purple is my favorite color, you know."

"Blue is mine," Charlie added.

Lisa gasped. "My goodness... I never thought of that. My two closest friends are represented in my bracelet. Blue and purple intertwined around my wrist." She held Charlie's hand with her free hand. "A perfect circle, a perfect bond that can never be broken. No matter how many years go by, no matter what happens, nothing and nobody can tear us three apart."

A tear ran down Tracy's cheek. "I love you guys."

Charlie and Lisa began to tear up also. It was hard enough to hold back already. "I love you, too," they both said.

They paused for another moment.

"We should let you get some rest," Lisa offered.

"Okay," Tracy said.

She started to walk away.

"Just one more thing," Charlie told Tracy as he took her hand by both hands and crouched down closer to her. "Remember when we were kids and you said that you believed in me?"

"Of course I do. I've told you that many times since then."

"Remember when you said that you knew I was going to do something important? That you could just tell?"

"Yeah," she said with a slight smile, "I remember it like it was yesterday. I've been so proud of you."

"I still believe in you, old friend," he whispered.

Her lip quivered and her eye began to water.

He continued with tears of his own, "Hang in there. We're about to do something important."

"For me?"

"Who better?"

He kissed her hand.

Charlie and Lisa went home completely exhausted. They still hadn't eaten supper. Lisa heated up the food as Charlie cleaned up the broken vase and set the living room back in order. The picture of the three amigos had fallen on the floor during the scuffle. Charlie picked it up. The frame was shattered. It was hard to see his favorite picture in such an awful condition. It felt like something sacred had been destroyed. He carefully removed the picture from the glassy remains. Just as in real life, under the terrible damage done to his friend was still a beautiful person.

"I believe in you. Whatever the heck it is that you're going to do, I know that you're going to do something important. I can just tell."

"What do you mean?"

"I believe in you. You're one of the good guys."

"So are you. You said that I helped you a lot, but you helped me a lot more."

"How did I help you?"

"You were a friend to me when nobody else would be, except Lisa. You've been kind to me all along. Even now, you're telling me that you believe in me just when I need to hear that. But, let me tell you something. I believe in you, too."

"Why me?"

"Because you're you. You're a kind and thoughtful friend. You say that you think I'm going to do something important someday, but I say that you already are."

"I don't know about that..."

"I do. You're a real friend. That's a hard thing to find."

"Tell ya what. What if I keep believing in you and you keep believing in me? How does that sound?"

"Sounds perfect."

"I love you, Charlie—as a friend, of course."

"I love you, too—as a friend."

Charlie wiped tears from his eyes.

After eating supper they gathered in the living room. It was time to talk about the night's events.

"I'm going to be very honest about this, Lisa. I hope we're thinking the same thing. If we're waiting to know it when we see it..." He choked up. "...we just saw it."

"Are you sure?"

"Are you not? This is Tracy we're talking about here. She's not just our oldest friend, she's the closest thing to a sister either one of us has ever had. Our kids call her 'Aunt Tracy.' She's been there for everything. She's family, Lisa." His eyes overflowed. "What did you say when we were kids? We have to look out for family. We didn't look out for her. She's our sister. You couldn't ask for a more noble purpose than this."

She held his hand.

"It's not that I don't understand where you're coming from or disagree with you, I just want to make absolutely sure that this is what we're going to do. I've been convinced for years that we needed to find your dad."

"The fact of the matter is, we don't know what happened to him. We only know a date. We don't know the circumstances or a time. We could make a good guess and be completely wrong and really mess up the past thirty years. There's just too much that we don't know about it. Even the police couldn't find anything. But, *this* we know. *This* is obvious. We can fix this."

"How? Do we go back to earlier tonight and stop Robbie before he gets to her?"

"No. If we stop him, he will find another way. We would only delay the inevitable."

"So, what do we do? Go back further and keep him from getting hurt in the game?"

"That's more like it."

"No," Lisa said while pondering. "That's not enough. The problem runs deeper than that. He didn't get this way by having one injury. There's a bigger problem that needs to be fixed."

"We just have to figure out what that is and how to fix it."

She closed her eyes. "I remember things... I remember things that he told me in the past, things that Tracy talked about as well. The two of us know him better than a lot of others do." She looked him in the eyes. "I know what we need to do. I know where we have to go."

He nodded. "I'm following your instincts."

"We save Tracy..."

"...by saving Robbie," he finished her sentence.

"Everyone deserves a second chance."

Charlie put his hand on her bracelet. "For friendship."

Lisa looked to the picture on the shelf. Charlie turned around and did the same.

She said, "For family."

After a good night's rest, they spent the next day plotting how they would carry out their mission. They went back to the thrift store knowing what to buy this time. That night, they met at Ilene's with the boys.

"I'm sorry to keep doing this, but we have to do this just one more night," Lisa said.

"We'll make it up to you," Charlie promised. "This weekend is the 4th of July. We'll have some good family time like we used to. It's the last holiday until a certain someone goes away to college."

"I'm going to miss our family times," Sammy said.

"Me, too," Elijah chimed in.

"I think we all will," added Ilene. "You guys are all grown up. Time is still moving forward. We have to roll with the changes."

"So, we'd better make this one really count," said Elijah.

"We will," Charlie said.

"We'll see you tomorrow," said Lisa.

Just as they were starting to walk away, Sammy said, "Are you ever going to tell us what this is all about?"

Charlie and Lisa looked at each other and back to Sammy.

"When the time is right," Charlie answered.

"What's wrong with right now?" he asked.

"It's just too complicated right now," Lisa replied. "After this is all over, maybe then we can be a little more upfront. Just hold on a little bit longer. Just trust us."

"Will we get to see the study?" Elijah asked.

Lisa and Charlie exchanged glances again.

"When it's the right time," Charlie confirmed.

The boys nodded.

"One last hug before you go," Ilene said as she stood up.

She hugged each of them and then said quietly, "I know."

"How do..." Charlie started to say.

She took each of them by the hand and looked him in the eyes. "I know. Just be careful, okay?"

"Okay," he said with a nod.

"Now, go be the miracle." She looked at Lisa. "Both of you."

"You got it," she said.

They waved at the boys and Duke again and left. They couldn't figure out exactly how she knew. She may not even be as right as she thought. But, they knew that she knew. Mom was always right.

Wednesday, June 30th, 2004. Charlie and Lisa brought everything they needed to the Shifter, including the Time Vests. Lisa's mind was totally at peace with their objective.

"There's something I've been thinking about lately," she told Charlie.

"Oh? What's that?"

"I was wondering if certain dates have meaning, like it's all a part of a grander scheme."

"I've often wondered that same question myself. I'd say if it did, then this day would be proof."

"Why's that?"

"Have you forgotten what day it is? It's Tracy's birthday."

She smiled. "Happy birthday, Tracy. We gotcha something you'd never imagine."

He laughed.

"Oh! We almost forgot the song," she said. "Beach Boys?"

"She was always a fan of Simon and Garfunkel. I've already taken care of it."

"Of course you have. Like a best friend... or a brother."

He smiled and held out his hand. "Ready for an adventure, Sunshine?"

She took it and stepped into the Shifter with him. "Ready as always, Mr. Blue Sky." She shut the door.

"Time to save our girl."

"Time to shine."

The Shifter hummed to life. The blue energy began to work its way around the sphere. The beautiful sound of "Bridge over Troubled Water" played. Charlie always knew how to pick 'em. Lisa closed her eyes and breathed calmly. Her thoughts took her to another time when she and Tracy shared their love for each other.

"I wish you didn't have to move away. I'm sure gonna miss you, Lisa."

"I'm gonna miss you, too."

"Have you said your goodbyes to Charlie yet?"

"No, not yet. We're gonna wait until right before we leave. I think that's when it will hurt the most, though."

"It won't be the same anymore."

"That's why you have to stick with Charlie. You'll still need each other."

"There's something I never told you. I've always wanted to, but I didn't know how."

"You can tell me anything."

"Before you and Charlie came along, it was hard for me to make friends."

"Why?"

"Because I was different. My mom had it worse than me or Tamika ever did, but there are still some people who make fun of us and call us names. Like there's something wrong with being half Asian. You and Charlie never said anything about it at all, almost like you didn't even notice. That's always meant a lot to me. You were just my friends, no questions asked. So, others started being better about it, too."

"You know what I see when I look at you? My beautiful friend. The sister I always wanted."

"I love you, sister."

"I love you, too, sister."

Lisa and Charlie looked into each other's eyes as the song was reaching its climax. They both had tears.

"If you love someone, anything's possible," she said.

"Love changes everything."

They put their hands on the walls and absorbed the energy.

They both called out, *"TRAAACCCYYYY!!!"*

They were saturated in a blinding blue flash.

They opened their eyes. They smiled lovingly at each other.

"We did it," he said.

"Are you sure?"

They both looked around.

"What?! What happened?!"

They were still inside the Shifter.

"How did that not work?" Lisa asked. "We did everything the same as we practiced."

Charlie took the remote out of his pocket and pushed the button.

"I think we're out of power," he said as the door opened. "Good thing I had this remote or else we'd really be stuck."

"Out of power?"

They stepped out of the Shifter. Sure enough, all the lights and computers were off.

"We must have blown a fuse or something," Lisa suggested. "I'll go check the fuse box outside."

The little light that came through the windows gave her enough to find a flashlight to make it down the stairs. Charlie used another one to search the room for answers. Everything was plugged in properly. Nothing seemed out of the ordinary, just no electricity. He was just as bewildered as he was disappointed. It never was a problem before.

"I don't get it. What could have gone wrong?"

He picked up a vest to see what the clock said. It was still on the time and date that it was before.

"CHARLIE! YOU HAVE TO SEE THIS!"

He hurried down the stairs to see what Lisa was referring to. She stood at the front door with a perplexed look on her face.

"What is it?"

She opened the door. His eyes squinted as he tried to see what she thought was such a big deal.

"Let's step outside," she said.

The answer became clear. Charlie looked at his surroundings almost in a state of shock. He searched for the words, but only two would come to mind.

"Go ahead and say it; I know you want to," Lisa said with half a smile.

She knew him too well.

"Great... Scott."

They looked at the vest. The clock was starting to finally change. It was true that it needed more time to adjust when it had further to go.

"It worked," she said.

The clock read 8:00, January 24th, 1985. They stood in the field... along with their house.

CHAPTER 26

"How did this happen?! This can't be happening! This is bad. This is really, really, really bad." Charlie ranted as he paced the living room.

"Look at the bright side," Lisa said from her seat on the couch. "We made history. We have the first time-travelling house."

"You know what this means? It means that it's historically bad."

"Charlie, come on. You're making me dizzy. Sit down and let's talk about this rationally. Maybe we can figure this out."

He plopped down next to her with a sigh. "Okay. Let's sit on this couch that shouldn't be here in a house that shouldn't be here and figure out what went wrong."

"Hey, we just survived a murder attempt and went back in time. I think we can handle this."

He looked into her eyes. How could she be so calm?

"Okay," he said. "I looked at all the wires and nothing seemed out of place. The machine obviously worked..."

"...it just worked a little *too* well."

"I don't get it. We tried this several times without any trouble."

"It's like the energy got outside the walls of the Shifter."

"That's exactly what it's like. But, that's not possible. The walls are solid."

"Maybe we should take another look."

They went upstairs to examine it again. Charlie knocked on the sphere.

"Like I said, solid."

"I don't see any crack. And, we had the door shut all the way, right?"

"Of course. Remember how I opened it with the remote?"

"That's true. I'm absolutely baffled."

Charlie's eyes widened. "In all the excitement, I almost forgot." He walked over to the video camera on the tripod. "I recorded it so we could see ourselves time travel later."

"That's great! Maybe we can get some kind of clue from the tape."

"One problem with that-- we have no way to watch it. No power means no video. What a cruel twist of irony. We actually have a TV and VCR with us, and yet we can't use them."

"The crystal! Maybe it can power it up enough to watch it."

"Worth a shot."

They took the crystal out of its position at the bottom of the Shifter. The blue looked extremely pale.

"Something's not right," Lisa said.

"I was afraid of this. The energy is totally depleted. After all the testing we did, moving the house nineteen years backwards took too much out of it. Our situation just got more complicated."

"What about the vests? Couldn't we use those crystals?"

"We have it programmed to bring us back to our time. If we do get it to work again, then we'll need that energy for that purpose. It would be better not to use it if we can help it."

"You're right. Maybe we should just concentrate on the mission first."

"If we don't restore power to the crystal and the machine, then we have a bigger problem than this mission. Without the crystal or any electricity, the vests won't get the message to send us back. We'll be stuck here."

"And, even if the vests did get us back, we still have the house with the machine here."

"Now you're getting it."

"We can still do what we came for."

"This is going to have to take priority. We can always come back and try again."

"I don't see why we can't do both."

"Don't you see, Lisa? We're only supposed to fix a couple of problems in the past. It's bad enough that we came back to the time when we were about to get together. It's going to be tricky enough to not interfere with our past. But, now we have a major change that could affect others."

"How could it affect others?"

"Think about it. Someone's driving down the road on their way to work just like any other day. They go past this field that they've seen a thousand times. Then suddenly, they realize on their way home that there's this two-story house that didn't used to be there. Something like that doesn't just happen overnight."

"I can see why that would raise a few eyebrows."

"It's worse than that. What if someone gets curious? What if someone wants to come check out this oddity? It might even make it to the news."

"That really is a problem. Hopefully no one will notice."

"Yeah, hopefully they won't... but, they might. The longer this house is here, the bigger the risk that someone will find it, whether or not we're in it." He motioned to the Shifter. "And, the bigger the risk that someone finds this."

She nodded. "You're right. We're Protectors. We have to keep that from happening. So, what do we do first?"

"First, we have to somehow find out what's on this tape. If we know what caused it, then we can change it."

"Right. Let's head downstairs and sit down. I think the fatigue is starting to catch up."

As they descended the stairs, Charlie said, "We might want to crack the blinds open a little to get some sunlight in here. We don't want to run the batteries down on these flashlights."

"Good thinking. We're going to need them when it gets dark."

"Whew. Let's sit down first."

They sat on the couch feeling more tired than they should have.

"Weren't we supposed to just feel a little fatigued and sleep for awhile?" asked Lisa.

"Yeah, that's the way I took it from what the notebook said."

"Maybe we should go lie down in the bed."

She just stared at him.

"What's wrong?" he asked.

"I can't move my legs."

His eyes widened. "Neither can I!"

"I can't move my arms."

He pointed his finger. "It's the fatigue! It's actually worse than we thought." His arm fell.

Lisa's speech became slurred. "It's more like..."

"...pawawysif," Charlie slurred as he tried to say "paralysis."

Their limp bodies fell over as they fell asleep.

"Charlie, wake up."

"Huh? Mom?"

Charlie woke to find himself on the floor in a puddle of drool. He tried to recall what happened to bring him to this peculiar situation. He slowly sat up. His mom wasn't there. He saw Lisa on the couch in a position that only a chiropractor could appreciate. He carefully stood up. He got a bit dizzy and caught himself. His stiff legs inched over to Lisa.

"Lisa, wake up."

"Uhnnn." She moaned. "I don't wanna go to school."

"No, Lisa. We're not going to school. Wake up. You're at home."

She opened her eyes. "Charlie." She wiped her mouth and stretched. "Ow. What happened?"

"We fell asleep. The time travel effects caught up with us."

"Aw, man. That wasn't a dream?"

"I'm afraid not. Come on, we have work to do and we've lost a lot of time."

She stood up. "Whoa," she said as she wobbled. Charlie caught her.

"Don't worry. That will get better."
They popped their necks and backs at the same time. "Whew," they both said in unison as they felt relief.
"What time is it?" asked Lisa.
She looked at her watch out of habit.
"You can't go by that. It's a different time here."
She looked at her phone.
"No cell phone service, either. They didn't have cell towers in 1985," he reminded her.
"Oh, yeah. It's all coming back to me now."
Charlie picked up the time vest and said, "It's 12:45 PM on January 25th."
"Oh, so we slept for a few hours. No wonder why I'm so hungry."
Charlie gasped. "No, we didn't sleep for a few hours. It's the 25th. We slept for over a day."
"Holy cow! Okay, so we really have lost some time."
"It will be okay. At least we already accounted ahead of time for some time lost due to what just happened and needing to walk to town to get a rental car. Maybe we should go ahead and eat something real quick before we do that. But, first, let's synchronize our watches."
They set their watches to the correct time.
"I'll see what we have to eat," Charlie said as he headed for the kitchen.
Lisa began opening blinds. "Hey, Charlie..."
He wondered what it could be this time. He went back to Lisa.
"One of our problems is solved," she said.
They went outside.
"Okay, so I get that the carport is attached to the house, but how did the car come along, too?"
Lisa pointed down. "It's on the slab, which runs up against the house."
"So there's still a good possibility that the plumbing and wiring are intact under the house, just not hooked up."
"Probably so."
"Good to know. So, we just saved some time and energy with this little surprise. Let's go back in and figure out what we're doing."

As they looked through the kitchen for food, it became clear to them that no matter how much history they might change as scientists, they would always be domestic partners in search of what to eat.
"We need to get a cooler to save this food from going bad," Lisa said as she looked in the fridge.
"We could almost put it outside. It's cold enough."

"Yeah, we're going to have to get a motel like we originally planned. It's going to be freezing cold here. Plus, we kind of need plumbing."

"Hopefully, we won't need to do that for too long."

They made sandwiches and sat down at the table.

"So, how do we watch this tape?" asked Lisa.

"We need to find someone with a VCR. We didn't have one yet."

"We did! We could take it to our house."

"Not if Annie is home."

"What day is it?"

"Friday."

"Great! She always goes grocery shopping on Fridays."

"We'll just have to see if she's home or not. Hopefully, we'll catch a break."

After quickly finishing their lunch, they drove to town.

"If Mom is gone, then you can use my key to sneak in the back. I'll keep a lookout."

"You have to keep your distance. The second she sees the car parked there, it's already too late."

"Especially since we're driving her old station wagon. Well, not old to her."

"Exactly. We have to figure out a better way."

"I know! I'll drop you off and go to the grocery store myself. It's not very far. I can keep an eye out for her there. When she starts to leave, I can call the house from the payphone to give you a heads up."

"That will give me just enough time to sneak out the back and walk down the block where you can pick me up. Sounds like a plan. I think this will work."

"As long as the tape actually shows something."

"Let's pray that it does."

When they arrived at the Duvall house, they saw that the station wagon was indeed gone.

"Perfect timing," remarked Charlie.

"Of course, we don't know how long she's been gone. She might have just left or she's on her way back."

"We have no time to lose."

They drove up to the alley. Charlie got out and brought the key, camera, and cords with him. Lisa switched to the driver's seat.

"See you soon," she said right before driving away.

Charlie looked around him nervously. No neighbors in sight. He swiftly and quietly unlocked the door and entered the house. He made his way to the living room. At least he was in familiar territory.

"Okay, let's see what we have here."

He picked up the TV remote while making a mental note to put it back exactly the way he found it. He turned on the TV. A soap opera was playing. Charlie rolled his eyes. He took the video out of the camera and tried to put it in the VCR. There was another tape inside.

"You've gotta be kidding me. She's recording this. Not you, Annie. When did you become a soap fan?"

In the meantime, Lisa arrived to the store. She ducked down as much as she could in case someone recognized her. Sure enough, the station wagon was there. When she finally found a place to park, it was too far to see the car or even have a clear view of the entrance. She knew that she would have to go in. She found sunglasses in the glovebox. She looked in the mirror. It still didn't seem like enough to conceal her identity. She pulled her hair back. Still not enough. What Robbie said was true-- she didn't age much in the past nineteen years. What would ordinarily seem to be a blessing was more like a curse in this particular scenario. She looked at the back seat to find anything that could help.

"No wonder why you couldn't find your jacket, Elijah. If you put things back where they're supposed to go..." She reached back and grabbed the black hoodie. "But, I'll let it slide this time."

Meanwhile, Charlie plugged in the camera and rewound the tape. He switched the TV input knowing that it wouldn't interfere with Annie's program. At least he had the foresight to bring the extra cord. He connected it from the TV to the camera. When the tape was finished rewinding, he played it back. He turned the volume of the TV down while noting where it was before. He watched as he and Lisa stepped into the Shifter and the door was shut. Simon and Garfunkel began playing as the energy started circling the sphere. He carefully scrutinized the image on the screen, looking for anything that appeared contrary to their intent. As the video progressed, he didn't spot anything unusual. When it finally came to the point of time travel, it still appeared to work perfectly fine, with the exception of the entire room becoming enveloped in blindingly bright, blue energy. Then, the image became mostly dark. Charlie shook his head.

"I have to watch that again."

Lisa stood at the entrance of the store wearing her son's black hoodie and sunglasses. Her beautiful blonde hair was completely concealed as well as half her face. She took a deep breath.

"Let's do this."

After walking into the store, she paused for a moment. "Mr. Sandman" by The Chordettes played overhead. She snickered.

"It's almost like they knew I was coming," she said to herself. She officially felt like she'd stepped back in time.

As she proceeded, the smell of fried chicken in the deli caught her nose. The recent addition of a video rental department had posters of "The NeverEnding Story," "Robin Hood," and "Sixteen Candles." Familiar logos of bread, soda, and even the store itself were back to the way she remembered them from her youth. Prices were much lower. The store's very layout was different than what she'd grown accustomed to. The employee uniforms had gone through changes as well with everyone wearing aprons. It was truly a blast from the past. She kept her head down and avoided eye contact as much as possible while she searched for her mom.

"Need any help finding something?" a friendly worker asked.

"No, I'm fine," she quietly answered as she swiftly walked by.

And there she was. Annie was inspecting the meat section. Lisa thought fast and grabbed a newspaper ad on a nearby stand. She held it up to her face and pretended to look at the sales. She took a peek at her mom. Seeing her in her thirties again was surreal. She was beautiful and lively. Annie clearly had no clue that she would become a grandparent in a little over a year. It suddenly occurred to Lisa that they were the same age. *"Holy cow. She's young and I'm getting old,"* she thought. Annie made her selection and put it in the cart. It was nearly full. Lisa knew that there wasn't much time left. Annie continued her shopping while Lisa hid her face again. She stealthily followed after her.

Charlie played the video again and stood closer to the screen. The cause of their predicament still wasn't clear. He rewound it to the last minute, thinking that what he was looking for must be in those final moments. Again and again he watched that last minute. Then, he noticed something. He rewound it again and slowed down the speed.

"AHA!"

He did it again... and again and paused.

"Now I'm onto something."

Lisa kept her distance as she carefully observed Annie.

"Excuse me, Sir?" she heard her say. "Could you do me a favor?"

Lisa looked around and noticed that no one else was in the aisle. She was actually talking to her. At least the hoodie tricked her into thinking that she wasn't her daughter. But, a male was completely unexpected.

"You're a little taller than me. Could you get this down for me?"

Lisa really wasn't that much taller, but she was still the taller of the two. Her heart beat faster. Could she really act her way into fooling her own mom that she was a man? She would have to find out post haste. She set the paper aside and held her head down, hoping that the hood would disguise her face a little bit more than it probably did. She walked towards her mom with a slightly exaggerated masculine gait.

"It's this one on top," Annie informed her.

Lisa stretched the arm closest to her mom towards the shelf, blocking any clear look at her face.

"The one on the right," Annie guided her.

Lisa grabbed it and gave it to her.

"It's my daughter's favorite cereal. She would disown me if I forgot to get some more. Thank you very much."

"No problem," Lisa replied in her husky Dad voice that she used when playing with dolls as a kid. She surprised herself. After Annie walked away with her cart, Lisa breathed a sigh of relief. "That was way too close!"

She picked up the paper again and continued in her guise. She walked down the aisle and around the corner.

"Are you finding everything okay?" another employee asked.

"Uh huh," she answered simply.

She saw her mom get in line for the checkout. She knew that it would buy her a little time to call Charlie and get the heck over to the house.

"I can help you over here," another cashier offered.

Annie changed to another lane with no one ahead of her.

"Oh, snap," Lisa said as she saw the speed of the cashier. She made her way out the door. She dug some change from her pocket and put it in the slot on the payphone.

"Oh, John!"

"Oh, Marsha!"

Charlie sat enthralled by the soap opera. He considered making popcorn, but knew that the smell would be noticeable. The phone rang. He abruptly shut off the TV and ran to the kitchen. He started to reach for the phone, but stopped.

"What if it's not Lisa? Someone else could be calling for Annie. Better not take any chances."

The phone rang again. He cleared his throat and picked up the receiver. In his best feminine voice, he said, "Hello?"

Lisa cocked her head back. "Charlie? Is that you?"

"Yes," he answered. He cleared his throat again and repeated in his usual voice, "Yes."

"Why are you talking like that? Never mind; it's not important right now. Mom is in the checkout *right now!* It won't be long, so I'm coming to get you right away. Please tell me that you found something."

"Okay, Lisa. I did find something. I'll explain later."

"Okay. Just get out of there!"

"I'll meet you down the block."

"Perfect. See ya."

She hung up the phone. Out of curiosity, she decided to peek in and see how close it was until her mom was done checking out. She did have a lot of things after all. She walked back in and looked towards the registers. She felt a hand on her shoulder.

"Come with us," she heard a man say.

Her stomach sank. She turned around to find three managers. They escorted her to a nearby office.

Charlie already had his stuff ready to go before Lisa called. He went back to the living room to get them. First, he turned the TV back on and adjusted the volume back to where it originally was. He shut it off and set the remote back to where he found it. He picked up his stuff and went out the back door, carefully locking it and making sure that no one saw him. He began to walk away.

"We've been watching you," one of the managers said. "You've been acting suspiciously."

"I didn't do anything," she said in her real voice.

"What's in your pockets?"

"You think I'm a shoplifter? I've never stolen anything in my life! Here, look." She started emptying her pockets. "Keys, some change, just standard pocket stuff."

"Why are you wearing that hood?" asked another manager.

"Because I'm cold."

"And the sunglasses?"

"It's too bright in here."

Another one interjected, "Why did you go outside and use the phone and come back in?"

"Because I needed to call my husband. Now, you guys have nothing to accuse me of and no proof of any kind. I know my rights. You can't legally hold me here."

She opened the door.

"Sorry," one of them said.

"Well, you just lost my business, mister." She stepped out and then popped back in. "Your produce section stinks anyway."

She hurried towards the door. Mom was already out of sight. She frantically scanned the parking lot. The bagger was adding the last of Annie's bags to the trunk. Lisa sped to her car and started it up. She was about to back out when she saw someone walking behind the car. "Come on, come on!" she said. As soon as they were away, she backed up and took off like she was in a race... because she was. Lisa knew that she had to get far ahead of Annie so that she wouldn't spot the very same car with her own daughter driving it. If she were to drive by Charlie walking down the road, that would have also been a terrible inconvenience-- especially if Charlie mistook who was driving. It was too late. Annie was ahead of Lisa. She kept thinking that her mom might spot her in the rearview mirror.

"Time for a different approach," she said. She took a different road, hoping to catch Charlie on time. "Please, please be walking this way and not the other."

She saw Annie cross the intersection up ahead, the one right before the house. Lisa took another right.

"Charlie!" she said as she rolled down the window. "Get in quick!"

He got in and they took off again.

"I was wondering why it was taking so long," he said. "I had to turn around and start walking this way in case you were coming from a different direction."

"Thank God you did. You don't know how close that was."

Lisa started to drive back home. As they reached their street, Charlie asked, "What are you doing?"

"Oh, right! I just went this way out of habit. I guess I'm still pretty frazzled." They slowly drove past their house. "It's so weird. There's two of them."

"Yes, two houses, two cars, two of you, and two of me. That's why we have to be extremely careful."

"Believe me, I'm convinced."

As they drove home (that is, the one in the field), they told each other what happened.

"That really was close," Charlie said with wide eyes as he exited the car.

"So, let's recap," Lisa said as she did the same. "Yesterday, we time travel with our house, car, and everything we own. Then, we slip into a twenty-eight hour coma. Today, having awoken from our slumber, we set out on a little adventure that gets me almost accused of shoplifting and both of us nearly getting caught by Mom. Boy oh boy, we are off to a flying start."

"It's okay, Lisa. We had some close calls, but everything worked out fine. Now, let's go inside and get the answers we're looking for."

"I could really go for some good news right now."

They went in.

"We need the flashlights and the lantern. I want to make sure that there's enough light to see it," Charlie stated.

After retrieving what they needed, they entered the study.

"We'll need to open the blinds in here, too, just this once."

When they opened the blinds, it occurred to them that this was the first time they had seen the Shifter in the sunlight.

"We really should get the crystal to soak up some rays," Lisa suggested.

"Good idea. It wouldn't hurt for all three crystals to get some sun. Every ray of sunshine can help. But, before we do that, let's keep it in place while we investigate."

"Just what are we looking for?"

"I saw in the video that the energy started to come out at the bottom, like there was a leak."

"I still don't see how that's possible."

"Remember, anything's possible."

He turned on the lantern and knelt on the floor. Lisa followed suit.

"Is that a hole?" asked Lisa.

"Where?"

"Right here, in the floor," she said with a pointed finger.

They got on their bellies to get the closest view that they could.

"You're right. How did that get there?"

They looked up at the machine right above it. Lisa pointed a flashlight on it.

"Is that a crack?"

"I'll be danged. It's just a small one, but a crack nonetheless."

They looked at each other.

"How the heck did that happen?!" Lisa asked. "This is supposed to be bulletproof!"

Then, it dawned on them. "Robbie," they said in unison.

"When I wrestled him for the gun, it went off. With everything that happened, we didn't even think of looking where the bullet ended up."

"Here it is," Lisa said as she found the bullet on the floor. "It must've bounced off the Shifter."

"It was pretty strong for it to go all the way through the ceiling, the floor, and then crack this thing. Imagine what it would've done to us."

"I still don't get it. How could this penetrate it at all? It's supposed to literally be bulletproof. You've seen how strong this stuff is and how hard it was to put it together."

"That's just it. Aluminum oxynitride is some super strong stuff, but we have something even stronger."

"The crystal."

"Exactly. We still don't know just how powerful this thing really is. I think what happened was with all the testing we did, along with adding our weight to it, the energy from the crystal eventually broke down the integrity of the walls it was passing through."

"It weakened it. That makes sense."

"Remember, this was originally meant to be a one-time use thing. We added the vests to the equation, and therefore more testing."

"It's my fault."

"No, it's not your fault. We just underestimated how powerful the crystal really was. I mean, come on. There's really no way we could even research it. There aren't many of us who even know it exists."

They sat up.

"So, what do we do now?" Lisa asked.

"The crack still isn't that big. I think it will hold up for one more trip back."

"Should we fix it?"

"No. We need it to leak the energy and bring the house back with us."

"That's true. That is, if we can get the energy back to the crystal."

"We have no choice but to try." He removed the crystal from the machine and looked at it again. "I have a feeling that it's gonna take awhile."

They brought the ladder over and put the crystal back on top of the Shifter to be near the solar panels.

"It's like a battery that needs to be recharged," said Charlie. "Only this one will probably take a lot longer than just a few hours."

"So, our original mission should move forward."

He nodded. "I agree. It would be for the best. The way things are going, we may not be able to make it back here again. We'd better make this one count."

"We need to get that cooler and the motel room. We're going to need a place to make some calls."

"Right. We still need to get a rental car, too. I think it will come in handy to have two cars. We'll also need a way to still call each other at any time."

She snapped her fingers and pointed. "Beepers. We can send each other messages."

"Good thinking. They did have those at this time. Let's go get the rental and the beepers. Then, we can split up. You can take care of the food and anything else we might need from the house. I'll go get the motel room and go shopping for a generator to get some electricity to this thing."

"Sounds like a plan."

They met again that night at the Chesapeake Motel. It wasn't as nice as their home, but at least they would have heat during the cold winter night.

"I went to every hardware store in town and couldn't find a generator," Charlie said as he slumped on the bed.

"Aw, man."

"You wouldn't know about this, but right before you moved back here, there was a big ice storm. A lot of people lost power. We never did, but at least half of the town did. The stores haven't had any in stock since."

"That's terrible timing for us," she said as she sat next to him.

"Yeah, it is. I'm going to make some calls tomorrow. Surely somebody will have one somewhere. I might even have to go out of town to find one."

"Things were a little easier in 2004, huh? We could've found something on the internet within minutes. I'm starting to really appreciate how good we had it in our time."

"Yeah, we may have gotten a bit spoiled. Not only when it comes to gadgets, but also our basic technologies like electricity."

"Or plumbing. Speaking of which, I'm ready for a shower. This has been a long day."

"Agreed. I think I'm going to unwind with a little TV. Maybe I can find an old show that was on for the first time."

"Sounds good. See ya in a bit."

Charlie started flipping channels. Somehow, he couldn't quite concentrate on the TV. His thoughts wandered into what he was doing at the same time in another location. January 25th, 1985. It didn't take long to realize why this date was significant. Lisa had just finished gathering her stuff to take to the shower.

"Why did you choose this date?" he asked.

"You remember it, don't you?"

"How could I forget?" He turned off the TV.

"It was when I had my first date with Robbie."

"I know. I was there. You don't know how painful that was for me."

"I didn't realize at the time that you loved me. And, I sure didn't know that you worked at Wigner's. If I knew either of these facts, I wouldn't have done the same thing."

"Is that why you chose this date? Did you want to change it?"

She sat down next to him. "A part of me knew that I shouldn't, but a part of me wanted to. If I could prevent a relationship with Robbie, then it could change a lot of things."

"That's exactly why you shouldn't do it."

"I know that now. I realize how much even a small change could have bigger repercussions."

"It was one of the hardest things I'd ever experienced. I was in love with you for years. I finally started to think that I wouldn't see you again, then you came back. I still didn't know what to do about that. I was afraid I would scare you away. Seeing you with someone else was already hard, being the waiter on your first date with him was a punch in the gut. When I left that night, I went to the park. You know that bench that we go to sometimes? That was where I went. I sat there and thought about everything. I prayed and I cried." His eyes began to water. "That was the night that I gave up. I couldn't keep trying. In my mind, Robbie already won. I sunk into a deep depression. The only way I overcame it was by talking to Sam. He convinced me to keep trying."

"I'm sorry, honey. I didn't realize it was that hard on you. I'm sure this has done nothing but bring up those painful feelings."

"It has. But, as painful as it was, it had to happen. As tempting as it might be to change those parts of our lives, as easy as it might seem, it is imperative that we keep our past the way it is. We had to live through it all to get where we are. If we change any of it, it will jeopardize our entire future. Our kids might not even exist. We can only change the lives of our friends in a way that doesn't directly affect us, and pray to God that we're doing right by them. This is a heavy responsibility that we bear. We only get one chance."

"You're absolutely right. I'm so proud of you for always doing the right thing no matter what. It's one of the best things about you. Plus, you have excellent taste in women."

He laughed. "Well, you're not wrong."

"We'll just stick to the main plan I had. I think that will actually work. Just remember one thing."

"What's that?"

"Robbie didn't win." She kissed him. He smiled. "What was meant to be is what happened. That depressed seventeen-year-old was rewarded for his patience. Both of us were."

She stood up and took his hand. She smiled and motioned with her head. "Come hither," she said.

He chuckled. How could he resist?

Saturday the 26th. Charlie and Lisa woke and enjoyed the motel's continental breakfast. When they returned to their room, they discussed the plans for the day.

"None of this is going to be possible to fix overnight. It's going to take a few attempts to make this right," Lisa said. "There's just too much to overcome, and Robbie is stubborn. So, maybe these next couple of days should be more focused on the time travel situation. I can't really do too much just yet until school starts anyway."

"I agree. Let's try to locate a generator and go from there."

"I just had a thought. Why couldn't we use the car battery?"

"It will take a lot more power than the voltage of a car battery to get the machine running again."

"But, we only need to run the machine, not the whole house. Maybe we need more than one battery."

"No, I thought about that. We actually need to run the Shifter and the computers, but it takes all the power we had from the house. Using only a car battery would be like taking a shower with just a few drops of water. We need a heck of a lot more power for a sustained period of time to get everything running properly. A generator is the best solution."

"I see. And what if we can't get enough solar power to energize the crystal?"

"Then we're still stuck."

She shook her head. "At least we can fix the other problem soon." Her eyes widened. "I think I left my diary at the house."

"We'll need that."

"Without that, I won't remember all the details of what happened when. I don't have the perfect memory that you have."

"I didn't even know that you had one until the other day."

"I only used it up until we were together. I kind of outgrew it after that. I wrote down all my thoughts about you, Robbie, pretty much everything. I need to go get it."

"I'll go with you."

"Don't you need to stay and make calls about the generator?"

"I can still do that. A lot of places aren't even open yet."

"Okay. Let's go home."

When they got to the field, they drove up to the house. They started to head for the door when they saw another car drive by.

"We still have another problem to fix," Charlie said. "This house is still visible to anyone driving by. It's just a matter of time until someone gets too nosy."

"You're right. I think I have an idea. Come with me."

They walked up to the street and looked back to the house. There was still a good distance from the road.

Lisa said, "We can't exactly make it invisible, and we can't just put a tarp over it. We have to still obscure the view."

"What do you have in mind?"

"Something that we pass every day-- a billboard."

He smiled. "Yes! A billboard! Anyone who drives by will have their focus drawn to the sign instead of the house."

"If we make it big enough, they might not even see the house at all."

"That's a great idea! Let's measure it."

They went back and got the tape measure. They stood on the road and framed their vision with their hands as a movie director would do. They went back a few feet into the field and measured it.

"There's no way we can completely obscure the view of the house," Charlie said, "but, we can sure draw their attention away for those few seconds. Brilliant idea, Lisa."

"Thank you. One question-- what about the owner of the property?"

"You're right. There has to be someone out there who owns this land. Let's just hope and pray that they don't see it for awhile. We have to make sure that whatever we end up putting on the billboard doesn't trace back to anyone, either."

"True. So, what next?"

"Let's get your diary and head back to town and rent a trailer. Then, you can take me back to the motel where I'll stay and make calls. You can go to the lumber yard and pick up the materials. Then, we'll go build this thing."

"Right on."

After a series of disappointing phone calls, they went to work on building the sign. They tried as best as they could to finish it before sunset. They stood back and looked at their almost finished product.

"All it needs is some paint," said Charlie.

A car drove by from the other direction.

Lisa said, "It just occurred to me that we have this pointed at an angle for only one direction."

Charlie put his hand on his head and said with a sigh, "You're right. It might only do half as good as it should."

They said simultaneously, "We need another one."

When they got back to the motel, Lisa looked again at her diary.

"Tracy called me tonight to see how my date with Robbie went."

"What did you tell her?"

"I didn't really write down many details about that. I don't really remember it that much, either. The diary talks more about the date itself and how I felt."

"How did you feel? What else did you do after the restaurant?"

"We just had dinner and that was it. I had him take me home. Seeing you there just reminded me of how much I really wanted to be with you instead. I was nice to Robbie on the outside, but on the inside, I was very much torn."

"Do you know when Tracy called?"

"It was sometime at night. That's all I really remember."

"Think about it. Was it before or after sunset? What else was going on?"

She closed her eyes and thought about it. "I'm not sure what difference it makes."

"It makes all the difference. If you could call her before she calls you..."

"...then I could discourage her from being interested in Robbie. I just don't know if I can remember it all that clearly. Nineteen years ago was a long time. Plus, I tried to forget some of these things anyway. I was much happier to be with you."

"Memories can be tricky. You don't have to have a perfect memory to recall everything, just something to remind you. The good news is that we're actually here at that time."

"Too bad we can't just go back to my house and jog my memory that way."

"Yeah, we can't do that, but you're on the right track. Being in a familiar environment can trigger those memories. It could be the temperature, a scent, a sound, a visual of some kind. Just keep your eyes closed and concentrate. What was going on that night when Tracy called? What were you doing?"

She squeezed her eyelids tighter and tried to picture it in her mind.

"I think I was doing homework."

"Okay, good. That's a good start. You were at home, right? Were you in your room?"

"I remember talking to her on the phone in my room. But, I was in the other room when she called and I went to my room where it was quieter."

"That's really good, Lisa. That means that there was something noisy. What was making the noise? What room were you in?"

"I was at the dining room table. I think Mom and Dad were watching TV."

Charlie turned on the TV. "Was this what was on?"

"I--I don't know. Doesn't sound familiar."

He turned the channel. "Whatchu talkin' 'bout, Willis?" came from the TV.

"Okay, that sounds right."

"Your parents watched 'Diff'rent Strokes'. Good to know. Was this on at the time, or was it earlier or later?"

"I do remember this being on."

"If it was any later, 'Double Trouble' was on. That was about twin girls."

"I don't remember that."

"I bet a lot of people don't. Anyway, I think it's safe to say that it was around this time."

"I think you're right." She opened her eyes. "I'd better call her before it's too late. Good thing there wasn't any caller ID."

"Hello?"

"Tracy? It's Lisa."

"That's funny! I was just about to call you. What are you up to?"

"Just taking a break from homework."

"Me, too. So, anything else going on? Weren't you going out with Robbie last night?"

"Yes, I did," she said with a giggle.

"What was that like? What did you do?"

"He took me to Wigner's."

"Isn't that where Charlie works?"

"Yeah, he was our waiter. I didn't even know he worked there."

"That must have been kind of awkward."

"Why do you say that?"

"Oh, never mind. Was he nice? Did he pay for the meal?"

Lisa knew that she couldn't talk like he was a jerk only for her to see otherwise at school. The only thing she could do was to tell the truth and hope that it would make her accept that she was with Robbie.

She laughed. "Yeah, he paid. He was really nice. We had some good conversation and laughed a lot. He was a perfect gentleman."

"Man, I'm kind of jealous. I hope I can find someone like that."

"Are you kidding? Of course you'll find someone. You're the best."

"If you say so. What else did you do?"

"We just went out to eat, and then he took me home. That's it."

"Any good night kiss?"

"No, we didn't kiss. I'm not ready for that. We're just getting started. There's still plenty of time."

"It sounds like you want to keep going out with him."

"Yeah, I think I'll see how this goes."

"Well, I'm happy for you. I hope it works out."

"Thanks, Tracy. I have a good feeling about it."
"That's good."
"Well, I'd better get back to my homework."
"Me, too, though I'd rather be doing anything else. Like hugging a cactus."
She laughed. "Yeah, I know the feeling. At least we're coming to the finish line. See ya later, babe."
"See ya."
She hung up the phone and said to Charlie, "I hope that worked. I wonder what she meant by it being awkward?"
"I think I know. She figured out when we were kids that you and I were meant to be together. She knew that I loved you without me telling her. Looking back, I wonder if she knew about you loving me."
"She might have guessed it, but I never told her. I kind of wondered back then if she had feelings for you."
"She did at first when we were little, but she stepped back and let us figure it out."
"She really is a great friend. I wonder if she already has any feelings for Robbie and she's stepping back all over again."
"That's exactly what she's doing. I've seen how she looks at him. That could be one of the reasons why we've always gotten along so well. We have this unspoken thing in common-- hiding our feelings for someone while someone else is with them."
"It's not an easy thing to go through, I'm sure, but we still have to discourage her from being with him. It's for her own safety."
"What happens when the two of us are actually together? Would things still play out the way they already did?"
"Not if my plan for Robbie works. I still can't say for sure what will happen until some questions are answered. The future is still up to him."

Sunday, January 27th. Charlie and Lisa worked all day at building another billboard. When they were finished, they stood back and appreciated their effort.
"I still have no idea what we can paint on this," Lisa said.
"Yeah, that is another complication that we don't need right now. We'll come up with something soon enough."
"At least it's up there. That should do the trick. It will still take the attention from the house even if it's not painted."
"I just had a thought," Charlie said with a bit of panic in his voice. "All this time worrying about people seeing the house... but, we didn't think about the other side of it."
"What do you mean?"

"I mean, while we're here in 1985, the house is missing in 2004."

"We have it programmed to bring us back a minute later."

"Yes, we do... but, that's if it actually works."

"So, we have to get the power back and return to 2004. I know it's a big problem, but we're working on it."

"That's just it, Lisa. It's a bigger problem than we initially realized."

"The house, I know. We didn't bargain on that being a part of the equation."

"Think about it. What if we don't make it back? Or, if we do, what if it's not a minute later? It's one thing for us to being missing for a bit, but an entire house? How could anyone explain that?"

"I see your point. The neighbors would notice." She gasped. "The kids! What are they going to think?! They knew that we were working on something in the study. Mom knows, too."

"Police will be called..."

"It makes the news..."

"It becomes a legend. They make up wild conspiracy theories about us. They might even make movies about it. While we're here in 1985, there's a whole other future happening in 2004 and beyond. One without us in it."

"We removed ourselves from the timeline! It all becomes chaos!"

"Exactly. The longer we're here, the more time is changing in the future as well as the past. It can set off a chain of events that would be hard to set right unless we get back right when we're supposed to. Even if we do, there's still the risk of a paradox."

"How so?"

"Our younger selves might not build the machine. Or, they might build it, but not use it at the same time that we did."

"Yeah, that would be pretty unlikely."

"And very much a problem. We would be trying to get back to an empty space... that might not be empty."

"This is heavy. Maybe this whole thing wasn't such a good idea after all."

"Too late for that now. We have to deal with the situation that we have at hand."

"What should we do? Maybe we need extra help. We could go to Arizona and see The Protector. Maybe we could trade out the crystal."

Charlie shook his head. "No, it's too risky. We'll lose a lot of time on the road when there's still work to do here. If we see The Protector, he won't know who we are. Even if he knows by some kind of spiritual awareness, I don't think he would give us the crystal for one that's totally depleted of power. We're supposed to be Protectors, too. He might see us as unworthy of bearing the responsibility if he sees that we let the crystal be drained."

"You might be right about that. We would also need to make sure that the crystal in the past is exactly the way we need it for the future."

"That's exactly why we can't tamper with the ones planted in the trees, either. Any change like that could throw everything into jeopardy."

"So what do we do? We're already in jeopardy. I don't see any way that we can do anything without it being some sort of risk."

"You're right. Every single thing we do, even our very presence here in this time, is a risk. That includes this idea..."

"Do you know who can help us?"

"There's only one man who can help us now."

He picked up the notebook.

"You mean the one who wrote it? Do we dare?" she asked. "How do we even know where to find him?"

"Everything happens for a reason, Lisa." He looked into her eyes. "I know exactly where he'll be."

CHAPTER 27

Monday, January 28th, 1985. Charlie sat in the rental car across the street from the First Bank of Chesapeake. Unsure of what time the mystery man would be there, he made sure to be there before the bank opened at nine. He kept a careful eye out for him, not even sure who it was or what he would look like. He just knew that he would recognize him if he saw him, especially if it turned out to be himself as he originally theorized. He only used binoculars when the view was a little unclear. Time dragged on slowly as he anticipated this arrival, all the while hoping that no one would get suspicious of his presence across the street.

An hour turned into two and two became three. If he didn't know for sure that this person would be there that day, he would have already given up. His stomach growled. He took out the sandwich that he packed. After finishing his lunch, he waited and watched some more. A few minutes later, he saw a man in a suit step out of a car. He was holding an envelope. Charlie used the binoculars.

"What?! It can't be! That doesn't make any sense!"

He recognized this mystery man, though he could hardly believe his eyes. He waited until he exited the building again.

"I have more questions than I have answers."

"So, did you find him?" asked Lisa when Charlie returned to the motel.

"Yes."

"And?"

He sat on the bed. "It's not who I thought. Or, maybe he is. I don't know. I'm confused."

She sat next to him and put her arm around him. "You look pretty troubled about this. How bad can it be?"

"I just don't know what to think or believe anymore. I didn't expect this."

"Who is it?"

"I can honestly say that I'm not sure anymore."

"Did you talk to him?"

"No. I just watched from the car. I'm still trying to process who he is."

"Maybe I can go with you. Do we even know where to find him again?"

"I have a pretty good idea. I'm going to wait awhile and follow him to see where he goes next. Maybe then we can go see him together. I just want to be sure about something first."

"Okay. Whatever you think is best." She kissed his cheek. "Try not to worry too much about it. This could still be a good thing. We might still get the help we need to get back."

He looked into her eyes. "Or, we might destroy everything else in the process."

They went back to the house. They brainstormed ideas for what to put on the billboard, but Charlie's brain was raging another kind of storm. After awhile, he took her back to the motel. It was time to get to the bottom of the situation.

Three o'clock. Charlie sat in the rental car with sunglasses on to keep his face partially hidden. He didn't have to wait long. He witnessed the same man from the bank get into another rental car and drive away. He carefully followed him. A thousand thoughts clouded his mind as he drove to where he felt in his gut would be their destination. A few minutes later, he was proven right.

Charlie returned to the motel room.

"How did it go?" Lisa asked.

"Just like I thought," he replied, visibly startled.

"Did you talk to him this time?"

"No. I want you to come with me. It's time for some answers."

She grew more concerned. As they walked out the door, Lisa headed for the car.

"We won't need that," he told her.

She made a quizzical face and followed him as they walked around the corner and across the lot to another set of motel rooms.

"He's right here?!" she asked.

"I expected as much," he said.

"I don't think you expected any of this."

"No, but once I saw who he was, then I just knew. But, I still have a lot of questions."

"We don't have to do this now," she said as they stood at the door. "Maybe we're tampering too much with things."

"No, I already know too much. There's no turning back now."

He took a deep breath before knocking on the door. Room 426. The blinds moved in the window.

"Who is it?" asked the voice on the other side of the door.

Charlie and Lisa looked at each other for the right answer. Surely it would be a surprise that he had visitors. She shrugged.

"An old friend," Charlie answered.

The door slowly crept open. The chain still remained on the door. Charlie tried to see through the crack. The other man did the same thing.

He gasped and shut the door. “You can’t be here!” he nearly shouted.

“But, I am.” He quickly thought of a response. “I know that you’re not one to turn away from helping someone. You’ve already helped me a lot...” The chain could be heard to come undone. The door cracked open again. “...Mr. Whitfield,” Charlie continued.

“Sorry, Charlie. I was caught off guard. I didn’t think anyone knew I was here.”

“It’s okay, Mr. Whitfield. We really need to talk to you about something,” Lisa said.

“Who’s that with you?” he asked.

He cracked the door open a little further. Lisa peeked out over Charlie’s shoulder.

“Come on in,” he said as he opened the door. He looked like he’d seen a ghost. Charlie and Lisa walked in and shut the door.

“I’m sorry to surprise you like this, but we’re running out of ideas. You see, we’re in a bit of a jam,” Charlie said.

“W-w-wait a minute,” Sam said with a raised finger. “Something’s not right.” He squinted and looked them over. His eyes widened. “You’re not seventeen, are you?”

They shook their heads.

“You can’t be here! Get out! Get out now!! You could ruin everything!”

He tried to push him towards the door.

“We don’t have much of a choice!” Charlie replied. “We can’t change the fact that we’re here.”

“Well, go do it somewhere else. The risk is too great!”

“Charlie!” Lisa said. She put her hand on Sam’s shoulder. They looked into each other’s eyes. “Charlie.” She smiled. “It *is* you.”

Sam ducked his head and walked towards the bed. She followed him.

The younger Charlie asked, “You were me all along? How could you do it? I trusted you.”

The older Charlie turned back to him. “I did what I had to do. I had to become someone else to get through that stubborn head of yours.”

Charlie chuckled. “I was pretty stubborn back then, I admit. I had no idea that it would take a visit from my future self to talk some sense into me.”

“Well, I’m still trying to do that, in case you’ve forgotten. I’m not done working on your 1985 self. You really shouldn’t be here. It could mess up everything that I’m trying to do.”

"We're going to be careful," Lisa said. "We're going to stay away from our past selves so that we don't ruin it. Believe me, we had some long conversations about even time travelling in the first place. We wouldn't have done it if there wasn't a good reason... a noble purpose, like you said in the notebook."

He chuckled. "The funny thing is, I just put that notebook in the bank today. You really picked an interesting time to go back." His face grew more serious. "Why *did* you go back? Nope, forget it. I don't want to know. I shouldn't know too much about the future. I'll just trust that there's a good reason. There must be something that I left undone." He looked down again and noticed Lisa's ring. "I already know too much. And, just when I wondered if what I was doing was even working."

"Oh, it works," Charlie said. "All of it works. Everything you talked to me about, the time machine, all of it. And, we don't want to interfere. But, there is something I feel compelled to tell you." He stepped up closer to him. "Thank you." Tears came to his eyes. "I know I told you that before... I mean... I told you later... from your perspective...I-I wanted to tell you as Charlie, not as Sam. Not as a character. I wanted to tell you that what you did for me-- for us-- we have never forgotten."

Sam took his hat and glasses off. "I guess I don't need this disguise anymore."

Charlie took out his wallet. "I know that you don't want to know too much about the future and all that. I also know that this whole thing can't be easy for you. Maybe you just need some encouragement. After all, this isn't your future anyway-- it's ours." His lips quivered and the tears increased. "I want you to see just how important it is for you to keep going." He showed him a picture from his wallet. "We named him after you."

The older Charlie tried to hold back his tears, but he couldn't.

Charlie showed him another picture. "Here's our second born, Elijah."

"They're beautiful."

He sat on the bed and wept. Lisa sat next to him and put her arm around him.

The younger Charlie said, "If it wasn't for you, it wouldn't be possible."

"I'm overwhelmed. I didn't expect that at all," he said through his tears.

Lisa said, "What happened, Charlie?" She gently pulled his chin towards her with her free hand. She wiped his tears and caressed his cheek. "There's so much pain in your eyes. What have these beautiful eyes seen?"

He looked down. "I can't tell you."

"What was it?"

"Please, whatever you do, don't make me say it."

"We weren't together where you come from, were we? You came back and fixed it. But, there's something else. Something happened."

He looked into her eyes. "I can't."

"It was me, wasn't it? Something happened. Something so bad that you had to risk everything to fix it. You're the only one who could love me like that." Her eyes filled with tears. "My hero."

His tears returned as he held his head down again.

She said, "I'm going to tell you something that I'm sure you've never heard me say before. I don't care if it messes up anything or what happens. You deserve this. I want you to look me in the eyes when I say this." He looked her in the eyes. "I love you, Charlie. I love you with all my heart."

"I love you, too."

She looked over to the younger Charlie. He nodded his approval. She looked back to him and said, "You deserve this, too." She put her other arm around him and kissed his lips. Though startled at first, he put his arms around her and kissed her back. The younger Charlie felt only a little awkward.

The older Charlie said, "I've gotta say, this was not how I expected the day to go."

Lisa laughed. "I didn't expect to ever see two of you in the same room."

Charlie sat next to his older self. "The reason why we're here is because we really could use your help with a problem."

"What might that be?"

"Let's just say that we figured out a way to go back when we're done with our mission, but things have gone a little caca."

"How much is 'a little caca'?" He held up his hands. "Wait a minute. I probably shouldn't know about this."

Lisa and Charlie exchanged glances. She said, "We're not going to get into the details of why we're here, but we may have a little issue in how we get back."

"I never said anything about that in the notebook. I had a rough idea, but I couldn't quite work out the details. My mind has been a bit Swiss cheesed at times."

"Well, we figured it out," she said. "But, now our situation has become complicated."

He squinted his eyes. "How complicated?"

Charlie said, "Well, we kinda sorta brought back the machine with us..." The older Charlie's eyes grew wide. The younger man continued. "...along with the house."

"WHAT?!?" He stood up and faced them. "The house?!? You brought back the whole house?!? How could you be that careless? I gave you specific instructions..."

"Yes, I know, and we followed those instructions to a tee and tested it out several times, but we still had a mishap that caused the energy to leak out."

The older man paced the floor. "This is great. This is just great. Coming back here to a time when I'm already changing the past and then dropping a house on it is just a lovely, wonderful surprise. I thought I was dealing with Doc Brown, but you really turned out to be Dorothy."

"Hey, it was an accident," Lisa interjected, "cut him some slack. It was beyond our control."

"I suppose this makes me the Wizard who has to provide a way to get you back to where you belong. You can't just click your heels this time."

"I get that," said Charlie. "And, we're working on it. The biggest problem we have is with the crystal. Since you're the only one who knows how it works, we thought you might have an answer for us."

"That's just it, guys. I don't know much more than you do."

"How did you get three crystals? Are there really three of them, or did you go back in time and get more?"

"No, there's only one blue crystal." He sat down between them. "I knew that there was a chance that you two might figure out how to make a return trip through time. I went back to see The Protector. I thought maybe he had another blue one that I didn't know about or had some other way to do it. He used the white crystal to split the blue one into three parts. The one that you have is the complete version."

"How did he do that?" asked Lisa.

"Yeah, that has to be the toughest substance on the planet," added the young Charlie.

"That's the weird thing about it. He didn't cut it or break it in any way. He just waved the white one over the blue one. It was like some kind of magic."

"What else can the white crystal do?" asked Lisa.

"I don't know. I just have a feeling that only God himself is more powerful than that crystal."

Charlie replied, "No wonder why The Protector has to watch over it."

"What exactly is the problem with the crystal?"

"The energy is used up."

The older Charlie groaned and shook his head.

"Do you know a way to get the power back quickly?" asked Lisa.

"No. Only storing up enough solar power. The amount that you need could take months, maybe years."

"Not exactly the answer I was hoping for," Charlie admitted.

"I don't know what to tell you. I'm sorry I can't be of more help. I'm sure with our collective intelligence, we can find a solution eventually. But, I really do need to focus on what I came here for. Without succeeding at that, your problems will disappear on their own, if you know what I mean."

"Yeah, I know what you mean. We won't interfere with your mission."

"And, I'll stay out of your way as well. You can still come to me if you really need to."

"At least you're staying at the same motel."

He chuckled. "I guess we still think alike, no matter what age difference."

"There is still one thing that you can help us with," added Lisa. "It has to do with our mission."

He gave her a somewhat stern look. "Proceed with caution."

Charlie and Lisa made plans the rest of the night. Having another Charlie as an ally would certainly make things easier in some ways, however, much more caution would have to be exercised. Between Charlie's perfect memory of the events that would happen beyond Sam's knowledge and the memories recorded in Lisa's diary, they could fulfill their mission on a schedule. As long as they could still solve the time travel issue, they were sure to succeed... as long as they didn't cause any paradox along the way.

Lisa tossed and turned that night. It was enough to cause Charlie to begin waking up. Lisa suddenly sat up and cried.

"What happened?" Charlie asked as he put his arm around her.

She quickly wrapped both arms around him tightly and said, "Thank God you're okay."

"Of course I'm okay. You just had a bad dream." He put his other arm around her and kissed her cheek. "Do you want to talk about it?"

She took a couple of deep breaths.

"We were kids in the dream. We were at the beach in Heatherton. Everything seemed nice at first. We were building a sand castle and having a good time."

This dream sounded eerily familiar to Charlie.

She continued, "What gets me is how real it felt. I could feel the sand and the sun. I could hear the ocean. It was like I was there."

"Some dreams can be like that. Your own memories have a lot to do with it."

"We built the sand castle really big. We stood back and admired it. Then, Amanda came and knocked it over."

This dream was becoming way too familiar to Charlie. He could guess what would happen next, but he listened to her instead.

"We built the castle again, but then Robbie came and hit it with a bat. He wasn't a kid, though. He was the same age as he is now."

"You mean seventeen?"

"No, I mean our age."

That was a difference that Charlie noticed. "What happened next?" he asked.

"We went back to work on the sand castle. We were almost done, but your mom said that you had to go. You didn't want to. You looked really sad. After you walked away, I finished the sand castle." Her voice became shaky. "That's when I saw the wave coming. I was too scared to move, too scared to scream. I just stood there paralyzed. It swallowed me up. I couldn't breathe. I tried desperately to swim to the surface. Once I did, the water became sand. I was in a giant hourglass. It was filling up fast. That's when I saw it." She started crying and shaking again. "There was a hand reaching out to me."

Charlie remembered this all too well. He was almost afraid to ask, "Whose hand was it, Lisa?"

She looked him in the eyes. "It was yours."

A chill went down his spine. "How do you know it was me?"

"You were wearing your dad's watch. You needed my help. I tried to save you, but I couldn't. That's when I woke up." Noticing how visibly shaken he was, she said, "It was just a dream, right? Please tell me it was just a dream."

"It was just a dream. But, I think I should tell you something. I had this same dream before."

"What?! How is that possible? When?"

"January 28th, 1985... when I was seventeen."

"That's... that's today. That's right now! You were having the same dream at the same time when you were younger. That's not possible! That doesn't make sense."

"I don't understand it, either. It was the same dream, except for Robbie's age and you being called away by your dad. Are you sure that was me in the hourglass? It was my dad when I dreamed it."

"It was you. I could feel it instinctively. What does this mean? How could two people dream the same thing at the same time at different ages? What are we getting ourselves into, Charlie? Are we in trouble?"

"I don't have the answer to that. I know that when I dreamed it before, Sam told me that the wave represented my depression and that the hourglass represented the years that have gone by mourning my father."

"What if it's something else? I haven't been depressed, but I have felt disappointed."

"About what?"

"About this situation that we're in. I thought this was my time to shine and really help people, but we've been stuck trying to solve other problems. Maybe I'm not good enough, I don't know."

"Of course you're good enough. You are the absolute best. We have a plan and it's going to work. Tomorrow is when you start the process. You will make a big difference. Nothing is going to stop you. Not a wave, not an hourglass, not even time itself. You are the sunshine that is needed here at this time in history. We built the sand castle together and we built the machine together. We're in this together."

"Always together."

"We just have to make the sand castle bigger than the wave."

She smiled and said, "Here comes the sun."

Tuesday, January 29th. Lisa and Charlie pulled up to the high school.

"Are you sure you don't want to come in and reminisce?" asked Lisa.

"I'm sure. Maybe I'll do it if I really need to sometime, but having three of me there at the same time? That's a little too risky. I'll just go back and try to figure out our energy problem some more."

"I understand. Okay, how do I look? Ridiculous?"

"You look like you fit in."

"I'm a little nervous."

"You should be. Remember, there is still another version of you in there, too. Maybe a little nervousness will keep you alert."

"You're right. I have to be very careful that I don't run into myself or make anyone think that I'm her." She changed her voice to sound like a valley girl. "I have to like, totally blend in fer sure."

Charlie laughed. "Just don't overdo it. This is still Kansas, not California."

"Like, don't have a cow, dude. I've got this."

"I know you do. I have complete faith in you."

They gave each other a quick kiss before she got out of the car and took her backpack from the backseat.

"See ya later," he said.

"Later, dude."

She put on her sunglasses. It was time to put her acting skills to work.

As she entered the building, the memories of 1985 came flooding back. She chuckled internally as she noticed all the heavily hair-sprayed girls and others with ponytails on the sides of their heads. Neon colors were in abundance, as were windbreakers and sweaters. She wore a plain white shirt, stonewashed denim jacket and matching jeans, pink shoes with the socks showing prominently, white hoop earrings, and a black porkpie hat. She decided not to alter her hair this time. Hopefully, the hat and sunglasses would still be enough of a disguise for the short time she needed them. She still remembered where everything was and made her way to Sam's office.

Another girl passing by stopped and gave her a big, brace-filled smile. "Bodacious jacket! And, that hat is totally gnarly!"

"Thanks, dudette!"

"Much better than what some of these others wear. Like, they have no sense of fashion."

"I know, right? Like, gag me with a spoon!"

She laughed with a screech. "Yeah! Like barf me out!" She laughed again and walked away.

Lisa said to herself, "Why did we ever talk like this? Grody."

She reached Sam's office and went in.

"Can I help you, Miss?"

She took off her sunglasses. "Charlie, it's me."

"Lisa? You had me fooled for a second. You look like Debbie Gibson."

She smiled. "You say that like it's a bad thing."

"No, not at all. Although, I would exercise caution. Someone else might think you look like her, too. Then again, her first album didn't come out for a couple of years, so you might be okay."

"It's kind of scary that you know that."

He sighed. "It's a blessing and a curse."

"Did you find the forms I need?"

"Yes," he answered as he handed a file to her. "Take the whole thing. I've already read it."

"And memorized it, I'm sure."

"You know me very well. I have to admit, it's still very odd for me. Where I come from, you never knew that side of me at all. I never saw so many sides to you, either."

"Keep that in mind, Charlie. What you do here makes a huge difference. You were right about us all along. Now, it's my turn to make a difference for someone else."

"Say no more. I'm getting too many ideas as it is. I guess with all the memory loss I've had, I must have forgotten to take care of this issue myself."

"Memory loss? You?"

"Yes, Lisa. I didn't anticipate that whenever I change something in the past, it would also affect my memories of it. The more my younger self makes different decisions, it affects me adversely."

"How adversely?"

"I think maybe I shouldn't say too much. Just be extremely careful with how you handle things."

"I will. We both will." She sat down. "There's something else I want to talk to you about. I hope it doesn't mess with the space-time continuum or anything, but I just don't know what to make of it. I really could use some peace of mind."

He sat at the desk. "I'll do my best."

"I know Charlie was here earlier. He told me about it. I mean, my Charlie told me that he came to see you when he was younger."

"I guess it can get a little confusing, but I know what you mean."

"So you know about the dream."

"Yes. He was pretty shaken by it."

"I… I had the same dream."

"When you were younger?"

"No. Last night."

"I… I don't know what to say. Did you dream it before at all?"

"No. I only dreamed it last night. Charlie never told me about it, either."

"I don't understand. People don't just dream the same dream like that. I wonder why I never dreamed it when I was younger."

"You didn't? That doesn't make sense. He remembers it vividly. Are you sure it's not because of the memory loss?"

"I'm very sure. The only way I can make any sense of it is the fact that I didn't have any time travel in my life before."

"Maybe there's something more to this. Maybe we're doing something we're not supposed to."

"I hope that's not the case. Everything looks like it turned out right. My advice to you is to not worry about it and focus on the mission. That's something you can control better."

"The thing that makes me worried about it the most is the biggest difference between my version and his."

"What's that?"

"His dad was reaching out to him in the hourglass. In my version, it was someone else." Her lip trembled. "It was you."

"Are you sure?"

"You… he was wearing his dad's watch."

"Well, see, then it still could've been Dad."

She shook her head. "I knew it in my gut."

"Well, I don't have his watch, so that proves it."

"Mom gave it to him on our wedding day. I'm sure you saw him wearing it."

He reluctantly admitted, "I did. Look, Lisa, just because this dream felt so real doesn't make it so."

He got up and walked over to her. She stood up as well. He put his hands on her shoulders and looked into her eyes.

"I promise I won't die in a giant hourglass." He chuckled. "The very idea is absurd. Every version of your husband is going to be okay."

She nodded her head. "Maybe it's just a warning to be careful."

"I think you're right. I think it's just a warning. So what do we learn from this? We have to be careful. Good thing we already are. We don't have to be worried about some dream or anything that may or may not happen in the future. We can control that. You can control that. You get to make a better future here in the present. Or, the past as it were." He laughed. "It all gets a little convoluted these days."

She smiled. "You're right. The future hasn't been written yet."

He looked at his watch. "You'd better get going. If you're doing what I think you're doing, then you don't have much time to get ready."

"Yeah, I'd better get to it. Thanks, Charlie... I mean Sam. I have to get used to calling you that around here."

"You're going to be fine. Just focus on the mission."

She nodded and headed for the door.

"One other thing, Debbie," he said with a smile.

She turned around and smiled back.

He said, "I could get lost in your eyes."

She laughed at his song reference. "Only in my dreams," she said slyly as she slowly put her sunglasses back on.

He smiled as she walked away. His smile went away as he thought back to their conversation. "For once, I hope your dreams don't come true."

She quickly travelled to the bathroom. She opened up the file and studied the forms as fast as she could. She took a deep breath and looked in the mirror.

"Okay, Electric Youth. Time for a change."

She took another outfit from the backpack. She slipped out of her clothes and into a nurse's blue dress. She looked into the mirror again. She pulled her hair up with a hair tie and carefully placed a red wig over it. She wished that she could wear it down to help disguise her better, but knew that she would have to pin it back to fit the requirements of a nurse. Black horn-rimmed glasses were finally added to aid in hiding her identity.

"Oh, Tracy. Be thankful for your modern day scrubs."

She entered the school gym. Several stations were set up for physical exams.

"Oh, good! I thought we were going to be shorthanded," a nurse said as she walked up to Lisa. "We had one who got sick. Let me get you set up."

She took her to one of the stations. Within minutes, Lisa had familiarized herself with the instruments she would need as well as the paperwork once more.

"Just don't be nervous. I have to be a different person," she said quietly to herself. She took another deep breath. "Okay, let's do this."

She brought Robbie to the station.

"So, Robbie Kunkel, you're a strapping young man," she said in her best southern accent.

"Yeah, I was born to be an athlete," he said with a chuckle.

"Let's see just how tall you are."

She measured him and wrote down the results. "5'11". That's just under six feet. You really are a biggun. Now, let's get your weight."

He stepped onto the scale. "What's your name?" he asked.

"Oh... uh... it's Jennifer Park-- I mean Sarah. Sarah Jennifer Parker. Everyone just calls me Jenny."

"Okay, Jenny. I was just wondering since you're getting all this information about me. Didn't want it to be too one-sided."

"Yeah, I guess you should at least know my name," she said with a nervous laugh. She wrote down the results. "180 pounds. That sounds pretty healthy."

"All muscle, too," he said with a wink.

"Is he flirting? Why is he being charming? At least he doesn't think I'm his girlfriend," she thought to herself.

"Where are you from?" he asked. "I like that accent."

"Oh, just some lil' ol' place I'm sure you've never heard of."

"Somewhere in Oklahoma, I bet."

"You nailed it," she said with a smile. "Now, let's check your blood pressure. Just sit down here for me."

She put the cuff on his arm and started pumping. Other than that, she had no idea what she was doing. Robbie didn't have to know that. She went back to the papers and looked at the one from the previous year. She wrote down the same results on the new form. She knew that he already passed his physical before, so it wouldn't harm anything to just copy it. She worked her way through the list.

"Let's check that pulse."

She copied the results.

"Now, let's take a look at those peepers."

She held the light and tried to mimic what she saw Tracy and others do before. "Everything looks good there. Now for your ears." She did a similar performance and wrote it down. "Let's listen to your ticker." She put the stethoscope on him and had him breathe in and out. She wrote it down. It was time to start getting to the point of her reason for it all.

"I looked over the form that you filled out at home ahead of time. Everything there sounds good. Are you a football player?"

"Baseball."

"Oh, that's nice. I reckon you're pretty good."

"Yeah, that's what they say. I'm going to play for the college next year and hopefully make it to the big leagues someday."

"Oh, would you look at that. I'm talkin' to the next George Brett."

He laughed. "I hope so."

"Your parents must be very proud."

His smile began to fade. "Yeah. Yeah, they are."

"That didn't sound very convincing. I see that your dad signed the form. Is your mom around?"

"No. She left a long time ago."

"Aw. I'm sorry to hear that. I'm sure your dad's proud of you."

"Maybe."

"Ya know, part of the exam comes with some questions I need to ask you. I hope you answer them honestly. It's really for your own good. I'm here to help, ya know."

"I know," he said with a nod.

She looked at the form. "Do you feel stress or under pressure?"

He hesitated. "Yeah. Sometimes. It's been getting better lately since I have a new girlfriend."

"Oh, yeah? I bet she's really nice."

"Yeah, she is. I feel a lot happier around her."

"What about when she's not around? Maybe I should ask the next question on the list. Do you ever feel sad, depressed, hopeless, or anxious?"

"I used to. I guess I still do sometimes. Playing ball helps. I've been looking forward to the season starting."

"I see. Do you feel safe at home?"

He looked down. "I try to stay away."

She shook her head. She felt bad for him. She knew there was always something wrong with his home life, but never knew the details. Her instincts were right.

"Have you ever tried cigarettes or tobacco?"

"Just once."

"Have you ever tried alcohol?"

"No. I don't ever want to touch that poison."

Given what she knew of him from her time, she was surprised by his answer. "Why not?"

"I've seen what it does to people."

"That's a good answer. You don't want that getting in the way of your baseball career."

"Are there any other questions?"

"No. We'll just move on to the next thing."

There actually were a few other questions, but she didn't want to push any further. She knew that she struck a nerve. She copied the rest from the previous year's form. Surprisingly, he answered her questions much more honestly this time than he did before. Her discomfort was giving way to more confidence as she saw that there was hope.

"It's time for some stretches," she said. "You've done this before; you know what to do."

He stood up and did everything by memory. She pretended to know what to look for and copied the results.

"Very good, Robbie. Well, we're gonna wrap this up. I'm gonna make a note here about some of the things you told me. I hope you understand."

"You're just doing your job."

"Yes. Just doing my job. I mean-- no. No, it's not just my job. I like you, Robbie. I like you very much. I think you're a nice, charming, intelligent young man with a lot of ambition. I think you have a few issues that need to be worked on so that you can be a lot happier. I'd hate to see anything pull you down. Which is why I'm gonna recommend that you see a counselor."

"A counselor? I don't know about that."

She knew that there was no way he would volunteer to do such a thing. This was her way to nudge him in the right direction.

"How do you feel about me? You seem like you were being pretty honest with your answers."

"That's different. You're not a counselor."

"What if I told you that my sister is?"

"Really?"

"Yes, really. She's really good. She just happens to be taking a position here tomorrow. You'd really like her. I think it would be very wise to go talk to her."

"I'm really not one to open up about my feelings too much."

"I understand that. I think you should at least try it once. She knows what she's doing. Do you trust me?"

"I guess so. I don't really have a reason not to."

"Then, you don't have a reason not to trust her, either. I think it will do you a lot of good. Don't you want to be happier?"

"Yeah. Okay, you talked me into it. I'll give it a try."

"Great! I don't think you'll regret it."

"What's her name?"

She had to think fast again. Coming up with names on the spot wasn't her strong suit. Since Jennifer Parker was already in her head, she thought of another name from the same movie.

"Lorraine... Lorrie. We always called her Lorrie. Lorrie Parker."

"Okay. If Lorrie is as nice as you, then I don't see what harm it could do."

"That's wonderful. I'll tell her to expect you. Well, I guess that's everything I need from you. You're a very healthy young man. You passed with flying colors. With exception of the counselling part of it."

"Uh... I think you forgot something."

"I did?"

"You know..." he motioned downwards.

She looked down. "OH! Oh, that!" She nervously chuckled. "Silly me. How could I forget that? Such an important part of the exam." She looked at the form. "There it is in black and white-- 'genitourinary'. I just skipped over that part, didn't I?" She actually did it on purpose and hoped that he wouldn't notice. Now, there was no getting out of it. She tried desperately not to show how nervous she was.

"That's okay. We all make mistakes," he said as he pulled his pants down.

She put on gloves and tried to tell herself that it was all for Tracy.

"Just look straight ahead and hold still."

She thought if she kept him from looking down, then he wouldn't see her with her eyes closed.

"Turn your head and cough."

He did as she said. She quickly headed back to the papers while taking her gloves off and throwing them away.

"Everything tests out fine," she said as he pulled his pants up.

"Am I good to go now?"

"Yes. Yes, you are free to go."

"Thanks, Jenny. Good talking to you."

"Yes, it was so nice to meet you. I wish you all the best with everything. Take care now."

He started walking away.

She said, "Maybe I'll see you on a baseball card someday."

He laughed. "Yeah, I hope so. And in the papers."

He headed for the exit.

"I just hope it's good news," she said. Then, she went back to feverishly apply hand sanitizer. She shuddered and made a vomit noise. "All for Tracy. This is all for Tracy. Man, I love that Tracy. Oh, the things I'll do for that Tracy. Yes, sirree. Whew! Boy, oh boy."

Another baseball player walked in.

"Ugh. I should have called myself Olivia. Let's get physical."

"You've been washing your hands for five minutes," Charlie said in the motel room.

"I wish I had something to wash the images out of my mind," she said with a shudder.

"At least you achieved what you were trying to do."

"Yeah, yeah." She shut the water off and dried her hands. "I wish it didn't have to include touching... things. One of the guys thought it was a good thing." She made a disgusted face. "Trust me, you don't wanna know. I'm just glad it's over."

She reclined on the bed next to Charlie.

"So, on the bright side, you get to finally counsel Robbie tomorrow."

"Yeah, I think I'm even more nervous about that."

"Didn't you say that he responded well to you today?"

"He did, but I'm going to have to ask some really tough questions. He might not want to go very far and give up too soon. It's going to take a few sessions, I think. There's just a lot riding on this. Especially Tracy."

"If there's anyone who can help him, it's you. I think today already proved that."

"I hope you're right. I just have to be careful."

"I wish we could have a breakthrough on the energy problem. I can't find a single generator anywhere. I guess we still have a little time, but I'm even more worried about the crystal. It may not be nearly enough time at all."

"At least it's still soaking up the sun. That's about all we can do right now. We still need to do something more about that billboard, too."

"I'll take care of all that. Just concentrate on helping Robbie. You're the only one who can do it."

"You know, that brings up a good point. There was another version of life when I wasn't with you. I can't even imagine that. You're the only one who can do it for me."

They smiled and looked into each other's eyes.

"I'm pretty sure the other me was never with anyone else, either. It was such a miserable thing for both of us that it just had to be fixed."

"I'm so glad we had our happy ending."

They kissed.

"I have a crazy idea," Lisa said. "I think it would help cleanse my mind from other things."

"Oh, yeah? What's that?"

She rolled on top of him. "What do you think?"

"Hmm. This could help, yes."

They kissed again.

"What would happen if I got pregnant?" Her eyes widened. "What if I conceived in 1985 and gave birth in 2004? Wouldn't that be awesome?"

"It sounds interesting, but I'm not sure that it would be safe for the baby. The machine was hard enough on us. I think it would be too dangerous."

"Yeah, you're right."

"But, you get points for creativity! It would definitely be a first."

"Maybe we can still come up with some creative things," she said with a mischievous smile.

"I'm willing to try."

Later that night, Sam, the older Charlie, woke up startled. He sat up.

"Why am I dreaming this now? What's this all about?" He started to cry. "Why can't I save him?" He looked at his watch and remembered what Lisa said. "Maybe it's not up to me."

CHAPTER 28

"Mr. Whitfield?"

"Yes, come on in. How can I help you?" He squinted. "Wait a minute. Lisa?"

She smiled. "I had you for a bit."

"You're getting pretty good at this," he said with a chuckle. "Although, I have a feeling you're not a student this time."

She wore a dark gray blazer and matching long skirt with a white shirt and black heels. A dark brown wig with a tinge of gray covered up her blonde hair. Big, round, black framed glasses distracted from her eyes. She carried a purse instead of a backpack.

"Like it?" she asked as she twirled.

"Yes, I do. You look very professional and mature. The gray hair was a nice touch."

"Thanks. I took that out of your playbook."

"Well, this gray is natural. I think. It showed up after my first attempt with the machine."

"Oh. It must have put a strain on you."

"You don't know the half of it. So, Lisa, what should I call you now?"

"Now, I'm Lorrie Parker. I'm your new assistant guidance counselor."

"Oh, really?" he said with great surprise. "Was I not getting the job done?"

"Let's just say that you'll need me to take care of a situation. I promise I won't interfere with anything you're doing."

"I trust you. So, how does this work? Do we take turns?"

"First we're going to need to see Mr. Foltan to make it official."

"I was just thinking the same thing."

Wednesday the 30th. Lisa told Charlie more of the details on their way to Mr. Foltan's office, but not too many. She knew that he would have to know a least a little bit to be prepared.

"Ah, Mr. Whitfield. Good to see you."

"You, too, Mr. Foltan."

They shook hands.

"Who's your friend?"

"Lorrie Parker," she answered as she shook his hand. Her southern accent surprised Sam.

"She's here to help with counselling," Sam told him.

"Was there a letter about this? I don't recall hearing anything about it," Mr. Foltan said with a quizzical look on his face.

Sam looked to Lorrie. She replied, "No letter."

"No, no letter this time. Just personal recommendation," Sam explained.

"I've heard a lot of good reports about you, Whitfield. It sounds like you've been doing a great job and helping a lot of people."

"Thank you, Sir. I do what I can."

"I'm a little surprised that you would need help. I thought you had everything under control."

"Well, it's just that..."

"If I may, Sir," Lorrie interjected. "Some of the girls are reluctant to talk to a male counselor. We saw the need to provide another option."

"Yes," Sam added, "we knew this would be a great way to solve that problem. She's really great, too. Very experienced."

"And, I would be working as a volunteer. I would just be here for a couple of weeks anyway."

"Volunteer, huh?" Mr. Foltan replied. "I like the sound of that."

"I just want what's best for the students," she said.

"I think that's what we all want," Sam added, trying to nudge the principal a little more.

He thought for a moment. "Well, Mr. Whitfield, if you say this is what's best, then I'm inclined to agree. You're the expert." He held out his hand. "Welcome aboard, Miss Parker."

"Thank you, Sir. We're gonna get along just fine," she said with a handshake.

"Are you from Oklahoma?"

"Why, yes I am."

"That's what I thought. I graduated in Tulsa. Whereabouts are you from?"

She thought fast. "Ponca City."

"Oh. Sounds like a thicker accent than what I've usually heard from there."

"We moved around a lot."

"Okay, fair enough. I take it you're starting today?"

"Yes, I wanted to get started as soon as possible."

"You two can share an office."

Lorrie and Sam looked at each other for the best response.

"If it's possible, could we have another one?" she asked.

"It's more of a privacy thing for the students," Sam reasoned.

"We don't have any more free right now. I'm sorry." He thought for a moment. "Tell ya what. If you end up needing to see a student at the same time, just use mine. You can come and kick me out." He smiled.

"I appreciate that," she said.

"That's very generous of you," Sam said.

"Anything for a fellow Okie. I have a good feeling about you."

"Thanks, Mr. Foltan. I won't let you down."

As they walked away, Sam said, "I'm really impressed. You did some quick thinking in there. I think you really won him over."

"That easily could've went a different way. Thanks for coming with me. I knew you would give me more credibility."

"Nah, it was your southern charm."

"Oh, fiddle-dee-dee," she said with a laugh.

"So, what's next?"

"I don't want to interfere with anyone who might come to you for help."

"True. We don't know when someone will walk in."

"So, I will give you my beeper number. That way, when someone comes to talk to me, you can send them to Mr. Foltan's office."

"Good plan. I think we can make this work."

They walked a little further when Lisa asked, "Are you okay? You seem like something is on your mind."

"Oh, I'll be okay."

"It's okay to tell me. I really am a counselor... and in another time, your wife."

They entered his office and shut the door.

"I had the dream last night," he said.

She gasped. "No way! How is that possible? Are you okay?"

"I'll be okay. It was very intense. I just didn't expect to have that dream myself."

"It *is* just a dream... right?"

"I hope so. I really hope so." He sat at the desk. "There's something else I'm nervous about."

"What's that?"

"Tonight's the night that I go talk to Mom."

"Oh! As Sam?"

"Yeah. Talk about trying to be someone else."

"That would be tough. She knows you so well. Charlie did tell me that you did that. It just puts a whole new twist on it now that I know who you really are."

"It's more complicated than you know. I can't get into that, though. I can't change anything I'm meant to do. My reality affects your husband's past."

"And, it affects me, too."

"Exactly. I know that you mean well and that you want to help me, but I have to just do everything the way I would've done it without you here. No matter how difficult or lonely it might become."

"I understand. I'll limit our contact as much as possible."

"It's the best thing for everyone. I don't think I'll be here much longer anyway."
"It's a sobering thought. Once we start changing the past, it has consequences that affect us."
"That's why you have to be extremely careful. At least you have an advantage that I didn't have."
"How so?"
"You have a partner."

In the meantime, that partner was back in the study making notes and pacing.
"How can I get more solar power? There is far too little time to get so much. I can't exactly put it in the sun itself..." He considered it for a moment. "Nah. That's too impossible. What can we do? There has to be a way."

That afternoon, Lisa received a page. She politely informed Mr. Foltan that she would need his office. It was time for Miss Parker to shine.
"Miss Parker?"
"Yes, come on in. You must be Robbie. So nice to meet you."
"You, too."
They shook hands.
Lorrie said, "Go ahead and have a seat and we'll get started."
She sat behind Mr. Foltan's desk while Robbie sat in front.
"This is kind of awkward for me. I'm not sure what to do," Robbie admitted.
"That's okay, Robbie. We're just here to talk, that's all. Why don't you tell me a little about yourself?"
"I'm not sure what there is to tell. I'm a senior... I would've actually graduated by now if I wasn't held back in second grade."
"So, you're eighteen?"
"Yes."
"Anything else?"
"I have a new girlfriend named Lisa and I play baseball."
"Oh, yeah? What position?"
"Second base. Do you know much about baseball?"
Oh, the irony. Having a baseball coach for a father, Lisa knew as much as Robbie did about the game, perhaps even more. But, that would have to remain a secret.
"I know all the main stuff, yeah. I've even been to some games."
"That's cool. I plan on going professional after college."
"That would be really neat. Kansas City?"

"Yeah. Maybe work my way up through the minors first."

"Where are you going to college?"

"I was originally thinking of going to Kansas City College, but now I'm not sure. Lisa's dad is the coach here, so I might end up staying here. I don't know. I guess I'll see how it goes with her."

Lisa wasn't sure if Robbie was with her because of her dad or not. He seemed to truly like her at the time, but now as an observer knowing that he ultimately went to Kansas City, the full truth wasn't clear. What if going to Kansas City was what led to worse problems? Still, their relationship was young and couldn't be tampered with too much in case it ruined everything that Sam was doing to help them. The situation was extremely tricky, so she had to be extra cautious and try to help Robbie in other ways.

"It seems like you have a lot going for you. Nice, smart, good-looking guy with a promising baseball career and a girlfriend. So, what brings you to me?"

He looked down as he was clearly searching for how to express his feelings. "I've had some depression."

"That's okay, Robbie. It's okay to admit that. I know it may be hard to talk about it, but it's normal."

"It doesn't feel very normal. Like you said, I have everything going for me."

"It's normal for someone your age to feel this way. You're at a major turning point in your life. You're not a kid anymore. You're a man. That brings a lot of new responsibilities and tough decisions. I know from experience. I went through it, too. Most people do, whether they admit it or not. It's not easy to be this age. I totally get that. That's why I'm here. You're free to talk to me about anything you want."

He looked her in the eyes and said, "I appreciate that."

"You're safe here."

He nodded.

"How often do you get depressed?"

"Not very often anymore. I used to get it all the time. Lately, things have been going better, so I've been happier. Sometimes something will cross my mind, but I try to think about something else."

"That's good. Once you give in to it, it's hard to pull out of it. If you can change your thought process and focus on something positive, that will help you a lot. What do you think about to keep from getting depressed?"

"Lisa. And baseball." He chuckled. "There's really not anything else."

"I see. Well, keep doing that. Before Lisa came along, I'm sure it was just baseball."

"Yeah. It's actually helped a lot. I'm glad the season is coming up soon."

"I'm glad that you have that to look forward to, but we still need to get to the bottom of the situation and try to prevent you from being depressed with or without baseball. Wouldn't that be nice?"

"Yeah. Man, there's so much I could talk about. My mind is just all over the place right now." He rubbed his head. "I'm feeling all kinds of things right now. I don't know if I can handle doing all this yet."

"That's okay, Robbie. You don't have to do this all at once. I never expected you to. Years of problems don't just go away in a day. But, that's okay. We have plenty of time. I'll be here tomorrow if you want to talk."

"I don't know. Can we make it Friday? I think I have more time then."

"Sure, sure. Same time?"

"Yeah, I think that would work."

"Let's do that."

They stood up and shook hands.

"Thanks, Miss Parker. I have a feeling that if anyone can help me, it's you."

"We'll get all this worked out together."

He smiled and said, "See you Friday."

"Can't wait."

He left the room. She said to herself, "the future depends on it."

"How did it go?" Charlie asked later at the motel.

"Pretty good."

"What did you talk about?"

"I can't tell you much about that. Confidentiality, you know."

"Oh, yeah. Of course."

"We didn't get very far, but that's okay. I was just trying to get him to dip his toes in the water for now. He needs to get more comfortable around me to dive into the hard stuff when he's ready. I think we made a lot of progress towards that. I feel optimistic about it."

"That's good. I know you will be the one who can help him."

"One thing still bugs me. I can't say too much to get the information out of him and possibly mess up everything. I have to get around it somehow."

"What are you talking about?"

It dawned on her. "I have to test him. But, I can't be Lisa or Lorrie. I have to see if he really likes me or if he's just with me because of my dad. It would help to know how to steer him in the right direction."

"How are you going to test him?"

"With my feminine charms," she said reluctantly.

"Uh... excuse me?"

"Nothing will happen... I just have to, you know... be seductive."

He searched for the words to express how flabbergasted he was. "Seductive? You're going to seduce him? How?"

"Don't worry. I know what to do."

"You do?! How?! Have you done this before?"

"Well, no... but, I've seen movies."

"I can't believe this. There has to be a better way."

"Relax. Don't you trust me?"

"Of course I trust you. It's Robbie that I don't trust."

"You can be there, too. Remember that spy kit that we got Elijah awhile back? You can listen to the whole thing from the car."

"Because that's not creepy at all..."

"If something doesn't go right, you can intervene. Don't worry. I think this will work."

He sighed. "Okay, Lisa. I trust you. We'll do whatever you think is best. You know Robbie better than I do."

"Thank you. It's not exactly something I look forward to, ya know. It's just something that has to be done."

"Okay. Where are you even going to do this?"

"The one place that I know he'll be tonight. But, first, we need to go back to the house. I have to get the right outfit to play the part."

Charlie waited in the living room as Lisa changed. He didn't like the idea of his wife trying to tempt someone else, but with the spy equipment in hand, he did feel more secure in the situation. If Robbie did anything too inappropriate, he would come to the rescue. Besides, Lisa had already proven that she could defend herself against him when he was at his violent worst. He had years of rage built up in a prison, yet she was able to knock him down. This Robbie was still nice, a friend even. Just a teenager. Maybe there wasn't anything to worry about. Then, she walked in. She seemed to walk in slow motion with her hair blowing in the wind as it happened in the movies. Pat Benatar's "Heartbreaker" began playing in Charlie's mental jukebox. She wore black heels and a black mini skirt that showed off her shapely legs. A white tank top plunged a bit to highlight her cleavage. A black leather jacket was over that, with a black beret topping a straight red wig and lipstick to match. She pulled her sunglasses down and asked, "What do you think?"

Thoughts? What were those? Charlie's jaw hung open in vacuous speechlessness.

She laughed. "Too much?"

He finally remembered what this was all about. Thinking that Robbie wouldn't be anything to worry about because he was still a teenager suddenly changed to worrying about it *because he was a teenager.*

"It's... uh... you look fantastic. Very... seductive."

"Thanks. Judging by your reaction, I must have gotten it right. Let's see what Robbie thinks."

"Okay, let's get this over with, Heartbreaker."

She chuckled. "That reminds me of that song."

"If the heels fit."

"Barely," she said as she stumbled a bit as they exited.

When they arrived at their destination, Charlie said, "Let's test out the equipment first."

"Good idea." She inserted the earpiece and covered it with the wig. "Can you hear me?"

"Yes. Can you hear me?" he said through his piece.

"Yes. Let's test it out when I go inside just in case."

"If one of them doesn't work, then we can use the beepers."

"Roger that. Okay. I'd better get in there."

"Are you nervous?"

"Tremendously. But, I think it's only half as much as you."

"Just be careful."

"I will. The only real danger might be if I run into my other self."

"Wait-- what?"

"How do you think I know where he is? I was here with him."

"Maybe this isn't such a good idea after all."

"Relax, honey. I can take care of myself. All I really have to do is play another part."

"All right. Just don't take too long."

"Okay." She got out of the car. "Time to bring on the sexiness." She began to walk like a model and stumbled once again.

Lisa was naturally sexy, but it came from her intelligence and personality, not just her looks. Charlie wondered if she would come off as a fake if she tried too hard.

Lisa played "Heartbreaker" in her mind as she tried to feel more confident as this new character. She reached the door of the library. A sign said, "SHH! Please be quiet while people study." As soon as she opened the door, the music in her head got quieter and Pat Benatar was reduced to a whisper.

"Can you hear me?" she whispered to Charlie.

"What?"

"Can you hear me?" she said a little louder.

"I can hear you."

"Good. Now for a look around."

She carefully made her way towards the back of the room where she knew she studied with Robbie. She still kept a lookout for anyone else that might need to be avoided. When she got there, she quickly hid behind a shelf.

"Okay, I found them at the table," she quietly informed Charlie.

"Now what? You can't just go up and talk to him when you're there."

"I know. I have to get him away somehow."

She watched her younger self take a drink from her bottled water.

"I remember!" she said. "I had to go to the bathroom. I remember it because I was kind of embarrassed."

"That's good. It doesn't give you much time, though."

"Actually, come to think of it, he went at the same time. Maybe this won't be as easy as I thought."

"I have an idea. I'm coming in. Keep an eye on them."

"Okay."

Lisa watched as the two talked quietly with the occasional joke.

"It's all coming back to me now. Man, this is so weird."

"Hey, Heartbreaker," Charlie said in Lisa's earpiece. "How close are they to getting up?"

She noticed her younger self's slight squirming. To the untrained eye, it may not mean anything, but she knew herself.

"Any time now."

"Okay. I have the problem fixed. I put an 'out of order' note on the men's bathroom. That will make Robbie have to go to the one upstairs."

"That's really great thinking." She saw Lisa start to stand up. "Okay--it's happening."

"Get upstairs right away and wait for him. I'll keep an eye on the other you."

"Got it."

She rushed for the stairs. Charlie hid behind one of the shelves and waited for them to come by.

"Out of order?" asked Robbie.

"There's one upstairs," Lisa informed him.

"Right. I almost forgot about that. I'll see you in a bit."

Lisa went in.

"It worked," Charlie told Lisa. "Robbie's headed your way."

"Great. I can do this."

She took a deep breath. She got into position across from the bathroom next to a bookshelf. She quickly picked up a book and pretended to read it.

"You can do this. Just be confident."

As Robbie approached her vicinity, she casually looked towards him. She slowly pulled her sunglasses down a bit. Eye contact was made. She smiled seductively and raised an eyebrow. He smiled and nodded. He grabbed the bathroom door and pushed. It didn't open. He looked back to her. He chuckled nervously and pulled it open. She winked at him. He chuckled again and entered the bathroom.

"He just went in," she told Charlie. "I've already made eye contact with him and made him nervous. I think this is going to work."

"That's good. Just make sure it doesn't work *too* well."

The younger Lisa came out of the bathroom.

"Your other self is already done. She's heading back to the table. I can't stay in here much longer and risk her seeing me without any disguise or make the librarian wonder why I'm talking to myself. I'm going back to the car. Make this count."

"I hear a flush. Okay, gotta go."

A moment later, Robbie was back. They exchanged smiles again. She purposely dropped her book.

"Oops! I am so clumsy," she said in her best French accent.

"I'll get it," he said as he rushed over.

"I can do it."

She bent over with her rear extended towards him. *"I can't believe I'm doing this,"* she thought with disgust and embarrassment. She picked up the book and turned towards him again. The look on his face told her that she was doing something right.

"You're French?" he asked.

"Oui. I am... how you say... foreign exchange student."

"That's really cool. I never see many people from other countries here in Chesapeake. My name's Robbie." He held out his hand to shake. "Robbie Kunkel."

"Bonjour. I am Babette," she said as she shook his hand.

"Babette. That's a lovely name. Do you have a last name?"

Why did she always have to come up with names on the spot? She thought for a brief second and quickly responded.

"Uh... Benatar."

"Benatar? Like the singer?"

She gave him a quizzical look. "I do not know this singer."

"Oh. Maybe she's just popular in America."

Listening in the car, Charlie raised an eyebrow and mouthed, "Babette Benatar?"

It was time to turn up the heat. Lisa said, "There is so much about this place that I have yet to learn." She put her hand on his bicep. "Perhaps I need big, strong homme to teach me." She put her other hand on his shoulder. "And, maybe I can teach you what you only read in books."

Charlie's and Robbie's eyes both widened.

Robbie chuckled nervously and said, "That sounds nice and all, but..."

"You look nervous. Did I say something wrong?"

"Well, it's just that I have a girlfriend..."

"No."

"Yes, and she's really great and she's downstairs right now..." he gently took her hands off him and continued, "a--and I really should get back to her."

"Oh. That's too bad," she said with a pout. "She must be very speciale."

"Yeah, she is." He started to walk away.

"Au revoir, Robert. Ce qui aurait pu etre."

He looked back and said, "Uh... so long." He waved and descended the stairs.

"What did that mean? That last French part?" Charlie asked.

"Ce qui aurait pu etre? It means 'what could have been'."

"No kidding. Let's get out of here."

When she got into the car, Charlie couldn't hold back any longer. "Babette Benatar?!"

"I was nervous! That was the only name that popped in my head. No thanks to you for calling me 'Heartbreaker.' I had that song stuck in my head."

She playfully hit his arm and they both laughed.

"You might as well have said 'LePew'."

"Hey! My French was spot on. And, I really did make him squirm."

"He wasn't the only one. I'm glad I didn't have to witness it with my eyes." He began to drive back to the motel. "So, are you satisfied?"

"Yes. I think I proved that he actually does like me."

"Or, maybe Babette just isn't his type."

"No, he was attracted to me. I sense it even when I'm Lorrie or Jenny. That was another reason why I had to do this. It proved that he might be attracted to other girls, but he's still loyal to just one."

"Then again, he could just be attracted to one and sees something similar in all of your characters."

"I didn't think of it like that. That very well could be true. At least he hasn't figured out that we're all the same person."

"No, but he might if you're not careful. You can't slip up even once."

"That's why I'll need to just be Lorrie around him from now on. Southern accent, glasses, and brown hair with gray in it. Different mannerisms, facial expressions, walk, the whole bit."

"You've done a great job so far. I just wish there was a way to know how much it works."

"Yeah. We can't exactly see the future right now."

Charlie slowly grinned slyly. "Maybe we can."

"What do you mean?"

"Change of direction. We're going back to the house first. There's something we need to pick up."

He picked up the newspaper that documented Robbie's attack. "We have to change this headline. If we do that, then we'll know that we changed the past."

"Great thinking! We could actually see it change. But, that's not enough. The problem is deeper than that." She retrieved the old scrapbook and opened it. "This is the true test of changing the past. His injury, the DUI, all of it has to change. It has to be more than the violence that he inflicted on us and Tracy, even more than Tyson Fredericks."

"We have to keep him from getting hurt in that game."

"It's not just that. It's a complete change of thinking that has to happen. There's something deeper and worse than that injury. I just know that he's going to tell me about it soon. I have to help him with whatever pain he's experienced that lead to him becoming this man. He went down the wrong path. I have to keep him on the right one."

"Are you sure it didn't all start with the injury? He seemed fine until that moment. That's when we can historically say that it all went downhill from there."

"No, there's something more. That was just the catalyst for giving in to his inner conflict. That conflict is already there. I'm going to do my best to put an end to it."

"I hope you can for Tracy's sake."

"It's not just for Tracy's sake. Don't you see, Charlie? Robbie still has goodness in him. He's not a born monster."

He nodded. "I know you're right. There's still hope."

"Today has reminded me of the kind of person I used to know him to be." Her eyes teared up. "I'm going to help Robbie because he's worth saving."

CHAPTER 29

"Wake up, Charlie."

He fumbled for the light next to the bed. He saw a tape recorder on the nightstand. There was a note that read, "In case you forget." He started to play the tape.

"Charlie, this is you. This is a recording to help you remember some things in case you forget what's going on. Some of this may sound unbelievable, but this is you and this is real. Today's date is January 30th, 1985, but it should be the 31st by the time you wake up. You are not from this time. You are from 2015. You came back to 1985 to put right what once went wrong. You're going by the name of Sam Whitfield. You're the counselor at the high school where you've been helping your younger self. Lisa desperately needs your help. If you don't make a big change soon, Lisa will still have a miserable future. You've been making great progress with your younger self, but time is running out. You may have to get more aggressive in your approach."

He turned it off without finishing it.

"Same as I recorded last night. Maybe tomorrow, I'll actually need it." He glanced over at the hat and glasses on the table. "How much longer, Charlie? When does the curtain come down on this performance?"

Meanwhile, Lisa was getting ready for another performance of her own. Before leaving, Charlie had to tell her something important.

"I remember this day very well. Today was a turning point."

"How so?"

"You know how the 25th was when I gave up? Today was when Sam really talked some sense into me. He got me to admit what I was so afraid of. This was the day when I finally started to see how much I was about to lose if I didn't try harder."

Lisa put her hand on his shoulder and said, "So, no matter what, I can't interfere with anything that happens. I have to stay away from Sam as much as possible."

"Our entire future depends on it."

"Maybe I shouldn't even be there."

"I think it will be okay, as long as you steer clear of both versions of me. It was in the afternoon, so definitely keep your guard up then."

"I will. Nothing is going to ruin it."

She gave him a kiss and left.

Charlie said to himself, "And, if I don't get this crystal problem solved, then we still won't have a future."

As the day went by, several girls were referred to Lorrie for counselling. She always kept the pages with Sam short and simple, never crossing paths with him physically. So far, so good. She thought it might be a good idea to even stay away from Robbie unless he came by. It was now eleven o'clock, and it was time once more for Lorrie to borrow the principal's office.

"Hi, come on in. I'm Lorrie. What can I help you with?" she asked a timid young girl.

She slowly sat down. "I didn't know where else to go."

"Well, you came to the right place. I'm sure I can help you. What's your name?"

"Noreen."

"A beautiful name for a beautiful girl."

She looked her in the eyes. "You really think so?"

"Of course. Now, what's the matter, sweetheart?"

She looked down again. "Well... you see... there's this bully."

"You're safe here, Noreen. It's okay for you to tell me. They aren't going to know. Okay?"

She nodded her head.

Lorrie continued, "What did they do?"

"She calls me names. Says things to get under my skin."

"Has she ever hit you?"

"No, but she's talked about it. She's talked about jumping me after school." A tear rolled down her cheek. "I can't take it anymore. I shouldn't have to be afraid just to go to school."

Lorrie got up and went to her side. She crouched down and put her arm around her.

"No, you shouldn't have to be afraid. And, you don't have to be afraid anymore. You did the right thing. Now, we can put an end to this."

"Are you sure she won't know I told you?"

"I'm sure. Even if she did figure it out, we won't let anything happen to you. She won't get away with this behavior anymore. But, you'll have to tell me who it is first."

"I don't know if I can."

"It's going to be okay. What if you're not the only one? What if she's doing this to someone else? What if she gets worse? You may be the only one brave enough to speak up."

"You think I'm brave?"

"Yes, I do. You're the one who's going to stop a serious problem just by having the courage to come here today to tell me. But, I can't do much without knowing who she is."

Noreen nodded. She paused for a moment, then looked her in the eyes. She said softly, "Amanda DiPino."

Lisa's blood turned cold. She couldn't reveal how shaken up she was inside. "Thank you for telling me. I'm proud of you. It just so happens that I know who she is."

"You do?"

"Her reputation precedes her. Don't worry. Her bark is worse than her bite most of the time. She will be dealt with swiftly and effectively."

She smiled. "Thank you. I feel better already."

"Good. You're going to be fine, Noreen. I'll personally see to it. Amanda's behavior will be a thing of the past."

After Noreen left, Lisa sat at the desk and processed this information. She knew that the protocol was to inform the principal when there was a case of bullying, but under the circumstances, she decided that Charlie should be told first. She paged him to tell him that she was coming home.

"What's so important that you had to rush back here?"

"We have another complication. A girl came to see me. She's been getting bullied."

"That's terrible. But, why leave early to come tell me? Shouldn't you report this to Mr. Foltan?"

"There's a good reason why I wanted to come see you. You might want to sit down."

He sat on the couch. "Okay, what's going on?"

She sat next to him. "Charlie... the bully is Amanda."

His heart began to race. "I--I thought she was doing better."

"Maybe she did for awhile, but it looks like she's back to her same old tricks."

"You'll have to tell Foltan."

"If I do that, he's sure to suspend her or even expel her. I think we can do better than that. Imagine if I wasn't there today. This poor girl was so afraid to speak up. I don't think she would've told Sam or anyone else. I guarantee you that this originally went by without anyone putting a stop to it... and this girl paid the price. We're Changers, aren't we? We're here to change this situation."

"So, you want to convince Mr. Foltan to have Amanda go to you for counselling?"

"Not quite." She held his hand. "I think you're the one to help her."

"Me?! How could I do it? She used to bully me, too. This whole thing is bringing back bad memories. I would be a nervous wreck around her."

"You know her better than I do. Remember how you told me that you tried to be friends with her? You made a connection. You got through to her when no one else could. You told me that she never bothered you again after that. You have a gift, Charlie. I've seen it countless times. You know just how to look into someone's heart. You are the perfect one to do this. Besides, it would also bring closure. You could finally overcome those bad memories."

"That's if it actually works. She might not listen to me. She's not a little girl anymore."

"You know how I told you that she said something about you that made me so mad that I slapped her?"

He chuckled. "Yeah, I remember that. I was really surprised."

"Do you know what she said?"

"You never told me. I've always wondered."

"She said that you were a wimp. I knew that wasn't true. I saw a boy who was always trying to do the right thing no matter what. I saw a boy who had a struggle that few kids would have to go through with losing a parent. I saw you keep trying every day to go on with your life, no matter how hard it might be. I never once saw you as a wimp. I saw you and Mom as the strongest people in the world. *That* is why you're the only one who can help her. You're the only one who has been strong enough to take everything she dishes out and still show her love."

He stood up.

"Where are you going?" she asked.

"I have to hurry. I have to find the right suit, add some gray to my hair, and put on a fake goatee. That is what heroes look like these days, right?"

She smiled. "That sounds about right."

Lisa went back to school and resumed her duties as Lorrie. Charlie arrived at the school fifteen minutes before three so that he wouldn't interfere with his own past. His own version of Sam met with Lorrie in Mr. Foltan's office.

"Sir, we've been informed of a student who's been bullying at least one other student," Lorrie said.

"Oh, yeah? How were you informed?"

"A girl named Noreen came to tell me about it. She's been pretty scared."

"Who's the bully?" asked Mr. Foltan.

"Amanda DiPino."

"And, you know this for sure?"

"She's had a history of this behavior when she was younger."

"Well, if you're certain that she's guilty, then I have no choice but to expel her."

"Expulsion? Are you sure it needs to be that severe?" asked Sam.

"In all my years of being a principal, I have never tolerated a bully. Not once. I have prided myself in keeping my school safe from threats. Whenever I see a problem like this, I nip it in the bud. Remove the troublemaker and you remove the problem."

"With all due respect, Sir, we believe that this particular situation would only get worse if she was expelled," said Lorrie.

"Oh, really? Why's that?" he asked very skeptically.

"Her educational career would suffer."

Sam added, "Plus, we have reason to believe that her home environment is potentially unsafe and would make it more harmful for her personally if she was there more often."

"Reason to believe?" Mr. Foltan asked. "If the situation is as bad as you think it is, then perhaps we need to get the authorities involved."

"We thought that we could at least talk to her and see what she has to say about it. We could provide counselling for her either way," Sam said.

"We just want what's best for all the children," Lorrie added. "Even bullies should get a chance to be heard. I think with the proper care, Amanda could be reformed. She has caused problems, but it would be better to get to the root of the problem rather than to just dismiss her as another statistic."

Mr. Foltan leaned back in his chair and thought for a moment. He sighed and said, "I've always thought of these bullies as weeds that needed to be separated from the rest of the garden so that everyone could grow. I like you, Mr. Whitfield. In the short time you've been here, I've heard how much you've helped some of the students just by giving them someone to talk to. On your recommendation, I agreed to let Miss Parker assist you. You both seem to be highly capable at your jobs and you really care about the students. You don't see this bully as a weed. You see a flower that needs more care to fully blossom. That's a different approach than I'm used to, but it sounds like one that might work if done right."

"It would be better to at least try. We wouldn't want to fail Amanda any more than we would want to fail Noreen if we didn't do our part to help her," Sam said.

"All right," Mr. Foltan responded. "I'm going to give you a chance to get through to her before we do it the other way. Miss Parker, I hope you're as good as he says you are."

"Actually, I was going to let Mr. Whitfield handle this one."

"Oh? Why's that?"

Sam replied, "She's very capable, but I've had more experience with bullies."

"I see." He looked at his watch. "It's a bit late in the day to do anything, so tomorrow I expect you to deal with this Amanda as soon as you can. I'm putting a lot of trust in you, Whitfield. Don't make me regret this."

"I won't. She's going to change. You have my word."

Later at the motel, Charlie and Lisa discussed how to juggle their responsibilities and not cause a problem by having two Sams. They decided that he would need to see Amanda in Mr. Foltan's office. The conversation changed from the logistics to the heart of the problem.

"How did you know that there was trouble at home for Amanda?" Lisa asked.

"I don't know for sure, but I've always had that suspicion. I always knew that she carried some kind of pain. I guess I'll find out soon enough."

"I wish there was some way to find out if it's going to work. We have the scrapbook for Robbie, but nothing for Amanda."

"Yeah, it's weird. I can't remember anything about her after high school. Can you think of anything?"

"It's a complete blank."

"Did she move away? Did she get married?"

"I don't know. I don't even remember seeing her at the store."

"Is there anything in her file that could give us a clue?"

She looked again. "Just a lot of stuff that we already knew. She was held back in the fourth grade, she's never been a great student, but she's gotten by... her parents have different last names, so I guess that's something we didn't know."

"Were they never married, or did they get divorced?"

"It doesn't say. It just has DiPino for her dad and Untereiner for her mom."

"Untereiner. Why does that sound familiar?"

"It is a unique name."

He closed his eyes and repeated it, trying to recall how he knew that name. "Untereiner. Amanda Untereiner."

He opened up the scrapbook.

"Is there something in there?" she asked.

"I don't know. There's something vaguely familiar. Like I've seen it before..."

He skimmed through the various newspaper articles about Robbie. He came to one from 1990.

Lisa said, "That's when Robbie went to prison. Is there something about her there?"

"I don't see anything, but my gut says otherwise."

"Maybe it was on TV?"

He began to carefully peel the article from the scrapbook.

"It's on the other side," he said.

"You remember reading that?"

"Just a quick glance, I think. Sometimes, I read things all the way through, and other times, I just skim. I don't forget anything, so I have to pick and choose how much information I want to absorb."

"That's got to be a pain sometimes."

Charlie's heart sank as he read what it said. "Not as painful as this." His voice was shaky as he read aloud, "'Former Chesapeake resident Amanda Untereiner, 23, was found dead in her home yesterday.'"

"NO!" Lisa reacted. "It can't be!"

"'There was no sign of struggle, and evidence suggests Miss Untereiner committed suicide.'"

They both began to cry. She held him tight.

Charlie asked, "How did this happen? How did we miss it? Were we so caught up in our own lives that we didn't even notice she was gone?"

"We lost track of her. Apparently, she moved away and changed her name to her mom's. We were so busy with the school and the kids, that we didn't see it."

"I never would have thought it was that bad. I wish we could have seen it coming."

She looked him in the eyes. "We do see it coming now. We're still five years away from her taking her own life. You can still help her. We can change it."

"We *will* change it."

Friday, February 1st. Lisa was prepared to talk to Robbie that afternoon, but first, Charlie needed to talk to Amanda that morning. As he sat at Mr. Foltan's desk, he recalled one of his worst memories of his encounters with Amanda.

"I bet you were scared all day. Well, there's something I want to tell you, but you can't tell anyone, okay? I'm serious, Charlie. Promise me you won't tell."

"Okay, I promise."

"Good. This is just between you and me. You seem like an honest guy, so I believe you. Okay, here goes."

He remembered the pain from the punch to his stomach as if it just happened.

"Your goody-goody little girlfriend ain't here to defend you anymore. Watch your back, freak show—things are gonna change. Welcome to my world."

She was a manipulative liar when she was nine years old. She could get under the skin in ways that Robbie never did until their last confrontation. He could only imagine how much worse she may be now. He knew that his childhood fear of her would have to be put aside to remain strong. He'd outsmarted her before, after all. He was reminded of Matthew 10:16, "Behold, I send you forth as sheep in the midst of wolves: be ye therefore wise as serpents, and harmless as doves." He couldn't change what happened between them in the past, but with some wisdom, he could still prevent a dark future.

She walked in and sat down. "Where's the principal?" she asked.

"It's just going to be you and me."

"Who are you supposed to be?"

"I'm Sam Whitfield, the guidance counselor."

She scoffed. "Guidance counselor. Foltan won't even come punish me himself."

"I'm not here to punish you. I'm here to help you."

She laughed. "How do you think you're gonna help me? Rearrange my schedule? Tell me which college to go to? Please."

He completely expected her to challenge him. He knew how to counter everything she said. His past experience with her was actually his secret weapon.

"I'm here to listen to you."

"Well, you can listen to me not talk to you."

"I have one question first. How many students are you bullying?"

She rolled her eyes.

"Too many to count?" he asked.

"I'm not telling you anything."

"Well, I was hoping we could do this the easy way. We're just trying to get an accurate number of how many it is. If it's a certain amount, you'll just have to go to the juvenile detention center."

Her eyes grew big. "Wait-- what? Juvy?"

"Of course. Bullying is a very serious offense, Miss DiPino. If you have enough victims, then you're considered a serial bully and the law moves pretty swiftly for someone like that."

"The law?! Victims?!"

"Yes, victims. How many are there currently? Ten? Twenty?"

"How many would it have to be?"

"Good question. I'm not sure." He reached for the phone on the desk. "I could give them a quick call and find out exactly."

"Three!" she blurted out. "It's just three. Stephanie, Noreen, and Mark."

"Hmm. I think three is still within the jurisdiction of the school. I can still help you when there's only three. But--and this is very important--you have to immediately cease from all bullying."

"Okay, I will."

"I mean it. The whole school will be keeping an eye on you. If anything happens, I'll know."

"Wait a minute. Why you? Why isn't Mr. Foltan doing this?"

"You know why it's not him? Because he was going to expel you."

"So? That just means I don't have to come to this stupid school."

"This 'stupid school' is more important than you think. If you were to be expelled, it would go on your record. You're a junior, right?"

"Yeah."

"I've seen your file. You were held back. Do you really want that to happen again? You wouldn't have enough credits to pass."

"No. I could always drop out."

"Are you sure that's what you want? If you get expelled or drop out, it will not only go on your record, but you'll have a harder time finding a good-paying job. Everyone wants someone they can count on, not someone who'll give up. I don't want that to happen. I told Mr. Foltan that I would do everything I could to help you so that you don't go down that path. I'm offering you a chance to change your course before it's too late."

She folded her arms. "Doesn't matter anyway. I'll never get to do anything important. I'll just end up in fast food or the mall like everyone else."

"What do you actually want to do?"

"Like I said, it doesn't matter."

"I think it does. I think it matters very much."

"Why should it matter?"

"Because *you* matter."

She scoffed and rolled her eyes.

"Don't believe me?" he continued. "Then why would I be here?"

"Because it's your job."

"No. I'm here because I convinced the principal that a bully matters as much as the one getting bullied. I think there's more to you than just being a bully."

"I still don't have to tell you anything."

"It might be an awfully awkward thing to just sit there silently while I do all the talking."

"Just like class."

"And, just like class, you'll have to keep coming back until I say that you're ready to move on."

"You can't do that!"

"Oh, but I can. All you have to do is cooperate. As long as you don't bully anyone, it will make it go by faster. I'm not just trying to get you to quit bullying, but to get to the bottom of why you do it. That's why you'll need to start opening up to me about things."

"You can't make me do that."

"No, and it doesn't have to all be today. But, think about it, Miss DiPino. I'm offering you the chance to talk to someone about your problems confidentially."

"What makes you even think I have problems?"

"Because for all this tough act, I still see something else. I see pain in your eyes. You've been hurt and don't know what to do about it, so you lash out at others who don't deserve it. Well, let me tell you something. You don't deserve it, either. This vicious cycle has to stop."

She looked down without saying a word. He could tell that he was getting through to her. Just like when they were kids.

He added, "Let me just ask you this-- when was the last time someone just sat and listened to what you had to say? When was the last time someone said that your opinions and feelings matter?"

She struggled for the words. "I-- I don't remember."

"It's time for that to change. Just give me a chance to help."

"We'll see."

"We'll ease into the harder things later. One question I want to ask again for now. Just a normal question that anyone would ask. What do you want to do? If you could do anything you wanted for a living, what would that be?"

She hesitated. "I would be an artist."

He was surprised by the answer. "That's very good. Do you have anything I could see? I'm just curious."

She took a notebook out of her backpack. She stood up and put it on the desk. She thumbed through a few pages before settling on one to show him.

"That's really good," he said as he admired her colored pencil drawing of an eagle. "That's amazing. I had no idea that you could do this. How long have you been drawing?"

"I've been drawing all my life, but I never got serious about it until high school."

"Are you in any art classes?"

"Yeah, but I don't usually show people my stuff."

"Why not? You have real talent."

"I don't know. I guess I don't want it to get picked apart. It's personal to me."

"Well, I'm very glad you showed me. I really appreciate that." He suddenly had an idea. "It's a great coincidence that you did, because I happen to know someone who's hiring for a big art project."

"Really? I don't think I'm ready for something like that."

"I think you are. You never know until you try."

"I bet they want someone with experience."

"You just told me that you had a lifetime of experience. I'm sure it won't be a problem. They really need someone tomorrow."

"Tomorrow? That's a little soon."

"Did I mention that it pays $500?"

Her eyes widened. "$500?! I've never seen that much money before. Are you for real?"

"Yes, I'm for real. Do you have a car?"

"Yeah... kinda."

He took a piece of paper and started writing. "Meet me at this address tomorrow morning at nine. I'll lead you the rest of the way from there. You'll have all the materials you need and lunch will be provided. Be prepared to be there all day. It's a real job, you know."

"Why me?"

"Why not? You're an artist, aren't you? Now, you can do what you wanted. I knew there was more to you."

That afternoon, Robbie came back to talk to Lorrie. He still seemed unsure of how to express himself. Lisa knew that she would have to guide the conversation.

"You told me that baseball helps to keep you from being depressed. How long have you been playing?"

"Since middle school. I found out that I liked it and kept getting better at it."

"What makes you so good at it?"

"It's funny that you ask that, because I've noticed that everyone tries to figure it out without even asking me. They always think they have to hit harder, run faster, throw with more accuracy, but they're missing the most important, basic principle."

"What's that?"

"Keep your eye on the ball. I know everyone says it, but I don't think everyone actually does it. That's what makes me good at it. I watch where the ball is going and how it's spinning. I can catch it almost every time and throw it where I want it to go. I can tell when a pitcher is getting tired and sloppy. I just keep my eye on the ball. I think that's how it keeps depression away. I have something else to focus on."

"I'm glad you've found that solution."

"Everyone needs to have something that they're good at, right?"

"That's very true."

She knew how this would turn out later. He was clearly dependent on playing ball to be happier, but she also knew that he would need to find another way to achieve that if his path remained the same.

She continued, "So, what do you do when it's not baseball season?"

"I still have Lisa," he said with a smile.

"I'm sure she's a wonderful girl, but you told me that she was new to your life. What did you do before she came along?"

His face grew more serious. "Before she came along, it was a lot harder."

"What is it that made you depressed?"

He looked down as he searched for the words. He said quietly, "I kept getting hurt."

"How did you keep getting hurt, Robbie? Who hurt you?"

"There are always girls who like me. Sometimes I even fall in love. Maybe I'm just more mature than they are, I don't know. They always find some other jock instead of me. They don't want to know the real me. They can't handle all my problems."

It was clear to Lisa that his problems stemmed from something much deeper than high school romantic entanglements. She couldn't push him too hard. He had to volunteer his information at his own pace.

"I think those girls are foolish," she said. "Anyone would be happy to be with you. I think you're right, though. They're not as mature as you are. They're still playing high school games instead of taking life seriously. That's okay. It just narrows down the kind of woman you should be with. You should be with someone who can handle your problems and maybe even bring some healing."

"I think I might have found that with Lisa."

"Well, I can't say that for sure having never met her, but all I can tell you is to be careful and take your time. It's all still new and you're both young. If it works out, great, but if it doesn't, then don't give up. The right one will still be out there somewhere."

"You're right. I really do hope it works out with her. I've never known anyone else who was so kind, smart, funny, and beautiful. I really don't want to blow it. I think that's one of the reasons why I'm here. I don't want to scare her away like all the others."

An already awkward situation just became even trickier for Lisa. She said, "I'm glad you see it that way. I'm going to help you as much as I can. But, I can only help you as much as you're willing to let me. I still have a feeling that there's a lot that you're holding back. I'm not going to make you say anything you don't want to, but if you truly want to get better, you'll have to be open about some things, okay?"

"Okay."

"I think we need to wait until Monday before we start getting into more of it. That will give you some more time to think. How does that sound?"

"That sounds good. It's hard for me to talk about this stuff. I know I need to, but I might need more time to ease into it, like you said."

"We're going to get all this figured out together. Just keep your eye on the ball."

He smiled and said, "I always do."

Lisa and Charlie talked later about their experiences without breaking confidentiality. They knew that their counselling schedules would have to avoid his younger self's meetings with Sam on Tuesdays and Thursdays. They noticed that the headlines still hadn't changed, but realized that it was still early. There was still time for the future to be rewritten.

CHAPTER 30

Saturday, February 2nd. Charlie woke up and turned to Lisa. They smiled lovingly. Charlie said, "Okay, campers, rise and shine, and don't forget your booties cuz it's coooold out there today."

"Dang it. Every year. Every single year. And, this year, I get it twice."

He laughed. "That's right, woodchuck chuckers-- it's..." He waited for her to finish the sentence with him.

"Groundhog Day," she said reluctantly, but alertly. Charlie was more enthusiastic and said it with gusto.

"Come on, Lisa. This is going to be a great day. We're actually back in the past on Groundhog Day. How cool is that?"

"As long as we don't have to keep reliving it every day."

"I know what you need." He held out his hand. "Put your little hand in mine." She did. He continued, "There ain't no hill or mountain we can't climb."

She rolled her eyes and groaned. "I fell for it." She shook her head and laughed.

He proceeded to sing "I Got You, Babe."

Charlie as Sam arrived at the predetermined location. He knew that he couldn't give Amanda the actual location for the project, so he had her follow him the rest of the way. They pulled up to the field and got out of their cars.

"A billboard?" she asked.

"Two of them."

"What do they want me to put on them?"

"That's up to you."

"It could be anything I want?"

"Within reason, yeah. It still needs to be professional and worth the money they're paying. Which reminds me..." he took out his wallet and handed her some cash. "This is half. You get the rest when it's done."

"I don't know what to do. What if they don't like it? What if it's not good enough?"

He put his hand on her shoulder. "Of course it will be good enough. Do you want to know how I know?"

"How?"

"Because it will come from your heart. Instead of painting whatever you're told, it will be what you want it to be. It will be your vision."

"I can't think of anything to do. I don't want to mess this up."

"You won't. I believe in you. All you have to do is block out everything else and do whatever comes to you. Just like a true artist would do."

"Okay, I'll try," she said with a sigh.

"I know you will." He started taking paint out of the trunk of the car. "You have all day, even more if you need it. Something will come to you." She joined in and they set the last of it on the ground. "You have all the supplies here. I'll be back later with lunch."

"This is crazy, you know. Who's the one behind this, anyway?"

He couldn't tell her that it was him, so he gave a different answer. "It's for the city. Don't worry. You've got this."

He waved as he drove away. Only time would tell if this plan would work.

When Charlie got back to the motel, Lisa told him, "I've been reading my diary. Do you know what happened today?"

Charlie thought about it and answered, "I worked all day. What about you?"

"This was the day when Robbie came over and showed his baseball tapes to Dad. It's when Dad really wanted him to play for him."

"And, he still didn't do it?"

"I think the only reason why he didn't was because you and I ended up together."

"So he went to KC just because of that?"

"That's the biggest reason, yes. He was on the fence for awhile, but that's what did it for him."

"Do you think he is still meant to go to KC, or was he meant to stay here all along?"

"It's hard to say. If he would've stayed here, I think Dad would've won more games and probably would've gone to the championship."

"And, maybe he wouldn't have done all the other things he did."

"What would make him stay here? He's still not going to end up with me, and we dang sure don't want him to end up with Tracy, either."

"I don't know. All I know is that the headlines still haven't changed."

She sighed. "It's frustrating. I'm not sure what to do. I'm trying, but I just can't make him talk about things that he doesn't want to talk about. I still think that will be the key to changing everything. It has to come from a change within."

"You'll get there. We still have some time."

"I hope so. At least you're making progress with Amanda."

"Yeah, I feel hopeful about it. At least we got her to paint the billboards."

"That was a good bonus. Who knew she was an artist?"

"I had no idea. As long as I can get her to tell me other things, I think she'll be okay."

"I hope we'll be okay financially. We're spending a lot of money here lately."

"I know, but it will all be worth it."

"Good thing I asked Sam if we could have some money. He said that he wasn't going to do anything with it." Then, it hit her. "Wait a minute. He also joked that even when we're not married, he still has to give me money."

"What's so strange about that?"

"We keep overlooking a big fact about him. Why did he have to come back here and be your counselor? What did you talk about?"

"He's the one who convinced me to tell you how I feel."

"Exactly. He's the one who brought us together."

"We already knew that."

"Yeah, but don't you see? Where he comes from, we weren't married. Think about it. What did we do instead?"

"I would have went to Kansas City College like I planned before you came back."

"And, I might have still been with Robbie. Remember when we first talked to him in the motel? He was hiding something. I knew that something happened to me." She picked up the scrapbook. "These headlines would've been about me, not Tracy."

"Oh, wow. I never thought of that. He came back here to save you, just like we came back to save Tracy."

"Robbie and I must have stayed together, maybe even got married. I can't even imagine being with him instead of you. I can't even imagine what that did to your other self."

"Enough to make him build a time machine."

"Well, the cycle ends here. No more people getting hurt. I'm just going to have to get a little more strategic in getting him to open up to me."

"Should we keep him from going to your house?"

"No. Baseball and I are the two things that bring him some happiness. We can't mess with that, at least not yet. We also have to be very careful not to change things in our own past that could keep us from getting together."

He shook his head. "This whole thing is going to give me an aneurysm. So much we can do, yet so much we can't do. I could literally walk over there and talk to myself right now."

She laughed. "Yeah, this is pretty nuts. We could even go to Wigner's and pretty much cause a disturbance in the space-time continuum."

"Yeah, I'm glad we've been able to dodge that one so far. Whatever we do, we just have to be very precise. Nothing can be left to guesswork."

"The future depends on it."

"Lives depend on it."

A few hours later, Charlie took lunch to Amanda. She had made some progress, but still hadn't done much. She told him that she was still trying to figure it out. Later that night, Charlie went back to check on her again.

"Sorry I didn't get it done," she said. "I'll have to come back next Saturday, if that's okay."

"That's perfectly fine. It is quite an undertaking. At least you did get a lot of it."

"I just couldn't think of what to do. Then, I remembered what you said, that it was for the city. Do you think this will work?"

The billboard on the left said, "Welcome to Chesapeake," and the one on the right said, "Now Leaving Chesapeake."

Charlie said, "I think it's perfect."

"I wish I could think of something to put on the rest of it. This town isn't really known for anything."

"Maybe it will be someday."

"That doesn't help me now."

"Well, Miss DiPino, you have a week to figure it out. I'm sure something brilliant will come to you in that time."

"I hope so," she said with a sigh.

"You've done a good job. Time to go home and relax. See you on Monday."

She groaned. "Do I have to?"

"Yes, you have to. It will be okay."

"Fine. See you Monday. I guess."

Sunday, February 3rd. Lisa was pleased to see that the previous day didn't repeat. After having another continental breakfast, she got out her diary and Charlie had the scrapbook.

"Still no changes," Charlie said.

"Tomorrow might be better," Lisa replied. "What did you do today-- when you were younger, I mean?"

"I worked on that," he said as he pointed at the notebook.

"Wow. I forget that you were already doing that even then."

"It has to stay that way. We can't do anything to interfere with that, or we're in serious trouble. What were you doing?"

"I went with Robbie to have lunch after church, and then we studied."

"Isn't the library closed on Sundays?"

"Yes. We went to the park. Don't worry-- it wasn't our spot. It seemed like a good idea, but it was a little windy. After that, we went to see a movie and he took me home."

"I remember Mom telling me that she was there when you got back."
"That's right! That's when she met Robbie."
"She told me that I needed to know what I'm up against. I had to do something fast, or else I'd lose you. I told her that I had some ideas."
"I'm so glad you did. It was starting to get serious with Robbie, but I was still in love with you."
"The rest is history."
"Or, the present. Depends on how you look at it."
"Yeah," he said with a chuckle. "We just have to stay away from ourselves when we have times like this or we won't have a future."
"So, what do we do today?"
He thought about it. "There's not much we can do until tomorrow."
"Wait a minute. Are you telling me that we can have a day off?"
"Yeah... I do believe so."
She laughed. "What do we even do with ourselves?"
"We don't have to be Lorrie or Sam or anyone else. We can just be."
She put her arms around him. "Sounds perfect."

After their much deserved day off, Sam and Lorrie were back to school on Monday the 4th. It was time to make a real difference. Amanda arrived in Mr. Foltan's office to speak to the younger Mr. Whitfield as usual.

"Good morning. Ready to make some progress?"
She rolled her eyes.
"I see. Don't you want to get better?"
"There's nothing to get better from. I like being me."
"I'm not so sure about that. I see a conflict in you. I think you're doing something that a lot of people have done, including myself. You're your own worst enemy."
She scoffed. "I don't hurt myself. I just do what I have to do."
"Even if that means hurting other people."
She looked down without saying a word.
He continued, "You're better than that, Amanda. I think you're much better than that."
"I wouldn't be too sure about that."
"No? You know what I think? I think that this whole tough chick bully image is an act. Yes, you are tough, and yes, you are capable of intimidating people, but I don't think that's who you really are. I think you're a much more sensitive and caring person on the inside. You have a lot of pain that you carry with you, and instead of admitting it and being honest about yourself, you act out."

She folded her arms and said sarcastically, "Boy, you just have me all figured out, don't you?"

"You just proved my point."

"Well, I have to be tough. I don't have much choice."

"There's nothing wrong with being tough, but when you use it to hurt others, that's when you've crossed a line. There's an old saying-- 'your right to swing your fists ends where my nose begins.' I still don't think that you truly want to be that person. It's one thing to be tough, it's another to be strong. I think you have an inner strength that you have somehow misused. Why should your problems become a different problem for someone else? Do you think that Stephanie, Noreen, and Mark deserve to suffer because you are suffering? Is that fair to them?"

She paused before admitting, "No."

"I think you have a lot that you keep bottled up, and then it comes out in destructive ways. It's hurting others and it's also hurting yourself. If you don't work on what's eating away at you, things will never get better. I'm not here just because you've been a bully. I'm here because Miss Parker and I saw that you were someone worth helping. You have the opportunity to fix this situation, but it won't happen unless you allow it. You have to want better for yourself."

"I'm not sure how."

"You can do it by tapping into that part of yourself that you keep hidden. Just look at your art."

"What about it?"

"Why don't you let others see it or even know about it?"

"Because it's personal."

"What makes it so personal? Don't you think others would enjoy it?"

"I don't know what they'll think. Probably won't be good enough."

"Your first statement was right. You don't know what they'll think. I can guarantee you that it's good enough."

"Yeah, well, I don't want to find out the hard way that it's not."

"I get that. I'm glad that you've found something positive that you can do to deal with things. You're on the right track, but you're still missing the point. Bottling it up won't solve anything. Hiding your art because of what people might think is the same as hiding your true self from the rest of the world. I know that you're a good person. You've been through some hard things. Going into this shell won't make it better. You need to start dealing with whatever it is that's gotten you to this point."

She looked him in the eyes. "I don't know if I'm ready."

"What if you told me next time?"

She nodded.

"All I want to do is help."

She stood up and said, “I know. That’s why I keep coming back.”

Later that day, it was Lorrie’s turn. Robbie walked in and sat down.
Lorrie said, “You look like you have a lot on your mind.”

“I think I’m ready to start talking more about the hard stuff.”

“Okay, Robbie. You just say whatever you need to say.”

“I just don’t know where to start.”

“Maybe I can guide you there. Is it something about your parents?”

He looked down. “Yes.”

“What’s been so hard for you?”

“I think what’s hardest for me is how I’ve had to grow up.”

“Why is that?”

“My mom left when I was twelve.”

Lisa knew that he always tried to change the subject whenever it came up when they were dating, but she never knew what his home life was truly like. She could only guess that something was wrong.

“I’m sorry to hear that. Do you know why she did?”

“She couldn’t take it anymore. She was always fighting with Dad.”

“What did they fight about?”

“You name it, they fought about it. Anything and everything. I hated it. I would try to ignore it or drown out the noise, but I couldn’t. Sometimes I still hear it.”

“It’s really sad when parents do that. They don’t realize just how much they’re hurting their own kids. It’s not fair.”

“It might not have been so often if he wasn’t drinking all the time.”

“It’s a terrible addiction. I’ve seen it hurt a lot of people.”

“There would be times when he’d try to quit for awhile, especially if Mom threatened to leave, but he would always go back to it.” He shook his head. “I wish he would have loved his family enough to fight it. He chose to fight us instead.”

“Do you have any idea why he kept doing it?”

“Sometimes he would go on a rant about life being a disappointment and nothing ever going right. He talked about no one ever understanding what he’s been through and no one will ever know how bad it was. He always talked about it, but still wouldn’t really talk about it, you know? Like he was the only one suffering. He didn’t see the irony.”

“Was he in the war? I’ve seen some people who were and sounded a lot like that.”

“Not that I know of. I can see why Mom couldn’t put up with it anymore. I don’t blame her. I just wish she would’ve took me with her. I’ve been stuck dealing with him.” His eyes teared up. “I haven’t seen her in years.”

Lisa's heart broke for him. She said, "I don't understand how a parent can do that. I just want you to know that it's not your fault. Okay?"

He looked her in the eyes. "Okay."

"I mean it. It couldn't possibly be your fault. You just got caught in the middle of something that never should've happened in the first place. You know, you're old enough now that you could still try to get in touch with her and have a relationship again."

"I hope so." He looked down again. "But, I'm not gonna hold my breath."

"Someone wise once told me that if you love someone, anything's possible."

"Was that from a fortune cookie?" He shook his head. "I'm sorry, Miss Parker. I don't want to be rude. I know you're trying to help. I just don't know what's possible anymore. It seems like the more I try sometimes, the worse things get. I try to be confident and act like I have it all together, but deep down, I know the truth." His tears increased. "I know I'll never amount to anything. I keep trying, but there are two people who will never see it. And, that hurts worse than anything."

"They will see it as long as you keep trying. You're going to accomplish everything you set out to do as long as you don't give up."

"How can you be sure? No one knows the future."

"The future is whatever you make it. If you're giving your best, you will definitely amount to something. Only by giving up will you fail. Your past shouldn't decide your future. A lot of people have overcome struggles to get where they wanted to be. Life isn't always easy or fair, but it can be wonderful when you let it. Someday, you'll be able to look at all your accomplishments and say that you did it because you wouldn't give up. You can't change what your parents have done, but you can decide what *you* do. You have control over that."

"I know I definitely never want to start drinking. It's not worth it."

She hoped he really meant it. "That's right, Robbie. I'm glad that you can see the problem and avoid it. That reminds me of what a preacher said, 'It's better to avoid what you might not have the strength to resist.' Just because your dad went down that path, that doesn't mean that you have to follow. Just because he complains about the way his life has gone, that doesn't mean that you'll end up the same way. You get to make that choice."

He nodded and said, "I know you're right. It's just that sometimes the bad memories get the better of me. I feel like I'm already defeated in a way." He looked down again and shook his head. "I haven't even told you the worst of it yet."

"It's okay, Robbie. You can tell me."

"I don't know. Maybe I've said enough for one day. I don't want to get depressed." He stood up. "I can't get into it right now. It hurts too much."

He started to walk away.

Lisa stood up and said, "You don't have to tell me anything you don't want to, but you can't run from your problems, either. They'll always find a way to come back and defeat you until you find the strength to face them."

He paused.

She said, "At least come back tomorrow."

"Wednesday," he said. He looked back to her. "I'll try to do it then."

"Okay. I'll be ready for you."

He nodded and walked away.

She said, "I'm ready to end the pain."

That night, Lisa and Charlie talked about their day, trying not to give away too many personal details about Robbie and Amanda. They checked the scrapbook.

"What?!" asked a bewildered Lisa. "Why hasn't this changed? With everything he said today, I can't believe he still went down this path. Maybe it's my fault. Maybe I'm not doing this right."

"You can't go there, Lisa. You're doing the best you can."

"Am I? We have proof that he still makes the same choices. We have proof that I failed him."

"Whatever happens, it's still his choice. You can't blame yourself. There's still time. These headlines can still change any day now. For all we know, maybe it takes longer for some things in the future to catch up."

"I hope you're right. It's not just his future I'm concerned about, you know. Let's not forget Tracy. Or, Amanda for that matter."

Charlie said, "I think Amanda is making progress, but there still needs to be a permanent change before her future still ends up in the paper. I have a little less time than you do to get this right."

"What do you mean?"

"I mean that my future self's time as Sam is coming to an end. I can't keep going back to the school as Sam after he stops doing so."

"Why not?"

"Because there would be a chance that my younger self would run into him. After we said our goodbyes, I couldn't rely on him anymore. I had to take everything he said and apply it to a new future-- the one that we live now. I can't very well show up again as Sam and undermine the finality of our time together. Do you know what my younger self talked to Tracy about today? We talked about my wanting to ask you to the prom. Can you believe it? I finally found the confidence to let her in on it. We can't take the chance of interfering with anything that I did from now on."

"I totally understand and I agree with you. I hope we can make the same kind of difference for Amanda and Robbie as Sam did for you. When is his last day?"

"I'll never forget it. It's this Thursday. He was never seen or heard from again except when he saw my mom a week later."

"I wonder what he did in between."

"Probably just hid out in his room. Maybe I'll ask him when the time's right."

Tuesday, February 5th. Sam woke from a night of strange dreams. He sat up shaking. He watched as his hands trembled before he held his torso and groaned with pain. He stood up and caught the bed before he fell over. His head pounded along with his heart. He slowly stumbled his way to the mirror, pain affecting his every move. He gazed at his pale reflection, the visage of a man unfamiliar. His breathing grew more panicked. It took all of his strength to hold onto the sink long enough to ask himself a burning question.

"What's happening to me?!"

When Lisa arrived at the school, she went by Sam's office. The door was locked. She waited to see if he was just running late. After half an hour, she knew something wasn't right. She didn't want to say anything to Mr. Foltan yet, so she found a phone in the teacher's lounge.

"Hello?" Charlie asked from the motel phone.

"We have a new complication. Sam isn't here."

"Oh, yeah-- that's right! This was the day when he didn't show up."

"So, it happened this way before?"

"Yeah, he said on Thursday that he wasn't feeling well."

"Maybe you should check on him."

"I don't know... I might cause a bigger problem."

"At least go see if he's at the motel."

"Okay, I'll go look. Hold on."

He set the phone down and went outside. He came back and told her, "The car is still there."

"Okay, good. I just hope he's all right."

"He does come back to school, so I'd say he will be all right. It might not be wise to go see him. Try not to worry about it."

"Okay. I just hope that my being here doesn't change anything too much."

Lisa had Mr. Foltan unlock the door with a spare key. She spent the rest of the day dealing with a little more than the usual amount of counselling duties. That afternoon as she sat at the desk, a special visitor came by. She immediately became nervous.

"I'm here to see Mr. Whitfield. I have an appointment."

"He wasn't feeling well today. Sorry about that. I'm the temporary assistant counselor."

"Oh. Well, I hope he gets better. Maybe I could still talk to you for a minute if you don't mind. I could use a lady's advice."

"Sure, sure." She held out her hand. "Lorrie Parker."

He shook her hand as he said, "Charlie Jordache."

"Nice to meet you, Charlie. Have a seat."

"Man, I hope I don't mess this up. Why did this have to happen today?" she thought.

"There's this girl I like. Actually, that's not even the right word. She's with this other guy, but I've known her for the longest time. I wanted to ask her to Prom, but I'm so nervous I can't find a way to do it. She's probably going with him anyway, but I still feel like I need to ask her."

"Even if she might say no?"

"That's what I'm afraid of. But, I'm becoming more afraid of what would happen if I don't even try. I just hope I'm not already too late."

She knew that she had to choose her words carefully so that he wouldn't do anything at the wrong time. "You're not too late. Even if she's already going to Prom with this other guy, that's not the end of the world. You could still have a chance. Just don't give up."

"Do you have any idea what I could say to her?"

"Only your heart can tell you what to say. Just speak from your heart and be yourself. I'm sure it will all work out."

"That's what Sam said. I just don't know if I can even compete with this other guy. He's tall and good-looking, athletic, popular..."

"That's all just superficial stuff. You know better than that. It's the heart of a person that matters. You seem like you have a good, caring heart. I'm sure she sees that in you."

"I want to ask you this, but I want you to be honest."

"Okay, shoot."

"Do you think I'm good-looking?"

She smiled. "Yes, Charlie. I think you're a very good-looking guy. Not that it matters."

"Thanks. I know it doesn't matter, but I still worry about that. She's so pretty, and all the guys like her..." He squinted. "Actually... she looks a lot like you."

Her heart beat even faster than it already was. "Really? I--I don't know what to say..."

"You have a similar smile. You look like you could be related."

"Wrap this up quick! He knows you too well!" she thought as she struggled for a good response. "I highly doubt that we're related. I'm not from around here."

"Oh, yeah-- the accent. She's from California and just moved back here again. You're probably not related then."

"Yeah, probably not," she said as she tried not to smile the same way. "Listen, Charlie, I'm sure any girl would be happy to be with you. It sounds like this particular girl must be quite a catch, so you just hang in there and don't give up. Okay?"

"Okay. I'll keep trying. I just don't want to mess this up. She means too much to me."

"With a heart like yours, I'm sure the future is very bright."

"Thanks, Miss Parker. I'll give it my best." He stood up. "Tell Mr. Whitfield I said, 'hi' if you see him."

"I will. Nice to meet you."

They smiled and waved as he walked away. She breathed a sigh of relief and put her head on the desk.

"If this kind of thing happens again, I might go gray for real."

"Man, that was too close," Lisa told Charlie later.

"What was?"

"Your younger self coming to talk to me. I was scared to death that I would change something too much in our past."

"What are you talking about?" he asked with a laugh. Then it dawned on him. "Oh, that was you! That's why I thought you looked like Lisa. That's so crazy!" He laughed again.

"You remember that?"

"Of course I do."

"This is heavy! I did change your past! You remember something that didn't happen before. I actually changed your memory!"

He laughed. "What changed memory? That's the way it always was. I went to see Sam like usual, but he wasn't there. So, I ended up talking to Miss Parker instead. I just didn't realize it was you." His face grew more serious. "Wait a minute. That doesn't make sense. How could you have been there as Miss Parker when I was in high school?"

"That's what I'm trying to tell you, Charlie. I wasn't there originally. I was there today and changed it. This is a new memory for you, but you remember it as though it was always that way."

"A new memory? That really is heavy. It's all so confusing."

"Do you feel okay?"

"Yeah, I'm okay. I'm just processing this."

"This is exactly why we can't interfere with our own past selves. This time was safe and you still ended up talking to me about Prom, but another time might not be so good."

"You're absolutely right."

"This might even happen to me. Maybe you should read my diary and notice if anything changes. In fact, we shouldn't keep holding back information from our counselling. I know that confidentiality is important, but if we change something and don't even realize it, then we're doing this blindly."

"I agree. We have to work together as a team for Robbie and Amanda alike. There's far too much at stake here to keep adding variables. If we share with each other what we know, it could improve our chances of success."

"Oh, wow. I just thought of something. If memories work this way for you, just imagine how much of this is happening to Sam. He might not know what to believe at times."

"I think you have a good point. That may be why he didn't make it to school today. It might be catching up with him."

"That poor man. And, he's doing it all for me."

"He's been doing it all alone."

On Wednesday the 6th, Mr. Foltan came by Sam's office.

"How's it going with the bully situation?"

"The bully situation?"

"Yeah, I think her name was Amanda something. I haven't heard any reports that she's caused any more trouble, so I assumed that you were making progress."

Unfortunately, he was asking the wrong Sam. Though he was bewildered, he thought quickly. "Oh, yes, Sir. Making a lot of progress. I plan on making even more... progress."

"Glad to hear it. Looks like you were right. Keep up the good work, Whitfield."

Mr. Foltan walked away. Sam said, "What the heck was that about?"

Later that morning, Amanda begrudgingly sat at the desk in Mr. Foltan's office.

The younger Sam said, "Good to see you again, Miss DiPino."

She rolled her eyes.

Sam said, "Having a rough day?"

"Not really."

"Then why did you roll your eyes? Did I say something wrong, Miss DiPino?"

"That. That's what you said wrong."

"I'm sorry; I don't follow."

"I'm tired of being called that."

"Miss DiPino? Is that not your name?"

"No, it's not my name. It's my stepdad's name. I hate it."

"Okay, I'll just call you Amanda from now on. I take it that you don't like your stepdad."

"He's a jerk."

"What makes him a jerk?"

"Do we really have to talk about this?"

"What else should we talk about? We're here to solve your problems. It sounds like this is a big one. You said that you would start opening up more today. I'm going to hold you to it."

She sighed. "Well, if you really have to know, he's lazy. He just mooches off of Mom. He can't hold a job for nothin'. He doesn't do much around the house. Mom has to work more to make up for it, so I have to take care of the kids."

"Kids? Do you have siblings?"

"Yeah, I have a brother and a sister. I'm the oldest. I never thought I'd have to be a mom."

He was quickly reminded of his own childhood. "Unfortunately, too many kids have to grow up too soon. It's a heavy burden to bear."

"Yeah, well, I didn't ask for it. I love my brother and sister, but this ain't the way it's supposed to be."

"I'm sure your mom is doing the best she can. I'm also sure that she appreciates what you do to help."

"I don't know. It's not like I see her much. She spends more time with him when she's home."

His mind began to connect the dots. "How long have they been together?"

"Since I was a kid."

"Was it always this hard for you?"

"Not always. It got worse over time. And, sometimes it's not as bad."

"Did it start getting worse again recently?"

"Yeah. They've been talking about getting married."

He was astonished. "They haven't been married all this time? Why do you have his name?"

"Because Mom insisted. Just like always, no one listens to me."

"I'm listening now. It sounds to me that you've been largely neglected. You haven't had the attention that you need, and when you do get it, it's because you've done something negative to achieve it."

She smirked. "Yeah, that's about right."

"What you've been through isn't fair. You deserve better than that. You've bottled this stuff up for so long that it's almost second nature.

It doesn't need to be that way. You really need to talk to your mom about your concerns."

"She won't listen to me."

"Have you really tried?"

"Yeah."

"When? Recently or a long time ago?"

"It's been awhile."

"You don't know that she won't listen. I don't know if she should be with this man or not. I don't know enough about him. But, your opinion is valid. You have to both communicate how you feel. No problems ever get solved by sweeping them under the rug. It only makes it worse. You've already channeled them into being a bully. You're better than that, Amanda. Think about your siblings. Don't you think that they look up to you? Shouldn't you speak up for them, if not yourself?"

"Yeah, I guess so."

"You're worth it, Amanda. You just have to start communicating with your heart."

"How do I do that?"

"By being honest."

"Like you said, it's almost second nature."

"It's time for that to end. You've kept things buried inside, you've lashed out at innocent people, and you've even done it to yourself. You don't even have to tell me that for me to see it. The pain has to end. You've been a prisoner of it for far too long. The truth will make you free."

"How did it go with Amanda?" Lisa asked Charlie as they shared a lunch in the car.

"Better. I think she's finally starting to have a real change of heart."

"I hope Robbie opens up more this time. We're so close I can feel it. I think I know what his biggest problem is, but I can't make him tell me. I really want to help him, but he has to make that effort."

"Same with Amanda. If there's anyone who can do it, it's you."

"I know, but it's harder than I thought it would be."

Lisa's heart weighed heavily as she prepared herself for what she believed Robbie would talk about. If she was right, this could be the beginning of the end to a lot of pain.

"I always have a hard time knowing how to get started," Robbie said.

"I know it's hard for you to talk about these things, but we both know that it's necessary."

"It's just that I've held this all back for so long, I don't know anything else. I've never told anyone the things that I'm telling you. It's really hard to just let it out that easily."

"I understand, Robbie. I didn't want to push you. Experience has taught me to let people know that it's okay to talk about it and give you time to get comfortable. I've seen this all before. I think I know what you're holding back, but I don't want to push you or put words in your mouth. It's your choice to tell me. I know it's hard to break that barrier and say it out loud, but when you do, it does become easier."

He nodded. "You do make it easier." He closed his eyes and took a deep breath. "Okay, here it is. I told you that my parents fought a lot. I told you that my dad drinks and my mom left. Well, the biggest reason why she left, the thing that pushed her too far, was during one of their yelling matches... he hit her." His eyes teared up. "I saw it happen. I can still see the look on her face. It was shock more than it was pain. That's all it took. Just that one time. She left right then and there and never came back."

"I'm so sorry, Robbie."

"He's talked to her on the phone and stuff, but he couldn't get her to come back. It didn't make things better. It wasn't a wakeup call. He just hit the bottle harder. There have been times when we could get along, but it's rare. He has this old car, this '65 bug, and we would work on it sometimes. I don't even know why he keeps it. He doesn't drive it, he just keeps it in the garage. Just a hobby, I guess. He would show me how to do stuff, but he would get frustrated. This one time, he'd been drinking again, and..." He looked down and teared up again. "...he hit me. I didn't even do anything. I was only twelve."

It was exactly what Lisa feared was true. She said, "You never told anyone?"

"I was afraid. I thought he might do it again if I told someone. It didn't matter because he still did it again anyway. He kept doing it off and on for years. I finally got too big for him and he stopped. I think he's afraid that I could hit him back. I try to avoid him anyway."

"I really appreciate you telling me. I know it was hard. I hope you realize that it wasn't your fault that he did that. You never deserved it."

He nodded. "I know. I had to keep telling myself that it was his addiction. I tried to talk to him about it a couple of times, but it just made him mad. Man, I can't wait to just get out of that house. I have to get away. I have to start over."

"So, are you talking about moving to Kansas City for sure?"

"Maybe. I don't know. Lisa's here... and, I really like her. I can see it working out with her. I don't know if she would want to move. She has her family here. She might want to get married sometime, but I do know for sure that I don't ever want to have kids. I don't want to take a chance that I would do to them what was done to me. I don't ever want to turn into my dad."

He cried.

"I think the fact that you know that you don't want to be like him will keep you from doing that. You are not him. You have been through a lot of pain, but that doesn't have to ruin you. He doesn't have to have that power over you anymore. You have pushed through it so far, and you can keep doing it. You have dreams, you have ambition, and you can start over, just like you said. You can make a new future. You don't have to worry about having kids and being like your dad. You are not him. You can determine to be better than that. The cycle ends now."

He nodded his head and wiped his eyes. "I'm trying. I just wish he could be proud of me. I wish I could have parents cheering me on for doing a good job. I never know if I'll be good enough for that."

"Of course you're good enough. I'm sure your dad is proud of you in his own way. Maybe he also has a hard time communicating how he truly feels. All you need to do is hold your head up high and do your best, no matter what anyone thinks. Everything else will fall into place."

"I know you're right. It's just hard."

"At least you talked about it. Doesn't it feel better?"

"A little bit. But, it also brings back too many memories. I've tried to move past them."

"Bad memories can't be buried to go away. They have to be dealt with properly."

"I think that's part of Dad's problem. He just buries them. Tries to drown them. He blames everyone but himself."

"You know that doesn't work. You have to talk about these things. I won't always be here. Even if it's someone else, you need to talk to someone."

"I will. I'm just... I'm just all over the place right now. I think I've said enough for today. I want to be able to concentrate on my classes."

"Sure, Robbie, I understand. I think this was a big step in the right direction for you. A big step towards overcoming everything. I'm proud of you."

"Thank you. Sorry for blubbering in front of you."

"Oh, you don't have anything to be sorry about. It took a lot of strength to tell me what you said. That strength will get you through anything."

"I'm sure gonna try."

He stood up and started to leave.

"See you Friday," she said.

He looked back and gave her half a smile and a nod.

She knew that this was the breakthrough that was needed, yet it somehow didn't feel right.

"I still remember it," she said to herself. "I guess it's gonna take more time. What else will it take?"

Thursday the 7th. Charlie knew that this day was too important to risk interfering with his past. He stayed away from the school and talked to Lisa about steering clear of both of his counterparts. She wholeheartedly agreed. Her responses to Sam's pages were kept simple. She helped other students that day, but still had one in particular on her mind.

Charlie replayed his memories of this day the first time he lived it. Sam telling him that he wasn't well took on a deeper meaning. He still had questions. It was time for answers before it was too late.

"Well, looky here," Sam said when he opened the motel door that night. "I already said my goodbyes earlier."

The younger Charlie said, "Yeah, the whole time travel thing can have its share of twists and turns."

"Don't I know it. Come on in."

He entered the room.

Sam asked, "Do I dare ask what brings you by?"

"We had an incident the other day when you weren't at school. Because you weren't there, my younger self talked to Lorrie instead."

"Oh, dear. That clearly wasn't meant to happen. I hope it didn't throw anything off."

"I don't think it did. Lisa was very careful about what she said. But, it did cause something interesting to happen. She never did this before, yet I remember it happening when I was seventeen. What she did here in 1985, I remember it as a thing that happened years ago."

"Your memory changed. You'll never know a time when you didn't talk to Lorrie. It's now a part of your permanent history." He chuckled. "It's pretty fascinating, isn't it?"

"Yes, it is. However, it does raise some questions."

"Like what?"

"You don't remember any of that, do you?"

"I came from another time. It's not a part of my history."

"See, I think it is. I think your memory would also have to change."

He sighed and scratched his head. "Okay, you got me." He sat down on the bed. "Here, pull up a bed."

Charlie followed suit.

Sam said, "Want to know why I wasn't at work that day?"

"You said that you weren't feeling well."

"That was true. I didn't want to have to tell you the whole truth. See, I woke up that day in pain. It wasn't the first time, but it was one of the worst times. And, I don't mean a little sore, either. I mean excruciating, agonizing pain like I've never felt in my life. I don't even know how to describe it. When I looked in the mirror, I didn't even recognize myself. Who was this old man? What was happening to me? I didn't have the answers. This is happening more and more."

"What's causing it?"

He pointed at the night stand. "You see that tape recorder over there? Tonight, just like every night, I'm going to record myself telling myself what the date is and what I'm doing here. I have to resort to a tape to tell me who I am in case I forget."

"I can't imagine how hard that must be."

"I've gone my whole life... heck, so have you... not being able to forget anything. Even if I wanted to, I couldn't do it. Now, I'm forgetting things left and right. I forgot to even play that tape for awhile that day. Know why I had to tell you goodbye today? Because I know that each day I wake up, I'm going to become more and more incapacitated. I had to get you to a point where you can handle changing your own future without any more guidance from me. Apparently, you end up doing that. I don't know when or how, but you do."

"Your memories change based on what I do."

"Bingo. The more you need me, the better I feel. My mind stays as sharp as yours. But, the more you become independent of me and change how you do things, that's when it starts affecting me adversely."

"So... the more you achieve your mission, the more I change my attitude and actions, the more you suffer."

"I always knew this was a one-way ticket. I wasn't sure of how it would happen exactly, but I knew that I wouldn't survive it. This version of me-- this future-- can't and won't exist."

"Are you saying that..."

"Yeah, kid. I'm dying. I'm fading out of existence."

"So, that's what happens to you? Are you scared?"

A tear rolled down his cheek. "I'm terrified. I don't know when it will be, but I know it will be soon. I know that each day might be my last. I keep reminding myself that it's all for Lisa. It's all so that you can save her from what she experienced. Dying isn't what scares me as much as not knowing if I'll save her before it happens."

"You do. We both do. Remember? You've talked to her. We end up getting married and having kids. I showed you the pictures. Remember?"

His tears increased. "I remember now. Sometimes, I don't know what's real and what's not. What's a memory, and what's just a dream. It's all scary and confusing. At least I know that it all works out. You'll never have to go through this. You'll never be alone like me."

"Maybe I shouldn't stay much longer. I don't know if I've already told you too much."

"This might sound weird, but could you stay just a little bit more? I haven't had anyone to talk to."

They were the saddest eyes he'd ever seen. "Sure. Whatever you need."

"Now, I don't even know what to talk about. There's not much that we don't both already know."

Charlie hesitated, but went ahead anyway. "There's something I have to ask you."

"If it's about the future, forget it."

"I understand that it's not good to know too much, and I understand that the future may still change."

"Anything about your future is entirely different than mine. There's no way you can run with anything I tell you. It will all change."

"Then, it might be okay to ask."

"I think I know what you're going to ask anyway."

"Then, I might as well say it. Do you know anything more about Dad?"

He looked down and shook his head. He reluctantly admitted, "I don't know anything more than what we knew when it happened. I didn't want to have to tell you that."

"Maybe that will change with Lisa."

"It doesn't hurt to be optimistic, but don't get your hopes up. You might be better off moving on with your life."

"What year are you from?"

"2015. Before you can even ask, I'll tell you that there aren't any flying cars. Hate to burst your bubble. Some other predictions came true, but I'll let you find that out for yourself."

"Wow. It really took you awhile to build the time machine."

"It sure wasn't easy. It took years of research to even find out about the crystals and where they might be. You had it made. You got to piggyback off my work, and had a partner to boot."

"That did make it a lot better," he said with a smile. "Thank you."

"While we're on the subject of changing the past, there is one thing that I want to tell you that could make a difference. Something that you could do that I never did."

"What's that?"

"You could use your full potential."

"I feel like I am with Lisa by my side. She brings out the best in me."

"That's all well and good, but there's something else that you're still hiding. Something that she doesn't know. Not even Mom knows. You can't hide it from me. We have the same brain."

"What are you talking about?"

"You know full well what I'm talking about. The part of you that you don't let anyone see. The part that you're still not sure about. Maybe it's a little scary. I'm talking about the voice you hear when no one is around."

It was like he saw right through him. "You're right. I've still never told anyone about that."

"It's not Mom, and it's not Dad. You know who it is. You have to start listening more. You have to embrace your full potential, Charlie. Mom was right all along. There's a reason why God made you this way. You have to use your gift."

"I'm not even sure how."

The older Charlie suddenly grabbed his head and looked very distressed.

"What is it? Are you okay?" the younger man asked.

"You have to listen to me, Charlie. You have to open up and not fight it."

"How? What is it?"

"I see it, Charlie." He began to cry. "I see it. I don't know when... but, I see it."

"What is it? What do you see?!"

"You have to do this." He looked into his eyes. The younger Charlie saw fear and desperate urgency. "The world is gonna need it."

"The world?! What do you mean?! Your future and mine aren't the same. You said so yourself."

He shook his head. "No, no, this... this is beyond that. This... this is bigger. This is your destiny. They need you!"

"Who needs me?! You're not making sense."

He grabbed his arm. "The world is gonna need *all* of you."

"You mean others?"

"You're not the only one who can do it."

"Dad?" Lisa asked as she sat up in the bed. No one was there. "I guess I must have dozed off. I thought I heard someone. Maybe I was dreaming."

CHAPTER 31

Friday, February 8th, 1985. Charlie woke from a night of little sleep. His older counterpart's words haunted him. He knew that he wasn't at his best, but whatever it was that he saw was clearly genuine and disturbing. He would never forget the look on his older self's face.

"Are you going to be okay?" Lisa asked.

"Yeah. Why do you ask?"

"You tossed and turned all night."

"I had a lot on my mind. Had a hard time getting to sleep."

"I know the feeling. Today's a big day. We need to see some major changes in Robbie and Amanda very soon. Plus, we still don't have a generator or a functioning crystal. We really have a lot on our plate."

"Yeah-- too many plates spinning at once."

She chuckled. "That's more like it. But, at least there's two of us to handle it." She kissed him. "Always together. 'For we walk by faith, not by sight.'"

It was the reminder that he needed. The older Charlie may have seen something, but it was still faith that would guide them through it all. The bigger picture was too much to process for the time being, so they would have to focus on the current needs. And, it would take all the faith they could muster.

Charlie sat at the desk as Sam for what he hoped would be the last time. He couldn't risk undoing his past by his presence, but he also couldn't risk Amanda's future being ruined, either. He knew this would have to be the day that she changed her direction, but it was ultimately up to her.

"Good morning, Amanda," he said as she walked in.

"Good morning," she replied with more pleasantness than usual.

"Ready to get those billboards finished tomorrow?"

"Yeah, I guess so," she said as she sat down.

"Have you decided what you wanted to put on them?"

"I'm still thinking about it. I have a few ideas."

"I'm sure you'll come up with the right one." He was surprised by how much different she sounded. It seemed like she was actually being herself. "Did you talk to your mom?"

"I tried to, but she was too busy."

"Keep trying. Don't give up."

"I will."

She seemed like she meant it. "Is there anything else you want to talk about?"

She hesitated for a second. "Well… I've been thinking about what you said about being honest. I realized that I've told more lies than I can count. I also realized that it really was hurting people… even myself."

"Sometimes it may seem easier to lie, but honesty is always the better option. It really is a choice."

"I thought about what you said about being myself. I saw myself going down this path that I didn't want to go down again."

He knew what she meant, but he had to ask as Sam. "What do you mean by 'again'?"

"I was being a bully and hurting people. You were right. They didn't deserve it. I did that to someone a long time ago, and I had to pay for it. I got held back because I was cheating off him. I used that as an excuse to hurt him even more, but it was my fault." She started tearing up. "Even after I beat him up, he said that he felt bad for me. He wanted to be friends… even after all I did to him. He gave me his hand to shake, but I told him that I didn't know yet." Her tears increased. "I felt so bad about it. I never picked on him again. I was so mean to him. He didn't deserve it. He was a really nice kid and he was already going through a lot." She sobbed.

Charlie tried with all his might to hold back his own tears.

She continued, "I was so terrible to him. I promised myself that I'd never treat anybody like that again. Well, that was another one of my lies. I was good about it 'til recently. You were right. I don't want to be this person. It's all I've known. I'm tired of the guilt and the pain that I've caused. I wish I could change it. I'm so tired of it."

Charlie was completely blown away. Still trying to hold back his emotions, he said, "You *can* change it, Amanda. It's not too late. You can't change the past, but you can make a better future. You can still change your direction, just like you want to. You can still talk to your mom as honestly as you've talked to me today. I think it would help a lot. You can still choose not to hurt anyone. You could still go back to Stephanie, Noreen, and Mark and apologize to them. Maybe you can even be friends."

"I will. It might not be easy, but I know it's the right thing to do. After all I did to them, I can at least do that much. I just hope it's not too late to apologize to Charlie."

He never would've imagined that she would say such a thing. He said, "It's never too late to do the right thing."

"I still see him around the school once in awhile. He hasn't seemed very happy, either. I think I really got to him back then." She started to tear up again. "The truth is, I was kind of jealous of him. He was smart and had a really good mom. I thought he was an easy target at first. I could make him do what I said. I thought he was weak. He was actually strong. He was a lot stronger than me."

"I think today is when you take back control of your own strength. It took strength to tell me everything you said. It will take strength to apologize. It will take strength to talk to your mom. It's your choice. You get to choose this path. Once you start going this new direction, I don't think you'll ever want to look back. Instead of getting attention for all the wrong reasons, you can now get it for the right ones."

"I will. It starts today."

"Congratulations, my dear. You made it out of here."

"Yes! It worked!"

"What?!"

"I'm kidding!" she said with a laugh.

He breathed a sigh of relief. "Don't scare me like that! You had me going."

"Speaking of going, I'd better get out of here." She stood up. "Maybe I can get at least one of my apologies in before the next class. See you tomorrow, Sam."

"Can't wait."

She walked away smiling. He took the newspaper clipping out of his pocket. She was no longer in the news.

"Oh, thank God!"

He took off his glasses as he began to cry.

"Finally some good news."

He leaned on the desk as his tears overflowed. A weight that he felt for decades was finally lifted. He was right about her all along. She wasn't someone to hate, she was someone to love.

"Love changes everything."

A little while later, he had gathered himself together enough to make a quiet exit. As he walked down the hall, a familiar face made eye contact. He hoped that he could avoid talking to him, but there was no way out of it.

"Hey, Sam," his younger self said. "I thought you weren't coming back."

"Charlie! What a surprise. I still had one more student to counsel today."

"Oh, I see."

"It was a good thing I did. I shouldn't tell you too much, but just know that it ended up being good for me as well. That's what happens when you communicate honestly with people. You never know when you'll hear exactly what you needed to hear."

"I'll remember that."

"I know you will. I think you'll be in for some big surprises soon if you speak from your heart and listen just as well."

"I hope so. I'd better get going. It was good to see you one last time. Maybe our paths can cross again someday."

"You never know what the future will bring."

They smiled and parted ways. The older Charlie said under his breath, "...or, the past..."

That afternoon, Lisa prepared for her usual appointment with Robbie. She sat at the desk thinking of the best way to guide him. As the time on the clock ticked past the appointed time, she grew more concerned. She waited a few minutes longer in case he was running late. She tried to think back to what was happening at that time when she was younger. She still remembered being with him at lunch and for some of their classes. She thought back to the days that followed. She remembered that on Sunday the 10th, she had her first semi-date with Charlie. Even without the perfect memory that he had, she couldn't forget such an important time.

"Come on, Lisa, think. What else was going on?"

She remembered what Charlie said about memories.

"A familiar sight, sound, smell, or anything else that could trigger a memory. Let's see... I went to the mall with Charlie. We looked at clothes, got hot fudge sundaes, and tossed some pennies into the fountain. We went to the park... but, what about Robbie? He wasn't there. Ilene came over to our house and we talked about him. It felt awkward. Charlie must have known that Robbie wasn't there because of Mom. That's why he made his move. That sly dog," she said with a chuckle. "But, why wasn't Robbie there? Did I talk to him at all? Think! Think!"

She looked at the phone on the desk. She put her hand on it and closed her eyes. She tried to imagine it as the one she had at home.

"I tried to call him, but he said he wasn't feeling well. We never did do anything together that weekend." It dawned on her. "He wasn't sick. He was depressed. That's why he didn't come talk to me today. Even when he needs to the most, he's running the other way." She shook her head and sighed. "This isn't the way, Robbie. We were making such good progress. It was so close. You have to fight it, man. You have to let me in."

She decided to start using Sam's office for the remainder of the day and beyond. As the clock inched closer to three, she took care of a few more students. One of them was Noreen. She informed Lorrie that Amanda came to apologize to her and that all was well. This good news did bring her spirits up substantially. Just as she was about to close up for the weekend, someone else came to talk.

"I'm sorry it's so close to the end of the day, but I was hoping I could talk to you about something if you have a minute."

"Sure. You can have as many minutes as you want."

"My name's Tracy," her old friend said as she held out her hand.

"Lorrie," she said as she shook it. *"Why do I have to keep getting into these situations?"* she thought. "How can I help you?"

"I have this friend. And, when I say that I have this friend, I don't mean the proverbial 'friend' who is really myself. I mean that it really is my friend."

"I see," she said with a laugh. "I'm glad you cleared that up."

"Sorry. I'm a bit nervous. It's actually about two of my friends. There's this one, who's a boy, and he's in love with the other one, who's a girl. The only thing is, he's too nervous to say anything about it. Plus, she has a boyfriend now, so that doesn't help matters. They're going to the prom together. I've known these two for a long time. I've always known that he's been in love with her. I could never tell if she felt the same way about him. If she does, she's really good at hiding it. I don't know why she wouldn't, cuz like, you know, they really should be together. It's really obvious to me. I would be very surprised if she didn't have some kind of feelings for him. I mean, come on. He's really rad. I had kind of a crush on him myself when I was little, but I knew better, so I didn't do anything about it and just quietly cheered them on."

Lisa tried to hold back her smile. She really was a great friend.

Tracy continued, "So, anyway, the reason why I'm telling you all this is because I have a bad feeling that things aren't going to go right. Should I get involved? I love these guys to death and I don't want to see them end up miserable. What do I do?"

She had no idea what to say. All she knew was that she had to choose her words very carefully. "First of all, I think that you're an amazing friend to want to help them. I think that maybe you should give it a little more time and see if this young man tells her how he feels. Valentine's Day is coming right up, so you never know."

"Yeah, maybe you're right. I don't want to mess up anything, but I don't want to stand back and watch them make a mistake, either."

"If it's meant to be, then it's meant to be. Let love take its natural course."

"That makes sense, but what if she ends up with the guy she's dating instead? I just don't think they're right for each other."

"What's wrong with him?"

"Oh, nothing's wrong with him. It's just not the same. He's actually a really good guy. I admit... I kind of had a crush on him, too."

"Do you think that you would be a good match with him?"

"I can kinda see it. It might not be such a bad thing. I think he wants to go to Kansas City in the fall, though. I'd rather stay here."

Lisa knew that she couldn't reveal too much. "Well, whether he's right for you or not, it sounds like these other two are right for each other. My advice is to quietly cheer them on as you've already done. If Valentine's comes and goes and things still don't look right, then maybe you should start dropping some hints."

"Okay. I wish it was all easier than this. Why does it have to be so complicated?"

She smiled. "Where's the fun in that?"

She laughed and said sarcastically, "Oh, yeah. So fun." They shook hands again. "Thanks, Lorrie. I feel better about it now."

"I'm glad I could help."

"Goodbye," she said as she walked away.

"See ya later."

Tracy paused. "My friend always says that."

Lisa's heart beat faster.

Tracy said, "Cool." She left the room.

Lisa breathed a sigh of relief. "Sister, you don't even know the meaning of 'complicated'."

Charlie and Lisa talked about their experiences for the day. Lisa was thrilled to hear that Amanda finally had her breakthrough and was no longer headed for a grim future. She felt less optimistic about Robbie. Despite Charlie's assurances that she would still make a difference, she worried more and more that she may have only made things worse.

Saturday the 9th. Charlie arrived to the field as Sam once more.

"Did you figure out what you would add to the billboards?" he asked Amanda.

"I'm still debating it."

"Too many good choices?"

"Nothing that feels right."

He rubbed his chin, careful not to pull the fake goatee off. "I'm not an artist, but I do know what it's like to be creative. I know that you can't do what you're told to do. You have to do it your own way. You have to come up with something from the heart."

"I agree."

"Maybe the problem isn't a lack of inspiration. Maybe it's just a lack of confidence."

"I've been afraid this whole time that it won't be good enough."

"Is it really your art that you're not so sure about, or is it yourself?"

"Maybe it's both."

"Listen, Amanda. You just had a major breakthrough yesterday. I can't emphasize this enough." He put his hand on her shoulder. "This is your time. Now is when you prove yourself."

"Are you sure I'm good enough for this?"

"You've done a great job so far. As long as you do what's in your heart, then it's going to be just fine."

She nodded and looked back to her canvas of sorts. "I need to stare at it for awhile and see what it needs to be."

"I can't wait to see it."

Later that day, Charlie came back. Amanda smiled when he walked up to her.

"You did it!" he exclaimed.

She chuckled somewhat nervously.

"How does it feel?" he asked.

She smiled even bigger and said, "It feels great."

"Now, look at it. Just stand back and look. You did that."

As they looked at the signs, Charlie glanced over at Amanda. He had never seen her so happy. They watched as a car drove by. The driver looked back towards them.

"Did you see that? You're turning heads! People are already noticing the great job you did."

"Do you really think it's that good?"

"Oh, Amanda. It's perfect. This will be here for years. Generations will drive by and see what you've done. That's something to be proud of. I'm proud of you."

She held her head down. "No one's ever been proud of me before."

He put his hands on her shoulders. "My dear girl. That's all gonna change."

Her eyes began to water.

He continued, "You've done something that will stand the test of time. Let this be a reminder to you. Whenever you feel like you're not good enough, just think of these signs. You have a whole town that will think that you're good enough. You did that. You did it with your talent, your vision, and your heart. You did it by just being you."

Tears ran down her cheeks.

He said, "You can't change the past, but you can make a better..."

"...future," she replied.

"You can be just like your art. You're the only one who knows what's inside you. Once you let that out, we get to stand back and be amazed. It's there inside you for a reason. You are here for a reason. We want to see what you can do. You're the only one who can do it. No more bullying, right?"

She looked him in the eyes. "Never again."

"You get a new start. No more Amanda the bully. No more of the Amanda who doesn't think she's good enough. You're Amanda the artist. The one who can be whatever you choose to be."

She looked back to the image on the sign. "Amanda the sunflower."

He smiled. "I like that. Sunflowers symbolize happiness. You're free to be happy. Just like you've always wanted."

She hugged him and started to cry again. "Thank you for not giving up on me."

"My pleasure. Just don't give up on yourself... Sunflower."

"She really did it!" Lisa enthused as she admired Amanda's art a little while later. "Everyone will definitely notice this instead of the house."

Charlie said, "She did an amazing job. Even better is her transformation. She even thanked me for not giving up on her."

"That's the best news we've had in a long time. How do you feel? Does it give you a sense of closure?"

"It does." He searched for the right words. "I feel free."

She hugged him. "I'm so happy for you, honey. For both of you. You were the only one who could've helped her and she was the only one who could've helped you. Sounds like a miracle to me."

"It goes to show you that anyone can change-- even Robbie."

She let go and looked him in the eyes. "The jury's still out on that one."

"No, it's gonna happen. I'm sure of it. You're so close to seeing another miracle."

"I really hope so. We just have to be a little more patient, I guess."

"All in due time."

"Yeah, about that... we don't have much of it left. We still don't even have a way to get back yet. There has to be a way to get power to the crystal faster. If only we had more time."

"Oh, the irony. A time machine without time."

"We have to think outside the box. How can we buy more time or increase the solar output?"

"I don't think we can. And, we definitely can't stay here long after we change the past. We don't know what that would do to us. We'll probably see the headlines change..." suddenly a thought occurred to him. "The headlines change in the future because it changed in the past."

"Yeah? So? We know that already."

His eyes got wider. "We can still see it now because we're from the future... even though we're in the past."

"Yeah, I get it. What are you trying to say?"

"When did we get the notebook?"

"That was 1995."

"How did we get it?"

"It was at the bank."

"It was planted in the past for us to find in the future."

"Okay, I see what you're getting at, but how will that do us any good? How would we get it in the future if we're stuck here?"

"Look around. We're not all that came from the future."

She smiled. "The house! Of course! There's another one in the past. We can hide the crystal somewhere in the other house in this time and find it in this house."

"Now you're getting it."

"That sounds great, but where could we hide it without it being found too soon? How would we still get enough solar power if it's in a closet?"

"Hmm. Good points. Maybe it needs to be outside... like on the roof."

"We couldn't do that. We had to install solar panels, remember? Surely, we would find it before it's time."

"Maybe we should take a look."

They walked over and looked for any place on the house that they could possibly hide it without their younger selves or someone else finding it. Then, they realized that what they really needed to do was to look at the other house. They drove to their house's 1985 counterpart and checked for anything that was similar or different-- at least from their perspective in the car.

"Maybe we could just hide it in the car," Lisa suggested.

"Nah, some mechanic would find it."

"Or, the crystal would make the car run so well that Mom never sells it to us."

"Point well taken." Charlie squinted. "Do you see something that still remains consistent from then till now?"

"The paint?"

"Something on the roof-- the chimney."

"Was it still in use though?"

"No, they completely removed the fireplace in the 70s. I remember that from the paperwork when we bought it. They still kept the chimney for the looks. The bottom is sealed."

"Wouldn't we still possibly see the crystal in it when we're on the roof later?"

"There's still one thing that would help conceal it. Something that has also remained over the years."

"The antenna," they said in unison.

Charlie said, "In our time, we just use cable, but it's possibly still in use now. I don't know. Remember how we thought of using it as a part of the time machine? It's so weather-beaten now that it's no good. It just sits there in the chimney as a last beacon of the past. Enough to hide the crystal from sight, but not enough to completely block the sun from reaching it."

"So, how do we go about planting a crystal up there without the current resident noticing?"

He smiled. "By getting permission."

Sunday the 10th. Charlie arrived at the house with a rented truck and new ladder. Charlie wore a hard hat, flannel shirt, and tool belt on his jeans. He knocked on the door, which in itself felt ironic. The lady of the house answered.

"Sorry to bother you on a Sunday, Ma'am," he said with his best southern accent. "I was hoping I could get up there on your roof to take a look at that there antenna."

"I'm sorry-- who are you?"

"I'm from the Wichita Lineman & Electrician Company. The name's Glen." He suddenly had Glen Campbell's "Wichita Lineman" playing in his head, but knew that he couldn't use such a well-known name. "Glen Benatar."

"Like the singer?"

He laughed. "Ma'am, you're not the first one to notice that. There are a few other people in the world with that name. My parents, for instance."

She laughed. "Well, I reckon that's true."

"Yes, Ma'am," he said with a laugh. "Wee doggies. I just need to get up there for some routine maintenance if it ain't too much trouble."

"This won't cost me something, will it?"

"Oh, no, Ma'am. It was just time to make sure it's running properly and maybe give it a little tweak. Shouldn't take much time atall. Who knows? Ya might even get an extra signal from Arizona."

"That would be nice. You can go ahead and do whatever you need to do."

"Thanks, Ma'am," he said with a wink.

He got out the ladder and set it up. He started climbing up.

"I never was a big fan of heights," he said to himself.

Meanwhile, Lisa was on the roof of their house in the field. There was no way she would stay up there without their ladder in case she needed to go to the bathroom. She looked in the chimney. Still nothing.

"I hope it doesn't take long, Charlie. I never was too big on heights."

As he nervously climbed up the slanted roof to get to the chimney, he had to remind himself not to look down. When he finally found his footing at the chimney, his curious nature got the best of him.

"Holy shingles!" he said as he saw how high two stories really were.

He took a few deep breaths and calmed his nerves. He took a look inside the shallow chimney.

"Would you look at that," he said as he carefully pulled a nest out. Inside were three robin's eggs. He thought it was odd that there would be such a thing at that time of year, but knew there must be a good explanation. He looked for a good place to set it down, but the roof was slanted in both directions.

"Well, this is a bit precarious."

He finally set it on the opposite edge of the chimney for the time being. He took the crystal out of the tool belt.

"I don't think anyone is going to look for you up here. I just hope this works."

He gave it a kiss and set it in the chimney. Then, he looked the antenna over and didn't see anything wrong. He gently put the nest back in place.

Lisa suddenly had a feeling. She looked into the chimney.

"There you are."

She took it out and smiled. The bright blue was finally back.

"So good to see you healthy again."

Charlie arrived not too much later.

"It worked! Yes! It actually worked!" he enthused when she showed him the newly rejuvenated crystal. "Now, we have our ticket back home."

"I hate to break it to you," she said. "There's still a little problem."

"What problem?"

"It's way better than it was, but it's still not at full capacity. It should be glowing."

He looked at it again. "You're right. Maybe it will be enough? I don't know. I had a feeling that the antenna might take away from some of the power. On the other hand, the lady who lived there probably had years of extra channels."

"That was our best shot at getting it powered up. What do we do now?"

"I'll see if I can figure out how much more power it would take and go from there. Hopefully, it will be enough. At least we're much closer than we were before."

"If anyone can figure this out, it's you."

While Charlie tried to solve the mystery of the crystal, Lisa tried to solve the mystery of what it would take to finally change Robbie's future. She knew what he'd been through and what would happen later. She knew that talking about his problems should help, but did it? The outcome remained the same.

"What am I missing here?"

She looked through the scrapbook, searching for anything that could provide an answer. She thought back to the days referenced in the old newspaper clippings.

"There was something about the way he said things. That look in his eyes. This has changed him. Without baseball, he's going to lose all of his sense of purpose."

"He was a good man once. How could it have gotten this bad?!"

"The good man we once knew, the friend we once had, he no longer exists. I tried to tell you guys. He died that day when he got hurt. The old Robbie stayed on the baseball field. He was never the same after that. He died that day, and I watched it happen. If only I would have tried harder. If only I would have been there for him..."

She closed her eyes and thought much further back.

"What's wrong, baby girl?"

"One of the boys at school tried to touch me."

"WHAT?! Who?! I'll kill 'im!"

"No, Dad, it's okay. I ran away and told a teacher. He took care of it."

"I'm glad you knew what to do, but you're obviously still upset."

"It just made me realize that sometimes I'm too trusting. Some people are good at hiding what they're really like."

"Don't go blaming yourself now."

"I'm not. I just... I just feel like I need to know how to protect myself. What if I get in a situation where I can't run? I don't want to be a victim. I want to be able to fight back."

She thought of what her Tae Kwon Do instructor taught the class.

"What if someone is much bigger than you? You still have the advantage. 'How?' you might ask. Is it because of your fists? Is it because you can kick? No. It's your mind. You have knowledge. You know something that he doesn't know. You know what you're capable

of. Your techniques will work against him, but it's your knowledge that gives you the real advantage. Knowledge is power."

She went upstairs to see Charlie.

"Any news?" she asked.

"Not yet. Just a lot of brainstorming. I think I'll need some electricity tomorrow to try some things. What about you?"

"A lot of brainstorming, too. I'm still trying to figure out how Amanda can change, but Robbie is still not there yet. I can't make him do anything, and if he doesn't come to counseling tomorrow, then we're going to have to get a lot more creative. I did figure out that we do still have an advantage."

"What's that?"

"We know what he doesn't know. We know what happens later. The only question is how to prevent it. I knew all along that it would take a change of heart, but how exactly do we get him to do that? It seems like everything we've talked about should have worked, but it only made him more depressed."

"Maybe he needs to go through that first before he comes out stronger. I know that's how it worked for me. Think about it. This was the night when we first went out together. Why? Because he wasn't there. Maybe he was already depressed that day. We don't know that he isn't doing what he already did the first time around."

"You might be right. I just keep thinking that there's something we're missing. I think about how he got hurt in the game, and that's when everything went downhill. We know that we probably can't prevent that from happening, so I have to work with him on changing how he responds to things. But, what if that's not enough? Remember how Tracy said that he was never the same after that? Baseball is his dream. There's no way we can take that away from him. We know that it doesn't work out, but he still needs that to keep him going."

"Maybe he needs a back-up plan."

"Like another job?"

"Yeah. You know how broke he was in the minors. He needs another skill."

"That might help, but there's still something else that keeps coming to mind. Who else knows what happens later?"

"My other self. But, we can't go entirely by that."

"Why not?"

"Because it was different. Where he came from, you were married to Robbie."

"How do you know that we were married?"

"Sam told me when I was seventeen. I finally put the pieces together. He said that there was someone he loved who ended up marrying someone else who became abusive. He was trying to keep me from making the same mistake of not telling you that I love you. I didn't know at the time that we were the same person talking about the same woman."

"Here's what I think. We need to fully combine what I know and what you know from every possible past and future. Even considering that, there's still someone else who knows what happens and would help."

"We can't talk to Sam about it now. Too much is at stake in our own past to interfere with it."

"I'm not talking about him. Who else knows Robbie well? Who else was there to see him rise and fall? Someone who has insight that we didn't have?"

"Tracy."

She nodded her head.

Charlie said, "We can't involve her in this. She's the reason why we're here."

"We said from the beginning that we had to save Tracy by saving Robbie. What if she's part of the solution?"

"No. She can't be. That's what got her hurt. We have to keep them apart."

"We already know that she has feelings for him. We already know that they have an off-and-on relationship with each other later..."

"We also know that she broke up with him because he was too focused on baseball to maintain a relationship with her."

"Maybe he was just too scared to really commit because of everything he's been through watching what happened to his parents."

"He still married you anyway in another time."

"That's true, but he also had my dad as a coach. It was just a different scenario. The point is, he's in a position right now where he could go either way. I might get through to him and influence a change of heart like you did with Amanda, or he might end up making the same mistakes. We're running out of time. Something has to happen to tip the scales the right way."

"What if you're wrong?"

"If I'm wrong, then we'll know by the headlines and our memories. We would still have a little time to fix it. But, what if I'm right? I've gotten to know Robbie a lot more as Lorrie than I ever did as my younger self. I've seen a whole other side of him. He's told me things that he probably never told me in some other version of reality. Things that he probably never told Tracy, either. We have that knowledge now. We know where he's coming from. That's huge! I understand him now. Yes, I worry about what could happen to Tracy. I love her. But, you know what? I love Robbie just as much." Her eyes began to water. "There's nothing about him that tells me that he's not deserving of love or capable of loving someone. He's so close to having that change of heart, of having that new direction. What did it take to get through to Amanda?"

"I didn't give up. I saw her heart past all the negative stuff and brought out the best in her."

"Exactly. What did you think of her even as a kid when she would hurt you? Didn't you say that you saw the pain in her eyes?"

He nodded. "I did. I thought she was only acting out of her pain. She wasn't someone to hate, she was someone to love." He chuckled. "The funny thing is, I learned it by your example."

She smiled. "Don't you see, Charlie? You were absolutely right about her. It took the same thing it took to get the two of us together. The same thing that made us start the school. The same thing that we teach our own kids. There may be challenges, pain, worries, doubts, and fears... but, the one thing that's bigger than any of that, the one thing that conquers all is *love*. It has been and always will be the answer. Love changes everything. What if the thing that we're missing isn't about keeping Robbie and Tracy apart? What if they were actually meant to be together?"

He put his hand on her shoulder. "For everyone's sake, I hope you're right."

"I have to try."

"How exactly do you play matchmaker without messing up our history?"

"Very carefully and very strategically." She smiled. "My wheels are already turning."

CHAPTER 32

Monday, February 11th, 1985. Lisa woke with a smile. She got out of bed and faced the day with a newfound optimism. Today would be the day for change. Before she left the motel, the phone rang.

"Hello?" Charlie answered.

Lisa couldn't hear what they said on the other side, but watched as Charlie's smile grew larger.

"I'll be there as soon as I can. Thanks." He hung up the phone.

"What was that about?"

"We have our generator!"

"YES!!!"

"One of the stores got one in. That's one big pressure relieved."

"I knew today was going to be a good one!"

"It's not a bad start, that's for sure. I'll go pick it up and take it to the house. I'm going to spend the rest of the day trying to solve the rest of the problem."

"We're a huge step further than we were. I have faith in you."

"Right back at ya. You'll help Robbie just the way he needs."

They hugged and kissed.

"Go get 'em," he said.

Lisa as Lorrie helped more students in Sam's former office. One thing she noticed throughout the day was a sense of excitement for the big Valentine's Day Prom on Thursday. Some were more nervous than excited. She tried not to be one of them. However, she did become increasingly more nervous to see if Robbie would actually keep their appointment. Her concerns were put to ease when he walked in at the right time.

"Sorry I wasn't here Friday," he said as he sat down.

"That's okay. I'm just glad you came back. I was really concerned."

"I'm sorry if I made you worry. To tell you the truth, I was depressed. Bringing up all the stuff in my past was bringing me down. I realize now that I should've came to talk to you. That's when I needed to the most."

"Talking about these things isn't easy, but it's necessary. I have to know what's bothering you to know how to help you."

"Well, I'm here now."

"Is there anything you want to talk about?"

"I keep getting this sense that I'm not good enough. I know it goes back to my parents, but I can't shake it. I keep thinking that I have to try harder, like I have to prove something. Maybe I can eventually be good enough to make it to the majors and be good enough for Lisa."

"I think you're already good enough."

"Thanks, but I'm just not sure."

"I've been doing a lot of thinking. I think that you've been putting all your eggs in one basket. In other words, I think that you've been so set on one thing that if something bad were to happen, you'd be completely devastated."

"What's wrong with setting goals?"

"Nothing at all. I'm all for it. I just mean that you should keep your options open."

"I thought you believed in me."

"Of course I do. I just think that you're setting yourself up for a fall if you put all your hopes on one thing. Let me put it this way. You want to play for the majors. Do you think that will happen right away?"

"No, I'll probably end up in the minors first for awhile after college. But, you never know."

"Exactly. You never know. You want to make a living doing this, right?"

"Yeah, sure. That would be great."

"You may not be aware of this, but the minors don't pay much. Like, not much at all. It's not all year long, either."

"So, I'll need a job."

"That's right. You do still plan on having a girlfriend, right?"

"Yeah."

"Then you really, really need a job. You need something to fall back on."

"I've actually been thinking about that lately. I'm tired of borrowing money from Dad."

"If you want to get out, like you said, then that's a big part of it. What else are you good at?"

"I don't know. I've done some yard work here and there."

"You said that you helped your dad work on his car. Do you know enough to do something more with that?"

"I never really thought of that. I guess I know a few things. I could always learn, too."

"That's the kind of job that needs help year-round." She reached into her purse, pulled out a business card, and gave it to him. "These people are good. You might give them a call and see if they're hiring."

He looked it over. "Whitson Automotive? I've seen that on Main Street. Zachary Whitson-- I wonder if he's related to Tracy Whitson? That's Lisa's best friend."

"Wouldn't that be a great coincidence?" She knew exactly what she was doing.

"Yeah. Maybe she could put in a good word for me." His smile became serious. "I still don't see how this would solve the problem of being good enough."

"Whether you get this job or a different one, it would give you the chance to take more charge of your life. Instead of relying on your dad or what may or may not happen with a baseball career, you would still have something that you can point to as an accomplishment. One that would give you more independence."

"Have you ever felt like you're not good enough?"

"More often than you would think. A lot of people go through that. It doesn't just come from abuse. It could be peer pressure or any number of reasons."

"How do you overcome it?"

She smiled. "By helping others. If someone else has become better, then I know that I've done something right. I don't worry so much about being good enough, it's more about making sure that I don't fail anyone."

"Like me."

"Especially you."

"Why especially me? Am I that bad?"

"No, Robbie. You're that good. I see the most potential in you."

He searched for the words to say. "You don't want me to try to get this job because I might fail at baseball. You just want me to succeed no matter what."

"I want you to succeed at everything you set out to do."

He looked down and said quietly, "You really do care about me."

Her eyes grew misty. "Very much."

"I'll do it. I'll apply for this job. Whatever you think is best."

"I do think that would be a good idea."

"All right." He stood up. "I'll give it my best. See you Wednesday."

"I can't wait."

She smiled and waved as he walked away. She finally felt like he was going in the right direction. Then, a thought occurred to her.

"He really looks up to me. I'm not just a counselor to him. I'm a mother figure."

When Lisa arrived at the motel, Charlie enthusiastically greeted her.

"Good, you're finally here! I've discovered something!"

She laughed. "You're really reminding me of Doc Brown right now."

"I take that as a compliment. And, you're not far off. Oh! But, first, how did it go with Robbie?"

"Very well. I think things are starting to get better."

"Awesome!"

"I'll tell you about it later. Let's not lose your enthusiasm!"

"Yes! The discovery!"

They walked over to the bed where the crystal was.

"As we know, the crystal is powered by the sun. For reasons we haven't been made privy to, it's just the way it is. We've managed to get most of the power back, but it's still not enough. So, I brainstormed and paced and tried to figure out what to do. That's when I discovered this..."

He turned on the radio. "One of These Days" by Emmylou Harris played. The crystal began to pulsate the blue glow.

"Wow!" Lisa exclaimed with a laugh. "I don't believe it! Does it know any Jackie Wilson?"

Charlie replied, "That is a deep cut movie reference and I'm extremely proud of you for coming up with that."

"Thank you."

"To answer your question, it should work with Jackie Wilson, The Beach Boys, or anything else just as well. You know what this means, right?"

"If we get some mirrors, we could make a really cool disco ball? Just kidding."

"It means that the crystal responds to other forms of energy."

"I thought it was only solar power."

"So did I, but The Protector never told us it was the only way. It's the main power source, and by far the most effective, but not the only one."

"It must be one of the reasons why we need music when we use the Shifter. It enhances the power."

"I think you're right about that."

"So, what do we do? Keep playing the radio 24/7 to get enough power stored up?"

"According to my calculations..."

"Okay, I'm gonna stop you right there. Sorry to interrupt, but that is one of my pet peeves. Every time the nerdy character in a movie is about to explain something he pushes his glasses up like this and says, 'according to my calculations.' It's just so unoriginal."

He stared at her for a moment. She did have a point.

"Sorry," she said.

He cleared his throat and attempted to continue. "Based on my data..."

"Much better."

"Thank you. Based on my data, we don't have nearly enough time to build up enough power by music, even if we played it 24/7. But, there is another alternative."

He turned off the radio and started up an electric fan that he brought from home. The crystal pulsated once again.

"Wind power? Not bad."

"It still wouldn't be enough."

"What if we put it outside in the sun, put the fan on it, and blared music non-stop? Would that be enough?"

He shook his head. "Sadly, no. According to my... uh .. based on my data, we need a heck of a lot more energy than even that would provide."

"How much more? Don't tell me-- 1.21 gigawatts."

"Not quite that much, but still a lot. We would need roughly 10,000 kilowatt-hours."

"How are we gonna get that? If you say, 'a bolt of lightning...'"

"No, no, we won't need lightning. If only it were that easy."

"That easy?! What exactly do you have in mind?"

"We'll need more wind power. The only way we can get that much of it would be from a..."

Her eyes grew big. "No freaking way!"

"I'm afraid so, Lisa," he said with a pained smile.

They said in unison, "tornado."

"Are you crazy?!" she asked emphatically. "An actual tornado?!"

"Maybe a little bit crazy. And, yes, an actual tornado."

"How do you suppose we get a tornado?" she asked "They're not exactly available at the store. We're not going to make one, are we?"

"No, we won't have to do that. There won't be enough time."

"You've actually considered that option, haven't you? This is crazy! We'll have to catch one somehow. What do we do, use a trailer park for bait? This is crazy! Lunacy! Madness, I tell you! And, did I mention, incredibly dangerous?!"

"It's okay, Lisa. Believe me, I get the concern, but it's going to work out."

"You already have a plan, don't ya?"

"You know how I have that perfect memory?"

"You've mentioned it once or twice."

"Well, see, we're here at just the right time. A tornado is going to rip through Stubbville. Thankfully, no one was seriously hurt. It was all over the news."

"I kind of remember that, now that you mention it."

"We were a little preoccupied, but I remember it mostly because of when it happened."

"Didn't it happen on Valentine's Day?"

"The day before."

"That's only two days from now. You're serious about this, aren't you?"
"It's our best option."
"So, we know the time and place. How exactly do we harness these 10,000 kilowatt-hours?"
"Very carefully."

Tuesday afternoon, February 12th. Charlie and Lisa arrived just outside the small town of Stubbville, Kansas. They parked the car in a field similar to the one back home.
"This looks like a good spot," Charlie said as he exited the vehicle.
"Are you sure?" she asked.
"The tornado will cut a path right through the middle of town. All the news reports said that it came from the west. We're definitely standing on the trail that it will take before it gets there."
They brought the crystal over to a nearby tree.
"You didn't know this tree was here, did you?" she asked.
"No clue. I'm just glad it is. Makes it easier."
They wrapped a chain around it and held the crystal to its trunk. Lisa put a lock on the two links.
"That's about the best we can do on short notice," he said.
"What if the tornado uproots the tree?"
"That's still a possibility, but at least Old Blue has a chance of not flying away too far to find."
"Did you just name the crystal?"
"Huh. I guess I did."
"Old Blue. Simple, descriptive, and catchy. I like it."
"Works for me."
Lisa's face grew more serious as she looked towards the town.
"Those poor people have no idea what's coming. We could warn them."
"I'm afraid we can't do that."
"Why not? Wouldn't it be better to save the town from a disaster than to sit back and do nothing? We have a moral obligation."
"I understand completely, but we just can't do that this time. What if we warn them now? No one would believe us. Even when they hear the siren tomorrow, they still might not believe it."
"The boy who cried wolf."
"Exactly. No one died before. No one was seriously injured. There was some destruction of property, but they rebuilt. Believe me, I thought all about this. Suppose we warn them and someone does believe it. Maybe they panic. They do something different than what they would have done before, and this time, they get hurt. We don't

know all the details of a town full of people. As hard as it may be, the simple fact is that we stand a greater chance of saving them by not telling them. We have to let history play out the way we know it will."

She nodded. "You're right. We can't rock the boat with so many variables. I just wish there was a better solution."

"Sorry, honey, but there are just some things that are too big for even time travel to solve."

Wednesday the 13th. With their time coming to an end at an alarming speed, Lisa hoped that the big problem she faced wasn't too big to solve. Robbie's newspaper articles in the scrapbook remained unaltered. This day may be the last chance she would have to talk to him. It was time for the Changer to see real change.

"How are you, Robbie?" she asked as he approached her desk.

"I'm doing pretty good," he replied with a smile. "I have Prom with Lisa tomorrow and a job interview on Friday."

"That's wonderful! Congratulations."

"Thank you. I asked Tracy, and she said that Zachary Whitson is her dad. He actually did mechanic work in the army and went to Vietnam."

Of course, this wasn't news to her, but she still replied. "Wow, that's very interesting." Hearing that he talked to Tracy sounded very hopeful.

"Thank you for steering me in the right direction. I have a good feeling about the interview."

"So do I. It sounds like Mr. Whitson would be someone good for you to work with." While things were going so well, she decided that it was time to bring up the subject. Maybe it would spur him to action. "Now, the bad news. I hate to have to tell you this, but tomorrow will be my last day here."

"Really? Why?"

"I was here to help Mr. Whitfield temporarily until a permanent counselor could take over. He's already had to leave due to his health. It was always meant to be short term for both of us. Don't worry; a new counselor is coming soon."

"It won't be the same."

"I'm sorry about that, Robbie. I've really enjoyed getting to know you and trying to help you the best I know how. I'm going to miss everyone here. It's just time to go back home."

He nodded. "I understand. You've really helped me a lot with my problems, but I'm still not sure if I can ever fully overcome all the bad memories."

"Unfortunately, I can't erase those memories. They will still be a part of you."

"I wish I could forget it and move on."

"I know you do. I completely understand. The best you can do is to make better memories to overpower them."

"I'm just afraid that no matter what I do, even if I become a big baseball star, I'll still have my dad's voice in my head telling me that I'm not good enough."

"Think about what you're saying. If you become a big baseball star, then you would have overcome it. You're not going to get anywhere without trying. It just takes time. You'll get there."

"I know you're right, it's just easier said than done."

"Do you get straight A's?"

"No."

"But, you still give it your best. Do you win every game?"

"No."

"But, you keep trying. Do you ever strike out?"

"Yeah, plenty of times."

"But, you keep swinging. And, if you don't get this job, then you apply for another one. That's the way life works, Robbie. You win some, you lose some. It's never going to be perfect, but it's still worth the effort. You might get bummed out by losing a game, but how do you feel when you win?"

"It feels great."

"And, it happens more often than not."

"I see what you're saying. I have to focus on the positive."

"That's right, but it's more than that. What if something really bad happens? What if it's not just a game, but the championship and you let the whole team down? What if you got hurt? What if you kept giving your best and it just didn't work? Then what?"

"I--I don't know."

"You think it's rough to have your dad's voice in your head? What if you get famous? What if you're in the news and everyone has turned against you? What if the cheering crowds have turned to booing and calling names? Can you handle that? Are you strong enough for that?"

"I don't know. I-- I think so."

"What makes you strong, Robbie? What others think of you?"

"No."

"Then, what is it?" She knew this would be the time to really put him to the test. She stood up and began shouting, "He's a bum! He's a loser! Get him out of here! He can't play! Where'd he learn to throw? You play ball like a girl! Fire him! Throw him out of here!"

She could see his shock turn into anger.

"You know it's gonna happen," she said. "You know they're gonna say it. You know it's gonna remind you of your dad. What do you do, Robbie? Get mad? Get even? What do you do?"

He stumbled over his tongue.

She pounded her fist on the desk. *"WHAT DO YOU DO?!"*

He stood up and yelled, "I PROVE THEM WRONG!!"

She smiled.

He tried to catch his breath. "I prove them wrong."

She nodded and said, "Who are you proving wrong? The crowds? Your teammates? Your dad? Is that enough?"

Tears came to his eyes as he said, "I have to prove it to myself."

"Because you're good enough?"

"Yeah. Because I'm good enough."

She smiled as a few tears of her own began to surface. "You're dang right you are."

She came around the desk and put her hands on his shoulders. They looked into each other's eyes.

She said, "What do you do if you strike out? Do you throw the bat down and sit on the bench and pout?"

"No. I go back next time and try again."

"That's right. You might miss one, but the next might be a homer. True strength isn't about showing everyone how hard you can hit or how much you can dish out, it's what you can take. It's how you handle things. It's about trying again and again. It's about going to bed at night knowing that you gave it your best, and waking up the next day trying to make it better than before. Make it better than the last game... make it better than your past. That was yesterday. Tomorrow, you get a new chance to try again."

"I will. I just have to keep my eye on the ball."

She smiled and said, "You can do it."

They hugged.

He said, "Thanks for everything, Miss Parker. I won't let you down."

"I'm proud of you. I believe your future is very bright."

Meanwhile in a field outside of Stubbville, Charlie waited patiently for the big arrival. He brought one of the smaller crystals with him. He held it up to Old Blue. Just as he thought, they both pulsated when they were together, especially the smaller one. He didn't want to take a chance of Old Blue getting tossed away to where he couldn't find it, and especially not to be discovered by someone else. If it did end up airborne, the smaller crystal would be able to guide him to its location. He got back in the car and drove a few yards away from the tree. Close enough to still see it, yet far enough to be out of harm's way...

hopefully. "Now, we wait," he said. He was starting to get into a habit of speaking to the crystals as if they could hear him. In all honesty, he wasn't sure that they couldn't.

Minutes turned to an hour. He wasn't sure what time it was supposed to happen, only that it was late in the afternoon. He noticed the leafless branches of the tree moving in the wind. It had done so throughout the past hour. Every time it happened, he wondered if this time would be the moment he was waiting for. Another false alarm. Five minutes later, it happened again. This time, it didn't stop.

"So it begins."

Raindrops began to tap on the car. He turned the key and activated the windshield wipers. The rain fell harder. It became more difficult to see the tree through the downpour. Was it really a downpour? It seemed to be coming towards him sideways. He increased the speed of the wipers only to see that the tree also increased in movement. Then, he heard the sound of thunder, but it didn't sound right. This thunder didn't come and go. It persisted in its roar. He grew more nervous. After a minute or so, the rain stopped. The branches quit swaying. The roar ceased. He thought for a second that it was another false alarm. Maybe he was wrong about the location. Then, he noticed that the sky had a green tint.

"The calm before the storm."

The sky grew darker. The roar returned. Bits of hail started pelting the car. His heart beat a little faster. The wind rocked the car. Then, he saw it. The dark cloud swirled viciously in the distance. He started to drive in reverse. It approached faster than he ever anticipated. As it came closer to the vicinity, he saw how much bigger it was becoming. His heart nearly beat out of his chest. The massive size and ever-increasing speed quickly showed Charlie just how outmatched he was. To be in its path would mean certain death. He saw the blue light of the crystal fly away.

"There goes the crystal!"

The tree blew over.

"Holy Helen Hunt!!!"

He shifted the car from reverse to drive and turned around. He put the pedal to the metal, trying desperately to outrun the unstoppable force. His vision was becoming more obscured by flying dirt. He looked for any sign of the crystal. Something big caught his attention as it flew by the windshield.

"Is that a hog... or a cattle?"

He didn't have time to figure it out. He looked to the smaller crystal. It wasn't pulsating. He knew that he must be too far from Old Blue. He tried to change course to the left in case it wasn't traveling in a straight line. The crystal pulsated just a little. Maybe this was the right direction. The tornado kept its destructive pace towards him as he retreated as fast as he could in the opposite direction. The crystal pulsated even more in this strange game of Hot and Cold. His view through the window was completely overtaken by dirt and debris. Still he drove blindly and furiously into the unknown, hoping that he wouldn't run into anything or lose the crystal. He drove so fast that it felt like the wind was pushing him forward. He suddenly realized that he indeed wasn't touching ground anymore.

"JESUS, TAKE THE WHEEEEEELLLLL!!!"

The car flew like a bullet through the darkness. Charlie silently prayed with all his might that he wouldn't get sucked into the vortex. Before too long, the car dropped back on its tires. The harsh jolt made Charlie hit his head on the steering wheel. Thankfully, he wasn't as far from the ground as he feared. He drove onward, veering to the left to try to get out of the twister's destructive path. He looked over to the passenger seat again to check the crystal. It wasn't there. He looked up to the windshield again. He couldn't see anything anyway, so he looked back to his right. He finally saw it on the floor. There was no way he could reach it without taking off his seatbelt. He decided it was just fine where it was. It glowed more and more.

"I must be getting close."

The dirt that clouded his view decreased. He looked into the rearview mirror. He had finally gotten far enough away to see the tornado moving in a different direction. More accurately, it was still going in the same direction towards the town, but he was no longer in its crosshairs. He still drove fast in case it changed its mind. The crystal pulsated just as strongly as it did when he held it next to the other one earlier. He slowed the car down and observed his surroundings. No trace of Old Blue. The smaller crystal still behaved the same way. He came to a stop.

"That's funny. It should be here."

Suddenly, the back window shattered and threw glass all the way to the front. Charlie screamed at the surprise. He looked back. Old Blue was in the backseat. He reached back and picked it up. He smiled as he held the bright blue, pulsating rock to his face.

"We're back, baby!"

He looked at the glass all around him and the hole in the window. He noticed that the antenna had blown off in the storm as well. He thought of how rough the outside of the car must look.

"Sorry, rental car people. Good thing I paid extra for the insurance."

Lisa paced throughout the motel room. She was already worried about the tornado, but she became more and more concerned that something didn't go right. She called his pager multiple times, but she realized that the weather might have interfered. The doorknob began to rattle. She rushed to the door.

"Thank God!!" she exclaimed as she threw her arms around Charlie. "I was so worried about you."

"God was definitely looking out for me. Take a look at the car."

They let go. He stepped back so she could see the damage.

"Whoa! You survived that?! You don't look so hot, either! What happened?"

They came in and shut the door. Charlie was still shaken up from the incident.

"Well, there I was outside of S-Stubbville. I waited awhile for it, then the w-wind picked up and the tree was shakin' like a leaf. Only there were no leaves."

Lisa quickly realized that she would have to ask him again sometime when he was more coherent. "Uh-huh... go on..."

"It started raining sideways. I turned on the windshield wipers. Woot weet, woot weet, woot weet." He made motions with his shaky arms. "I tried to keep an eye on the crystal, but it was hard to see with either of my eyes. The wind kept coming down harder and the rain kept blowing. Then, there was the thunder. Only it wasn't thunder. It was a freight train that sounded like thunder. Then, it stopped. The rain stopped. Maybe it was over. Praise be to The Lord! But, then I noticed something. Skies ain't normally green are they? It's the calm before the storm! It got dark. The wind blew harder. The hail came at me. The car was shaking. It was hail, hail, rock, and roll."

Lisa tried to stifle her giggles.

He continued, "The roaring thunder sound was back. Like someone done ticked off the MGM lion. And, if that wasn't scary enough, I saw it. The black cloud of doom. I-I put the car in reverse. There was no escaping it. It kept coming faster and bigger. The crystal flew off the tree!"

"Oh, no!"

"The tree was knocked down!"

"Snap!"

"I knew I was next! I turned the car around and drove it like I stole it. I saw something fly by. Was it a hog? Was it a cattle? I'll never know. Dirt was flying as far as the eye could see. Except there was so much dirt, I couldn't see anything."

"Huh?"

“I used the smaller crystal to try to find where the other one was. You know, like a radar. I kept driving to get away from the big spinny dirt monster… and then, it happened. I flew.”

“You flew?!”

“IIIII FLEW. It picked me up and threw me like a football. You’d think it would be fun to fly, but noooo. I’m 88% sure I need to change my pants.”

Lisa covered her mouth as she tried hard not to laugh at that one.

“Now, I never intended to get killed by a tornado that happened nineteen years ago, so I started to pray like never before. Pretty sure I used small words like ‘help.’ It didn’t take long before I fell back on the ground. I kept driving, and then I saw that it was going a different direction than me. I tried to find where the crystal was, because I really didn’t want it to end up somewhere else. Because driving in the dark and nearly getting sucked up by a tornado is clearly the only way to do this. I saw that the little crystal was glowing like it did earlier. It must be here! I stopped the car. BAM!!”

Lisa jumped.

“The crystal flew through the back window.”

He took both crystals out of his pockets and put them on the table. Lisa’s eyes lit up as she smiled.

“It worked!” she said.

“Crystal Blue Persuasion is back in business!”

They hugged again and laughed.

“OH! I almost forgot to tell you!” she said. “Robbie had a major breakthrough today! I think we’re on track to a mission accomplished!”

“That’s great!”

They let go.

“We should celebrate. I’ll order a pizza. How does that sound?”

“Yes, have some.”

He walked over to the bed.

She said, “You poor thing. You went through quite an ordeal.”

“Yeah, I need to rest for a bit.”

He plopped down on the bed face first.

Lisa chuckled. “Rest, brave warrior. You earned it.”

“Uhnn,” he replied. He stayed motionless for a few seconds. Then, he started getting up. “I’m 100% sure I need to change my pants.”

CHAPTER 33

"I have something for you," he told Lisa with a mischievous grin.

"For me?"

"Happy Valentine's Day."

He pulled a bowl from his backpack and gave it to her.

"What in the world?" she asked with a laugh.

She opened the lid. Her eyes bulged bigger than he'd seen in a long time.

"No way! Is this what I think it is?" She smelled them. "Your mom's chocolate chip cookies!" She took a bite. "Mmmm! So good! These are the best cookies ever! I haven't had these in forever. Thank you so much."

"You're welcome."

"Man, it takes me back. Remember when we first met? You brought some over with your mom."

"How could I forget? It was the best day of my life."

"It was?"

"Of course it was. It was the day I met my best friend."

"Oh, Charlie." She stood up and hugged him. "Still the best friend a girl could ever have."

The older Lisa watched carefully from a cracked door as one of her favorite memories played out in front of her again. It was a bit risky to watch, but hard to resist. She quietly closed the door. Little did the younger Lisa know that she would finally get to reveal her true feelings for her best friend later that night. The older Lisa smiled. It was almost like living it all over again.

"Happy Anniversary, Charlie," she said quietly. "I wouldn't change a thing."

Thursday, February 14th, 1985. For another great love story to unfold, it would almost certainly have to happen on Valentine's Day.

Meanwhile, Charlie arrived at the field. The "Now Leaving Chesapeake" sign greeted him. He wasn't about to leave Chesapeake, but he was very close to leaving this particular version of it. He admired Amanda's work once more. It certainly wouldn't be the last time. He drove the battered rental car up to the house. He got out and double-checked the trees. The crystals were right where they needed to be. He went back to the car and started bringing everything back to the house that they'd brought to the motel. Today was checkout time.

Lisa's counseling sessions were much fewer this time. She realized that Prom was the strongest concern on the minds of the Senior class. Mr. Foltan stopped by, however.

"I heard a nasty rumor that today was your last day."

"Oh. Yes, it is. Sorry, I meant to tell you that sooner. I guess I've been too preoccupied with work."

"I understand what that's like."

"I've really enjoyed my time here. The students have been amazing and you've been wonderful."

"I've talked to the teachers, and they've reported much better behavior and attention than they've ever had. The bully situation was not only stopped, it's as if it never happened. Amanda DiPino seems to be truly reformed, and the victims have also come out better. Please tell me that there's something I can do to convince you to stay permanently."

She smiled. "Although that's very tempting, I'm afraid I have to decline. It's time for me to go back home. I'm needed there."

"Can't blame me for trying. I hope I can find someone else who's half as good as you and Mr. Whitfield."

"I'm sure you will."

He held out his hand. "Miss Parker, it's been an honor."

She shook it. "The honor is all mine."

He smiled and winked. "Take care now."

"You, too."

He walked away.

She said in her normal voice, "See ya later."

Charlie put the small crystal back into the Time Vest. They were both powered up and ready to go. He put Old Blue in the window to make sure it soaked up some more solar energy before the big event. He checked the generator and the computers again. Everything was ready. The time machine was back in business. The only thing remaining was a little more time.

Lisa watched from the distance as her younger self walked up to her locker with Robbie.

"What do you have there?" asked Robbie.

"These are some cookies that Charlie brought me. His mom made them. She used to make them a lot when we were little. I think she did it for me more than anything. Want one?"

"Sure."

They each had a cookie before she put the bowl in her locker.

"Man, this really is good," he said between chews.

"Told you so."
The older Lisa's mouth began to water.
"You two were pretty close, I take it."
"Me and Charlie? Of course we were. You know that."
"No, I mean his mom."
"Yeah, we were. Ilene is like a second mom."
"Must be nice. Since you were all so close, did you and Charlie ever... I don't know... like each other?"
"Like boyfriend and girlfriend?"
"Yeah. I've always wondered about that."
She laughed. "We were just friends. Trust me."
"If you say so."
"Come on. Let's get to class."
The older Lisa hid her face as they walked past her. She said to herself, "You're a good little actress, never showing anything you don't want him to see."

As he descended the stairs, Charlie felt something weird. He began to get dizzy. He quickly stumbled his way to the couch. His thoughts were getting fuzzy.
"What's happening?"
For some reason, his mind wandered way back to 1977 after he was pummeled by Amanda.

"I used to wonder why you were so mean to me. Then I realized that there must be something that's bothering you... some kind of pain."
"What do you know? You don't know anything about it."
"No, I don't know. But, I do know that it's not too late to do the right thing."
"What do you know about pain?"
"I'm all alone, aren't I?"
Little Charlie held out his hand to her.
"Can we be friends?"
"I don't know yet."

Another memory was forming in his mind. It was confusing at first, like it was a dream. He looked over to the shelf that held their favorite pictures. That's when he saw it. He walked over to get a closer look. His mind flashed back to another memory in 1985. February 14th, to be precise.

"Hey, Charlie."
"Hey, Amanda."

"I've been doing a lot of thinking. There's something that's been bothering me for years."

"Okay… you have my attention."

"I was really unfair to you when we were little. You were always nice to me, but I treated you like dirt. I never forgot how much I hurt you. I've felt bad about it ever since."

Tears came to the older Charlie's eyes just as they did for his younger counterpart and Amanda. It wasn't a dream at all. His mind was catching up with something that just happened.

"This isn't a trick, is it?"

"No, it's not a trick. No more tricks, no more lies. Just real tears and real honesty. I never did hate you. I was jealous of you. I wanted a mom like yours. I wanted to be as smart as you. I wanted to be liked. I didn't mean all those terrible things I said. You didn't deserve any of it. The way you just took it… man, I wish I was that strong." Her tears increased. "I am so sorry."

The older Charlie wiped his tears and picked up the picture from the shelf.

She took a piece of paper out of her notebook. "I made you something." She handed it to him. "This is how it should have went if I was stronger."

The older Charlie looked at what she gave him. It was a drawing of them as kids wearing the same clothes they wore that day. Her hand was shaking his.

She held out her hand. "I hope it's not too late."

He smiled. "It's never too late to do the right thing."

They shook hands.

He said, "You're stronger than you think… my friend."

The older Charlie fell to his knees as his tears overflowed. The painful memories of his past abuse by Amanda were becoming overpowered by the good memories of the past nineteen years. Memories of a friendship that would last for all time.

That afternoon, Lisa patiently waited for the clock to strike three. She pondered what to do if things didn't go as planned. Once in awhile, she would briefly help a student, but otherwise, she was alone with her thoughts. Then, the unexpected happened.

"Are you Miss Parker?"

"Y-yes," she stammered. Her pulse quickened. She'd been through her share of challenges lately, but this one might prove to be the most difficult. "How can I help you?"

"My name's Lisa." She shook her hand. "Lisa Duvall. I have a conundrum."

"You and me both, kid," she thought to herself. Then, she realized how ironic it was to distinguish herself from herself.

"What might that be?" she asked her younger self.

"I've heard that you were really good. My boyfriend has been coming to see you-- Robbie Kunkel."

"He's a fine young man."

"The problem is... I just don't know if I should be with him. I know he's doing a lot better now because of you... I just don't want to make it worse."

"What makes you feel this way?" As if she didn't know.

"There's someone else. We have this history together, and... it just seems like we're meant to be together. But, I don't know what he thinks. Maybe he just wants to be friends."

"You haven't told him how you feel?"

"I'm waiting for him to make the first move. I know it sounds old-fashioned, but I still think it would be better that way. The trouble is, I don't know if he ever will."

Talk about a conundrum. Lorrie tried to come up with an answer that wouldn't ruin everything that was meant to happen.

"Give it some more time. Let him make that first move. Maybe he's wanted to, but didn't because of Robbie."

"You think so?"

"Well, there's only one way to find out."

"I still have to wait? For how long?"

"That's between the two of you. Follow your heart. He may just surprise you."

"I hope you're right. He has been surprising me a lot lately."

"Just be a little more patient. I have a good feeling about it."

"Okay. Thanks for the advice." She started to leave, but paused. "You know, you really remind me of someone. I can't quite put my finger on it."

Her heart nearly pounded out of her chest. "Uh... w-we've never met before."

"I'm getting this weird feeling of déjà vu. It's hard to describe."

"Maybe it's not about feeling something that's happened before, but about something that *should* happen."

"Like destiny?"

"Trust your instincts, Lisa. You already know the answers. And, some you'll find out when it's the right time."

The young lady squinted her eyes and nodded. She slowly walked away.

When she was out of sight, Lisa stood up and said, "That's it-- I'm done. I can't take any more of these surprises." She grabbed her purse and started to head for the door. "'I'm getting this weird feeling of déjà vu.' Yeah, well, kid, try it from my point of view. That's right-- you will." She paused. "And, I remember it. I remember being her talking to me." She shuddered. "This is just too weird. *Too weird!*" She went out the door and locked it. "Mr. Foltan, you can have your key back, cuz I am outahere. I'm outahere and outatime."

When Lisa got home, she and Charlie recounted the events of the day. The conversation naturally segued into what the night would hold for their plans.

"It can all still work out, but it's still so up in the air," Lisa lamented. "Why haven't the headlines changed?"

"Because what happens tonight still has to happen first. Like you said, it's all up in the air. There's nothing set in stone right now. Things could go in any direction if we're not careful."

"I just wish it was a *little* more set in stone," she said with a sigh. "All the pieces of the puzzle are there, yet it still feels like there's something missing."

"Because it's out of our control. We can't force anything to happen. If Tracy and Robbie are supposed to end up together, all we can do is nudge them along. We can't make them fall in love. It's up to them."

"You're right. I wish there was more time. Robbie has made a lot of progress, but it's all still fresh. I truly think that Tracy could help him with his issues, but he has to be willing. If he gets the job with her dad, that would be a great way to give him the family connection that he's missing. I just wish we knew it was going to happen for sure."

Charlie nodded. "Back when I was in day care, there was this little boy who cried and cried. It took all morning just to get him to finally calm down and get distracted enough. It would start all over again the next day."

Her eyes widened. "How far back can you remember?"

"I don't remember when I was a baby, but I do remember everything else."

"Why was he crying?"

"Because he missed his mommy. He didn't understand why she was leaving him there. He was never truly happy until she came to pick him up. She finally stopped bringing him."

"I see. You're telling me this to say that only certain people can truly make someone happy."

"Well, that's part of it, but it's also very specific. That boy's name was Robert. I never realized until today that Robert was Robbie."

"Oh, wow. You actually knew him way back then?"

"Not very well, but I was acquainted with him. I still kept to myself, too, you know."

"He was missing a parent who would go on to leave him years later. His pain runs deep. I never realized how much you two had in common."

"His pain runs deep, but so does his love. You were right. He is capable. That's why we know that he really does need true love to help him. If you love someone, anything's possible."

"Love changes everything." Suddenly, a thought occurred to her. "Remember what Robbie said the night he came over?"

"Of course. But, you'll have to be more specific."

"He said that you stole me from him."

"That's not quite accurate."

"No, but that's the way he saw it. He also said that I hurt him worse than I think."

"What are you trying to say?"

"I'm saying that those events still won't change. I just figured out what the missing piece is."

"What's that?"

She looked into his eyes. "I have to fix my mistake."

"*Your* mistake?"

"It can't be Lorrie or Jenny or Babette or even Sam. It has to be me. I'm the only one who can do it."

CHAPTER 34

Charlie arrived at the school gym. Happy couples were still making their entrances.

"Hey, Charlie! You came!" enthused Tracy.

"A deal's a deal, right?"

Her date pulled her arm towards him.

"I guess we'd better go. See you around."

Charlie waved. He looked around for Lisa, but to no avail. Robbie stepped outside.

"Hey, Robbie."

"Have you seen Lisa?"

"No... I thought she was with you."

"She was, but she took off. I thought she was coming back, but I guess not. She was acting funny the last couple of days. I don't know what's gotten into her."

"Maybe she's not feeling well."

"If she wasn't, then she shouldn't have had me come here with her. I'm not chasing after her. Guess I'll find someone who actually wants to be with me."

He went back inside. Charlie went back to the car. It was time to follow his heart.

The older Lisa and Charlie ducked down behind a car as the younger Charlie drove by.

"There's our cue," she said.

Charlie, dressed as Sam, rushed to the door and went inside. He quickly scanned his surroundings for Robbie. He spotted him not too far away. Knowing that Robbie had never met Sam, he had to be more cunning.

"I'm looking for someone named Robbie," he said to other teens gathered in the area. "Has anyone seen him? Do you know where Robbie is?"

"I think I saw him a little bit ago," said Ethan.

"He's right over there," said Kaisha.

"Thanks."

He approached him. "Are you Robbie?"

"Yeah, who are you?"

"I'm Mr. Whitfield, the counselor. There's a young lady outside looking for you."

"Really? Must be Lisa. Why didn't she just come in?"

He shrugged. "You'll have to ask her. I'm just the messenger."

"Okay. Thanks."

Lisa nervously waited for him outside. She wore the very same dress that she wore that night when she was younger. Good thing it was in the closet. Her hair and makeup were fixed the same way. She hadn't aged much over the years, but she still chose a spot where she could stand in the shadows just in case. Of all the parts she played during their time travel adventure, being herself would prove to be the most challenging. She couldn't hide behind accents and wigs. Being her authentic self at seventeen was the only thing that would work this time.

"There you are," Robbie said. "I thought you left."

"I did... but, I came back."

"Are you okay?"

"Yeah, I'm okay."

"Good. Let's go to the dance."

"I think it would be better if we talked right now."

"Okay... what's going on?"

"I wanted to tell you sorry that I left. I didn't mean to hurt you."

"I admit, it did hurt... but, you're here now. It will be okay."

"I want to tell you why I left. This may not be easy to hear, but it's very important that we talk about this."

"You're worrying me."

"I know, Robbie. I'm sorry. I've been wrestling with a lot of thoughts lately. I need to tell you how I really feel. You're a great guy. I've really enjoyed the time we've had together. Anyone would be happy to be with you. The fact of the matter is, there's someone else."

"Charlie."

She nodded. "Yeah. I want you to understand that it's nothing that you've done wrong. You are a wonderful person. I really do care about you. That's why I came back." She took his hand. "You deserve to be treated better. I'm sorry for running off like that. I could've handled it better."

"How long have you been seeing him?"

"I haven't. I've been faithful to you. He hasn't done anything, either. You have to understand that we've been friends since we were five years old. I had to move away for awhile, but I came back. We have something, Robbie. Charlie and I have something rare." Her eyes teared up. "He's my true love."

"I have noticed that there was something there. A part of me wanted to be jealous, but another part of me just wanted what you have. I guess I'll never have that."

"Of course you will, Robbie. Just because I'm not the right one for you doesn't mean that nobody is. There's a gym full of girls right now."

"None of them are like you."

"I can think of someone who already has feelings for you."

"Really? Who?"

"Tracy."

"For real?"

She smiled. "Yes. For real. Don't tell her I told you, though. I know her really well. She's like my sister. You would be crazy not to give her a chance."

"This is all happening so fast. You're breaking up with me, then there's Tracy... I don't know. I might need some time to process."

"No! I mean... like the saying goes, 'there's no time like the present.' Word of advice-- with someone as awesome as her, don't let her slip away. Do whatever you have to do. Oh, and appreciate her. Always put her first."

"This is crazy. It's just a dance, you know. You make it sound like I have to make a big commitment already."

"You don't have to rush... but, don't miss any opportunities, either."

He chuckled. "You know what? I should be sad and hurt, but I'm not. This actually makes sense. I feel hopeful."

"It makes a ton of sense. I'm so glad that you're taking this so well."

"Honestly, Lisa, I just want you to be happy. You have to follow your heart, and so does Charlie. I wouldn't want to stand in the way of that."

"You have to follow yours, too. Don't give up when things seem to be going wrong. There's always hope. You can do anything."

He nodded and took a deep breath. "Well, I guess I'd better let you go. It's not entirely easy."

She smiled. "You said that you want me to be happy. Know what would really make me happy?"

"What?"

"If we were still friends. You don't have to let me go, because I'll always be here. I'll be the one cheering you on the loudest."

He smiled. "Sounds perfect."

Her eyes watered again. "Come here, ya big lug."

They held each other tight.

When they let go, she said, "You're going to be okay, right?"

"Yeah. I'll be okay."

"I'd better skedaddle. Following my heart and all that."

"Yeah, me, too."

She held her hands out towards the gym. "The future awaits."

"No time like the present."

"Aha-- there you go."

"Goodbye, Lisa," he said with a wave.

"It's not goodbye. It's only see ya later."

After changing into her Lorrie clothes, Lisa entered the gym. To the side were tables holding cake and punch. Balloons and streamers decorated the room with a distinctive Valentine's Day theme of red, pink, and white. The band played Cyndi Lauper's "Time After Time," which seemed rather fitting to Lisa. The crowd was large and filled with tuxedoed boys and corsage-adorned girls in beautiful dresses. She didn't see a single person who wasn't smiling. Happiness was in the air... as well as hormones and an almost overwhelming aroma of hairspray.

"So much big hair," she said to herself. "The 80's-- gotta love it."

She looked closely, but still didn't see a trace of her husband.

"Why, Miss Parker. Fancy meeting you here."

She turned around and smiled. "Ah, Mr. Whitfield. So good to see you. Looking rather dashing, I might add."

"Thank you, my dear. And, you are looking lovelier than ever."

He took her hand and kissed it.

"Why, Mr. Whitfield," she said through her ever growing smile. "You do flatter me."

"We never did make it to this dance the first time around," he said in his normal voice. "Of course, we were in the middle of something more important."

"True. We get a second chance. Isn't time travel grand?"

"It definitely has its perks."

The song ended and the band started playing "Head Over Heels" by Tears for Fears.

"I love this song," Charlie said. He held out his hand. "May I have this dance?"

"Oh, Mr. Whitfield," she said in her Lorrie accent, "what would the students think if they saw the two of us together?"

"Let them eat cake."

She took his hand and they began to dance.

He said, "Seriously, the cake is really good. You should have some."

"I couldn't eat right now."

"You? Turning down cake? Did we mess up the space-time continuum?"

"Very funny. I just can't think about food right now. I'm still focused on our mission. We don't have much time."

"Right. How did it go with Robbie?"

"Very well, actually. I think he's going to be interested in Tracy now. Only time will tell."

"That's good."

"Speaking of which, have you seen anything? Is Tracy still with her date? Is Robbie dancing with anyone?"

"Yes about Tracy, and no about Robbie."

"There are too many people here to even get a good look. We need to get closer to keep an eye on them."

"I agree. It might be easier than you think," he said as Tracy approached them.

"Lorrie! I thought that was you. I didn't know you would be here."

"Hi, Tracy! Mr. Whitfield and I are here to chaperone."

"Nice to meet you," Tracy said as she shook his hand.

"You, too."

"That guy over there getting punch is my date. His name is Tad."

They looked over to him. He drank a cup of punch in one swig and burped.

"Charming fellow," Sam remarked.

She made a disgusted face and looked into Lorrie's eyes.

"This guy's terrible."

"What's... uh... wrong with him?"

"He is so full of himself. He thinks he's God's gift to women. I wish I had the gift receipt to take him back for a refund."

She laughed. "Is he really that bad?"

"Well, let's just say that he's pointed out a few girls who he claims have been crazy about him. I am definitely not one of them."

"That sounds awful."

"Sounds like a butthead," Sam added.

"I've gotta get away from him. I saw Charlie when we got here. I bet I could dance with him instead. I haven't seen him since then, though. Come to think of it, I haven't seen Lisa, either."

Sam and Lorrie gave each other a knowing look.

"What about that young man you told me about the other day?" Lorrie asked.

"Who? Robbie? He's with Lisa."

"Is he? I've seen him here, and it looked like he was alone."

"Alone? That doesn't sound right. I wonder if something happened."

"Only one way to find out."

"Yeah. Maybe I'll ask him."

Her date came back and held out his elbow. She gave them a pained smile. "Thanks for the talk. See ya."

As soon as she walked away, Charlie looked at Lisa and said, "We've got to get her away from this Tad character."

"I think we need to give it a little time."

"You just said that we don't have much of it left."

"Well, you said earlier that we can't rush them, either. Let's just see how she handles it."

"Okay." He looked at his watch. "But, they'd better hurry."

They casually danced their way closer to the center of the crowd as the band played "I'm So Excited" by The Pointer Sisters. They saw Tracy dancing with Tad. She was smiling, but it didn't look like she was truly happy. Meanwhile, Robbie halfheartedly danced with another girl who asked. Lisa noticed that he would glance over to Tracy from time to time. She pointed it out to Charlie.

"Yeah, he's definitely keeping an eye on her," he said.

"Maybe he's too nervous to talk to her."

"Or, maybe he doesn't want to as long as Tad is there."

"We need a distraction."

As they tried to think of something, Lisa said, "I never noticed how naughty the lyrics to this song are."

"Aaaaand, now we can tell the difference between the young whippersnappers and us old-timers."

"We're not that old. Besides, look at the band. They look about the same age as the kids here. They're too young to sing about this stuff."

"I don't think anyone else notices... Mom."

"Look at the lead singer. He doesn't look so good."

"He's not the most handsome guy, I'll give you that..."

"No, I mean he doesn't look well."

"Yeah, you're right."

The singer very weakly sang, "I'm so excited... I'm so... sick."

He turned back and tried to rush offstage, but didn't quite make it. The band members quickly reacted.

"My drums!"

"My keytar!"

"My perm!"

"My eyes!" declared Charlie at the horrible spectacle.

"What's the name of this band, Simon and Barfchunkel?" Lisa quipped.

The rest of the crowd expressed their disgust.

"Not the distraction I hoped for. This is terrible! How can we have a dance without music?" asked Charlie.

"Oh, man! I just remembered. Tracy told me about this. She said that they all just kind of hung around for awhile until they got some more music. One of the teachers eventually found a tape of Lawrence Welk."

Charlie's jaw dropped. "That may actually be the saddest thing I've ever heard. We can do better than that. I think I have an idea."

"Don't tell me-- you're going to get up there and play 'Johnny B. Goode.'"

"If I could play the guitar, I would totally do that! But, no, I have another idea. There's a tape I borrowed from Mom in the car. It's the one that Sam left."

She smiled. "I see where you're going with this."

"While you go get that, I'll stall them."

"How?"

"By making up for another mistake."

Charlie as Sam headed for the stage. The janitor was a ready cleaning up.

He heard him muttering, *"I never in forty-three years saw anything like this. Sweet mother of mercy."*

He stepped up to the microphone.

"This is even worse than The Great Flu of '62."

Sam said, "If I could please have your attention."

The students obliged.

"While Old Lou cleans this up..."

"Gonna be awhile, young man. I don't think I have enough absorbent."

"...I want to assure you that we do have more music on the way very soon."

"I hope it ain't Bill Haley and His Vomits. I can't take no more."

"All right already," Sam replied. He turned back to the students. "We have a tape of good old... uh... *recent* hits that you're going to love. So, the party is just getting started!"

Some of the students cheered.

"For those who don't know, I'm Sam Whitfield, the guidance counselor. If any of you need to talk about what we just saw, I'm available."

They laughed.

"I thought I'd take the opportunity to tell you that due to health reasons, I will no longer be able to continue serving you. Miss Parker is also leaving. I know that may be hard for some of you to take, but this is the only option we have. I wish it didn't have to be this way. Rest assured, Mr. Foltan will find a wonderful replacement. I have really enjoyed getting to know you and helping as much as I can. It's been an honor."

He saw Lisa come in. "All right, looks like we're back n business. So, let's take a chance..." he made eye contact with Tracy and continued, "maybe find a little romance..." Some of the students whooped and whistled. The music began to play. "And, most of all... LET'S DANCE!!"

The crowd erupted into cheers. "Puttin' on the Ritz" by Taco filled the air. Charlie moved and grooved his way to Lisa. It was one of his favorite songs.

"You're really getting into this, aren't you?" she said with a laugh.

"Why not? We only get one high school prom," he said with a wink and a smile. "Besides, it always reminds me of 'Young Frankenstein.' Look around-- I'm not the only one who's digging it."

They observed many a teenager try to sing along and tap dance--including Tracy and Robbie.

"Too bad they aren't dancing together," Lisa said.

"They'll get there."

"I'm glad you're so confident about it."

"I have a good feeling about them. Just have faith." He laughed. "It's funny. I used to be the one who worried all the time."

"There's just a lot riding on this."

"I know. It is a serious situation. But, the night is still young. So are we... for this moment in time."

"Okay, I'll try to have fun."

Lisa started exhibiting her usually fun-loving self the more she danced with Charlie.

"Like when we were kids," she said as she once did when they talked about Prom the first time around, "only fancier."

"A lot fancier," he said without missing a beat.

She tap danced along with the song.

"You can tap dance, too?" Charlie asked in amazement.

"Nah, just a fast learner."

As usual, he couldn't quite keep up with her.

When the song was finished, "Automatic" by The Pointer Sisters began. They continued to have a good time dancing, but Lisa's thoughts drifted back to their friends.

"I think we could use that distraction pretty soon," she said.

"Yeah, I was just thinking about that. Maybe we can stop the music for an announcement of some kind."

"You have this tape memorized, right? When does it get to the end of this side?"

"Well, let's see... there were a few songs already at the beginning, including 'Come on, Eileen.' There's just one more song after this." He smiled. "The next side could start stirring up the romantic feelings."

"Great. I could go turn the tape over while you go back onstage."

"You know, with the way Tad was guzzling that punch, he might need a bathroom break soon."

"Perfect. I love your scientific mind."

"It comes in handy from time to time."

"Break My Stride" by Matthew Wilder played next. Charlie and Lisa thoroughly enjoyed dancing exuberantly to the catchy song. They watched as Tracy and Robbie each did so as well. Their partners looked like they were having fun, but still looked mismatched. When the three minutes were over, Lisa headed for the stereo as Charlie took to the stage.

"Hey, everyone! Are you having a good time?"

The cheers were enthusiastic.

"What a wonderful Valentine's Day Prom this has turned out to be. Do you like the music?"

They cheered again.

"We'll have the rest for you in just a little bit. I think we should also acknowledge the band. They did a fantastic job up until... well, you know."

Old Lou said, "I told you this was gonna take awhile."

Sam continued, "Let's give a hand to the band."

The crowd clapped and cheered.

"We're definitely the ones who could use a hand," Old Lou quipped as he and the band continued to clean up the mess.

Sam said, "And, how about these awesome decorations?"

They clapped and cheered again.

"We're going to take a little intermission before we start the music."

"Intermission?" Lisa asked aloud as she held her finger on the play button.

Sam repeated as if he could hear her, "Yes, intermission. This will be a good time to take a break. Maybe go to the bathroom or have some cake and punch. We'll be back in five minutes."

"He has something up his sleeve," Lisa said. "Maybe he sees something that I don't. Time to trust his instincts."

Sam walked offstage as the students started doing exactly as he said. He passed by Tracy long enough to hear Tad tell her that he was going to the bathroom.

Lisa said, "He's thinning the crowd. Most of them will do it because everyone else is doing it. But, not Tracy and Robbie. They're stronger-willed." She looked again at the list of songs on the tape. She smiled. "Music is powerful. He's carefully orchestrating the whole thing. I love that man."

He approached her at the stereo. "Sorry that I changed plans at the last minute, but I have a better idea."

"I believe it."

"I'll stay here and play the tape. You need to talk to Tracy."

"What would I say?"

"Like you said before, she's the key to all of this. The problem is, she doesn't know it. She needs an extra nudge in the right direction. She's too nice to tell off Tad and too nervous to talk to Robbie. For all she knows, he's still dating you."

"There's a barrier that has to be lifted."

He put her hand on her shoulder and said, "You're the only one who can do it."

She nodded.

Lisa returned to the main floor and found Tracy sitting off to the side.

"Hey, Tracy."

"Hey, Lorrie. I had to sit down for a minute. I really shouldn't have worn these heels to a dance."

"I feel your pain, sister." She sat next to her. "Where's Tad?"

"He went to the bathroom."

"This could be a good chance for you to have that talk with Robbie."

"I don't know... I don't want to hurt Tad's feelings."

"What if it hurts Robbie's if you don't?"

She gave her a quizzical look. "Why would it?"

"I can't give away too many details for sake of confidentiality, but I'll just say that I have counselled quite a few people here. I know some things that would be very interesting to know if I were at liberty to discuss them."

"Color me intrigued. Is Robbie one of those people?"

"He might be."

"Hmm. You really think I should talk to him?"

"With everything in me."

Her eyes widened. "Wow. Okay... but, what about Lisa?"

"That goes back to one of those interesting things that I know. I know that's who you were talking about the other day."

"You do? What else do you know?" She shook her head. "No, I shouldn't know. Knowing some things before you should know it kind of takes the fun out of it."

"Sometimes knowledge is power. Sometimes you just need to know. For instance, I know why she isn't here. I also know why Charlie isn't here."

"Really?!"

"I have it on good authority that they are both following their hearts as we speak."

She gasped. "What?! Oh my goodness!! I can't believe it! It's really happening! Tell me this is true! Are you sure?"

"Pretty darn. But, you didn't hear that from me."

She acted like she was zipping her lips shut. "I won't say a word. You were right-- it really was Valentine's Day. Man, this will change everything. It's like a miracle."

"Love changes everything. It's good that you're concerned about Tad's feelings, but guys like him wouldn't think twice about hurting yours. He's going to be fine. Robbie, however, is not like him. He's pretty special."

They looked across the room. He was sitting alone with a sad look on his face.

Knowing Tracy's compassionate nature, Lorrie added, "That nice, young man over there just lost someone important to him tonight. He knows it. Whether or not, he says anything about it, it's starting to hit him."

She kept her gaze on him and said, "Aw, man. Poor Robbie."

"You know what Charlie and Lisa are doing right now? They're taking a chance. The kind of chance that only happens once. There's one thing you could do. The very least you could do, and it's something I hear that you're really good at."

She looked her in the eyes. "Anything."

"He really could use a friend right now."

Lorrie stood up and held out her hand. She said, "You're the only one who can do it."

Tracy took her hand and stood up. "What do I say to him?"

"Whatever comes naturally."

Tad walked up to them. "There you are. I bet you missed me."

The two ladies glanced at each other and back to him.

Tracy said, "Not at all."

She walked away. Lorrie tried not to clap.

Tad said, "Wait a minute. What are you doing?"

Lorrie said, "Something she should've done all along. You blew it, mister."

"But, she's my date."

"I heard you were quite the ladies' man. Surely it wouldn't be hard to find someone else."

He smirked. "Yeah. You're right. I can take my pick." He looked her over. "How about you, babe?"

She held up her fist. "How about you have some more punch?"

He gulped. "I am getting thirsty." He gave a fake smile and walked away.

Lorrie stepped closer to hear what Tracy said. Charlie began to play the tape. DeBarge's "All This Love" was absolutely perfect.

"Hey, Robbie."

"Tracy. How are you?"
"Pretty good. What about you?"
"To tell you the truth, not so good."
"I can guess why Lisa isn't here."
"Yeah. We broke up. She's with someone better."
"No. She's just doing what's right for herself. Just like I'm doing." She held out her hand. "Wanna dance?"
He looked at her hand and then into her eyes. "What about your date?"
She smiled. "I'm with someone better."
"Thattagirl, Tracy," Lisa said quietly.
He smiled. He took her hand and stood up. They walked over to the center of the room and began to dance slowly.
Charlie walked up to Lisa and put his arm around her. She looked into his eyes. Happy tears began to overflow.
"It's happening, Charlie. It's finally happening."
He took her by the hand and they joined in.
"How are your memories?" he asked. "Do you remember anything that happens to them after this?"
"I-- I don't. It's all fuzzy."
"Same here. They've definitely changed history, but it's not quite set in stone yet."
"So, anything could still happen."
"Technically, yes. But, look at it this way-- anything's possible."
"Only time will tell."

Tracy and Robbie danced somewhat awkwardly for the rest of the song. Lisa and Charlie figured that they were just nervous, and hoped and prayed that they would keep trying. The next song was "Say You, Say Me" by Lionel Richie.
"This is such a good song," Lisa said. "It's so perfect for them."
"Yeah, it's one of the best. It was in a movie called 'White Nights.' Did you know that this won Best Song instead of 'The Power of Love'?"
"No, I didn't know that. So, that means it came out in 1985."
"Yeah, it was..." his eyes widened and he gasped. "It was released in December!" He looked around the room at the unsuspecting crowd. "It wasn't out yet! No one has heard this song before! We have to stop the tape!"
"Whoa. Just slow down there. This is just a high school dance in an average-sized town in Kansas. So they hear it before anyone else? It's not going to ruin the space-time continuum."
He sighed. "I guess you're right. I overreacted a bit. It might be okay."
"That's all right. Let's just see what happens."

They kept their eyes on the would-be couple. They kept dancing. Sometimes they would say something and laugh. Neither Charlie nor Lisa could make out what they said.

"It looks like they have chemistry, but I just wish we knew if this was truly working," said Charlie. "My memories of it are still fuzzy."

"Me, too. If these two songs don't spark something, I don't know what would."

The song reached the bridge. The sudden change in tempo seemingly confused the crowd.

"Oh, no! They don't know what to do! No one's heard this and didn't know this part was coming! This is a disaster!" lamented Charlie.

"Maybe not. Look at 'em."

While everyone else looked confused or even stopped dancing altogether, Tracy and Robbie didn't miss a beat. They had just as much fun dancing to the faster pace as they did earlier, and had the audible laughter to prove it. This moment didn't last long, but it was like magic. When the song segued back to its slower tempo, their faces grew more serious. They looked into each other's eyes.

"I'm remembering something," said Lisa.

Tracy put her arms around Robbie's neck and leaned her head on his shoulder. They continued to dance slowly as he put his arms around her.

Lisa looked Charlie in the eyes through her tears. "This is their song."

Charlie smiled. "We did it."

"No." She returned the smile. "*They* did it."

"You're always right."

She held him tight and said, "They're gonna be okay."

They danced the rest of the song basking in the satisfaction of watching their friends falling in love. One of the most beautiful sights they'd ever seen.

The song came to an end. Tracy and Robbie slowly pulled apart and smiled.

"We should get going," Lisa said. "We don't want to be late."

The next song started.

"One more song?" Charlie asked as the lively music set everyone's feet boogying.

"'The Safety Dance.' How can I resist?"

"Not quite. Listen closer."

She laughed. "It's the 'Weird Al' version. You did it. You still managed to bring a 'Weird Al' song back in time. You brilliant, wonderful, beautiful, geek of a man. I couldn't possibly love you more."

"I love you, too. Happy Anniversary."

They joined in with the rest of the happy students and teachers. Charlie lip-synced in perfect harmony with Mr. Yankovic. They shimmied and swayed, rocked and rolled. Everyone clapped along at the right parts. It was all rather silly, but they loved every second.

"Can I cut in?" asked Robbie.

"Sure," Sam replied.

Robbie started dancing with Lorrie as Sam danced with Tracy.

"I think something is happening with Tracy," Robbie told Lorrie. "I just wanted to say thank you for everything."

"You're most welcome. I'm really proud of you."

"I'm gonna get it right this time."

He didn't know just how important those words were.

Lisa replied, "I know you will. I have a good feeling about you two. Now, get back to her."

He smiled and danced his way back to her. Sam went back to Lorrie, and they enjoyed the rest of the song. They looked at the new couple. They really did fit.

"They'll have quite a time together," he said.

"They're off to a flying start."

He looked at his watch. "This is fun and all, but we need to get out of here."

"Yeah. I miss the kids. It's time to go home."

CHAPTER 35

Charlie and Lisa returned to their house and parked the car on the slab.

"It's awfully dark," Lisa said.

"I came prepared. There's a flashlight in the glovebox."

They used it to light their path as they made their way to the front door. Their memories were slowly beginning to change. As they entered the house, they went over to the shelf to find the graduation picture. It was no longer just Charlie, Lisa, and Tracy.

"There's Robbie," Charlie said.

"The four amigos."

"Let's check the headlines."

Lisa opened the scrapbook and flipped to the stories about Robbie.

"He stayed here and played for Dad."

"They won the championship."

"The Champ Chargers." She chuckled. "I remember that now."

They checked for more news.

She sighed. "It says that he still gets hurt in the game."

"Aw, man."

She turned the pages.

"There's nothing about a DUI or hurting anyone."

"So, he still gets hurt, but he doesn't take it out on anyone else." He put his arm around her. "You did it, Lisa. He really did change."

"I'm starting to remember more."

"So am I."

They hurried up the stairs and stopped in front of Elijah's room.

Lisa said, "He still got hurt. There was nothing that could change it."

"But, he had Tracy with him. She helped the healing process."

"He had a job to fall back on. He worked with her dad and had a support system."

"They encouraged him to keep trying. They wouldn't let him give up."

"Neither did we."

"He went back and tried again."

Lisa opened the door. Charlie shone the flashlight as they walked in. He pointed the light at a poster.

"He became the All-Star of Kansas City."

He moved the light over to some other pictures on the wall. One was a crayon drawing of Robbie by a very young Elijah. Another was a photo of him in matching uniform with Robbie when they went to one of his games.

Lisa began to cry. "He's our son's hero."

"Good ol' Uncle Robbie."

When they entered the study, Charlie started up the generator. Lisa fired up the computers and the Shifter.

Charlie said, "I was thinking that we might not need the vests this time."

"That's true. We have to bring the whole house back with the Shifter, so we might as well save the energy. But, we already sent the signal back in 2004."

He checked his watch. "We barely have enough time to try to cancel it. Before we do that, we need to check something else."

He got on the floor and closely examined the bottom of the Shifter with the flashlight.

"Just like I theorized. Robbie changed course so much that he never shoots the gun that puts the crack in the machine."

"Without the crack, we can't get back. And, no, I didn't mean for that to rhyme."

"Good thing I planned ahead. But, we have to hurry or we won't even remember that there's a problem at all."

He picked up a gun from the desk. They hurried down the stairs.

"From this spot in the living room, if we point the gun at a specific angle, we'll match the other bullet's trajectory."

"Is that the same kind of gun?"

"Yes. I remembered it quite well. I knew we had to have one just like it to make sure it had the right amount of firepower to duplicate the damage. I marked the spot with tape, so I'll shoot it and we can be on our way."

She looked at the spot in question. Charlie held the gun up and aimed. He took a deep breath.

"I only get one shot at this."

His hand nervously trembled.

"Have you ever fired a gun before?"

"No, have you?"

"No, but I was in archery for a little while before track. Same basic principle-- aim and shoot."

"Wanna try?"

"Sure."

He handed her the gun and they switched places. She pointed the gun at the target. She took a deep breath.

"Here goes nothin'."

She pulled the trigger. A perfect bullseye. They rushed back upstairs.

"It worked," Charlie said after examining the Shifter. "Right on target as usual. Great job."

"Thanks. Now about those vests..."

“Yes! Now that we know the Shifter will make it, we have to cancel that before it’s too late.”

They pulled up the programming on the computer.

“The crystals are starting to glow!” Lisa warned.

“Almost got it.”

“Maybe we should put them on.”

“We need to bring the house and Shifter back. It will cause too much of a problem if we don’t.”

“Hurry!”

He pushed a few more buttons. “Almost... almost... THERE.”

The crystals stopped glowing. They each breathed a sigh of relief.

“We’ve got to quit cutting these things so close,” she said.

“It really gets the heart pumping, doesn’t it?”

She laughed. “Yeah, but I can come up with other ways of doing that without causing a time travelling incident.”

He held her hand and looked into her eyes.

“We sure had a good time, didn’t we?”

She smiled. “We had some ups and downs and some close calls, but overall... yeah. It was an absolute blast.”

"You might even call it an excellent adventure," he said with a sly grin.

She shook her head. "You and your movie references."

He laughed. "Come on. Ya gotta do it with me."

She sighed, "Oh, all right. You earned it."

They played an air guitar riff and laughed. They rose to their feet. She wrapped her arms around his waist as he put his arms around her shoulders.

“We’re officially Changers,” he said. “I could get used to that.”

“It does have a nice ring to it.”

“Watching you help Robbie, all the things it took, from costumes and accents...”

She laughed. “Don’t remind me.”

He laughed and continued, “...to just listening to what he had to say. I know it wasn’t always easy, but you handled it with the strength and courage and love that I’ve always known you to possess. In another part of town earlier tonight, the younger versions of ourselves were in the park. You did the same thing for me. You’re a true hero, Lisa. I don’t know anyone else that I’d rather go through time with.”

“Funny, I could say the same thing about you.”

“You’ve always been my Sunshine.”

“And, you’ve always been my world.”

“I love you.”

“I love you, too.”

“I’ll never get tired of saying it.”

"I'll never get tired of hearing it."
They kissed.
"What do you say, Lisa? Want to give this whole hero thing a try more often?"
"Like jumping around from time to time?"
"We could be partners in time. Helping others, changing the future..."
"Putting right what once went wrong..."
"And, be back before anyone knows we were gone."
"Sounds tempting."
"We're the only ones who could do it."
"Why don't we get back from this mission first, and then see what opportunity presents itself at the right time."
He nodded. "We'll know it when we see it."
"Mr. Blue Sky..."
"Sunshine..."
"Let's get back to where we belong."
"You're always right."

They went back to the computers and set the time and place.
"What song should we use?" She asked. "Something from Simon and Garfunkel again? The Beach Boys? Carpenters?" She smiled. "Maybe Lionel Richie?"
"Surprise me."
She picked a song and they opened the door to the Shifter. Lisa stepped in and Charlie followed, securing the door.

Before we can continue with the next part of Charlie and Lisa's story, it is at this time that some important information must be shared. Without the knowledge of these vitally important details, it would be harder to understand what is about to happen. We now must return back to earlier that night in another part of town. Seventeen-year-old Charlie and Lisa were professing their love for each other while Sam, the older Charlie, watched from behind a bush.

"The hard part is over. The rest will be easy," the younger man said. "Now that we're together, we can do anything. If you love someone, anything's possible."
Sam watched as everything he worked for, everything he lived for, everything he hoped for came true before his very eyes. He was right about her all along. From the second he first saw her, he knew. And it was ten times better than he imagined.
Charlie and Lisa brought their lips together in a kiss that expressed their love better than their words ever could. The years of waiting only

added more passion. The distance between them was no longer. They were together, and finally made whole.

Sam, the older Charlie, overflowed with emotion at the precious sight of true love. One of the rare moments in his life that he cried tears of joy. Everything he suffered was now worth it. He wiped a tear with his left hand. Then the strangest thing happened. He noticed something. His hand began to shake. He looked at it in total surprise, then looked back upon his younger self and Lisa. Suddenly, a vision appeared.

"No."

Several other visions flashed in his mind.

"Don't do this to them. They don't deserve it."

Thousands of feelings and thoughts overpowered him in an instant, bringing him to his knees.

"I beg you. Leave them alone!"

Tears gushed as he witnessed sights too horrible to express, like a glimpse of hell.

"Mom! Not her! Please!!"

His tears increased as pain ravaged his body.

"Who are you? Why are you doing this?!"

Pain tightened its grip and forced him to the ground face first. He'd never felt such excruciating agony in all his life. One thought overpowered all else-- he had to warn them. It took all the strength he had left to try to crawl closer to Charlie and Lisa on his belly. Inch by inch, he grabbed fists full of grass and pulled himself closer. He looked ahead towards them. It seemed like he was getting nowhere fast. To say anything of what he saw, to even let them know that he was from another time, could prove to be disastrous and paradoxical for their future. But under the circumstances, he knew that it would be even worse for them to walk unknowingly into this horrendous fate. Charlie and Lisa had no idea what was going on, and continued to savor the moment of their hearts' union. Sam knew that he had to try something-- anything-- to get their attention.

"Lisa!!" he called out. Fear had gripped his throat so badly that his cry sounded only slightly louder than a whisper.

He reached into his pocket for his keys. Maybe he could make enough noise to prick up their ears. His hand shook so much that he couldn't keep ahold of them. He tried to crawl again. He didn't get far before he was exhausted. He tried to snap his fingers, but his hands just wouldn't cooperate.

"Lisa!!" he attempted again. He could barely hear it himself. He tried again. *"Charlie!!"* Still no results.

He started to cry again. The visions became even worse. He winced with pain and grabbed his chest. Tears fell to the ground like rain. His eyes bulged as terror and panic consumed him. The physical pain was unbearable, but what he saw hurt immeasurably. He stretched forth his other hand, trying desperately to be seen. It trembled as much as his voice when he let out his final warning.

"THEY'RE... COMING!!!"

His arm fell. His face fell to the ground. The fear was too much to bear. His heart stopped. Charlie Jordache was dead.

The younger Charlie and Lisa danced and kissed, blissfully unaware of the tragedy that had taken place. Their joy was justified. It was a moment that took them thirteen years to reach. They would go about the rest of their time not knowing this event happened. They would be stepping into a time machine later with this warning still unheard. Even though he gave his dying breath to make them aware, unfortunately, they would have to discover it the hard way. Sam's lifeless body disappeared into nonexistence. No matter what age or version of Charlie and Lisa there would be, no one would escape the ominous threat of that final message.

They're coming...

The Crystal Blue Persuasion began circling around the sphere of the Shifter. No matter how many times they saw it, Charlie and Lisa were always impressed. The song began to play.

"That's weird," she said. "It was supposed to be 'Time in a Bottle.' That sounds like Aerosmith."

"It's 'Dream On.' Still a good song, but it doesn't make sense that it changed."

"Oh, well. I tried to be romantic, but at least we're still going back."

The Shifter started to slow down.

"Whoa. That's not supposed to happen," he said.

"Maybe it's not enough power after all?"

"I don't know. I thought for sure it was fine."

It slowed down to a stop for just a couple of seconds. It started up again.

"Whew. That was weird," Lisa said.

"It gets weirder. It's going backwards."

"What?! Something's really not right."

"If it keeps doing that, it's going to send us further back to the past."

It started to slow down again. They watched in bewilderment as it went forwards again.

"I don't like it," Charlie said. "Something's very wrong."

"Shut it down before it's too late."

He searched his pockets. "I don't have the remote."

They squinted through the flashing blue light circling them.
She said, "It's still on the desk."
Charlie rammed the door with his shoulder.
"What are you doing?" she asked.
"I have to try."
He did it again.
"This is bulletproof glass! All you're gonna do is hurt yourself!"
He stopped. "You're right." He looked down at the floor. "The crack! Let's stomp on it!"
They stomped and jumped on the crack. They stopped to catch their breath.
"It's no use. We're not making any impact," she said.
The energy spun faster through the sphere.
"I have a really bad feeling about this," he said.
"Me, too." Lisa walked closer to the door. "It feels like... there's a presence."
"I feel it, too. As strong as when we were in Arizona."
She tried to see through the sphere.
"I don't see the vests."
"I do. They're over here."
"What?!"
She rushed to his side.
"That's not where we left them."
"They're glowing again."
They pounded on the walls.
"HELP! HELP!" they yelled.
"There's too much noise. Whoever is out there can't hear us," she said.
"Or, doesn't want to."
The blue energy spun faster.
Lisa looked into Charlie's eyes. "I'm scared."
"I'd be lying if I said I wasn't. But, we're at the point of no return. Whatever is gonna happen is gonna happen. We have to stay calm and focus like usual so it doesn't make it any worse."
She nodded. "Okay."
As much as he knew he was right, being calm was still a lot easier said than done. There was a palpable sense of dread far worse than any he'd felt before. He knew that Lisa felt it just as much if not more. The music playing added an extra level of eeriness.
"So much for staying calm," Lisa said as she pointed to the wall. "Why is it purple?!"
They watched in shock as the blue became purple.

He said, “I have no explanation for that. Something is definitely not right.”

The energy spun faster.

Lisa looked even more frightened. “Is this the end?”

“I don’t think this is the end… but, I have a feeling that our lives are about to get a lot more complicated.”

The Shifter was reaching the final level.

“Whatever happens next,” Lisa showed him her friendship bracelet and continued, “forever means forever. Always together.”

They reached for each other’s hands. Suddenly, they were each pulled to the walls of the sphere. Their backs were pinned by a force that was so strong they couldn’t fight it. They tried once more to reach for each other, but to no avail. Their hearts beat faster as the energy was reaching a climax. Neither was able to speak or even be heard if they could.

Charlie mouthed, “I love you.”

“I love you, too,” was the tearful reply.

Lisa’s expression matched his own feelings. Pain, fear, and heartbreak were overpowered by only one thing-- love. They didn’t know what the future would bring-- or the past-- but, one thing would always be true. They would always be in each other’s hearts.

The song reached the end as the machine finally leaked the purple energy into Charlie and Lisa. With every last bit of strength she could muster she cried out, *“CHAARLIIIEEE!!!”*

They were gone in a flash.

CHAPTER 36

Charlie found himself on a linoleum floor.

"What happened? Where am I?"

He slowly started to rise, but dizziness gave him pause. He started to remember what happened, but not how he ended up in this position.

"At least it doesn't hurt."

He tried again. The dizziness faded away. He looked at his surroundings.

"A hospital? How did I get here?"

He looked down to see himself in clothes he didn't recognize and another strange addition.

"Why am I wearing the vest?"

The digital display still wasn't showing the time and date.

"How far back did I go?"

A more pressing question came to mind.

"Lisa! Where are you?"

He quickly examined his surroundings in the middle of the hall, trying to discern which direction would be the best to search. Suddenly, he heard screaming.

"LISA!! I'm coming!!"

"Oh, man, is my head spinning," Lisa said.

She slowly stood up, trying not to fall over. She looked around as her vision became clearer.

"What? Why the heck am I in a hospital?" She suddenly realized something. "Wait a minute-- where's Charlie?"

Charlie followed the sound of the screams to one of the rooms. He felt strangely compelled to walk in. Doctors and nurses were gathered around a bed. He stepped closer to get a look at the patient.

Lisa saw a nurse heading her way.

"Excuse me, I'm looking for my husband, Charlie. He's about this tall, brown hair, brown eyes..."

The nurse walked by without acknowledging her.

"Well, that was rude."

She saw a couple of doctors approaching. She rushed up to them.

"Excuse me, I'm looking for someone. Maybe you can help me?"

They didn't even look at her. She stepped in front of them.

"It's an emergency. It's my husband, and I think he's in trouble."

She got out of the way before they could walk into her. They kept walking and talking in their own world.

"What has gotten into people today? They act like they can't even see me." It dawned on her. "Maybe they really *can't* see me." Her heart raced and her breathing became panicked. *"Am I dead?!"*

Charlie stepped closer.

"Just keep breathing," one of the doctors said.

He finally got a good look at her face.

"What? How is this happening?"

Lisa tried to calm down.

"I have to figure out where I am. Or, *when* I am. And, why I'm wearing this vest. Why hasn't the date caught up yet?"

She heard a woman screaming.

"That doesn't sound anything like Charlie, but something tells me I need to be there."

She ran to the room. She was almost pulled in by force.

Charlie couldn't believe his eyes. "Mom?"

"You're doing great, Mrs. Jordache. Just keep breathing. You can do this."

"Since when are you pregnant?"

Lisa walked closer to the bed.

"You're almost there," a doctor said.

Lisa saw the woman in labor.

"Who the heck are you?"

She couldn't figure it out, but still felt compelled to be there.

"Congratulations, Mrs. Jordache, it's a boy."

"This is so weird," Charlie said. "This can't be happening."

"Can I hold him?"

"Of course you can."

They handed her the baby.

"Look at you. My little man."

She began to cry tears of joy. Charlie had goosebumps.

She continued, "Hi, little Charles. I'm your mommy. Your daddy couldn't make it on time, but you'll get to see him soon. We love you very much. We're going to take good care of you. I promise."

Charlie reeled back in shock. He began to breathe heavily.

"This can't be happening... th-this is impossible."

He looked around at the others.

"You can't even see or hear me, can you? It has to be a dream. That's the only logical explanation. This kind of thing can't happen."

He looked down at the vest. The numbers were finally starting to settle.

"It's a girl!" the doctor said.

Lisa had a weird feeling about this.

A nurse said, "Do you have a name for the baby?"

"What's your name?"

"Lisa."

She shrugged her shoulders. "Works for me."

"WHAT?!" the adult Lisa replied. "That's it? Just naming a baby on a whim? I'm glad you're not my mother." She started to walk away, but stopped. "But... whose mother are you? What are the odds that the baby is named Lisa?"

She walked into the hall looking for a clue. She didn't have to wander far to find a sign.

"Heatherton Community Hospital? I'm back in California?"

She rushed back into the room and stared at little Lisa.

"No, no, no. This can't be!"

She watched as the time on the vest came into focus.

"May 25th, 1967."

"May 11th, 1967."

Lisa exclaimed, "Great Scott!"

Charlie looked into the mirror, but saw no reflection.

"Ohhh, boy!"

We are now at the halfway point in the story of Charlie and Lisa. Everything else that follows will get complicated... well, let's face it. This is where it *really* gets complicated...

LOST IN TIME

About the Author

Jared Vaughn is the author of the acclaimed novel *The Longest Time*. It's a nostalgic story about a unique boy named Charlie, whose love for his childhood friend, Lisa, leads him to fulfill a heroic purpose. Readers of all ages have unanimously agreed that they "couldn't put it down" and eagerly awaited the sequel, *Another Time*. He loves to encourage dreamers in his writing workshops and panels at conventions, libraries, and schools, with a special emphasis on the youth. Jared's vision extends beyond *The Longest Time* series with his company, Time Honored Productions. Exciting additions to the Time Honored family are coming soon with the release of *Tobias' Travels*, a delightful story for all ages about a little robin that goes a long way. Cleverly written by Shoshanna Aaliyah and beautifully illustrated by Ray Gordon with Alli O'Neal, this is the first book in history that's written and illustrated by three teenagers, and will have a coloring book version available as well. Shoshanna also contributes to *Free Time Tales*, a collection of short stories by new writers of all ages. Jared's own spinoff of *The Longest Time*, *Invisible Touch* is also available exclusively in this collection. In addition to his writing and publishing, Jared is known for his cosplay. He has appeared at many conventions as Marty McFly beginning on Back to the Future Day, October 21st, 2015. He's quick to make you laugh with his impressions and costumes from all three films, often accompanied by Doc Brown and Jennifer. His cosplay has also included Clark Kent, Neo, George McFly, Westley/Dread Pirate Roberts, Inigo Montoya, Count Rugen, Ernest P. Worrell, Ted "Theodore" Logan, Robin, Gomez Addams, Louis Tully, the Hamburglar, the highly original Mario McFly, and many more to come. Whether he's riding a hoverboard or writing a story, Jared Vaughn is always looking for innovative ways to express his creativity and share the Power of Love. He encourages you to take Doc's advice--"The future is whatever you make it. So make it a good one."

About the Artist

Victoria Beasley is a freelance vagabond, taking jobs as they come for ten-odd years. Her greatest love is making art that tells or is in service to a story, whether it be through comics, illustration, character design, or book covers. She frames art for her day job and draws frames in her off hours. She lives with her tarantula, Persimmon.

If you're interested in reading some of Victoria's original comics, please check out the artist "iesnoth" on Webtoons.

If you'd like to see more of her art, search "iesnoth" on Facebook and Tumblr, or "iesnothsart" on Instagram.

If you want to offer Victoria her next paid artistic venture, she can be reached at iesnoth91@gmail.com.

Made in the USA
Columbia, SC
06 September 2020

17888771R20187